FIREBORN

BOOKS BY TOBY FORWARD

Dragonborn
Fireborn

FIREBORN

A Dragonborn Novel

Toby Forward

BLOOMSBURY
NEW YORK   LONDON   NEW DELHI   SYDNEY

Originally published in Great Britain in 2011 by Walker Books Ltd
First published in the United States of America in December 2013
by Bloomsbury Children's Books
www.bloomsbury.com

For information about permission to reproduce selections from this book, write to
Permissions, Bloomsbury Children's Books, 1385 Broadway, New York, New York 10018
Bloomsbury books may be purchased for business or promotional use. For information on bulk
purchases please contact Macmillan Corporate and Premium Sales Department at
specialmarkets@macmillan.com

Library of Congress Cataloging-in-Publication Data
Forward, Toby.
Fireborn / by Toby Forward.
pages   cm
Summary: Companion to: Dragonborn.
Summary: When an old, dying wizard steals magic from his twelve-year-old apprentice, Bee,
and releases a new, wild magic into the world, another apprentice, Cabbage, sets out to find Bee
and try to set things right again.
ISBN 978-1-59990-889-2 (hardcover) • ISBN 978-1-61963-053-6 (e-book)
[1. Wizards—Fiction. 2. Apprentices—Fiction. 3. Fire—Fiction. 4. Fantasy.] I. Title.
PZ7.F784Fir 2013   [Fic]—dc23   2013012055

Book design by Nicole Gastonguay
Typeset by Westchester Book Composition
Printed and bound in the U.S.A. by Thomson-Shore Inc., Dexter, Michigan
2 4 6 8 10 9 7 5 3 1

All papers used by Bloomsbury Publishing, Inc., are natural, recyclable products
made from wood grown in well-managed forests. The manufacturing processes
conform to the environmental regulations of the country of origin.

Golden lads and girls all must,
As chimney sweepers, come to dust.
—William Shakespeare, *Cymbeline*

<hr />

This book is dedicated to all those
who are no longer here for me to thank them.
I wish I had expressed more gratitude
when I had the chance.

FIREBORN

It's your birthday tomorrow,"

said Slowin.

Bee looked up. "Is it?"

Slowin picked up a piece of paper from Bee's desk. He crackled. That had been happening more recently. Bee drew away from him.

"What's this?"

Bee hated him to touch anything that was hers. "It's a list," she said, "of different types of wood."

Slowin dropped it back onto the desk. "You'll be twelve years old tomorrow," he said. "You'd better come over to the workshop after breakfast. We've got something to sort out."

His fingers had left a small, dark stain on the paper. Bee waited until he had left; then she sniffed it. The paper was scorched where his fingers had been.

The page was lined with lists. It had taken Bee most of the morning to think about it, write it out, but she took a fresh sheet, dipped the pen in the ink, and began to copy it all out again. She did not want anything that Slowin had touched or marked. Especially now. It was as though sparks were shooting off him.

The first time of writing, Bee had sorted out the names, dividing the different types of wood into how they would burn. Which ones were sweet-smelling; which made harsh smoke; which ones flared up with cheerful flames or smoldered in sullen lumps; which ones needed to be stored through the winter before they would burn; which ones could be used as soon as they were cut. She had a special section for kindling, another for woods that were good for leaving safely to burn slowly through the night. The names of the different trees were like a song to her. Ash and elm, elder, rowan, the slender poplar, the broad oak. Beech, sycamore, chestnut, and spruce.

This time she was just copying and didn't have to think about what she was writing. Her mind went on a journey, leaving her hand moving the pen.

Twelve years old. She had never had a birthday before. Well, she must have had some. Not that she remembered. No one had ever mentioned one since she came to live here with Slowin and Brassbuck. There were shining fishes of memories. If she tried to catch them, they slipped away.

Lime, birch . . . her pen trailed the ink.

There was a day when she sat on the ground outside her parents' house. The kitchen door was open to her left. Her mother making the red tiles of the floor shine. It was snowing. The first snow Bee had ever seen. She raised pudgy hands to catch the flakes, and she was puzzled when they disappeared, leaving a wet trace. She soon tired of this and thought of something better for them. Her father came up the path and found her. She was surrounded by a cloud of tiny flames, each one a snowflake. They fell to the ground and died, a never-ending storm of lights. It wasn't the snow Bee remembered best. It was the look of fear on her father's face and her mother's wet arms as she hugged her and cried.

Bee's fingers were stained black. That was the trouble with ink. No matter how you tried to be neat, some of it always managed to crawl up the pen and find your fingers. Apple, pear, cherry, plum. Damson and greengage. She smiled as she wrote the names of the fruit trees. A fish of memory darted through the green fronds of her mind. A cottage and a garden. Fruit trees and butterflies. The sun on her neck. She was older now. Her father arguing with someone she now knew was Slowin, the wizard. Her father shouted at him and he left. She tried to see her father's face, to remember what he looked like, but the fish flashed away.

Twelve years old tomorrow. And something to sort out with Slowin.

Brassbuck looked more like a machine than like a woman. The soles of her boots were studded with iron that sparked against the flint of the cobbles in the yard. Her jerkin and leggings were black leather, held together with iron rivets instead of stitches. Her hands and face were black with soot from the fires and furnaces that were everywhere in Slowin's workshops and his storerooms. And she was broad. Not fat. Strong and wide.

Brassbuck was afraid of magic. She had come to Slowin years ago, more years than she could remember. Slowin was just a local wizard then, and a bit of a joke. People said that he was emptied out. Brassbuck had come to ask him to work some magic for her. He found her jobs to do to pay him. After a while, she found it hard to leave, and she settled in. "I ought go back," she said one day. "But I'm not sure where I came from."

Slowin put his arm around her shoulders. "You can stay here, then," he said. "You carry on with your work, and I'll look after you."

To her surprise, Brassbuck was grateful for the offer, and she stayed.

There hadn't been much magic back then. Slowin charged a lot and gave very little. Often, people came back and complained. The spells they had paid for didn't work. They wanted their money back. If Slowin couldn't chase them off with a poisonous word, he would threaten them with Brassbuck. One man, a butcher, came to complain. He dangled a heavy, sharp meat cleaver from his hand, ready to help persuade Slowin to give back his money. He had paid for a spell on all his knives and saws and cleavers. To make them safe to use. There had been a young assistant, just learning the trade, and he had swung the cleaver to chop through the bone in a loin of lamb. His eyes and his hand didn't agree on the spot where the cleaver should fall and it had snapped his thumb off. The boy screamed, dropped the cleaver, and ran around the shop, spraying blood from the wound.

"It was your spell that made it worse," said the butcher.

"Nonsense. Get yourself out of here, or I'll make your meat rancid for a month."

"Over twenty years I've been in this trade. Cuts and nicks, hundreds, but no one has ever chopped off a finger or a thumb. Not until your useless magic turned the blades against us. Now, pay up. I want the money back for the spell, and I want ten times as much again to give to the lad. He'll need the money now."

Slowin looked around for Brassbuck, but she was watching from around a corner, interested to see what the butcher would do. She could always come and help later. It was lonely working for Slowin. Not many people called by, and she was enjoying seeing the butcher arguing.

"Have you got the money?"

Slowin hadn't, but he wasn't going to admit it to this fool of a tradesman. Slowin had no money and almost no magic. The butcher stared at him, waiting. Slowin looked away, hoping to see Brassbuck.

"I'm going to take the money," said the butcher, "or I'm going to take your thumb and give it to the boy."

Slowin tried to smile. "My thumb will be of no use to the boy," he said.

"Nor to you," said the butcher. "There's some justice in that." He waited. "What's it to be?"

"I've no money."

"Then I'll take your thumb."

The butcher grabbed Slowin's wrist and slammed it onto the

table. Slowin struggled and shouted out for Brassbuck. He kicked. He tried to bite the butcher's hand. The butcher swung his fist to the side of the wizard's head. Slowin fell back, dazed. Brassbuck thought it was time she stepped in and helped. The butcher held Slowin's wrist, raised the cleaver, and swung it down. A thumb rolled over and fell to the floor.

Slowin shrieked as the meat ax fell. The butcher stared at what he had done. Then, with a roar of pain, he jerked his hand away. The crippled spell that Slowin had cast on the butcher's knives had made this cleaver miss its target, too. He had chopped off his own thumb. The butcher ran out, yelling, leaving the cleaver buried in the tabletop. Slowin skulked away, found his room, lay on his bed, and curled up, hugging his knees to his chest. Brassbuck shrugged her shoulders, carried in a bucket with warm water and a cloth, and knelt down to clean up the blood.

She liked the pattern the blood made on the floor. A pool under the table edge. Then small dots radiating out. The thumb lay on the floor. She picked it up, looked at it. The thumbnail was bitten down to the quick. It was messy. Brassbuck wiped it on her jerkin and put it into her pocket.

She squeezed out the cloth and began to mop up the blood. The small drops were like dark jewels against the cobbles, round and gleaming. She touched one with her finger. It moved aside. She touched another. It lifted up and scurried away. Each time she touched one, it hardened, rose, and scrambled over the floor. The spray of blood was turning into beetles at her touch, red black, hard shelled, with clattering, angled legs. She trapped three

of them in her hands and put them in the pocket with the thumb.
She could feel them squirming in there. She liked it. It was company. Slowin was not much company; this would be better.

That was how the beetles first came there.

Bee just managed to get to the end of the list

before her hand started to shake. She sprinkled powder on the paper to dry the ink, blew it off, placed the paper on a pile of others, then scrunched up the original that Slowin had touched. She sat back in her chair and breathed deeply. Breathing regularly, slowly in, pause, slowly out, getting rid of all the air, then slowly in again, helped her to get her hands to stop trembling. When they had first come, she had tried to control the trembling, to tense her muscles. That had made her arms and back and neck ache. It had made her head thump with pain. And when she stopped controlling the shakes, they came back, worse than ever. She'd taught herself to breathe, to let her body go loose, dangle her arms. She closed her eyes and pretended that the shakes were running away, out of her fingertips, like water from a downspout.

It worked. The trembling stopped, and she was left with no pain, no headache. Bee tried to remember how long it was since the shakes had started. Two summers, at least. Three winters? They came more often now. They lasted longer.

She folded the paper and, on a whim, decided she didn't want anyone to see it. She rummaged in her box of writing implements. A penknife, feathers, bottles of different colored inks, and there it was, a lump of sealing wax and an iron seal.

She didn't need a candle to melt the wax. Holding it above the paper, she clicked her tongue and it burned steadily, red drops of wax trickling onto the folded edge. She put it to one side, took the seal, and impressed a mark in the soft wax, holding it there till it was dry and hard. Now no one would be able to look at the list without breaking the seal.

She smiled. The iron seal was pleasant in her hand, heavy, cool, curved, and simple. It looked like a pawn from a chess set, or a weight from a grocer's scales.

Fresh air helped. Bee made sure that nothing overhung the edge of her desk. She moved pens and paper, her dust shaker and the ruler, a small jar with clematis in it, a book and other bits and pieces that settle on a desk like sparrows on a fence. She closed her eyes, her lips moved, and the whole of the top of the desk began to shimmer. Opening her eyes, she smiled, licked her fingers to get rid of the ink, and went out into the sunlight.

Brassbuck was in the yard. Bee had to walk around her to get out.

"Going out?"

"Yes."

"Where to?"

"Nowhere."

Brassbuck crossed the yard with Bee. Beetles too slow to dart away popped under her tread. The iron studs sparked against the cobbles.

"Everywhere is somewhere," she said.

"Yes, but nowhere is everywhere as well," said Bee. "So that's where I'm going."

"I'll come with you."

"No."

Brassbuck stopped at the gate, and Bee passed through. The woman's black eyes followed Bee as she walked away. When she was out of sight, Brassbuck clattered back over the yard.

Bee had her own tower where she slept and worked and ate all her meals. When she had lessons with Slowin, or when he wanted her to help him with some magic, she went to his tower or to one of the others that housed his workshops. Slowin was working on many magical projects, each with its own tower.

Bee's tower was her own place.

Brassbuck or Slowin could go in if they wanted. Bee was not allowed to lock it. But she made it plain that she did not like them in there. For the most part, they stayed out. Brassbuck went in as often as she could when Bee was not there.

Brassbuck crossed the threshold into Bee's room. Bee would know she had been there and would be angry. Bee always knew. Brassbuck sniffed. The smell was unpleasant. Bee covered her floor with fresh rushes that she changed every second day. She mingled wildflowers and herbs in with the rushes. Clover and mint, thyme and marjoram, honeysuckle in the summer, lavender in winter. As Brassbuck's boots trod on the rushes, they released their scents. It was like walking through a meadow on a hot afternoon. Brassbuck wrinkled her nose in disgust.

She stood by the desk, eager to see what Bee had written. She wanted to shuffle through the papers, pull open the drawers, and see what was hidden there. Time after time she came to do this. Every time, she found the same. She had learned from her mistakes. If she tried to touch anything, the shimmering surface would clench, then lash out a whip of flame. Everything in the room was protected in the same way. Brassbuck pulled a savage face at the desk, then spat on it. The green gout of snot sizzled and stank for a moment; then it was gone.

Brassbuck went to find Slowin.

Seeing Slowin in his armchair by the fire, she held a beetle out to him as a gift, seemingly unaware that they were everywhere.

Slowin took it, chewed it once, and swallowed.

"Tomorrow?" asked Brassbuck.

"Tomorrow," Slowin agreed.

Brassbuck took the other chair, and they sat in silence, watching the flames.

"Will she do it?" asked Brassbuck.

"Will she do it? Doesn't she do everything I tell her?" Slowin jeered.

Slowin's Yard was a scab on a smooth cheek,

hunched round and black, surrounded by a high wall. Around it, fields and woods, a clear stream with trout and carp and chub, a line of hills, a dry stone wall lovely with lichen, and the red level of a road. Bee ignored the road, climbed over the wall, crossed the field, and made her way to the top of the first hill.

Looking back, she could see the yard. Looking ahead, the fields like folds in bedclothes, a farm, far off, even farther off a farm cart on the disappearing road, and farther almost than she could see, the Palace of Boolat, small as her fingernail, yet big enough to house over a hundred men and their horses and servants.

The strangest thing about the Palace of Boolat was that the first time she had seen it was in a book. It was a picture. Not long after she had come to learn from Slowin, when she was about seven; they had been working together from a book about magic in deep cellars and high towers.

"The magic gets damp when you're underground," he explained.

"So you need to understand earth spells. And when you are very high up"—he put his finger on the picture, showing her the very top of the tallest tower—"when you are high up, the air will carry the magic. So make sure you learn your lessons well when we look at air magic."

Bee wrinkled her nose, something she always did when she was getting bored. "That's a big house," she said, pointing to the picture.

"It's a palace," Slowin corrected her. "Now, your own magic is fire, like mine. Remember? But even fire magic needs to know about earth and air and water magic."

"What's a palace?"

Slowin sighed. "You can see it if you want."

Bee kicked her feet against the table leg. She put a small hand on the book. "Of course I can see it."

"No. You can see it from the hill outside."

And she could. And she did. For years, she made her way up the hill, to escape from the miasma of Slowin's Yard, feel the breeze on her face, and look across to the Palace of Boolat. She imagined a girl in the tower, looking out toward her.

"Are you watching me?" she said. "Can you see me now?"

"Sorry."

Bee stood up and stared around.

"Who's there?"

The sun was halfway down in the west, low in her eyes, not yet evening. She squinted.

"I can see you," she said. "I know where you are."

She made a turn all the way around. There was no one in sight. She wasn't sure now that anyone had spoken. She looked at the tower. It wasn't from there?

"I'm going back down the hill now," she said. "Don't follow me."

"Sorry."

It was a small voice, broken. It came from just over to her left. She stepped back, keeping her face to where she thought it had come from.

"Who are you?"

The grass and bracken crackled silently with unused magic. For weeks now it had been building up, as the air grew heavy before a thunderstorm. Bee felt her hair prickle. The voice hardly stood out from all the activity around her. It spoke again, and she worked out exactly where it was coming from, deep in a mound of ferns. The words were not clear.

"Are you a person or are you magic in the air?" she asked.

The laugh frightened her. It sounded like pain. She pulled the ferns aside and looked in.

"Don't hurt me," it said.

It was too late to say that. Something had already hurt it terribly. Bee drew back.

"Oh," she said.

"Sorry."

"Why are you sorry?"

She moved the ferns aside again. "What happened to you?"

She thought it was a person. The eyes looked human. The face was like a toad, lumpy and brown and shining with slime.

It was dressed in dirty clothes, torn and not really enough of them. Bee thought she might be sick. It had legs and arms like a person. And it wore clothes, so it must be a person. It spoke like a person. It just didn't look like a person.

It stared at her.

She stared back.

Something had happened to the crackling magic in the air and in the undergrowth. There was a sort of pool of nothing all around the person. No magic at all. The loose magic formed a circle all around it. Bee stepped forward into the calm circle. As soon as she was there, she realized how much on edge she had been before. She understood why her shaking hands had been so bad recently. A faint, dull ache behind her eyes that she had forgotten was there disappeared.

Just as the nights grow shorter at the end of summer, a little at a time, the change so small that you hardly notice it until suddenly it is winter, so the magic had been gathering for months now. A little at a time so that Bee had not realized how much there was until she stepped into this pool of quiet. The absence of magic. She smiled and relaxed.

"What are you?" she asked.

"Mattie," it said.

"Are you a person?"

"A boy."

Bee hesitated, then put her hand on the boy, just where his shoulder would be if it didn't look like a toad's skin.

"What's wrong?" she asked. "What happened to you?"

The boy lowered his head, and Bee could feel his shoulder shake as he began to cry.

"Can you feel it?" asked Slowin.

He grinned at Brassbuck and picked up a beetle from the floor, cracking it open for sheer joy and tossing it onto the fire, where it sizzled and flared.

Slowin prodded the fire with a long poker. The flames raced along it to his hand. He dropped the poker and held up his hand, brandishing it in victory, turning it to admire the blue flames. It blazed like a beacon, neither hurting nor burning him.

"I am fire," said Slowin. "I am become fire."

He lowered his head. The flames died. Slowin pointed at Brassbuck. His finger flared up and a stream of fire rushed out, then fell to the floor in drops of flame, which ran around like beetles.

"It's everywhere," said Brassbuck. "Everywhere." She was still now. The excitement was there, mingled with awe.

"I did this," said Slowin. "I brought this here. I. Alone."

Brassbuck watched the fire beetles run along the top of the poker and throw themselves into the fire and disappear, joined to it, one element.

"What about Bee?" she asked, and wished she hadn't. She remembered how Bee had come to be here.

After the fight with the butcher and the coming of the beetles, Slowin gradually got better. He didn't sleep all day. He ate proper food, not just beetles. He could leave the yard and even go on small journeys. Then he could work a little magic again. Not much. But it worked, usually. The spells didn't often go wrong. He made a little money from simple spells and charms. And that was it. He was a local wizard. People bought his spells. Sometimes they paid in food because they hadn't any money.

But Slowin wanted more magic. He was old, though not as old as many another wizard. He wanted to be younger again. He wanted to be strong in magic.

He experimented with the beetles because he knew they had a strange power. They were created by magic, out of blood. They had saved his life.

He tried eating nothing else but beetles. That made him sick. He tried grinding them to a paste. He tried boiling them in water to make a tincture. But they could not die in water. They bobbed around and scurried away when it was tipped out. They were made of blood and anger. Water could not kill them.

Slowin noted this about them with special care. It would be useful.

Nothing worked. He was just a tired, old wizard, weak and empty.

He was making a setting spell for a farmer's wife. Their milk kept curdling because they couldn't be bothered to store it in a sensible, cool place. Their dairy needed repairing, and they were too stingy to spend the money on it. Slowin was botching up a charm to stop it tasting sour. The woman was all gossip, and Slowin was hurrying to get rid of her, not really listening to her when she said, "And there she was. Not more than four years old. Five at most, sitting in the snow. And as it fell around her, she was turning it into candles."

Slowin paused. "Oh, it's just a story," he said. "I suppose you heard it from a tinker. Never believe a tinker."

"I told you, I saw it myself."

"Yourself?"

"I told you that."

"Tell me again," he said. "I was concentrating on the charm."

So she told him about the man who worked for her husband, laying hedges, driving the cows in for milking, repairing the barn, all the jobs that never go away on a farm. She told Slowin she was on her way home when the snow started and she saw the little girl, Bee, working magic like a real wizard.

"She's a natural, that one," she said. "She'll either turn wizard, or she'll be put to death before she's twelve."

Slowin finished the charm and gave it to her. "Lots of small children do a bit of magic," he said. "It clings to them after they're born. Then it goes with their baby teeth. She'll grow out of it."

The woman looked at him with contempt. "I've seen more babies than you ever will," she said. "I've had five myself, and two of them did baby magic. But not like this. This wasn't baby magic. This is the gift."

"When was this?" he asked.

"Near a year ago. It'll be worse now."

She gave him a frosty good day and left.

It was easy enough to find Bee. But it was a wizard's work to get her parents to let her come to him as his pupil. Not altogether honest work, either. They needed to be frightened before they let her go. Slowin saw to that. He was old and weak. That was the bad thing. The good thing was, the older he grew and the weaker he became, the more cunning he was. It was clever to make them afraid of Bee. But that would never be enough to make them let her go. No, the cunning work was to make them afraid for Bee, afraid she would hurt herself if she didn't go with him. That was how he worked it.

And so, Bee came to be his pupil, and new, young magic poured into the yard. So strong that it took him by surprise.

"By the blazing fire," he said, "she's got a gift like I've never seen before."

Brassbuck was glad to see Slowin excited. The old wizard grinned at her.

"Enough for two of us," he said. "More than enough."

From that day, the yard had seemed to have a hum in it, too soft to hear, too low to catch, yet always there. Until about a year ago, when the hum became a buzz and a crackle and spark. Silent, invisible, but growing.

Bee could see that it hurt the boy to sit,

hurt the boy to stand. Even talking made his face hurt when he moved his mouth. So she wouldn't ask him too much. She wouldn't make the pain more.

Slowin had told her that she should never work magic outside the yard. He didn't like her to use any magic unless he gave her permission, but that was like telling a bird not to fly, so he accepted things like the way she put fire spells on her belongings to protect them. But outside it was forbidden.

Bee didn't care. Not today. Not with this boy.

She put her hand back onto his shoulder, and she could feel the fire there. So she took a deep breath, and she dragged the fire from his skin and rolled it up into a ball in her hand. It was heavy and it was hot. She had to make strong magic to hold it there. She took her hand from the boy, made a fist, and clenched it over the ball of fire. It glowed so bright, she could see her blood and bones through her fingers.

The magic outside the circle hurled itself at them. The walls of the circle held firm. The magic snarled at her.

The boy fell back and lay on the ground, panting. "What did you do?"

"I took the hurt away."

He tried to get his breath back.

"What happened to you?" she asked.

"I was burned."

Bee knew that already. "How?"

Mattie touched his face with his fingers. He still looked surprised that it didn't hurt. He looked at his blistered arms, his weeping hands. It was hard to find a patch of skin that wasn't burned.

"I work in the kitchens," he said. "Turning the spit, washing dishes, sweeping floors, cleaning out the ashes from the ovens. All the dirty jobs. All the hot jobs."

Bee kept a tight grip on the pain in her hand. The effort was clear on her face.

"We'd been having a lot of trouble with the meat burning on the spit. So they sent for a charm to stop it happening."

"Who did you go to?"

"I don't know. They just said not to bother getting the wizard to come, but to send something that would do the job. To save money."

"That wouldn't work," said Bee. "You need a wizard to come there himself for that sort of job."

She couldn't look at him. She knew now why he was all burned.

"I know that," said Mattie.

"What happened?"

"It came in a special box," said Mattie, "with a piece of paper inside with instructions on it. We took the charm out of the box and followed the instructions."

Bee shook her head. She didn't want to hear any more.

"We put the charm right into the heart of the fire, below the spit with a whole wild boar on it, ready to roast."

"Where was this?"

"In the kitchen."

"No. Where?"

"Oh. In the Palace of Boolat. That's where I work."

Slowin gave Bee practice pieces to do. Exercises. Little spells and charms so that she could learn different ways of working magic. She didn't like doing it. She knew that they probably wouldn't work properly. She had to do them. She was his pupil. He took them away, and she never saw them again. Now she knew why. He sold them. She had made the charm that had made Mattie like this. The ball of pain in her hand grew hotter. It took a lot of magic to stop it from hurting her.

"Go on," she said.

"Well, it all went wrong. I was turning the spit, and the fire jumped up onto the boar. It was like a mad dog. The boar came back to life, and it was alight, a blazing torch. It wriggled off the spit. I tried to move. It was too fast. It jumped on me and then *I* was alight."

Bee made herself look at him.

"Everyone ran over. They threw water on me. They wrapped

me in wet cloths. They beat the flames out. The boar ran out of the kitchen, chased by the mad dog fire, howling. We never saw them again. When they took the cloths off me, I was like this."

He held out his hands. He lifted his burned face.

"Why didn't they look after you?"

"Why? I wasn't going to get better, was I? I couldn't work in the kitchen anymore. They said I'd die from the burns. It was either kill me then or throw me out. They let me choose."

The magic outside the circle had faded to a low growl, listening, while he told his tale.

"How did you get here?" asked Bee.

"Crawled. Walked. Just kept going. Doing something made the pain less for a while. Then I couldn't go any farther. Or at least I couldn't till you took the pain away. Will it come back?"

Bee shook her head. She made a decision. She had already used magic outside the yard once today; she might as well carry on now.

Bee thought back to the day she had made the charm that had burned Mattie. She remembered that she had used a stone, a smooth, green stone, to lock the magic up. She remembered the way she had worked the magic. Thinking hard, she tried to work out how she could turn it around. How could she make it as though Mattie had never been burned?

She looked at the area they were in, inside the circle. There were stones around. Just ordinary ones. Nothing like the deep green stone of the charm.

"How long ago did this happen?" she asked.

"A week. Two weeks. I don't know."

The magic trail was old now. Bee had a feeling that if she tried to trace it back, to undo it at the place where it had gone wrong, she might take a wrong turn. She might even summon up the dog fire or the blazing boar, or both.

No.

Not that way.

It would have to be new magic.

New magic and a new stone.

Bee found a pebble, almost white, almost round, black veins running through it.

She held it in her hand. Gently. Not squeezing. Trying to get to know it. The stone was cold. Underneath, where it had been against the ground, earth clung to it, damp, dark. It was the right one.

She rubbed the dirty side against her sleeve, then licked the pebble clean of anything that had not rubbed off. The stone glistened under her spit, coming alive with a shine it had hidden.

The magic saw what she was doing and it rose up, thrashing against the invisible walls of the circle.

Mattie cowered down.

"It's all right," said Bee. "It can't get in."

In her left hand, she held the cool pebble, in her right, the ball of pain and fire. She stood and balanced herself, keeping her hands far apart.

"Mattie," she said. "Are you frightened?"

"Yes."

"What of?"

Mattie hesitated. He started to say something and then stopped.

"Outside," he said at last, "it's magic, isn't it? Trying to get to us?"

"Yes, it is," said Bee. "It can't get in, though."

"It's noisy."

"Yes."

She waited for him to say more. "What are you frightened of?" she asked again.

"The magic. Out there."

"I'm not frightened of it," she said. "Don't be."

Mattie tried to smile. "Are you really not frightened?"

Bee didn't answer.

"What are you really frightened of?" she asked.

"You."

"Yes."

The magic crouched down and growled.

"Are you more afraid of me than you are of the magic?"

Mattie thought about this. Bee saw the answer come into his mind. Even with his face burned away, it had enough expression for her to be able to read it. He stared at her, shook his head, and stared again.

"Well," she asked, "which are you more afraid of—the magic, or me?"

She wanted him to say it so that she could see if she was right.

"You are the magic," he said.

At once, the magic outside stopped. The silence was startling.

Then, in a flash, it redoubled its violence, reared up, and lashed the walls of the circle.

"Do you want to be better?" asked Bee.

He nodded.

"Are you brave?"

He shook his head.

Bee smiled. "Never mind," she said. "I'll be brave for both of us."

"Sorry."

"Don't say you're sorry again. Stand up."

They stood facing each other. Bee held out her hands and opened them, palms up. The white stone lay still in her left; the pain and fire glowed blue white in her right. Mattie's face was hot with the intensity of the fire. It hurt his eyes to look at it.

"Take one," she said.

Mattie took the white pebble.

Bee let her left arm fall to her side. "I think that's the right one," she said. "I hope so."

"Don't you know?"

"No. The magic has its reasons. I'm not a proper wizard. I hope it's right."

Mattie looked at his pebble. "What if it isn't?"

"If it isn't, we're about to make a big mistake."

Mattie stepped back, nearer to the edge of the circle. The magic made a huge lunge at him, almost breaking through.

"Hush," said Bee. The magic backed away. Mattie stared at her in fear.

"I'm not the magic," she said. "Not really. I don't think so."

"You are," said Mattie.

"Perhaps you're right. Now"—she lifted her right hand—"do as I do."

Putting her hand to her face, she put the ball of pain in her mouth and swallowed it. Mattie did the same with the pebble, very quickly, before he became too frightened to do it.

She wasn't sure whether a long time passed or whether it was all over in an instant. The pain was more than she had ever imagined could be possible. It didn't eat her up; it made her a thousand times herself and made each new piece a perfect fire of pain.

And then it stopped.

Bee was lying on the ground, next to the clump of bracken.

The circle had gone. The magic crouched, snarling, ready to attack, waiting for a command.

Mattie stood over her.

If it was Mattie.

It felt like Mattie. Bee could tell that it was the same person. He looked so different.

She tried to sit up, fearing it would hurt. It didn't. She sat, holding her knees against her chest, ready for another attack of the pain.

"Are you all right?"

It was like Mattie's voice, without the croaky sound.

"Yes. I'm fine."

She tried to stand. It made her head dizzy, so she stayed where she was.

The magic was sniffing around Mattie's ankles. He couldn't

hear it anymore. Bee could. She could hear it. She could see it moving the grass, brushing the fronds of fern.

"I don't know your name," he said.

"It's Bee."

He laughed, so she did as well.

"Yes."

"I thought you were dead."

"I thought you were going to die."

"I was," he said.

"Yes."

"I won't die now."

"Not yet."

They were awkward, wanting to talk, not knowing what to say.

"Look," said Mattie. He held out his hands and arms. He put his hands to his face, stroked the smooth skin, opened his mouth wide, then grinned. "I'm back," he said. "Like it never happened."

"But it did," said Bee.

"I'm just as I was."

"Nothing is ever just as it was."

She tried standing up again. It was all right this time. "What will you do now?" she asked.

"I don't know. What will you do?"

Bee pointed down the hill to Slowin's Yard. "I'll go back there. It's where I live."

They looked at the high wall surrounding the group of squat, round towers, the cobbled yard, the lazy smoke.

"The magic's crackling down there," said Mattie.

"Can you see it?"

"Not exactly, but you know it's there, somehow. Active."

"Yes."

He bit his lip, looked at the magic fizzing in the yard. "Can I come with you?" he asked.

"No."

"Oh."

"I wouldn't mind," said Bee. "I'd like someone like you around. You just can't."

Mattie looked in the other direction, to the Palace of Boolat. "I'll go back there, then," he said.

"You don't have to. You can go anywhere you like."

"Except there." He pointed to the yard.

"Anywhere except there," she agreed.

The awkward silence came back.

"Then I'll go," he said.

"Yes."

"Thank you."

"No."

"Thank you for making me better."

Bee couldn't answer. She knew she had made his pain in the first place. If it hadn't been for her charm, he would never have suffered. She couldn't accept his thanks.

"I'll pay you back one day," he promised.

"There's no need."

He still didn't leave. "Did it hurt?" he said. "When you swallowed the thing?"

"I'm fine," she said. "It doesn't hurt at all."

She watched him go. She wondered how many days it would take him to walk back to Boolat, wondered what they would say when they saw him well again, wondered whether they would take him back after he had been touched by magic, wondered what story he would tell, wondered if he would forget her the way he would forget his pain. So many questions. So much to think about.

Her hands were shaking a little and she decided to sit for a while and watch him walk away before she made her way down the hill, back to Slowin and the yard.

Flaxfield liked harvest time

best of all.

"Come on, Cabbage," he said. "We're off to work."

Cabbage was twelve and had never been to harvest before. "Shall I pack some food?" he asked.

Flaxfield boxed his ears softly. "You and your food," he said. "Go on, then. But only enough for one meal. We'll be there by three o' clock."

Cabbage grinned at him and pushed his hand through his hair, sweeping it back from his eyes where it had fallen from Flaxfield's playful cuffing.

Bag packed. Boots fastened. Hat on. Just lock the door and they're ready to go.

Flaxfield used a key. He liked simple ways whenever possible. As the key turned in the lock, it grew hot, and Flaxfield pulled his hand away.

"That's odd," he said.

"What?"

Flaxfield looked at his hand. A small red mark where the key had burned it.

"I didn't put a locking spell on the door," said Flaxfield. "So it shouldn't get hot like that."

"Are you sure?" asked Cabbage.

Flaxfield tried the key. It was cool now. He turned it in the lock and dropped it into the bag at his waist.

"I think so," said Flaxfield. "I suppose I could have done it without thinking."

"Is it locked now?"

He rattled the handle. "Tight as a bowstring."

"Let's go, then," said Cabbage.

"Have you got your notebook?"

Cabbage patted the bag slung over his left shoulder. "And what was left of that beef. Some bread. I buttered it already. Apples, cheese, and a couple of bottles of water."

Flaxfield strode along, Cabbage half walking, half trotting to keep up.

"If you ever give up being a wizard, you can open an inn," he said.

"I'd like that," said Cabbage.

He didn't see the quick look of disapproval on Flaxfield's face and carried on talking. "But I'd want to do both."

The disapproving look gave way to a smile. "Both?" said Flaxfield.

"You know. I'll never not want to be a wizard. But wouldn't it be good to be a wizard with an inn?"

"What about the customers who don't pay?"

"Turn them into frogs."

"The chef who steals the food?"

"Fill him with air like a pig's bladder. Put him on a stick outside as a warning to others."

Flaxfield grinned. "He'd blow away in the wind. You'd be arrested for murder."

"Oh, he'd blow back. Thieves always do."

Flaxfield stopped and looked at Cabbage. "Where do you get these ideas from?" he said. "Have you ever met a thief?"

Cabbage shrugged. "Don't know. Just think of them."

They started walking again. Flaxfield had slowed down, and it was more comfortable for Cabbage.

"They just pop into my head," said the boy. "Thoughts."

"You'd do well to let them pop out again," said Flaxfield.

"What I'd do," said Cabbage, "is, I'd charge people for their rooms according to what their clothes were like. The same for their food."

"How would you do that?"

"Well, say someone came in and was wearing jewels and furs and expensive clothes. I'd make them pay a lot for their food and rooms. And if someone came in wearing worn-out old boots, they could have a meal for a penny and a bed for tuppence."

"Do you think you can tell what people are like by looking at them?" asked Flaxfield.

Cabbage thought about this.

"You'd have an inn full of beggars," said Flaxfield. "And what rich person would want to eat there and pay for them all? You'd be out of business in half a year."

Cabbage slid his hand under the strap of his bag and adjusted it so it wouldn't rub into his shoulder so much. He walked alongside the tall wizard in silence for a while. Flaxfield let him think it through.

"What's harvest like?" asked Cabbage.

"Hard work."

Cabbage frowned. "Magic work?" he asked.

"Hard work. Lifting. Cutting. Stacking. Tying. Dragging."

"Not for wizards," said Cabbage.

Flaxfield laughed and put his arm on Cabbage's shoulder for a moment.

"What would you do all day at this inn of yours?" he asked.

"I'd welcome the guests. And I'd sit and talk with them, find out where they came from, where they're going, what their business is."

"Do you think they'd tell you their business?"

"I could give them a special magic drink that would make them tell me," said Cabbage.

"Could you, indeed? Is that why I'm teaching you to be a wizard, so you can trick people and learn what they don't want to tell you?"

Cabbage blushed. "What will I do for the harvest?" he asked Flaxfield.

The wizard worked out the time by looking at how far the sun had traveled across the late-summer sky. "Are you hungry yet?"

Cabbage was always hungry, so they sat in the shade of a horse chestnut and started to eat their lunch. The bread was crusty and the beef was pink.

Cabbage spread out a blue-and-white-checked cloth and arranged all the food and the two bottles of water as though they were receiving guests at home.

Flaxfield smiled. He bit into an apple and popped a piece of cheese into his mouth so he could eat them together.

"Perhaps you should have an inn, after all. You like to spread a feast."

Cabbage grinned at him. "Just because we're in a field is no reason why we shouldn't do things properly," he said. Then he added a hurried afterthought. "But I'm not going to. I'm going to be a wizard."

Flaxfield tore off a piece of bread.

"Doing things properly is wizard's work as well," he said.

"Look at that," said Cabbage, pointing to his left. "It's memmonts, isn't it?"

Flaxfield stood and waved.

"Is it memmonts?" said Cabbage.

"Over here," shouted Flaxfield. "They can't hear us. Run off and get them, boy. Quickly. Tell them Flaxfield wants to say hello."

Cabbage looked sadly at the food. He'd only just got started and didn't like to leave it. But an apprentice knows better than to argue with his master. And he'd never seen a memmont before.

He ran off in the direction of the figures, swearing silently. It was the hottest part of the day and he was still hungry. Soon he was sweating and short of breath. And he didn't seem to be getting any closer.

One spell. One simple spell would have been enough to attract their attention, make them turn around and come toward him. If he'd been on his own, Cabbage would probably have risked it. But not with Flaxfield looking on. "No loose magic, boy," Cabbage muttered in Flaxfield's voice, as he heard it day after day.

He called out. The heavy afternoon air sucked in his words and they didn't carry.

"Hey! Over here!"

The memmonts, four of them, with two roffles, carried on. It would take forever to catch them up.

Cabbage put his finger into his mouth and blew.

Now, Cabbage had never been able to whistle. He had practiced for hours.

Flaxfield was sitting in the shade of the tree, eating their lunch, while a hungry, angry Cabbage was racing over a bumpy field in blazing sun, shouting at memmonts that couldn't hear him.

He looked over his shoulder. Flaxfield had his back to him, lifting a bottle of water to his lips. It was too much for Cabbage.

He plucked a stem of high grass, heavy with ripe seeds, put it to his lips, and made a whistling spell. Flaxfield would never know.

The whistle sped silently through the air, like an arrow. It hovered over the memmonts and the roffles, then burst open in a shrill explosion.

They stopped, turned, and looked at Cabbage, who waved and beckoned them over.

The rear memmont, the one nearest to Cabbage, trotted toward him, then bounded forward, then ran at full speed. As it approached, it began to change, from a shy creature the size of a small goat into the biggest dog that Cabbage had ever seen. Its head became longer and sharper, teeth yellow and jagged. The creature's legs were slender yet strong. Its tongue lolled to one side.

Cabbage turned and ran back to Flaxfield. He was still running when the huge dog leaped onto his back. Cabbage fell forward. The hard ground knocked the wind out of him. He banged his face against the earth. The last thing he heard was the savage growl. The last thing he felt was the warm saliva on his neck as the dog's head jabbed down at him, mouth wide, teeth bared.

Flaxfield prodded the dead memmont

with the toe of his shoe. Cabbage had never seen his face so hard, so set. The wizard leaned on his staff and looked at the roffle. "Sorry," he said.

Megawhim shook his head. "I've never seen anything like it," he said.

"Cabbage," said Flaxfield, "tell us what happened. All of it."

Cabbage looked away, then looked back at them. The tall wizard and the two roffles, only half his size, with their backpacks shaped like squashed barrels. Megawhim was standing next to Flaxfield, arms crossed, looking Cabbage in the face. Megapoir was stroking the three memmonts and drinking a beaker of apple juice. But Cabbage's eyes kept going back to the dead memmont.

It was his fault. The dead memmont. He had done it. He had killed a memmont and nearly got killed himself. He couldn't speak.

"Did you tie a donkey to a plum cake?" asked Megawhim.

Cabbage shook his head.

"Well, did you push a pig's tail up your nose and sneeze a sausage?"

Cabbage stared at the little figure.

"No. Why would I do that?" He appealed to Flaxfield. "Why would I want to do that?"

Flaxfield put his hand on the roffle's shoulder. "Just let the boy tell us," he said.

Cabbage started to speak, then coughed, stopped, tried again, and began to choke. The words were fighting not to be spoken.

Megapoir trotted over and handed him the beaker. "Try this."

"Thank you."

Megapoir trotted back to the memmonts, sat on his barrel, and stroked them again.

"I made a spell," said Cabbage. He told the story to Megapoir, ignoring the looks of the others. It seemed easier. The smaller roffle nodded and smiled at him, helping him to go on.

"I was hot and tired and couldn't run. I got a stitch. You couldn't hear me. And I was hungry. He"—Cabbage pointed at Flaxfield without looking at him—"was eating all our food. So I made a whistle spell."

Megapoir nodded.

"I can't whistle," said Cabbage. "So I had to make a spell."

"I can whistle," said the roffle. He put his fingers to his mouth and proved it. Very loud.

"That'll do," said Megawhim. "You'll have a cow with a blue hat and a piece of fish coming if you're not careful."

"Anyway, I made the whistle, then the memmont started to run at me. Then it turned into a dog and I ran away. I think it jumped on me," said Cabbage. "The next thing I knew, I was here."

Here was the courtyard of an inn.

"What happened to me?" Cabbage asked.

"You were . . . ," began Megawhim, but he was interrupted by Megapoir.

"You should have seen it," he said. He bounced up and down on his barrel, the sides bulging.

"The beast had its jaws open wider than your head. It was going to snap it off."

He didn't seem to notice Cabbage's shudder.

"There was all this drool dripping down on you. Then he"—the roffle pointed to Flaxfield—"stood up and pointed his staff at you both. The beast flew backward, tumbling over and over, like a pinecone, and when it stopped, it was a memmont again."

He paused, out of breath.

"Dead, of course," he added, his voice lower and his eyes wet.

A memmont licked his face. Megapoir made a small smile and put his head to the side of the memmont, breathing in its warm scent.

"Then we brought you here," said the other roffle. His voice was angry. "And what are we going to do now? Eh? Are we going to make a cat's cartwheel, or shall we sing a song of sandwiches?"

Cabbage put his hand to the cobbles. Cold, smooth, with rough mortar between.

"It was my fault," he said. "It's my fault the memmont's dead."

"Yes," said Megawhim. "Your fault."

"Yes," said Flaxfield. "I'm afraid it was your fault. It won't do to pretend. But there's nothing that can't be put right."

"I'm sorry," said Cabbage.

"I know you are," said the wizard. "I know. We'll sort it out. Don't worry. Here, young 'un," he said to Megapoir. "Can you get my apprentice something to eat and drink? He went without his lunch. We can't have that."

Megapoir jumped up and ran over to them. "Can I get him some food?" he said. "Can a fat dog find a pork chop? Come on."

He grabbed Cabbage and pulled him to the inn door.

"But what happened?" asked Cabbage. "How?"

"He'll tell you," said Flaxfield. He gave the roffle a hard stare. "He seems to tell a good story. He'll tell you all about it."

"What will you do?" asked Cabbage. "What about the memmont?"

For all his talk about running an inn, Cabbage had hardly ever been inside one. When he traveled with Flaxfield, they usually stayed at the houses of people he knew. Flaxfield seemed to know people everywhere, and they were always glad to see him, but he liked it best when Flaxfield didn't know anyone and they had to stay at an inn.

Cabbage liked rooms with many tables and chairs, settles by the fire, bottles of wine and casks of beer. He liked the beehive of conversation, the laughter, the door opening and closing as people came and went. He liked the stairs up to a strange bedroom. He liked to be in the midst of people without being with them.

"What's this inn called?" asked Cabbage.

He had to ask Megapoir twice because he was eating a meat pasty the first time and the roffle couldn't understand him.

"Sorry," said Cabbage. "Shouldn't talk with my mouth full, but I'm so hungry."

"The White Hart," said Megapoir.

The innkeeper pretended to tidy bottles and clean glasses. He never looked directly at them.

Cabbage lowered his voice. "It's not very nice, is it?"

"Why are you called Cabbage?" asked Megapoir.

"Why do all roffle names begin with Mega?" asked Cabbage, going a little red.

"Mine doesn't."

"It does. They all do."

The innkeeper came across to them. "Any more food?" he asked.

The man was small, with arms and legs that didn't seem to work with the rest of his body. His dark hair was short and combed close to his head. He smiled when he spoke to them.

Cabbage picked up the last piece of pasty and then put it down again.

"No, we've had enough. Thank you," he said.

"Nice to see someone enjoying the food," the innkeeper said, and disappeared into the kitchen with the dirty plate.

"It wasn't very fresh," Cabbage whispered. "I'm still hungry."

"It's not a good inn," said the roffle. "Look. There's no one here."

He sat back, put his hands behind his head, and looked straight at Cabbage. "We never call here, usually," he said.

"Do you stay at inns a lot?"

Cabbage admired his confidence and experience.

"As often as a snail makes a kite in a farm cart. How old are you?"

"Twelve," said Cabbage. "What happened to the memmont?"

The roffle leaned forward, his eyes newly bright with interest. "You did that," he said. "How did you do it? Why?"

"I didn't. Really, I didn't. What do you do with memmonts anyway? Were they yours?"

"No one owns memmonts. My dad and I were just collecting them, to take back."

"Is that your dad? I thought you . . . well, never mind. How old are you?"

He shrugged. "We don't count really. There are no years in the Deep World. No seasons. Not like seasons Up Top. I suppose I'm about twelve as well."

Cabbage grinned at him, pleased to discover the roffle wasn't another grown-up after all.

"We're going to harvest," he said. "I've never seen a memmont before. Or a roffle." He ran his hand through his hair. "Look," he said. "I'm sorry, but I can't remember your name. All roffles have names that are sort of the same."

The roffle looked over his shoulder, then back at Cabbage.

"It's Megapoir. But that's only my name Up Top. Really, it's Perry."

"Right. Can I call you Perry?"

"Only when there's no one else around. We have a lot of things we say and do Up Top that we don't do in the Deep World."

"Why?"

"To confuse people."

Cabbage didn't understand this, but he nodded as though he did. He was just about to explain why he was called Cabbage when the door opened and Flaxfield and Megawhim came in. Perry gave Cabbage a warning look and Cabbage winked at him.

"Beer," shouted Flaxfield. "Two, please."

The innkeeper popped up straightaway and poured two mugs of beer from a barrel on a shelf. Flaxfield watched him and waited till he had gone before he spoke again.

"He appeared pretty quickly," he said. "I wonder where he's gone now."

Megawhim pulled up a chair and sat next to Perry. "We've buried the memmont," he said.

Perry nodded. His eyes filled with tears.

Megawhim looked at Cabbage. "What did you do?" he asked.

Cabbage was put off by his abrupt manner and the way he stared, as though challenging him to a fight. He glared back. "It was my fault. All right? I'm sorry."

He turned to Perry. "I'm really sorry."

Flaxfield put his hand on Megawhim's shoulder, but he spoke to Cabbage.

"It's all right," he said. "Forget about whose fault it was. It happened. We just want to know what went wrong."

"I told you outside."

Megawhim slapped his hand on the table. "There's more to it than that," he said.

"Memmonts are such gentle creatures," said Flaxfield. "It would take a very strong magic to turn one into that, into that . . ." He searched for the right word.

"Into that wild beast," said Megawhim. "It nearly killed you. I've never seen a memmont like that."

"It wasn't a memmont," said Perry. "Not when it got to Cabbage. Not anymore."

"That it wasn't," said Flaxfield.

"And it wasn't going to kill him," said Perry. "It was just standing there, dripping on him."

"It would have killed him," said Megawhim. "Of course it would."

"Why didn't it, then?" Perry demanded.

"Wait." Flaxfield held his finger to his lips. They listened. He turned his mug upside down. The beer fell out, gathered into the shape of an ear, and flew across the room. The door sprang open and the innkeeper fell through. The ear splashed against him and soaked his face and neck.

"Did you want to hear something?" Flaxfield demanded.

The innkeeper smiled at them. The same false smile he had given Cabbage when he took his plate away. "I was just coming to see if you wanted more beer."

As he spoke, the side of his face began to hiss and bubble. The skin blistered and peeled off. He screamed and held his hands to his face. The beer was burning him and eating into his flesh.

Megawhim leaped to his feet. "That's a bit harsh, Flaxfield," he said.

Perry and Cabbage stared at the man in his agony. Perry put his hands to his ears.

"Stop it," said Megawhim. "Stop it. He was only eavesdropping."

Flaxfield strode across the room. He seized the innkeeper's hands and pulled them from his face. The man screamed louder.

Cabbage had never seen Flaxfield look helpless before. The wizard stared at the ruined face.

"I don't understand," he said. "I don't know."

The innkeeper choked and gasped for breath.

"He's dying," said Megawhim. "You've got to help him. You've got to make it stop."

"I can't." Flaxfield looked around, searching for an idea. "I can't stop it."

Cabbage and Perry filled a bucket of water

from the pump and carried it over to pour into the stone trough for the memmonts to drink.

"What do you think they're doing?" asked Perry.

Cabbage stepped back to stop the water from splashing on his feet.

"I know I shouldn't be," he said, "but I'm hungry." He pulled an apologetic face. "I mean, we just watched a man die, and I've never seen that before, and I should be shaken up, but really, I'm hungry."

"I couldn't eat anything," said Perry.

"You could watch me."

They found the kitchen.

"Why isn't there anyone here?" asked Cabbage. "A cook or someone? And no customers."

Perry opened cupboard doors and took out bread, butter, some eggs, a cold joint of mutton, half a cooked chicken, apples, a pie that had the edges of its crust missing where rats had nibbled it.

"It's not that much of an inn," Perry reminded him. "And it's afternoon. People will be at work, or traveling. It might get busy later."

He looked at the food, most of it stale and old. "I don't suppose people eat here if they can avoid it."

Cabbage pushed the pie to one side, cut a slice of bread, buttered it, and added a slice of mutton.

They could hear muffled voices from the other side of the door. Flaxfield and Megawhim talking. Flaxfield didn't seem to be saying much.

"Flaxfield shouldn't have killed him," said Perry.

Cabbage stopped chewing.

Megawhim was shouting now. After a pause Flaxfield spoke quietly.

Cabbage tried to swallow, chewed again. He spat the food into his open palm and threw it into the trash.

"I thought you were hungry?"

"I can't eat this muck."

Megawhim appeared in the doorway. "Come on. We're going home."

His face was angry. He grabbed Perry by the shoulder to hurry him up. The young roffle sprang to his feet and backed away.

"I want to know what's going on," he said.

"Home. Now."

Megawhim seemed to notice Cabbage for the first time.

"We haven't got time to plant a row of candle trees and wait for the moon to light them," he said. "Come on, Megapoir."

Perry glanced at Cabbage, then glowered at his father. "My name's Perry," he said. "And you can stop that roffle-talk. Cabbage knows all about it."

Megawhim crossed the kitchen and grabbed Perry. "You've been too loose with your lips," he said. "You won't be coming back Up Top for a long while."

"I'm not going back. Not yet."

Cabbage thought Megawhim was going to hit Perry. Flaxfield seemed to think the same. He stepped forward and said, "We should all talk, old friend."

The roffle rounded on him. "You killed that man. I don't want Perry anywhere near any of this."

"Please," said Flaxfield.

Megawhim hesitated.

"Please," said Perry.

"I want to talk as well," said Cabbage.

Megawhim stamped off. He yanked a chair out from the kitchen table and sat down.

"In here," he said. "I don't want to talk in the same room as the man you murdered."

Flaxfield gave a grim smile. "Thank you," he said.

Cabbage cleared away the food from the table and they all pulled up chairs, Megawhim mumbling complaints all the while under his breath.

"Flaxfield," said Cabbage, "why did you kill that man?"

At last, there was silence. They all looked at Flaxfield and waited.

He cleared his throat. "I did kill him," he said. "We all saw that."

Megawhim started to speak. Flaxfield held up his hand for silence. He looked directly at Cabbage. "You're my apprentice," he said. "Have been for six years."

"Yes," Cabbage agreed.

"Have you ever seen me hurt anyone or anything? Think hard."

Cabbage didn't need to think about it. "No."

"Good."

"Well, you have now," said Megawhim.

Perry glared at him. "Let him finish."

"Have you ever seen any of my magic go wrong?" asked Flaxfield.

"No."

"Good. Suppose," he said, "I pick up this kitchen knife." The knife had a bone handle and a long blade, worn thin with years of sharpening. "To cut myself a slice of mutton," he continued.

Cabbage knew the knife was very sharp because he had used it himself not many minutes ago.

"Now," said Flaxfield, "suppose that the terrible roffle here"—he indicated Megawhim—"suppose he grabs my arm, overpowers me, and plunges the knife into my excellent, if ever-hungry young apprentice." He lowered his voice to a whisper. "And the boy dies."

Megawhim glared at him. Perry and Cabbage listened, open-mouthed.

"Who killed the apprentice?" asked Flaxfield.

"He did," said Perry, pointing at his father.

"But I'm holding the knife," Flaxfield argued. "It's in my hand. I'm covered in his blood."

"It doesn't matter," said Cabbage. "He forced your arm. He's the one who stabbed me."

"Look here," said Megawhim. "This isn't right."

"No," said Flaxfield. "I'm sorry. It isn't nice, being accused of murder, is it? Especially by an old friend."

Megawhim looked embarrassed.

"Let's just say it wasn't you," said Flaxfield. "Let's say it was a stranger who burst in and did it."

"It still isn't your fault," said Cabbage.

"You're right," said Flaxfield. "But a knife is a dangerous thing. And anyone who picks one up should be sure he knows how to use it safely."

"Where's all this going?" asked Megawhim.

"I didn't kill the innkeeper," said Flaxfield. "I made an easy spell to make the door fly open. And I spilled beer all over him, to give him a soaking. He was listening in on us, and I wanted to teach him a lesson."

Megawhim grunted.

"I held the knife," said Flaxfield. "Someone else pushed it into him and killed him."

"What do you mean?" asked Perry.

Flaxfield turned a grim smile on him.

"Something made my key hot this morning. Someone changed the beer into something else. Something that burned right through his flesh. The pain and the attack killed him. But I did not do it."

Perry nodded.

"Megawhim?" said Flaxfield.

The roffle scowled. "I don't know why you didn't help him."

"That's the worst part," said Flaxfield. "It took me by surprise. And it was very powerful. It was like being hit on the head by someone who crept up on me from behind. If I had seen it coming, if I had been ready for it, perhaps I could have saved the innkeeper. I don't know."

He was still holding the knife, turning it over in his long fingers.

"It was the same with the memmont," said Cabbage.

He explained how it had felt when the whistle he had made with magic reached the memmonts.

"It was like when you've made a garden fire, putting on a few pieces of wood at a time, letting it burn steadily. Then, all at once, it flares up, out of control. Catches the side of the house or a tree. And it's off. Too late to stop it. It was like that. I made the whistle with the magic." He looked nervously at Flaxfield. "And I used just enough magic, no more. I was trying to hide it from you. Then, when it reached the memmonts, it slipped away from me and grew huge, and I couldn't stop it."

"Exactly," said Flaxfield. "That's just what it was like. Something else seized it and took over."

He gave a solemn look around the table. "Something very powerful," he added.

"Something wild," said Cabbage.

"I was lucky," said Flaxfield. "When I stopped the memmont from attacking you. But," he continued, "I only tried to stop it, not hurt it. I wanted to turn it back into a memmont. I thought I had just made the spell too strong. Now I know that it wasn't that. Whatever wild magic is out there killed the memmont."

"What does it mean?" asked Megawhim. He was quieter now.

"We have to find out," said Flaxfield. "But first, we should leave here."

"That's good," said Megawhim. "We're going home."

"There will be people arriving," said Flaxfield. "We must go before they get here."

"Are we just going to leave the innkeeper here?" asked Cabbage.

"I'll perform the Finishing for him; then we'll leave. We'll use the back door."

The late-afternoon sun was welcome after the gloom of the kitchen. Flaxfield moved quickly, his cloak floating out behind him. Megawhim stamped over to the three memmonts and prepared them for the journey home. Cabbage and Perry left the courtyard through the big wooden gates and sat on a grassy bank, looking up the road to see if any travelers were arriving.

"What's it like being an apprentice?" asked Perry.

"It's all right." He flapped a hand in front of his face to drive away the midges. "What's it like being a roffle?"

"I don't know. I've never been anything else."

"I can't really remember being anything else but an apprentice. Do you often come Up Top with your dad?"

"Mostly. There's only us, so I'd be on my own if I didn't."

"What about your mum?"

"She died when I was little."

As an apprentice to a wizard, Cabbage had been to lots of

houses just after someone had died. It was always sad, but it was worst when there were small children left without a mother or father. He started to say something to Perry and was interrupted by Flaxfield calling out.

"Cabbage. Cabbage!"

"Over here."

Flaxfield stepped through the stone archway leading to the inn yard.

"No magic. Understand?"

"All right."

"I mean it. Not even the smallest spell. Nothing."

"Yes. I understand. I'm not stupid."

Flaxfield didn't like cheek. Cabbage knew things were serious when the wizard ignored it this time.

"I'll come and talk to you in a minute," he said, ducking back through the arch.

"It's all right," said Perry. "It was a long time ago. I don't really remember her."

"What about school?"

Perry plucked at a small celandine. He snapped the stem, then pulled the petals off.

"I don't go to school. I help Dad find the memmonts."

As though he had called them, the memmonts appeared in the gateway. Megawhim followed, then Flaxfield.

The wizard beckoned the two young ones over to him. "We've had a talk," he said. He paused. "And you can stay with us," he said to Perry.

Perry slammed his barrel-pack down and jumped up on top of it.

"Until the harvest is over," said the wizard. "Then you have to go home."

"Thank you," said Perry.

"Thank your father."

Perry stepped down and went to Megawhim. "Thank you."

Megawhim snorted. "Just make sure you behave."

"I will."

Megawhim turned and clicked his tongue for the memmonts and walked off. They followed him, strung out in a line. They crossed the grass bank, turned left, and headed for a dry stone wall. "And look after yourself," Megawhim called.

Perry ran after him. His father caught him in his arms and they hugged. "Be careful," he whispered. "I'll be back for you when harvest's over."

"I'll get them to bake you a special pie, for the big supper," Perry promised him.

"You do that." Megawhim dragged his sleeve over his eyes and put his hand on Perry's shoulder. "You do that, son."

He stepped behind the stone wall. His head dipped down and the next moment he was gone, and the memmonts with him.

"I like stars," said Perry.

They were lying on their backs looking up into the night sky. Flaxfield was a little way off. He had built a fire and was cooking a rabbit on a spit.

"We don't have stars in the Deep World," Perry said.

This started so many thoughts in Cabbage's head, so many questions, that he didn't know where to begin. "They're almost better than magic," said Cabbage. "But sometimes they are too loud and I get confused."

Perry sat up and leaned against his barrel-pack so that he could look at Cabbage. "What do you mean?"

"When they're all speaking at once," said Cabbage. "I can't make out what they're saying."

Flaxfield threw some roots into a pot of boiling water that he had hung over the fire from his staff. "Won't be long," he called.

"What are they saying now?" asked Perry.

Cabbage sat up. "Nothing, of course. They're not saying anything tonight. That's what's so strange."

Perry was about to ask the next question when Flaxfield called them over. The rabbit meat was nicely crisp on the outside, sweet and juicy inside. It was hot, and they had to take care not to burn their mouths.

"What's it like in the Deep World?" asked Cabbage. "What's the sky like if there aren't any stars?"

Perry took another big bite of rabbit and chewed slowly, thinking. Flaxfield grinned at him.

"Oh, you have to ask a different question," said the wizard. "Roffles don't tell anyone what it's like down there. Or, if they do tell you, it's never true. Is it, Perry?"

They waited for Perry to finish chewing.

"I'm not supposed to," he said. "But Cabbage is my friend. I don't want to tell him stories."

Flaxfield gave them some boiled roots and leaves. "Make sure you eat these. And there are apples for afterward."

"What shall I tell him?" asked Perry.

Flaxfield put a gentle hand on Perry's arm. "You'll have to work that out for yourself."

"I've never had a friend before," said Perry.

"That makes it harder for you, then," said Flaxfield. "Now, sooner or later we need to find out what's going on. And to do that, we'll have to try a little magic and see what happens."

He tore the last of the meat from a rabbit bone with his teeth, threw the bone into the fire, wiped his fingers on the grass, and said, "Right, shall we do something very dangerous, or shall we go to sleep and hope for the best?"

Perry and Cabbage sat to one side

of the fire while Flaxfield prepared for the test. Cabbage explained a little about magic.

"It's not a game," he said. "And it's never there just to make things easier."

"What's the point of it if it doesn't make things easier?" asked Perry.

Cabbage frowned. This was the difficult part. It was so difficult, he didn't really understand it himself, so it was going to be tricky trying to get Perry to get the hang of it.

"It does make things easier, but that isn't the point of it."

"Well, what is the point of magic?"

An owl flew silently past then, swooping in the darkness and rising up, a vole twisting in its talons.

Flaxfield sat down next to them.

"We're ready," he said. "But perhaps you should finish telling Perry first. It will help if he knows at least a little bit about magic."

Cabbage had the feeling that the wizard was teasing him.

"I'm stuck," he said.

"What is the point of magic?" asked Perry.

The wizard laced his long fingers together and rested his hands on his knees.

"We're going to harvest," he said. "It's hard work. Back-aching, arm-aching, throat-drying work. With the sun hot on the back of your neck and the dust from the fields in your face."

Perry moved closer, listening carefully.

"Now, young Cabbage here, he doesn't like hard work very much."

Cabbage scowled.

"Cabbage would like it if I could weave a little harvest magic, so that the crops cut themselves and jumped up into the farm carts. He'd like a spell to winnow the grain from the chaff and tie up the stalks and bag up the wheat. That's what Cabbage would like."

"I'd like that," said Perry. Cabbage gave his friend a small, grateful punch on his arm.

"Could you do that?" asked Perry.

Flaxfield nodded. "I could. Or something like it. And if I did, the village would die."

"Would the magic kill the village?" asked Perry.

Flaxfield stood up. "Wait until harvest," he said. "Then I'll tell you, perhaps. Come on. Magic. We need to get a long way from the fire, I think. Over there, by the river."

The air was cooler in the dip. The river grumbled over round stones. Cabbage picked up a frog.

"No," said Flaxfield. "No creatures, Cabbage. If anything gets hurt, it should just be us. We've chosen."

Perry studied the wizard. He seemed tall to the roffle. All men do. His staff seldom left his hand, as though it were part of him. He did not so much lean on it as put it on the ground to balance himself. Without it, he would have looked as odd as a man standing on one leg.

"I think we should stand a little apart from one another," Flaxfield suggested. "That way, if lightning strikes, it will hit only one of us."

The boys backed away.

"And not under that tree," he added.

Perry moved to his left.

"That should do it. Now, have you noticed any wild magic since the innkeeper died?"

"No."

"No. But two sudden flashes of it together, the memmont and the beer, and that little moment with the key just as we left home."

He sighed.

"I think," he said, "that the wild magic isn't coming at us from outside. I think it just uses any magic it can get its hands on."

"What shall we do?" asked Cabbage.

"We'll make some magic," said Flaxfield. "Just a little bit. As a test."

Cabbage looked at the stars again. He strained to listen to them. The same, strange silence.

"Perhaps a small spell to put the fire out," said Flaxfield.

He pointed his staff toward the fire.

A few last flames licked up over the orange embers. He spoke to the fire, telling it to go to sleep. Perry felt the effect of his voice, though it was soft, almost too soft to hear.

The flames stuttered. The embers lost their deep glow. The fire sighed, died. Then it burst out, twice the size. It reared up, like a snake, slithered across the grass toward them.

Flaxfield lowered his staff and shouted a command. The fire twisted, slid away; with a flick, it came on again. It swerved around the wizard, rose up, and struck its fangs into Perry's leg.

He screamed.

It wound itself around his leg. His clothes flamed out. Flaxfield shouted again. The fire-snake drew its head back, bared its fangs at Flaxfield, black eyes bright in the glow from its own fire, then turned back and sank the fangs again into Perry. The young roffle's shrieks flew out like bats.

Cabbage hurled himself at Perry. He threw his arms around him and ran him off his feet. The flames slobbered over them both. The force of his charge carried them off the riverbank and into the water. They hit the surface, sank, dashed against the rocks, then emerged, spluttering, soaked, but the fire extinguished. A serpentine line of ash floated away on the surface, spread and vanished.

"Let's have a look at you," said Flaxfield. He hauled them out of the water.

Cabbage had no marks on him at all. Perry was not blistered or burned, and in no pain.

"Here," said Flaxfield.

Below the knee, on his left leg, Perry had a scorch mark, black and red, in the shape of a snake.

Flaxfield gave Cabbage a grim look. "No more magic, understand?"

Cabbage didn't need Flaxfield to tell him. The stars had already whispered it in his ear.

"Why do they call you Cabbage?" asked Perry.

The village was within sight now. Flaxfield walked ahead. The boys followed, keeping him in sight, out of hearing. Since the experiment with the fire, the wizard had been glad to let the two of them chatter away while he tried to think about what was happening.

And all the time, the disturbance around them became greater. Perry noticed it a little. Like the scent of something rotting close by but out of sight. Cabbage felt it more strongly. His skin tingled. His eyes were sore, and he rubbed them red. For Flaxfield, the disruption in magic was like a pain. It ached all the time except for the moments when it became like a knife, and it was all he could do not to cry out. He knew that whatever it was, they were moving ever closer to it.

It was midmorning when they saw the first line of people moving across the field of wheat. Red poppies dusted the yellow wheat, flames on blond hair. Scythes cut through the stalks and the wheat fell away in elegant fans on the ground. Cabbage had never seen anything like it. The sun jumped from the bright blades. The yellow wheat submitted to the reapers. It looked so smooth, so easy, so graceful.

"Are they using magic?" asked Perry.

Flaxfield shook his head. "We're late," he said. "I should have been here before they started."

He hitched his cloak up on his left shoulder and led them down to the field. No one noticed them until they were almost there. One of the women lifted her head from her work. She called out. The men stopped swinging their scythes, straightened their backs, and turned to see them approaching.

Flaxfield waved. Some of them waved back. Others leaned on their scythes. Some took the opportunity to sit. A few found flasks of water, drank, passed them round, and wiped their wet mouths on their sleeves.

Two men and the woman separated themselves from the others and walked toward them.

"Dorwin." Flaxfield greeted the woman first. She hugged him, which made Cabbage stretch his eyes. She was tall, and her straight hair glistened with sweat from the heat and work. Flaxfield shook hands with the men.

"Leathort. Rotack," he said. "It's been a long time."

"Flaxfield," said Rotack. "I'm sorry. We couldn't wait."

He removed his hat and wiped his brow. He wasn't old, but his hair had already grown tired of him.

"Of course," said Flaxfield. "I'm sorry. We were delayed. This is Cabbage, my apprentice. And this is Perry."

"A roffle," said Leathort, shaking hands with the boys. "It's a long time since I saw a roffle."

"We waited three days," said Dorwin. "Harvest's early this year." Instead of shaking hands with the boys, or hugging them, she stood between them and put her hands on their shoulders. "Perfect weather for harvest, but we waited. Then we had to start."

Her eyes were anxious on Flaxfield.

"I understand," he said. "Harvest won't wait."

"We've never started without the Harvest Spell before," said Rotack. Cabbage couldn't decide whether it sounded like an apology or a complaint. Or perhaps a challenge.

"If the fine weather held, the grain would have been scorched on the stalk," said Dorwin.

"And if the weather broke, the grain would have rotted," said Leathort. "We had no choice." He smiled.

"You had no choice," agreed Flaxfield.

"But you can start now," said Rotack. "Let's get some magic on this harvest."

He folded his arms and waited.

"That may be a problem," said Flaxfield.

Perry and Cabbage sat in the shade of the hedge and watched.

The harvest had restarted. The men with long-handled scythes swung the blades and sliced the wheat. The women followed, gathering the stalks and shocking them, poppies and grain together. Flaxfield, Leathort, Dorwin, and Rotack stood to one side, talking intently. The boys couldn't hear what was said, but they could see how it was going. Flaxfield was explaining about the disturbance in the magic and how it had slowed them down.

"So," said Perry, "why do they call you Cabbage?"

"Every wizard has a special name," said Cabbage. "It's a secret. And the only way to find your name is to go to be an apprentice to a wizard."

"Cabbage doesn't sound very special," said Perry.

"It's not my wizard name," said Cabbage. "It's a nickname."

"What's your wizard name?"

"When I was born, my parents called me Borton," he said, "except everyone called me Bort."

"What were they like?"

"I don't remember. I was very small when I went to Flaxfield. They have to send you to a wizard when you're little, or you could hurt yourself. Or someone else."

The reapers had finished a wide strip of wheat on the south side of the field nearest the boys. Now they turned and started to cut along the hedge on the next side, walking away from them.

"I want a go with one of those scythes," said Perry.

"You'd cut your foot off."

"Or yours."

Cabbage punched him and they lay back, laughing.

"Anyway," said Perry. "Why are you called Cabbage? And how do you get your wizard name?"

"Only a true wizard can discover a new wizard's name," said Cabbage. "And without your true name, you can never be a proper wizard."

"What happens to people who are born with magic who never get their wizard name?"

"Most of them, the magic goes away. Like being able to put your toe in your mouth. If it doesn't go away, you can sometimes just stop using it. And it sort of freezes. It's still there, part of you, but you forget about it."

"I don't see how that can happen," said Perry.

"Neither do I. It's like being able to speak but not saying anything. I don't think it happens much and not to people who are born with a lot of magic."

"Have you got a lot of magic?"

The group broke up. Flaxfield walked away from the others. He crossed the field diagonally, his cloak trailing over the ripe wheat. Dorwin and Leathort went back to work. Rotack crossed his arms and watched the wizard walk away.

"Your apprentice master learns what your name is while he's preparing you for the apprenticeship," said Cabbage. "Then, on the day you sign to be an apprentice, he tells you what it is."

"What if you don't like it?"

"It's your name," said Cabbage. "It's chosen you."

Rotack joined the others. Flaxfield, arrived at the other side of the field, leaned against a gate and watched the line of reapers turn the corner and begin at the third edge.

"He's worried," said Cabbage. "Look at the way he's watching them."

"There's something in the field," said Perry.

"Yes."

"How do you know?"

The two boys looked at each other.

"I'm a wizard," said Cabbage. "How do you know?"

"I can taste it."

"Can you?"

"No. I don't know. But I can't see it. I can't hear it. I can't smell it. But I know it's there. Like a taste in my mouth." He paused. "Or," he added, "do you know when you can feel that someone's looking at you, and you turn your head, and someone is? Do you know that feeling?"

Cabbage nodded.

"It's like that."

The shocks of wheat were around three sides of the field now, drying in the sun. The reapers turned to the fourth side. Cabbage could almost see it. Like a movement at the edge of his vision. Neither out of sight nor visible. It was the wild magic, sweeping over the wheat, kindling the poppies. Bubbling up from the ground. Crouched low in the stalks of grain. Running along the hedgerow. Everywhere.

Flaxfield was watching it, too.

The reapers had finished the fourth side

of the field when Dorwin broke off from the group and came over to sit with the boys.

"Can you move up?" she asked.

They shuffled apart and she sat between them. Her arms were hot against theirs. She kicked off her shoes and wriggled her toes.

At first, when Cabbage came to live with Flaxfield, there had been a woman there as well, Flaxfold, and she had taken charge of most of his teaching. It was a few years since she had left, and he had not spent any time with a woman since then. And anyway, that had been different. Flaxfold was old. She had gray hair pinned up at the back of her head, and the skin around her neck was creased and loose. Cabbage couldn't remember his mother, but Dorwin put him in mind of her. Except she seemed younger even than that. More like a much older sister. Anyway, he enjoyed having her close.

"Why do they call you Cabbage?" she asked.

Cabbage sighed. "Wizards have different names," he said.

"I know. But why Cabbage? It isn't your real name, is it?"

"He won't tell me," said Perry.

"You don't talk like a roffle," said Dorwin.

Perry shrugged. "It's too much bother," he said. "All that stuff about bottles and balloons and cats with bits of string."

"What are they doing?" asked Cabbage.

"Reaping the grain."

"Yes. Why do they do it like that?"

Dorwin settled down and explained. "Every field has the power to grow crops," she said. "But growing the crops weakens the power. It goes into the grain, spreads out over the whole field. So, when we harvest, we start in one corner, go around every side of the field and cut, then move in and cut again, making a smaller and smaller square every time."

"What's that for?"

"So the power of the field can't escape. Look."

She pointed her finger at the reapers and laughed. More than half of the field was cut now. The square of standing grain was small in the center. The boys followed the line of Dorwin's finger. Two rabbits bolted out of the stalks, white tails bobbing. They ran off in opposite directions. Almost as soon as they had reached the hedgerow, another one darted away from a different point.

"Everything in the field is being driven to the center by the reapers," said Dorwin. "As they run out of places to hide, they make a dash for it. We let them go."

"Looks like you can't stop them," said Perry.

"You're right."

She frowned and fell silent. The swish of the scythes filled the emptiness. The bent-backed women gathered the wheat and made the shocks.

"That's why we need the Harvest Spell before we begin," she said. "The power of the field is being driven to the center. When we get to the last cut, the power is in those few stalks, all clenched up into a small space. The Harvest Spell stops it from running out, like the rabbits."

The three of them looked at Flaxfield.

"That's what he's looking for," said Cabbage.

"Yes."

"What happens if it escapes?"

"Then the field is dead. Nothing will grow there."

"What happens when you capture the power of the field?" asked Perry.

"We weave the stalks into a special shape and keep it safe all winter. In the spring, the day before we sow the new grain, we bury it in the field, to release it."

"Can you see what's happening?" asked Cabbage.

Dorwin nodded.

"Tell me," he said.

"Can't you see it?"

"Tell me what you see."

The reapers had stopped for a break. The remaining square of uncut wheat was the size of a room in a cottage. No more than that.

Dorwin straightened her back.

"The air above the grain is shimmering," she said. "Like the air over a fire, but nothing's burning under it. It looks as though there should be smoke, but there isn't. It's not like the hot air from a roof on a summer day. It's twisting and swirling. I just don't know how it does that with no fire beneath."

"What about you?" Cabbage asked Perry.

"The same," said the young roffle. "Except I can see the fire as well."

"What's it like?" asked Dorwin. "Can you tell?"

"No smoke," said Perry, "but flames, high and fast, coming straight out of the wheat, but not burning it up."

"What can you see?" asked Dorwin.

"The same," said Cabbage. "The hot air, the flames."

"Is that all?" asked Perry.

Dorwin turned her face to him. Cabbage liked her attention, but it made him shy as well.

"No," he said. "That's not all."

She leaned toward him, and he could feel her breath on his face.

"What else?"

"Other things," he said.

The men picked up their scythes and moved through the wheat. As the blades sliced through, the fire that only Cabbage and Perry could see sprang higher.

"I've never seen anything like this," said Dorwin. "The shimmering. The field looks alive." She stood to see better. The boys sprang up with her.

Three shocks, four, a fifth, and all that was left was a single clump of wheat. They stopped.

Leathort took his scythe and stood ready to cut the last of the wheat with a single stroke. He looked across to Flaxfield. The wizard had moved from the gate and was standing in a clear space. Although the day was calm, with no breeze, his cloak swept back as though in a gale. He held his staff before him in both hands, steady on the earth.

Leathort waited.

Flaxfield nodded.

"He's going to make the final spell for the field," said Dorwin.

"He can't," said Cabbage. "He mustn't."

Leathort drew back the scythe, let it sweep around in front of him, and it clipped the last stalks. They fell silently. Before they touched the earth, Flaxfield pointed his staff at them. He said something loud but impossible to make out at that distance. A woman leaned forward to scoop up the last of the wheat.

"That's Homeput," said Dorwin. "She'll weave the Corn Catch."

Flaxfield lowered his staff. It had worked. The spell had caught the power of the field.

Flaxfield began to walk toward the reapers, smiling and raising his hand to wave at them.

As he drew close, Homeput screamed. She shook her hands and pushed them away from her, the wheat tumbling down. As it fell, it flared up, bright against the hot sun. Flaxfield began to run to her. One by one, the shocks around the field began to catch fire. Each poppy burst into life. The red poppies were flames sparking the wheat. The wheat glowed, then flared, then blazed. The flames crawled out and spread over the stubble. The reapers ran for cover, leaping over flame and swerving to avoid the flaring shocks. Leathort put his arm around Homeput and helped her away. She was still flapping her hands in pain. Flaxfield stood in the center of the field. He raised his arms and tried to control the fire. For a moment, a space around him died back, but the rest of the field burned brighter and hotter. All the reapers were now at the safety of the hedgerows.

"The harvest," said Dorwin. "The whole crop. Destroyed."

The circle of clear ground around Flaxfield was growing smaller. His attempts to drive back the fire were failing. There was no path through to the safety of the edge. The entire field was a sea of flame.

"He'll die," said Dorwin. "He'll burn to death."

Black smoke swallowed him up, and they couldn't see him anymore.

Dorwin drew her shawl over her face

and stepped forward.

"What are you doing?" said Cabbage.

"I'm going to try," she said. "Flaxfield."

"Don't," said Cabbage.

She stepped into the flame, beating it down with her feet. As though it had been attacked, the fire punched back at her. It wrapped around her. She fell back and scrambled to the hedgerow. Her skirt was ablaze. Her shawl was singed and smoking. Perry smacked the fire out with his hands. Dorwin gasped for breath, black smoke pouring down from her nose and out of her mouth.

"It's not just fire," said Perry.

She tried to answer. Coughed again. Shook her head.

Cabbage stared into the smoke, searching for something. He remembered the way the whistle spell had exploded over the mem-mont, remembered the hot breath of the beast as it leaped on him. Something was tugging at his mind. The beast had not actually bitten him, not touched him. It just stood, snarling. He had passed out, and when he came to, it was dead.

He stepped forward.

"Come back," called Perry.

Dorwin tried to grab his arm. He wrenched himself free and walked into the field, into the fire. The heat made his face sting. The smoke crowded round him, swirling against him. He walked on. Although it was hot, it did not burn. Although the smoke pressed against his face, he could breathe easily and his eyes didn't smart or begin to fill with tears. He walked on, unburned, unhurt.

He had to guess where Flaxfield was. He couldn't see through the smoke.

He called out. "Flaxfield."

The fire roared up, trying to kill his voice.

"Flaxfield."

"Cabbage? Stay away."

Cabbage turned to his left, followed the voice, and found Flax-field. The wizard's cloak was wrapped around his face. His boots were burning. He swung his staff around and around, as though driving away a pack of dogs. The fire backed off at each sweep of the staff, then came back with greater ferocity.

Cabbage stepped up to Flaxfield, took the wizard's hand, and said, "This way."

As long as Cabbage led Flaxfield, the wizard was safe. They pushed through the fire. It snarled and whipped at their legs. Flames lashed at Flaxfield's face like slaps, but they did not burn him. As they broke through to the edge of the field, they felt a push at their backs and were spat out of the furnace, toppling over and landing clear of the flames.

Hands grabbed them, pulled them clear. Perry and Dorwin ran around from where they had been searching for them. Dorwin hugged Cabbage. He squirmed away, not very forcefully, then allowed her to hold him.

"Flaxfield," she said. "Are you hurt?"

He shrugged.

"Are you?" Perry looked at the wizard, waiting.

"I have no injuries," he said. "No burns." His voice was the croak of a rusty hinge. "Something to drink," he suggested. "And for Cabbage"—he smiled at the boy and put his hand on Cabbage's arm—"something to eat as well?"

Cabbage smiled.

"Thank you," said Flaxfield. "Thank you for coming for me."

"He should have left you there," said Dorwin. "It was too dangerous."

"It was," said Flaxfield. "He should. But I am glad he didn't. Now"—he clambered to his feet—"we need to find out how he did it when I couldn't."

"Now, this is what I call an inn," said Cabbage.

Perry watched as a man at a nearby table speared a piece of batter pudding with his knife, added some beef and gravy, and popped it into his mouth.

While he was waiting, Cabbage looked around the room. It seemed that all of the village was in there.

"I'll have the chicken pie," he said, as one was put in front of Leathort. "No, the roast duck." He changed his mind, seeing the crisp skin and the shining fat. "Or, no, I'll have that pork chop with the crackling and extra gravy."

Flaxfield sighed.

"Please," said Perry, "may I have the roast beef and batter pudding?"

"The same as him, please," said Cabbage, pointing at Perry.

"Three roast beef, then," said Flaxfield.

He ordered the food and brought a mug of cider and two smaller mugs of apple juice back to the table.

"We'll eat," said Flaxfield. "Then we'll sort out what's going on."

He still smelled of smoke, and his cloak was scorched down one side. Gray ash smeared his cheek and neck and shoulders. Cabbage wondered why his hair and beard hadn't been singed.

"Is the harvest ruined?" asked Perry.

"Perhaps," said Flaxfield. "I don't know. That was only one field. There are others."

The food arrived, and they applied themselves to it with pleasure and enthusiasm. Even the greens were delicious.

"Is someone doing it to us, or is it just sort of loose? I don't understand," said Perry. "I mean, is all this wild magic that's going about hurting things? Is it like a dog that's been trained to attack, and someone's telling it to do it? Or is it like a wolf or a stoat, something that really is wild and out of control?"

"Good," said Flaxfield. "That's very good, Perry."

"Is it?" he said. "Really?" He grinned with pleasure.

"If it's controlled, then that's one thing," said Flaxfield. "If it's wild, then that's another. And we need to find out before we can work out how to deal with it."

"What is it like?" said Perry. "And what is it, anyway? And where did it come from?"

"Ah," said Flaxfield. "Where do things come from? That's the question, isn't it?"

Perry wasn't going to be put off. "Yes," he said. "And what's the answer?"

Flaxfield looked at him with approval. "You're persistent for a roffle," he said. "There are several answers. I like the one about Smokesmith best."

"Do you know this?" Perry asked Cabbage.

"Yes. It's one of the first things you learn."

"Do they know?"

Perry nodded his head toward the nearest group of villagers.

"No," said Cabbage. "It's a secret."

"I want to know," said Perry.

To Cabbage's astonishment, Flaxfield said, "Then you shall."

And he told the young roffle the story of Smokesmith.

People wanted to see themselves. They saw their reflections in water, but they were always imperfect. The water rippled and distorted the image. And you could never stand up and look at yourself. You could see your face in someone's eyes, but that meant having to stand close and look straight at them. It was curved and, besides, looking at yourself through someone else's eyes was too personal, too dangerous. Staring into another person's eyes changed you, and it changed the person you saw yourself through.

Smokesmith was a blacksmith and a weapon maker. He had a forge and a workshop. He made gates and trivets. He shod horses. He made spearheads and swords. The best knives in the world. Sharp enough to slice through an iris at the waterside without bruising the stem. He made breastplates and shields. He found a way of mixing the charcoal from the forge into the iron, folding it over and over and over until it was hard and strong. The blades of the swords, polished with killing, became bright. They caught the sun and threw it back. Men turned them over in their hands and could see themselves, fragmentary and in part, like looking into a flashing stream.

Now we are all used to being able to see ourselves. Glass in our windows. Our faces in the looking glass. Before that, no one really knew what he looked like.

Smokesmith made a shield with this hard iron. He worked at night when the others had gone home. He locked the workshop and lit the forge, the fire bright in the darkness. When the shield was finished, he polished it till it shone. He could see his face in it, like the reflection of a face in the eye. He hung it on the wall by its strap. He could stand back and see himself in the shield, head and shoulders. It was a new way of seeing. Nothing like it had ever existed before.

It frightened him. He painted over the shining surface so

that it couldn't reflect anymore. He locked it away. He made a special lock in his workshop that no one could open. And there he hoped it would end.

But secrets are like bears asleep in caves; they wake up. It is not easy to light a forge at night and go unnoticed. Soon word went around that Smokesmith had made something special. They said it was a weapon, a sword or a spear or a shield, better than any that had ever been made before.

The stories grew, and the sword became one that would kill every time it was drawn. That the owner of the sword could not die in battle. That the spear was made so that it never missed its target and that no one could draw it out from the dead body except the one who had thrown it. The shield was so light, a child could lift it, yet so strong that nothing could pierce it. Whoever carried it was safe from all harm in battle.

There was no deadly sword, no perfect spear, no invulnerable shield. They were all stories. One night, men broke into Smokesmith's forge and ransacked it, looking for the special weapons. Of course, they didn't find them. They found the chest with the special lock, and when they couldn't open it, they seized Smokesmith from his bed and dragged him to the forge. He opened the chest, took out the shield, and handed it over. When they saw that it was just an ordinary shield, they thought he was tricking them. They beat him and threatened to kill him if he didn't tell them where the secret weapon was.

Before Smokesmith could clean off the paint and show them

their reflections in the shield, the dogs began to bark, the alarm was raised, and the men ran off, taking the shield with them.

The king of that country heard what had happened and sent for Smokesmith. The blacksmith was frightened at what had happened and he told the king everything. The king immediately sent out search parties to find the robbers. At the same time, he returned Smokesmith to his forge. He sent men with him, guards, to protect him and to keep him prisoner. He gave orders to Smokesmith.

Smokesmith was commanded to make a panel for the king. One bright enough to reflect. One big enough to see a whole person in. One flat enough, not like the shield, to show a person exactly as he was in life. The armed guard kept him at work. And they kept his work secret and silent, so none should know what he was doing.

Cabbage put his hand on Flaxfield's arm. The old wizard stopped telling his tale. Silence rested over the inn like smoke. Flaxfield questioned Cabbage with a look.

"No," said Cabbage. "No one heard you. They've just stopped talking. It's all right."

"Flaxfield," called Leathort. "We need to talk."

Flaxfield took his mug of cider and crossed the room to Leathort's table. He looked over his shoulder and nodded to Cabbage, who jumped to his feet and followed him.

"Just you," said Rotack. "The boy can stay over there with the roffle."

Flaxfield sat and pulled a chair across from a nearby table. He gestured with his head for the boy to sit.

"The boy is my apprentice," he said. "He stays with me."

"Of course," said Leathort. "Welcome, boy. You did well today to save Flaxfield for us."

Cabbage sat, with an apologetic look over his shoulder to Perry.

"All right," agreed Rotack. "But make sure you keep quiet, apprentice."

Flaxfield smiled at Rotack. "I think the rule should be that anyone with a question or a good comment should speak. For the rest, let's all remain silent until we have something useful to say."

Rotack glared at him.

Cabbage smiled and looked around the table. He knew Leathort and Rotack. Dorwin sat to the left of Flaxfield. Opposite her was a man he didn't recognize from the field. She saw him looking and said, "This is Cartford. He's my father."

Cartford stared at Cabbage, then lifted his mug of beer and drank what was left in there. He was older than the others and big. Hands like the big, smooth stones on a riverbed and thick arms with old scars on them.

"We'll need more drinks first," he said. "I don't want to have to stop this talk for refreshment."

Perry trotted over. "I'll fetch what you need," he offered.

"How do you know what we want?" demanded Rotack.

"How does a squirrel know when to paint a pumpkin?" said Perry.

The men were circling each other with words, unwilling to say directly what they thought. Each was testing out the other, trying to see what strength his arguments might have.

"Rotack wants you to leave, Flaxfield," said Dorwin.

The sudden, direct statement silenced them.

"I didn't say that," said Rotack.

"I will," said Flaxfield. "If that's what's needed."

"No," said Dorwin. "That's just Rotack. The rest of us need you to stay."

"Stay?" said Rotack. "Stay and do what? Burn all our fields? Ruin all our crops?"

"It wasn't Flaxfield that burned them," she argued. "It was the magic, though. Wasn't it?"

"No magic," said Rotack. "No fire. Isn't that right? The field was harvested all right and done before he ruined it all with his spell."

Dorwin banged her fist on the table. "No. It wasn't that."

After a pause, Cartford said to her, "What was it, then? What destroyed the crop?"

"The field was full of fire already," said Dorwin. "Even before the spell. It was there. It was ready. It would have burned anyway."

"And you saw it, I suppose," said Rotack. "What? You're a wizard now, are you?"

"I saw the flames," said Cabbage. "I saw them."

"And did you tell Dorwin?" asked Leathort. "Before the fire started?"

"She saw the shadow of the magic," said Cabbage. "Just as you know there's someone following you when you see their shadow on the wall next to yours. That's how Dorwin saw the magic. She told me."

"Why didn't the rest of us see it, then?" Rotack demanded.

"I expect some did," said Flaxfield. "And they dismissed it."

"Did you?" said Rotack. "Did you see it?"

"No," said Leathort. "I didn't."

"Did you ever turn a corner and see a low figure crouched in front of you only to then see it was a bush?" asked Flaxfield. "Or hear a noise in an empty house, like a moan or a laugh and say to yourself, 'It was the wind,' or, 'It was the timbers creaking?' Did you never hear a voice behind you in the street and turn to see there was no one there? Well, Rotack? What do you say?"

"All of those things," he said. "Everyone does. That isn't magic."

"You say so," said Flaxfield. "So you say."

"It doesn't matter whether you go or not, does it?" Dorwin asked Flaxfield.

Flaxfield smiled.

"If it doesn't matter, let him go," said Rotack. "And we'll get on with the harvest."

"As easy as that?" said Cartford.

Cabbage was surprised to hear the big man speak. Save for a few questions earlier, he had held his peace.

"You think that whatever has slipped its leash will be tethered again if Flaxfield goes? Eh? And takes his boy with him, and the roffle?"

"There was no trouble before he arrived," said Rotack.

Cartford rubbed his chin with a rough hand. "No? Is that what you think?" He drained his mug and slammed it on the table. "And don't think I haven't noticed you, young roffle," he said. "Fill that up for me, will you?"

Perry scuttled off and held the mug beneath the tap on the barrel.

Cartford looked around him at all the faces in the room turned in his direction. "Anyone else here who saw the magic ripple over the field today? Anyone see the ears of wheat dip in the breeze when there was no breeze? Anyone see the poppies glow?"

Some heads nodded.

"Have you made fire this week, Rotack?" he asked.

"No."

"No. I thought not. No fires in the hearth in this weather. What do you think, Flaxfield?"

"These are not easy days, Cartford," said Flaxfield. "It's no shame for one not to see."

"You were always too gentle," said Cartford. "Perhaps that's good in a wizard. I don't know. Not much good in my trade. If you had lit a fire," he continued, staring at Rotack, "perhaps you would have felt this coming." He looked again at the people in the inn. "What do you think?"

A woman indicated that she wanted to speak. He nodded to give her permission, and Cabbage realized that it was no accident that Flaxfield had joined this table. These, for some reason, were the village leaders. Cartford exercised power here.

"I've burned a stew three times this last few weeks," she said. "And the fire under the pot is greedy."

A ripple of agreement from others showed that she spoke for them, too.

"I saw a creature in the fire," said a man. "And it didn't burn. It was as though it lived there."

"What sort of a creature?" asked Flaxfield.

"A beetle," the man said. "But not like any beetle I've ever seen. Bigger. Red-black and blazing. I took the poker to it, and it disappeared. But it was there. I saw it. Twice. It came back."

Others agreed and added their own stories.

Perry whispered to Cabbage, "I thought it was only when there was magic used."

"There's magic in every fire," said Cabbage. "Only a little. But enough for the wild magic to fasten on to."

"What about you, Cartford?" asked the first woman who had spoken. Cabbage took notice of the strength of her face. She had more courage, more confidence than the others. "What have you seen?"

"At my forge?" he asked.

It began to make sense to Cabbage what Cartford was and why he hadn't been in the fields. He was the blacksmith.

"You wouldn't want to know the things I see in the fire in my forge," said Cartford. "Especially these last few weeks."

Then Cabbage understood. It was like the shape out of the corner of the eye. Like the creak in the house. Like the shadow on the wall. They had all of them seen or felt something approaching, something there, something wrong. And they had all said it was just an imagining, just a mistake. Now it was too late. Now it was here.

"But I'll tell you this," said Cartford. "Flaxfield didn't bring it here. And it won't leave us if he leaves. If we want some magic done from time to time, and we all want that, there'll be no safe magic till this is sorted out."

Rotack scratched the tabletop with his fingernail. Leathort sighed. "What are we to do?" he asked Flaxfield.

"What do you do when you sting yourself with a nettle?" Flaxfield asked.

No one answered.

"Come on," he encouraged them. "You all know what to do. Tell them, Cabbage."

"Get a handful of dock leaves," said Cabbage. "Screw them up in your hands to bruise them and make the juice flow. Then smear the juice on the sting."

"But what if there aren't any dock leaves?" asked Flaxfield. "What then?"

Rotack laughed. "This is simple magic," he said. "Anyone does this, wizard or not. And there are always dock leaves where there are nettles. They grow side by side."

"So they do," said Flaxfield. "Side by side. Wherever there's a nettle, there's a dock. Wherever there's a sting, there's a salve. We've been stung. Today. We lost a field. So if we look around us, we'll see a remedy." He sat back, smiled, lifted his mug of cider as though making a toast, and drank it off.

"You'll have a long wait," said Rotack.

"Do you think so?" asked Flaxfield.

As he spoke, the door opened and a man and a woman came in, dirty and hot from a journey. Their tiredness was on their faces like dust. The man put his hand out to steady the woman. They looked around the room, surprised to see so many there. They stepped forward and were followed by a small woman, with gray hair and a busy manner. She ushered them forward, encouraged them in.

"Let's get you some food and a drink, a wash, and a place to rest," she said. She surveyed the crowd. "Busy today," she said. "Hello, Cabbage. Hello, Flaxfield. You're here at last."

"Ah, Flaxfold," Flaxfield said. "I was talking about you."

Was that story true?"

asked Perry. "The one about the shield and the blacksmith and the king."

Cabbage was still trying to recover from seeing Flaxfold again. Her arrival had broken up the meeting. Flaxfield left the table and started to talk to Flaxfold and to ask questions of the couple who had come in with her. Flaxfold shooed him away and hurried the two of them upstairs.

"They're tired," she said over her shoulder. "And hungry. No time for questions now." She patted the woman on her arm and said, "And I expect you'd like to wash and change, wouldn't you?" The woman thanked her and allowed herself to be led away.

It had always been the same with Flaxfold, remembered Cabbage. She looked plump and placid, yet somehow she got her way and she got things done. And they were done in half the time you'd have expected. While Cabbage was panting with the effort and the speed of it all, Flaxfold never seemed rushed or breathless.

Perry gave him a friendly punch. "Well? Is it true?"

"It's just one story about magic. There are others."

Perry looked disappointed. "So it didn't happen, then?"

The day had decided it had seen enough for the time being and night had taken its place. Cabbage and Perry sat in the garden of the inn, backs against the bricks of a stable block.

"It's a funny thing," said Cabbage. "This is a really lovely inn, but have you ever noticed how much nicer places look from the outside than when you're actually inside them?"

Perry hadn't and he asked Cabbage to explain.

"I can't," said Cabbage. "It's just that looking into the inn from here, seeing the candles burning, the reflections and the shadows, I like it more than I did when I was actually there."

Perry thought about it for a moment. "So," he said. "Did it happen or not?"

"The blacksmith and the shield? It might have happened. Probably it did. I don't know. But whether it was how magic came into the world? I don't know; that's different."

"How does it end?" asked Perry. "We didn't even get to the magic part."

"Flaxfield started to tell you," said Cabbage. "You'll have to wait for him to finish it."

He was trying to listen to the stars, and he didn't want to be rude to Perry and tell him to shut up. It was no good. They still weren't saying anything. It was difficult for Cabbage to not do any magic at all. Apprentices can't be stopped from doing something. Cabbage's favorite magic, when he was bored or resting, or if he had something on his mind, was to dangle his hand over the edge of a chair or from his knee and let stars fall from his fingertips and pile up on the floor beside him. When the pile was large enough, he made a tiny cat, the size of a wasp, fall from his hand and lick up the stars. It wasn't allowed, of course, but it's part of the nature of boys to fidget and to do what they're not supposed to do, and it didn't do much harm. Usually.

Talking to Perry had made Cabbage let his guard down. That and a full stomach after a good meal, the soft summer night air, and the long walk in the heat. He was thinking about the old stories and whether they were true or not. Sitting with his back to the sun-warm wall, his hand dangling from his knee, he forgot about the wild magic. Silent stars began to drop from his fingertips, landing bright on the night grass.

Perry tapped his arm and pointed to the inn window. Rotack was watching them. His face was dark with the light behind it, but they knew him from his shape, his size. He moved his head and said something to another person in the room. Then there were two of them looking out at the boys. Rotack raised his arm. Cabbage collected his thoughts and saw the stars falling from his fingers, the small heap of them on the grass.

Then it was all noise and rushing. The door swung open and slammed against the wall. Flaxfield strode out.

"Perry," he shouted. "Get away. Be quick."

The roffle scrambled to his feet and backed away. Cabbage jumped up, keeping his back to the brick wall.

Dorwin ran over to Perry and pulled him toward the inn.

Leathort stepped aside to let them through, but Perry slipped out of her grasp and ran back toward Cabbage.

"Come back," shouted Dorwin. Perry ignored her. Flaxfield put out his staff and, flicking it around, caught Perry's legs and took them out from under him. The roffle stumbled and fell, winding himself and grazing his elbows on the grass.

The heap of stars began to smoke. Cabbage watched the gray fronds rise up and swell and billow out. The smoke wound itself around his legs. He couldn't move.

"Run," shouted Flaxfield.

Cabbage looked at him, tried to lift his feet. He was fixed to the spot. At the base of the cloud of smoke, orange flames glowed and grew and licked up.

"Run," shouted Dorwin.

Flaxfield strode forward to Cabbage, arm upraised, brandishing his staff. As he drew near, a whip of fire lashed out and struck him on the cheek. He wrapped his cloak around his arm and raised it against the attack. Cabbage was alight now from foot to chest. The smoke rose higher and covered his face.

Flaxfield threw himself forward. A wall of fire stopped him and covered Cabbage completely, blocking him from view.

The flames lashed Flaxfield over and over, driving him back.

"For pity's sake," shouted Rotack. "Use some magic, Flaxfield. Save the boy. He's burning to death."

Flaxfield raised his singed face. "I can't," he said. "If I do, it will grow stronger and kill us all. I can't."

"Better we all die than watch this," said Dorwin. "Do something."

A black shape, the size of a large cat, broke through the flames, then disappeared back into them.

"What was that?" asked Dorwin.

Perry was clutching his shins and groaning from where Flaxfield had hit him. Flaxfield reached out a hand and helped him up. The heat from the flames drove them all back toward the inn. Perry buried his face in Flaxfield's cloak.

"Look," said Dorwin. "There it is again."

The black figure half emerged, then was swept back into the blaze. For a moment, the fire just there flickered, then died, leaving a hole in the wall of flame.

"No," said Flaxfield. "It's not possible."

"What?" demanded Leathort.

"Watch."

The wall was breached now. The shape moved around; a tail flicked.

"Is it eating the fire?" said Dorwin.

Flaxfield patted Perry's head. "Yes."

"Eating it?" said Perry. "No. That's horrible."

"Eating the fire," said Flaxfield. "You can look."

Perry moved the cloak to one side so that he could see with one eye. As the flames died back, the shape revealed itself as a large black cat. It moved unhurt through the fire, lapping the ground at first and then moving in and eating up the heap of stars that had started the blaze.

Cabbage stood, eyes closed tight, hardly breathing, back against the red bricks, which glowed with the heat. Smoke still curled around his ankles like morning mist. The cat flicked its tail, licked its lips, sat down, looked up at the watching crowd, looked back at the little heap of embers, licked up the last of them, and blinked.

Perry started to shout to Cabbage. Flaxfield raised a finger to his lips. The wizard spoke to Cabbage in a low voice. "Cabbage?"

He didn't move. His eyes stayed tightly shut.

"What's wrong?" asked Perry.

Flaxfield put his hand on the roffle's shoulder. "It isn't over yet," he said.

"But the fire's gone. And he's all right."

"Wait." He called softly to Cabbage again. Still no response.

Dorwin whispered to Flaxfield. He shook his head.

"Let me try," she said.

"This is magic I don't understand," said Flaxfield. "It's already killed a memmont and the innkeeper. It nearly killed me today. We don't know what it might have done to the boy. He may never recover. If we push too hard, it may flare up again." He called a third time, louder, "Cabbage."

A spark flew up from the ashes and burst into yellow fire. The cat pounced on it, seized it in its mouth, and shook it. The fire went out. The cat licked its paws.

"You did that," said Dorwin. "You're a wizard. Whatever you do has magic clinging to it. You'll feed the flames. Let me try."

She went to Cabbage. Perry broke free and joined her. He put out his hand and she took it in hers.

Before they could move to Cabbage, there was a scuffle behind them and Flaxfold jogged them to one side.

"Sorry," she said. "Oh, I am sorry, dear. But please could you just leave him for a moment?" She disappeared back into the house.

Dorwin squeezed Perry's hand to stop him going any farther. The roffle tugged at her.

"Let me try," he said. "He's my friend."

Flaxfield took his arm. "Let's see what she says," he advised. "If you want to save Cabbage."

Flaxfold led the new couple out of the back door. "These people have experience with this fire," she said. "I think they can help." She looked at them. "Is that right?"

"I don't know," said the man.

They had rested and eaten. The woman had brushed her hair. The man had changed his clothes.

"We can try," said his wife. "At least we can try, can't we? It can do no harm?"

Flaxfield stared at her. "You can try," he said. "But I can't promise that it will do no harm. This is new magic to me."

"See?" said her husband. "We could make it worse."

Flaxfold put her arm through his, linking like a girl with her boyfriend. "No," she said. "I think you should try."

Rotack moved to stand in their way.

"Who are they?" he said. "More wizards? Wizards have done damage enough today."

Perry tried to pull forward to challenge him. Flaxfold patted Rotack's cheek.

"Not wizards," she said. "Just a mother and father. Just people like you, but I think they can help."

While the scuffle was going on, the woman moved toward Cabbage. She glanced over her shoulder to her husband, who sighed and followed. She leaned forward and put her cheek against Cabbage's.

"He's cold," she said.

"Through all that fire, and he's cold," said her husband.

"Yes. It's just the same as her."

She looked over her shoulder. "What is his name?" she said. She frowned when Flaxfield told her. "No," she said, "his real name?"

"Cabbage will do," said Flaxfield. "If that won't wake him, nothing will."

"He should have a better name," she said.

"He has."

The man stood to one side and put his arm around Cabbage's shoulder. The woman leaned in again and rested her face on his.

"Cabbage." Her voice was soft against his cheek. "Come on. Let's go inside."

A shadow moved away from him, low against the ground.

"The cat," said Perry. "The black cat."

The creature had been so still, they had forgotten it.

The woman stepped aside so that it could pass. "Cabbage," she said.

The cat ran down the garden, away from them. Reaching an apple tree, it clambered up the sloped trunk, claws catching easily on the bark. It ran along a branch, leaped into the air and, in an instant, disappeared.

Cabbage jerked his head around. His eyes flashed open. He looked into the black night where the cat had been. He shouted, "No!" then looked around at the faces in the windows' light.

"Cabbage," she said. Her voice was still soft, her cheek still close to his.

Cabbage moved his head back, looked at her, looked at the man, looked back at her. "You're her mother," he said.

Flaxfield banged his staff on the ground with pleasure. "Now we're getting somewhere," he said.

They wouldn't leave Cabbage alone

and he was embarrassed.

The man's name was Pellion and the woman was Vella. They wanted to talk to him all the time. They wanted to know that he was all right after the fire.

The woman, Vella, kept apologizing to him.

"It's all right," said Cabbage. "I'm all right."

He couldn't remember anything about the fire. He wasn't burned at all. He didn't even have a cough after breathing in all the smoke.

Perry was most interested in the cat, but nobody cared about what Perry was interested in.

The men of the village watched him, but they kept their distance.

"Where did the cat go?" asked Perry.

In the end it was Flaxfold who sorted them out. She took Cabbage to a small room at the side of the inn. There was room for Pellion and Vella as well. Flaxfield sat near the window, looking out into the night, listening but not speaking. Perry kept close to Cabbage. The men went back into the inn parlor, grumbling, knowing they would get their chance later, probably tomorrow. Dorwin stood near Flaxfield.

"Is this inn where you went when you left us?" Cabbage asked Flaxfold.

She finished checking him for signs of injuries. He liked the feeling of her hands on his face and neck. It reminded him of when she had looked after him before.

"Are you sure he's all right?" asked Vella again.

Flaxfold took her hands and smiled at her. "There's nothing wrong with him," she said. "And even if there had been, it wouldn't have been your fault. What's done is done."

"Can I go to bed now?" Cabbage said.

Flaxfield laughed. Dorwin smacked his arm and said, "Behave, Flaxfield. Can't you see he's embarrassed? He wants to get rid of us all."

Flaxfield didn't seem to mind that Dorwin had treated him as though he were more Cabbage's age than an old wizard. Cabbage decided that people were very odd. But he was glad that Dorwin had taken his side. He didn't really want to go to bed. He wanted to know what was happening.

"All right," said Flaxfield. "We'll deal with the boy later. Flaxfold, what's going on with your visitors? Why have you brought them here? What do they know?"

Everyone turned their attention away from the apprentice and looked at Pellion and Vella.

"I found them," said Flaxfold.

"Were you looking?" asked Flaxfield.

She glared at him.

"I found them," she repeated, "when I was on my way back here from a journey."

"Where had you been?" asked Flaxfield. "Looking for someone?"

"They're looking for their daughter," said Flaxfold.

"Did she run away?"

Everyone shushed Perry and he went red. Cabbage moved closer to him, and they sat side by side and listened.

"Her name is Bee," said Flaxfold. "She has very powerful magic."

Cabbage understood straightaway. This Bee girl hadn't run away. She had been taken away. Like him. To be an apprentice. He stared at her parents.

"Why did you let her go?" Perry asked. It wasn't a challenge, just a simple question. "If you didn't want her to, why did you do it?"

"Hush," said Cabbage.

"No," said Vella. "He's right. It's a good question."

Perry looked triumphant for a moment, until he saw that the woman was crying silently.

"I'm sorry," he said.

She put her arm around Perry and drew him close to her.

"We didn't want her to go," said Pellion. "But we had to. It was the only way."

Flaxfield moved away from the window and stood in front of

Pellion. All at once everything in the room was about the old wizard. Nothing else mattered. It was as though a dragon or a lion had appeared. No one could take their eyes from him. No one could think of anything else. Cabbage knew then, before Flaxfield spoke, that the only thing he wanted was to be Flaxfield's apprentice. This was what he was made for. So when the wizard spoke, Cabbage agreed, before the words had left his mouth.

"You are right," said Flaxfield. "For a child who has real magic, lasting magic, an apprenticeship is the only way. You had to let her go. She would never have been happy otherwise."

Flaxfold's voice was soft, insistent. "But it needs to be the right master," she added.

Flaxfield looked at her and nodded. "And that is right, too," he agreed.

"It was the only way," said Pellion. He looked at Perry, who had asked the question. "You should have seen what it was like."

Flaxfold tried to calm him. "No one blames you," she said.

Pellion shook his head. "But we are to blame," he insisted. "It's all gone wrong, hasn't it? Listen," he said, "it was like this."

And he told them the story of why he and Vella had let Bee go, why they had to, before she hurt herself.

We always knew it was fire

that would betray her," said Vella.

It was one of those hot days that seem to be the real meaning of summer.

Bee looked out over the fields. The air shimmered just above the stubble from the cut wheat. Swallows dipped and looped in the air, skimming for insects. A single, small cloud hung in the sky. White on blue. Flour-soft on china-hard.

Pellion was coppicing half a mile away. Bee, five now, was thirsty. She went inside, stood on a stool, and poured herself a beaker of water from the jug in the pantry.

"Are you all right in there?" called Vella.

"Where's daddy?"

"In the coppice."

"What's the coppice?"

"You know, that clump of trees, where we saw the badgers."

"What's he doing?"

"Cutting back trees."

Bee carried her drink into the kitchen and watched her mother edging the hem of a nightdress. "Why?"

"To make room for new ones to grow."

"Is he thirsty?"

Vella looked out at the heat through the open door. "I expect he is. Shall we take him a drink?"

Pellion didn't hear them coming until they were right on top of him. The coppice was set on a slope, to the east side of the large field. Hardly bigger than a manor house garden, it gave a supply of firewood, logs for charcoal, saplings for hurdles, beech mast for pigs.

"Does it hurt the trees when you cut them?" asked Bee.

Pellion took the jug of cool water and drank from the neck. Not too much. Not too quickly. "No. It doesn't hurt."

"How do you know?"

"You should finish soon," said Vella. "You've been all day."

"It won't look after itself," he said.

"But how do you know it doesn't hurt them?" Bee persisted.

"Because they don't feel like us. They're trees, not people."

"They've got faces," she said.

"Don't be silly," said Vella. She wiped the lip of the jug with a swift, hard hand. "You mustn't say things like that."

"Is it part of the secret?" asked Bee.

"No, it's just silly." She changed the subject. "How long are you going to be?"

"Less than an hour," said Pellion.

"Can we stay?" asked Bee. "We can walk back with you."

"What do you think?" he asked Vella.

"All right," she said.

"Can I go and play and look for the badgers?"

"All right. But don't leave the coppice."

"I'll find you some faces," said Bee.

Vella spread her skirts out and sat with her back to a beech tree. Pellion picked up his ax and started to hack at the small shoots that would choke the vigorous growth of the new trees.

"It hasn't gone away," said Vella.

Pellion swung the ax. "What do you know of magic?" he asked. "We're doing all right with her." He flicked away a wasp that floated by his ear.

"It will eat her up," said Vella.

"She's managing it. She's all right."

"We can't help her, though. She'll need guidance."

Pellion stacked the severed shoots.

"You've heard stories," said Vella. "Of magic gone wrong. We all have."

"They're just stories."

"We can't let that happen to her. We need to find someone who can help us."

Pellion grabbed the ax and gripped it till his hands hurt. "Which is it?" he said. "Which do you want? Help us or help her?"

"Us. Both. All of us."

"Then it's to stay a secret. Anyone who comes to help her will take her away."

"It doesn't have to be like that."

"It's always like that. Remember your stories."

Bee could hear their voices as she left them behind. The trees looked down on her. They all had faces, of course. Bee knew that. It was silly of her mummy and daddy to pretend they didn't. Some of them were big faces, made up of burrs or bent branches that stared straight out at you. Some of them grinned. Some of them smiled. Some of them were so sad that Bee wanted to cry. Some of the trees kept their faces turned away. They looked up to the sky, or they looked in at their own hearts. Bee couldn't see these faces, but she knew they were there. After all, if you saw someone standing with his back to you, you didn't think he had no face because you couldn't see it, did you?

One tree had two faces. It had its own face, which was kind and a little puzzled. And it had another face, a blank, gray face with very faint features, smoother than bark, but scaly. It was a wasps' nest, fixed in a forked branch. Bee could just hear the noise like someone sawing wood.

Her parents' voices were angry. They were arguing. Bee didn't mind. She was used to it. They argued a lot now.

It was only a few minutes before she reached the end of the trees and looked over the barley field again. She turned back, wondering if she could remember where she had seen the badgers.

She had never seen a stoat before. She didn't know what it was. The first thing that brought her to it was the sound of the thrush. Bee saw the bird, thrashing crookedly, dragging a broken wing. The stoat was running down a tree trunk toward it. The thrush flapped its good wing and screeched louder. The stoat's fur was beautiful. Its body moved with a swift grace that made Bee want to pick it up and cuddle it, play with it and toss it a ball of wool. The stoat's eyes turned to her and she felt a stab of fear. It opened its mouth and Bee saw teeth that could snap through a rabbit's neck. It seemed to smile at her. Then she was forgotten, and it darted toward the terrified thrush.

Bee ran to the bird. She scooped her hand down to pick it up. The stoat jabbed its head forward, digging its teeth into her finger. She dropped the bird, screamed. The stoat released her, grabbed the thrush by the neck, and shook it. The bird was dead instantly.

Bee sucked her finger, more angry than afraid, more in fear than in rage. Wasps, excited by the movement and the blood, hovered near the kill.

Bee pointed at the stoat. A hundred points of flame swirled around it. The wasps flared up, unhurt. They swooped down on the stoat. It reared up, like a snake. It snapped at the attacking swarm. They were quick, darting down to sting and burn, then jabbing away. The stoat dropped the dead thrush, swerved, spun, and spat, escaping and attacking at the same time. The wasps stung and burned. The stoat screamed. Its fur was singed. Its skin scorched. When it managed to snap a wasp with its sharp mouth, it was worse than missing it. The fire from the wasp burned the stoat's tongue. The sting sank into the soft flesh of the animal's mouth. It tried to spit out the wasp, making it sting again and again.

The little creature darted, blind with pain and panic. It tried to find shelter in the mounds of dead leaves and twigs. The wasps pursued it, jabbing and wounding.

Bee stared at the terrified stoat. The thrush had died swiftly. This animal was being tortured to death. She shook her head.

"That's not what I meant," she said. "No. Stop it."

Tinder around the stoat was starting to catch fire.

"Please stop," she said. She pointed her finger at the wasps. "Stop."

The flames from the twigs grew higher. The red at the heart of the black deepened and glowed. It spread out and up, eating more wood around it, growing stronger. The wasps ignored it and carried on their attack.

Bee held out her hands with the palms to the blaze. "All stop now. No fire. Stop."

Vella heard her first. She rose to her feet and grabbed Pellion's arm. "Listen."

They ran toward the sound.

Bee stood, not moving, tears running down her face. Vella hugged her.

"I can't stop it," she said.

The screams of the stoat rose above the crackle of the flames, the buzz of the wasps.

"I hurt it." She sobbed. "I hurt it."

Pellion strode across and swung his ax down on the stoat, killing it with a single blow. The wasps, robbed of their purpose, hung over the body. The flames flickered, then died. The wasps drifted away, back up to the blank face of their nest.

Pellion kicked at the fire, scattering the wood and leaves. He swung his ax into the coppice floor, loosening the earth. He kicked the damp soil over the flames, stamped on them, loosened more earth, and repeated it again and again.

Vella hugged Bee and sang to her. A song without words, soft and slow. The child pushed her face against her mother and wept.

"I hurt it," she said.

"It's over now. We'll go home."

They left Pellion covering the fire. He would not cut more wood today. He filled buckets with water and made five journeys to the coppice, pouring it over the black scar where the flames had licked.

"Fire looks as though it's dead," he told Vella, "but it can still flare up hours later. Unless you deal with it properly."

"I know."

"Why couldn't I stop it?" asked Bee.

"Shush. It's all right."

They watched Pellion plod across the stubble, the leather

buckets heavy in his hands. A small feather of smoke rose from the coppice.

"The next week," said Pellion, "he arrived."

Vella had stopped crying quite soon after her husband had begun the story. Halfway through, she had taken her arm away from Perry and taken Pellion's hand in hers. When he paused, she picked up the story for a while and then gave it back to him.

No one interrupted. When it was finished, silence covered the room.

The telling restored Pellion and Vella. Their faces were composed. The tears had ended. Vella squeezed Perry's hand again. He did not move away, enjoying the sense of her arm against his.

"Who was it?" said Cabbage. "The visitor."

"It was the wizard who was to be her apprentice master," said Vella.

"Of course," said Flaxfield. "But who?"

"His name is Slowin," said Pellion.

"No," said Flaxfield. "Oh, no."

"Is she bound to him yet?" asked Flaxfold.

Pellion and Vella looked at each other.

"Is she? Quickly," said Flaxfield. "If she's not, it may not be too late to save her."

"It's her birthday tomorrow," said Vella. "She'll be twelve."

Bee's first thought was of Mattie

and what had happened to him.

He had swallowed the stone and she had swallowed the fire. Then she remembered what day it was.

Her birthday.

Bee didn't feel any older, but she did feel different.

Slowin said they had something to sort out today. Because it was her birthday.

She decided there was something she wanted to sort out with him as well. She wouldn't tell him about Mattie. She didn't want Slowin to know about that. She knew Slowin well enough to know that he would be angry with her for talking to someone else. But she would tell Slowin that she wasn't going to make any more spells for him.

She picked up her brush and started to run it through her hair. She had a small looking glass, no bigger than the palm of her hand. She spoke to her reflection.

"I've read books," she said. "I know what I should do and what I shouldn't do. I know more than you tell me, old Slowin."

She grinned and pulled a Slowin face.

Bee knew stories about other wizards. She knew that magic was not supposed to be wasted or sold. Not proper magic. You could trade in village magic, but not real magic.

"No more little spells," she said to her reflected face. "Not unless I keep them."

"Well," she said to herself. "Twelve years old today. Do you feel any different?"

She knew the answer before she asked the question, which was why she asked it.

"In a way," she answered. "But I don't know which way."

Growing up without any children to play with or talk to, and not liking to talk to Slowin or Brassbuck, this was a sort of conversation she had grown used to. She took both parts.

"Do you feel older?" she asked herself.

"No," she answered herself.

"Then how are you different?"

She paused.

"I swallowed the fire," she said.

"Does it burn?"

"No."

"Does it hurt?"

"Not now."

"Do you look any different?"

She looked as thoroughly as she was able with the small mirror. "I don't think so."

She hesitated before she asked the next question. It was frightening.

"Has it taken away your magic?"

This was what had been folded away in her mind ever since she had opened her eyes, but she hadn't known it was there until she asked herself.

"I don't think so."

"Don't you know?"

"No."

"How will you find out?"

Bee put down the hairbrush. She closed her eyes. Opened them again. Looked herself straight in the eye. Holding her breath, she let go of the mirror and lowered her hands to her sides. The mirror hung in the air in front of her. Bee smiled. She pursed her lips and blew gently at it. A halo of fire spread out, surrounding the glass. Her image was enclosed in the sun. She blinked. The flames turned into sunflower petals. She took the mirror back into her hand and the petals withered, died, and disappeared. Her face smiled back at her.

"No," she said. "It hasn't taken away my magic."

"Has it changed your magic?"

Bee put the mirror down and walked away.

"I don't know," she said. "I don't know how to test that."

"Perhaps nothing's different then, except the way you feel."

"You're probably right," she agreed. "Nothing's different."

She went through for her breakfast and *everything* was different.
There was a beetle on her writing table.

Bee quickly checked that the spell to keep them out of her rooms was still in place. Another beetle scratched its way over the threshold. Bee watched it struggle against the magic, legs waving as though in pain, then recover and disappear into the rushes and herbs on the floor.

She looked around. They were everywhere. Not many. Not like outside, where they swarmed. But there was hardly a part of the room where there wasn't a beetle.

Caught between anger and disgust, Bee sent swift spells hurling at them. She loosed her magic and sent them spinning and popping and flaring up and sizzling. Each one, as it died, left a wisp of smoke, a nasty smell, and a slimy, sticky mark.

She breathed heavily as though she had run a long way. She scratched at her hair, feeling the sharp legs of the creatures against her scalp, though she knew it was in her imagination. She scratched her body, feeling them under her shirt against her skin. She shuddered and she stamped her foot.

"Ugh," she said.

"What's this?"

Brassbuck appeared in the doorway.

"Get out!"

Bee sent a shock spell across the room. It hit Brassbuck between the eyes, and she staggered back. The beetles kept on clambering in. For every one that Bee killed, two, three, more followed. Brassbuck shook her head and righted herself.

"Happy birthday," she said.

"Are you bringing these in here?" Bee demanded.

Brassbuck hesitated, then came right in. Beetles swarmed over her boots.

"I followed them," said Brassbuck.

Bee drew in a deep breath. Instead of directing her spells at beetles one at a time, she made a picture of them all in her head and made the strongest spell she knew. The air stood still. There was a short, sharp silence, so complete that it made her ears hurt. She saw a puzzled look cover Brassbuck's face. The rushes and herbs on the floor glowed. Bee blinked. Every beetle in the room exploded. They split their shells. The soft insides sprayed out, snot green and pus yellow, vomit gray, stinking.

The silence gave way to their popping and a high, whining screech. The glow faded. Brassbuck looked at the ruin of the invading swarm.

Bee had beaten them. And they had beaten her. In killing them, she had destroyed her home. The tidy room, with its sweet-scented rushes, was a sticky, stinking mess. She could still feel them crawling on her skin. The thought of them lived on after their bodies had burst.

"Get out," she said to Brassbuck. She was tired. Her head ached. Her hands were shaking again. The buzzing and crackling of the loose magic was stronger than ever. It made her hair lift a little from her head. "Go on." Her voice was little more than a whisper. "Get out."

"But I brought you a birthday present."

"I don't want it. Get out."

Bee looked at her desk. Her books and pens were covered in a film of slime. Shattered wing cases and broken legs littered the surface.

"You've got it already," said Brassbuck. She had recovered. "I brought you the beetles."

"Just get out." Bee was so tired, she could hardly say the words.

"You'll be glad I did," said Brassbuck. "After you've seen Slowin this afternoon."

Through her feelings of sickness and pain, Bee was glad to see that the beetles outside that tried to cross the threshold tested the air with their feelers and then turned away. No more were coming in. She had repelled them, at least for now.

"I'm not going to see him," she said. "I'm too tired."

"Oh, you'll see him," said Brassbuck. "You have to. It's your birthday."

Mattie had never felt better.

He covered the distance faster than he had expected. He didn't need to stop and rest. He hardly needed to drink. Didn't need to eat at all. His legs never grew tired. He didn't know what he had swallowed, what magic Bee had put into the stone, or found in the stone, but he knew it made him stronger than he had ever been.

Always in front of his eyes, the Palace of Boolat.

He thought often of Bee. Kitchen boys don't have an easy life. He thought his mother had been a servant at the palace, but he wasn't sure. And no one seemed to know anything they could tell him about his father. He didn't even know how old he was. He thought he might be the same age as Bee, perhaps a year older. Not younger, anyway.

There'd be a new boy turning the spit when he got back. That was all right. He didn't want to do that anymore. There was no shortage of work. He'd try the stables. He liked the idea of horses. He forded a stream, enjoying the chill of the water after the heat of the sun.

After the stream, he climbed to the top of the hill and looked down at the silver curve of its path.

"Thank you," said Mattie, looking back the way he had come. Turning to face the palace, he paused, not knowing what to say. In the distance, figures moved across a field, harvesting. It was that time of year.

"Well," he said at last. "I've nowhere else to go. So I'm coming back. But I want more this time."

As soon as her head was clear of the ache, Bee left her room. She hated it now. She was too tired to clean it up, too sick at heart to want to. She wanted to be away from the beetles, away from leather-and-booted Brassbuck, away from Slowin, away from the yard. She wanted grass and breeze, the smooth coolness of a pebble, the whisper of leaves overhead, the scent of hay and the damp soft earth. She wanted to talk to someone her own age. She wanted to hug her mother. She wanted to cry. She wanted to laugh. She wanted to see Mattie. She wanted to chase after him and bring him back and say she was sorry for sending him away.

She ran out of the yard and up the hill, hoping he had come back.

The Palace of Boolat shimmered in the haze of the late-morning sun. A lost opportunity. A picture locked in a book. She sat and looked at it until her eyes could no longer focus and her head swam. And she cried. And she was twelve years old that day.

For years afterward, stories were told about that day. Mothers told their children to behave or Slowin would come and get them and take them away to his tower. Then the memory faded. They forgot about the tower. They forgot about the fire. They forgot about Bee. All they remembered was the storm. On wild nights, when the thunder was rolling in across the hills and the lightning was scaring the dogs, when the rain threw itself against the windows in an agony of exile, the people safe in their houses would smile and pour themselves another drink and say, "It's a real Slowin tonight." When the rain had stopped and they went back out and saw a blasted tree, its trunk split from the shaft of lightning, they would nod and say, "Old Slowin's climbed that tree." When a house was struck and the timber caught fire and the roof blazed and the building was destroyed, the neighbors would shake their heads and say, "Slowin slept there last night." But no one knew why. No one remembered who Slowin was or why he was the company of lightning storms.

Wizards remembered him. Wizards remember more than other people. Sometimes, wizards remember things that never happened, but that's a different thing altogether.

But even wizards didn't always tell the story the way it really happened. Their stories became entangled with the memories of the storm. Sometimes they said that Slowin was hiding in the cellar when it happened. But there were no cellars in Slowin's Yard. Just the towers and the cobbled floors and the beetles and the experiments and the fires. And Brassbuck. And Slowin. And Bee.

Slowin moved from tower to tower,

crackling and sizzling. He couldn't work. He couldn't read. His hands were all the time moving, touching the apparatuses for his experiments, picking up a tripod, adjusting a flask, running a finger along the mortar between the black bricks of the walls, snapping a beetle and tossing it onto the fire. His eyes darted fearfully from side to side, up and around, checking. Always not quite seeing someone or something that seemed to be there, just in the corner of his sight, until he turned to look, and there was nothing.

The crackling magic was beginning to irritate him. It irritated his mind, making him want to slap out and hurt something. He scratched his sides to rid himself of the feeling of something crawling over him. His throat was dry. Drinking made it worse. He snapped the head off a beetle, put the body into his mouth, and ate it. For a while it soothed the soreness. Then he needed another and another.

Two o'clock.

Twelve years old.

He had the papers all ready for Bee to sign. As soon as she put her name to them under his signature, she would be his apprentice. Bound to him for six years.

His name.

Her name.

But not Slowin.

Not Bee.

Slowin's name as a wizard was Ember.

He had always hated it.

The day his old master had told him his name and told him to sign it on his indentures, Slowin had argued. "It's not a proper name," he said.

"What do you mean?"

The master was puzzled. He was a gentle man. Soft-spoken, slow to answer, waiting always to see how the other person felt.

"It's weak," said Slowin. "I want a better name."

Slowin had not been the easiest boy he had ever had to teach. He had often thought of suggesting that perhaps it would be better if Slowin went away, if he perhaps went to the College at Canterstock instead. There he would learn to use his magic but never become one of the wizards of the Old Craft.

"You can't choose your name," he said. "Come. Sign. You will grow to like it."

"You chose it," said Slowin. He kicked the leg of the table and scowled at the man. "You chose a bad name on purpose."

"The name chooses you," said his master. "All I do is find out for you what it is."

Slowin picked up the pen and jabbed the nib on the paper of the indenture. He didn't write.

"What's wrong with Ember?"

"It's a dead name. It's what's left of a fire when all the heat has gone. It's an old name. I'm not old. I'm young. I want a young name. I want a strong name. I want a name that will let me do things. Things people will always remember. It's a weak name."

"Ember is your name," said his master. "And it will be weak or strong as you use it. Nothing is weak or strong of itself. Embers are the soul of the fire. Embers are what remain when the flash of the flames has gone. Put your hand into a flame for a moment and no harm will come to you. But wait until the flames have died. Wait until all that is left is gray ash covering red embers. Then put your hand in the fire and grasp the embers. You will burn yourself."

He looked at Slowin. "Do you understand?"

Slowin scowled.

"Lay some kindling on the embers and blow gently. The wood will catch. Add a few small lumps of coal, the blue flames will reappear. Put on a log and watch the flames rise up. Feed the fire, add more fuel. The fire will grow and live and burn down a whole town if you feed it. Because of the power of the embers. Do you understand?"

Slowin scratched the nib on the paper, spattering ink.

"And when that fire has burned itself out and no flames remain, turn over the ashes with your boot, let them fall, and see the embers reveal themselves gold vermillion. That is where the fire lives. Ember is a great name."

"I want a better one," said Slowin.

But he signed.

He knew better now. He knew that the name was, indeed, not the master's to choose. The apprentice brought the name with her. It was only for the master to discover it. But that had not stopped him from hating his name all his life.

And now he knew Bee's name. Today her wizard's name would be used for the first time.

Her name was Flame.

Sleep had come easily

and passed pleasantly for Cabbage, which was not always the way. When he woke, Perry was already up and dressed, sitting in a window seat eating toast and drinking milk.

"What happened to the cat?" Perry asked as soon as Cabbage's eyes were open.

"Eh?"

"The cat. What happened to it?"

Cabbage stretched, feeling more than a little like a cat himself. "It just goes away," he said.

"Where to?"

"Is there any more toast?"

"I can get you some."

"Please."

"And then you'll tell me where the cat went?"

"Yes."

"All right."

Perry finished his toast and carried his plate to the door.

"And some bacon, please," said Cabbage. "And a fried egg if there is one. And some mushrooms."

Cabbage sort of washed his face while Perry fetched the food. He didn't bother with his hair.

It was hot again. And the air crackled and fizzed more than ever. The sun was well over the horizon but not too high. Still fairly early.

"There's a big conference downstairs," said Perry, appearing with the food. "They want you down there."

"I'll eat this first. Are they in a state?"

"Does a pig make mud wagons and take monkeys to market?" said Perry.

Cabbage was halfway through the food and regretting he had eaten all the bacon while there was still toast and egg left.

"Where does the cat go?"

Cabbage swallowed his toast.

"Nowhere," he said. "There isn't a cat."

"That's not fair."

"No. But it's the answer."

Perry sat in the window seat again, weaving the sunlight through his hair. "If we all saw a cat. And if the cat ate the fire, then there was a cat, of sorts," he said. "Otherwise it couldn't have eaten the fire."

"Only if there was any fire to eat," said Cabbage.

"It was hot," said Perry. "The grass is all scorched and gone where it was. And there are black smoke streaks on the wall where we were sitting when it started."

"It was real enough to burn," said Cabbage. His plate was empty now. "But not real enough to burn me."

Perry stood up with excitement.

"That's just what they're talking about downstairs," he said. "Why you didn't burn in the field in the afternoon, or in the garden last night. Everyone else gets burned right enough."

"We'd better go and talk to them, then," said Cabbage. He picked up his plate and headed for the door. "Is there any more bacon?"

There was more bacon, but Flaxfold wouldn't let him have any. "You can have more toast when we've finished talking," she said. "And an apple."

It was the same group as last night, with the addition of Bee's parents. Again, Cabbage found himself drawn to Cartford, Dorwin's father.

"No one's working," said Flaxfield.

"It's Bee," said Leathort.

"We think it's Bee," Flaxfold corrected him. "That's what brought these two here. The wild magic is very bad in their house. Worse than in the areas around. They decided that it was Bee asking them for help, so they set off. They knew that Slowin lived somewhere in this direction. That's how I found them."

"How?" asked Cabbage.

Flaxfold took a deep breath. "I was on my way to Slowin's. I thought he might be able to help with the wild magic. He's a fire wizard."

Flaxfold quickly told Perry and Cabbage about Slowin. About his age and his weakness. She told the boys that she had almost forgotten about him, and when she did think of him, it was to wonder when he was going to die.

"When I got near to his yard, about ten miles off, I began to hear stories from the people around who were using him again for magic. I was surprised."

"We're going to see him," said Flaxfield. "Today."

"It isn't a job for boys," said Dorwin.

"I'm going," said Cabbage.

"So am I," said Perry.

"You'll do as you're told," said Flaxfield.

"You'll get eaten by the fire," said Cabbage.

This was the signal for a quarrel to break out.

"Whatever you say," said Dorwin, her voice clearing the others', "it isn't a job for boys. Flaxfield, you've a responsibility for Cabbage. You can't allow him to go into danger."

"It's a job for anyone who can do it," said Cartford. "Let them all go and see who can work. Let Flaxfield try first, and if he does it, well and good. If not, then . . ." He shrugged his huge shoulders. "Then someone else will have to."

"Whatever else happens," said Flaxfield, "we have to do it now. Today. Before she signs her indenture. After that, it will be too late."

Dorwin grabbed his wrist. "You don't know that," she said.

"You don't know that this is anything to do with Slowin or Bee. You're just guessing."

He laid a brown hand on hers. "You know it's about Bee," he said. "You know it's about Slowin. Watch."

He leaned back and took a sheet of paper from the table by the window. Taking a pen, he dipped it into the ink and wrote:

Slowin

Underneath he wrote:

Bee

He leaned back. Nothing happened. He frowned.

"That's not right," he said.

"See?" Dorwin squeezed his wrist. "It's not about them. Leave the boys here with me. Go and look for what's causing this. But go alone."

"All right," Flaxfield agreed.

Vella picked up the pen. She altered the last *E* of *Bee* to an A and wrote:

Beatrice

"It's her name," she said.

The letters smoked and smoldered. The paper kindled and flared. A small black beetle climbed out of the inkpot and toppled onto the table. Cartford lifted the inkpot, then hammered it down, crushing the beetle.

Dawn comes early at harvest time, so noon was still far off when they left the inn. Flaxfield rode alone. Dorwin took Perry on her horse. Leathort took Cabbage on his.

"We'll never make it in time on foot," Flaxfield had said.

"Bring those horses back safe," Flaxfold warned him.

"What about us?" said Perry.

She patted his leg and waved them good-bye.

Cabbage didn't like being on the horse. It looked good when you saw a rider. It wasn't so good doing it. It jolted. It hurt his legs. Looking down made him dizzy. On the other hand, you could see so much more from up here. Clear of the hedgerows, Cabbage could see a pattern of neglect and damage.

They rested and watered the horses by a stream. The sun was still just below the noontime high.

"We can't stay long," said Flaxfield. "We'll be too late."

"What if she's signed already?" asked Cabbage.

"If we're right," said Flaxfield. "We'll know when she signs."

"How?"

"I don't know. But the wild magic is growing worse. It's preparing for something. When it happens, we'll know."

They remounted and pressed on.

It was the horses who first let them know that they were getting close.

Dorwin's horse stopped so suddenly that he nearly threw his riders. Dorwin urged him on. He turned his head and scraped his hoof on the ground.

Flaxfield's was next. Leathort was barely twenty yards ahead when his horse refused.

"We're on foot from here," said Dorwin.

They tethered the horses and trudged on. The sun was nearing the hottest part of the day, and they were crossing open country with no shade.

Leathort was the first to stumble. He fell awkwardly on his shoulder and cried out. Perry was nearest and he stooped to help him. The roffle drew back with a frightened look.

"What is it?" said Cabbage.

Smoke curled out from Leathort's mouth and he was bleeding from his ears.

"Drag him back," called Flaxfield.

They pulled him back toward the horses.

"I'll look after him," said Dorwin. Flaxfield strode on. Cabbage and Perry trotted after him. Dorwin held Leathort's head in her lap.

"Get back," Flaxfield ordered the boys. "Stay with the others."

For a moment, Cabbage did as he was told; then he trotted on again. He had almost caught up with Flaxfield when the wizard stumbled. Flaxfield straightened himself and carried on. Only a few paces more and he staggered, put his hand to his head, and groaned. He stood upright, moved forward again, and stopped. His face was twisted with effort.

Cabbage ran up to him. "Are you all right?"

Flaxfield turned his gaze on the boy, but Cabbage could see that he didn't recognize him.

"Perry. Give me a hand," he called.

The roffle came up and together they moved Flaxfield back a little and let him sit down.

"Is he all right?" called Dorwin.

Leathort was trying to sit up.

"I think so," Cabbage called back. "There's no blood or smoke."

Cabbage's voice roused Flaxfield. He climbed to unsteady feet. "Where's he going?" Flaxfield pointed to Perry, who was walking on.

"Stop," called Cabbage.

The roffle stopped and turned. "It's all right," he said.

"It's dangerous," called Dorwin. "Come back."

"Try it," said Perry, beckoning to Cabbage.

Cabbage followed. He passed the point where Flaxfield had failed. He joined Perry. Together they walked on.

"Stop." Dorwin ran after them, tripped, fell, and rolled back, as though punched.

The boys walked back toward them.

"It's just here," said Perry, pointing to the ground.

"That's it," said Flaxfield. "We're going back. Come on."

"No," said Cabbage.

"Don't you cheek me," said Flaxfield. "Come here now."

"I'm sorry," said Cabbage. "Cartford said it's a job for anyone who can do it, didn't he?"

No one answered him.

"You can't do it," said Cabbage. "So we have to. Sorry. Go back. Wait for us at the inn."

They turned and walked away, ignoring the calls to come back. Flaxfield tried to follow them, but he was sent reeling back again. There was nothing for it but to return to the horses and wait and watch.

The boys didn't look back.

"Are you scared?" said Perry.

"No," said Cabbage.

"I am."

They walked on. The air was busy with magic. Sometimes Cabbage felt that hands were running over his face, like a blind man, searching. Sometimes it was a stillness worse than resistance. He could tell that Perry felt it, but only in a weaker way.

"A little bit," he said at last.

"What?" asked Perry.

"I'm a little bit afraid."

"Which way are we going?"

"Just follow the magic."

Bee followed the path

from her tower to Slowin's.

She didn't knock. She walked in. Slowin was waiting at his desk.

"Sit down," he said, not looking up at her.

"I don't think I want to be your apprentice," said Bee.

"I told you to sit down. I've got the papers ready."

"I want to go back home."

Slowin scraped his chair closer in. "You'd better sit next to me so I can explain as we go along," he said.

Bee felt her eyes fill with tears. "I said I don't want to be your apprentice," she said.

"I heard you. Now sit down and we'll sign these papers."

"You're not listening to me. I want to go home."

Slowin pushed the other chair to her, and she sat down. As soon as she had, she wished she hadn't, but it seemed stupid to stand up again so she stayed there.

"This is the only home you have," he said. "Now, let's get on."

Brassbuck appeared in the doorway. She leaned against it, watching.

"I'm not going to sign anything," said Bee. "You can't make me."

"I'll take her home," offered Brassbuck.

Slowin pushed his chair away. "All right," he said. "Take her."

Bee blinked in surprise. "You mean it?"

"Of course."

She stood up. "Thank you."

"Pack your things," said Slowin. "Don't bother coming back to say good-bye."

Bee felt she should do something, shake Slowin's hand, or something.

He picked up a document and studied it, ignoring her.

"How long will it take to get there?" she asked.

No one answered.

"Is it far?"

"Don't you remember?" asked Brassbuck.

"No. I was very little."

"Well, I don't," Brassbuck said. "I've never been there."

Bee wanted to cry again.

"Where is it?" she asked Slowin.

"What's that?" He looked up. "Are you still here?"

Bee wanted to punch him in the face. "Where's my home?" she said.

"Here, of course."

"No. My real home. Where my parents are."

"That's gone," he said. "They've gone. They're not there anymore. Didn't you know?"

"I don't believe you."

Slowin smiled. His face shone. Really shone. It hurt Bee's eyes to look at him. He was full of magic. Not his own. Magic from outside him. It was filling him, spilling out of him.

"Things change," he said. "Nothing stays the same. They've forgotten you."

"They wouldn't."

"They did. I told them they could come here every year on your birthday, to see you. They never came."

Bee went over and leaned in to him. She shouted into his face. "That's not true."

"Why don't you sit down," he said. "Don't get upset."

He helped her into her chair. She was shaking.

"Now. This is your home. Let's settle things properly. Here. Blow your nose. That's better."

Bee put her hand to her head to feel where the pain was.

"We'll sort this out. Then you can go and have a lie down. You'll feel better then."

The papers were in front of her. He put the pen into her hand.

"There. I'll just help you to start." He dipped it into the ink.

"If you'll just write your name here. Beatrice. Remember that's your long name, not just Bee?"

He indicated the place with his forefinger.

"Good, and now, underneath, you'll write your own special name, your magic name. It's—Ember."

His voice was unsteady as he said this. His hand trembled.

"That doesn't sound right," said Bee.

He laughed. "That's what I said, all those years ago, when my master told me what my name was. See how alike we are?"

He put his hand on hers as though he were going to move the pen and sign her name himself. "Write it," he said.

"It really doesn't sound right."

Slowin grew hot. His hand was burning her. "See? You're making the magic angry by arguing. This is a great moment in your life and you're spoiling it. Write. Before it all goes wrong. Quickly."

Bee wrote the word.

Overhead and distant, a crash of thunder. Slowin's hand cooled. His face dimmed.

"Good," he whispered. "Now, I sign here, as your master." He grabbed the pen and scribbled *Slowin* very fast. He breathed deeply, steadied himself, then, slowly and deliberately wrote underneath it, Bee's name in magic.

And the fire swooped low over them.

Slowin burst into flame. Brassbuck threw herself at him and covered him, trying to put out the fire. Bee was hurled back in her chair and sent spinning across the room.

The tower split from side to side and fell open to the sky, black as night.

The magic led them straight to the hillside

where Bee had met Mattie. The Palace of Boolat had been in view for miles. The yard revealed itself all at once when they were almost on top of it.

"That's it," said Cabbage.

"How do you know?"

"Can't you see?"

Perry had been itching and sore ever since they had left Flaxfield and the others. His skin was tender, as though he had fallen into a bed of nettles.

Cabbage had suffered more, felt more pain, inside his head as well as on his body. More than that, he could see it arcing across the landscape, lighting trees like torches. Perry only saw the wall and the towers of Slowin's Yard. Cabbage saw a boiling vat of magic.

"Do you think we're in time?" asked Perry.

"Only one way to find out."

As he said it, the sky cracked. A clap of thunder sent them reeling back, their hands over their ears.

Perry doubled over in pain. Cabbage withstood it better, staying upright, but white as wishes. Perry half stood and then fell properly, lying on his side.

Cabbage took his friend's arm. "Can you get up?"

Perry stared at him.

"Let me help you up."

Perry shook his head. He pointed to his ears. He shrugged.

The sky was on fire. No smoke. No flames. No heat. Just the swirling eddies of pure fire above them and around them.

"I've got to go down there," said Cabbage. "It's happening now. I've got to stop it."

His own voice sounded funny to him, so he had no idea how it must be to Perry. The roffle tried to stand again and stumbled and fell.

"I'll come back for you," said Cabbage. He pointed to the yard and then to himself and then to Perry. "I'll come straight back. All right?"

Perry nodded, then turned his face to the ground and lay still.

Cabbage ran helter-skelter down the hillside, keeping his balance by never stopping. He reached the gate, putting out his hands to stop himself from crashing into it.

Made it. Just in time.

He ran into the yard, drew a deep breath to shout to Bee, and the sky split wide open. For a moment everything stopped. The crackling and fizzing of the wild magic ended. The bright fire overhead faded. The air was still again, and his head was clear.

Then the magic spilled out over the yard. It fell from the skies. It rose up from under the cobbles, tearing them apart. It washed over the walls and covered the ground. It knocked him sideways and backward and lifted him up and let him fall. The last thing he saw before everything went black was the great central tower being ripped open and destroyed.

"I can't stand this waiting," said Flaxfield.

Dorwin folded her arms and looked with Flaxfield in the direction the boys had gone.

"My father says waiting is the secret of getting it right," she said.

"What does that mean?"

"I don't know."

"How's Leathort?"

"He's asleep under the tree. The bleeding's stopped. He's not in any pain."

Flaxfield winced. "He's lucky, then," he said.

Dorwin nodded. "How can they get through?" she asked.

Flaxfield picked up a small stone and threw it. It arced up, then seemed to hit a wall and bounced back. Dorwin picked it up.

"It's hot," she said.

"It's just a stone," said Flaxfield. "That's why it can't pass."

"I don't understand."

He leaned on his staff, eyes constantly on the distance, looking for any sign of the boys, any indication that they were succeeding, or returning.

"Magic," he said, "works on the dangerous edge of things. That's where it gets its power."

Dorwin pretended to understand.

"I was telling the roffle a story about where magic first came from," said Flaxfield. "It's from the edges. Where things are one thing and another thing."

Clouds sped across the sky, swift and white.

"There's no magic in the roffle world," said Flaxfield. "Not magic the way we know it. The Deep World is a place with light but no sun, water but no rivers, air but no wind. Towns and no people. Roffles are different. They're not quite people."

"That's why Perry could go on through?"

"I think so. I should have realized back by the river, when the wild magic attacked him and he wasn't hurt. It killed the innkeeper. And Cabbage. What's he? He's not a boy, not a man. Not a normal boy, not yet a wizard. He's an edge. He's an apprentice. Neither one thing nor the other." He gazed ever ahead. "They make a good pair for the job."

"They're just boys," Dorwin argued. "They shouldn't have gone. It's too dangerous."

"Perhaps you're right," he said. "Perhaps you are." He smiled. "Anyway, they've gone. And we couldn't stop them."

"Sometimes I think wizards are the worst people," said Dorwin. "You come from nowhere. You never stay. And we're left with whatever's happened."

"We bring only what you ask for," said Flaxfield.

"We didn't ask for this."

Flaxfield sighed. "This is different," he said. "This is new. I've never seen this before."

He raised his staff and indicated the sky, making sure that no magic traveled from it. Even so, the willow staff seemed to attract something from above him. A shaft of light stretched out from the tip of the staff to Dorwin's hand. They both cried out and jerked away. The staff glowed white like iron from the furnace. Flaxfield dropped it with a roar of pain. It sizzled and turned black. Dorwin touched it. The staff was cold, wet. Flaxfield frowned when she handed it to him.

"Listen," he said.

The thunder began far away and traveled toward them, growing in volume till it was more than Dorwin could stand. She ducked her head. Flaxfield lifted his cloak and covered her in it, keeping his own head high, staring into the sky, defying the noise. Even when the sky opened and the wild magic rained down, he did not look away.

Flaxfield stood at the edge of the magic storm, brushed only by the spatter of stray drops that drifted out that far. Bee was at the center, and Cabbage, in the yard, just a few paces away. Slowin and Brassbuck, next to Bee, were crushed beneath its rage.

Flaxfield felt the wild magic

as a sailor feels the sea spray on his face in a storm. Unblinking, he challenged it.

Bee felt the wild magic as a trapped rabbit feels the fire when a field is torched. She did not try to challenge it. There was no challenge to this. She was part of it. Something Slowin had done, some hurt to her, had released this fury.

Cabbage turned his mind into himself. He made no resistance to the magic storm. Where Flaxfield defied it, Cabbage allowed it to wash over him. And as he did, the fire became water against him. The more it attacked him, the more he accepted it. And the more he accepted it, the less it could hurt him. When the fury had passed, he stood, drenched and shivering with cold, but alive and unhurt.

. . .

Dorwin emerged from Flaxfield's cloak. She blinked in the sunlight, braced her shoulders, and tested herself for any bruises or broken bones. Nothing. Flaxfield still stared ahead.

"Are you all right, Flaxfield?"

She touched his face. His eyes looked blind, fixed.

"Over here!" shouted Leathort.

"Wait," she called. "Are you hurt?"

"No. I covered my head. I heard it, but it didn't come through this far."

"I'll be with you in a minute." She shook the wizard's shoulder. "Flaxfield. Speak to me. Are you all right? Are you blind? What happened?"

He moved his head, shrugged his cloak back into place on his shoulder. "No. No, I'm not blind."

She took his arm. "They'll be all right, Flaxfield. I know they will."

"I'm going to see," he said.

"You can't."

"Watch me."

Cabbage grimaced as he picked his way over the cobbles. He'd never seen so many beetles. And they weren't even nice shiny black beetles like the ones you saw on dry days, or the handsome stag beetles with their big horns. They were hunched and round like bedbugs. Huge bedbugs. With a single, sharp spike in the center of their heads. The rain of wild fire magic didn't seem to have harmed them at all. And they weren't shy like normal beetles. They didn't scurry away. They let you tread on them and then they swarmed toward your foot as though attacking. Cabbage tried to flick them away, but they kept on coming.

"You freaks," he said. "Get away."

All of the towers were ruined, heaps of rubble. Cabbage saw equipment and apparatuses in the wreckage, stuff that he didn't recognize, couldn't even guess at. Alongside it, tables and chairs, a desk, a floor strewn with herbs and rushes. The main tower, the largest, was the least destroyed, the most damaged. It had split so that the two sides gaped open, like hands held apart. He climbed over the piles of blackened bricks and into what was left of it.

Completely undamaged, clean and fresh as though nothing had happened around it, lay an indenture. The ink was still wet on the signature.

"That'll be important," he said. "I think."

Cabbage folded it and put it inside his jerkin. The corner was sharp and scratched him. He took it out and tried to fold it again. The paper was too thick and it wouldn't fold flat. He felt inside his cloak and drew out a small notebook. Opening the book, he put the paper into a pocket on the inside back cover.

The smell was the worst thing. Except for the sticky feeling underfoot. And the soot. And the sense that something was hiding, waiting, that the danger hadn't passed even though the storm of wild magic had blown itself out. Small fires still burned. Pockets of flame in the black ground.

Except for the white of the paper he had picked up, everything was black. Cabbage stood and looked around. Nothing seemed any different from anything else. Here, where the storm had been most fierce, there was no trace of anything he could recognize. Nothing but the melted, fused, and hardened residue of the fire.

Cabbage wasn't hungry. He hadn't eaten for ages, and for the first time he could ever remember, he was empty and not hungry.

"I'd be sick," he said.

His voice bounced off the broken curve of the wall, reminding him of the noise that had started the storm. And that reminded him of the deafness. And that reminded him of Perry. He should go back to him.

"I'm sorry," he said. "Really sorry. But I've got to stay here for a bit longer. I've got to find Bee."

He didn't even know if Perry had survived the storm. "Just wait," he said. "Please."

He rubbed his face with his hand and blinked.

"Right," he said.

It felt less lonely talking to himself.

He stood as near to the center of the tower as he could work out. He let himself relax and breathe deeply, ignoring the stink. He imagined a girl, about to be an apprentice. He didn't know what she looked like, so it wasn't easy.

Relax.

Breathe.

Think.

Don't think.

Imagine.

As the tension and fear dribbled away from Cabbage, his shoulders grew loose, his fingers hung at his sides. And, before he could stop them, stars dribbled down and fell at his feet, making a circle of light around him.

Cabbage flashed his eyes open and looked around in panic. The small fires flickered with no interest in him. The scorched surfaces huddled, dead and black. No crackle of wild magic. No fizz or tingle.

A small black cat appeared and licked up the stars. Pausing, it sat and looked at Cabbage. He smiled. The cat licked its paw, nuzzled its head against his leg, then stood and licked up more of the stars.

"That's right," said Cabbage. "Good cat."

He dribbled a few more for her, then closed his hand and watched her finish her meal.

When the stars were all eaten, the cat sat and looked up at him.

"All gone," said Cabbage. "Off you go. I'll see you again."

This was the time when the cat should disappear. In fact, Cabbage had never needed to tell her to go before. Still, she sat and waited.

"What is it?" asked Cabbage.

She licked her other paw, then rubbed it over her ear.

"You want more?"

He scattered a few tiny stars for her. She turned her head and looked at them.

"No?"

She moved a few paces from him, stopped and turned to look at him.

"What is it?"

He followed her. She moved more, to the left, picking soft feet over the hot ground. She walked around an obstacle that Cabbage couldn't see, but it was clearly a part of the ground she didn't want to walk on. She found a small, slightly raised piece of ground and walked up and down it four times.

"There are no stars there," said Cabbage.

She gave him that look that he had sometimes seen before when he had said something stupid, but never from a cat.

He bent down and laid his hand on the ground. It moved. He snatched his hand back and scrambled away from it on all fours, squashing beetles under his palms.

"Ugh."

He wiped the sticky mess on a different patch of ground.

"Now my hands stink," he complained.

The cat licked her paw.

"It's all right for you. Don't think *I'm* going to lick my hands."

He approached the low mound. Touching it again, he felt it rise and fall.

"Let's see," he whispered. "Show me."

The cat nuzzled against the ground near to one end of the

raised section. Cabbage found a split in the surface and tugged. The ground peeled away like a scab.

He was looking at a girl's face. Red, raw, blistered, but a girl.

"Now what?" he said. "What can I do?"

But the cat had gone.

Having a blacksmith for a father,

Dorwin was a good horsewoman. She had grown up with horses, so she quickly caught up with Flaxfield and then pulled ahead of him.

She could easily have ridden off, leaving him behind, but she stayed just a little in front. Partly to teach him a lesson. Partly because she wasn't entirely sure of the direction and she didn't want them to get separated. In the end, it was clear where they were going, and when she crested the hill with the Palace of Boolat in the distance and Slowin's Yard below them, she reined her horse in and waited for the wizard to catch her up.

She put her hand to her mouth. "The stink," she said.

Flaxfield was gasping for breath. He looked down at the yard. "Too late," he said.

"Are you sure?"

"I'm sure."

Flaxfield stared at the ruin. "I remember this," he said.

"When it was good?"

"It was never good," said Flaxfield. "Slowin was a poor wizard, a greedy wizard. He should never have been allowed to finish his apprenticeship." He shook his head. "But once a child has set off on that road, it's very hard to turn back. Not many masters would give up on an apprentice."

"How can he have allowed him to be a bad wizard? How can the master have given him that power?"

"I didn't say he was a bad wizard, but a poor one. It's like a horseshoe. You know the difference?"

"Yes, a poor horseshoe will wear through quickly, perhaps be thrown. A bad horseshoe will break, perhaps cripple the horse. The animal will need to be put down."

"Exactly. I don't know how or when, but Slowin turned from being a poor wizard to a bad one. We should have noticed. It's our fault."

It was time to be practical. Dorwin flicked her reins. "What about the boys?" she asked.

"Let's see."

Flaxfield spurred his horse and led the way down to the yard. This time Dorwin allowed him to stay in front.

Her worst imaginings didn't include the beetles. She drew her cloak around herself and shuddered.

"They're everywhere," she said. "What are they?"

"Nothing ordinary," said Flaxfield. "Nothing good. Try to avoid them."

The advice was welcome but useless. There was no avoiding them.

"Cabbage," called Flaxfield. "Perry?"

"Over here."

Cabbage ignored the beetles running over his hands. He looked up at Flaxfield.

"Is this her?" he asked.

Flaxfield dismounted and knelt by Cabbage.

"I've never seen her," he said. "But yes. It must be."

"She's not dead?"

Dorwin couldn't bring herself to dismount. Not with the beetles crawling around.

"No," said Flaxfield. "Not dead. But perhaps worse."

Cabbage touched Bee's cheek and winced. Her skin was so raw, so red that he felt he must be hurting her. He wanted to soothe her but didn't know what to do.

"We can't leave her here," he said.

"We mustn't move her," said Dorwin. "It could make her worse."

Cabbage had never seen Flaxfield so grim.

"I don't think she could be worse," he said.

Cabbage looked up at Dorwin. "What can we do?" he asked.

He saw Dorwin give a fearful look at the beetles. She braced herself and dismounted.

Cabbage showed her how he'd discovered Bee, and Dorwin peeled back the rest of the black layer that covered her. Cabbage waited for Bee to moan or complain, to wince. She made no movement at all. Her breathing was slow and regular. Her eyes closed. Her hands by her side, one open, one clenched as though holding something. Flaxfield left them to it and walked around the yard, prodding the ground with the end of his staff and listening. The beetles moved away from him.

"Can we get her to the inn?" asked Cabbage.

"She can't ride," said Dorwin. "We could make a litter."

"What's that?"

"A sort of bed. Tie her to it and let a horse drag it. It will be slow traveling, but it's all I can think of."

"Where's Perry?" asked Flaxfield.

Cabbage explained where he had left him. He pointed.

"We came from there," said Dorwin.

Flaxfield frowned. "No sign of him."

"He'll be all right," said Cabbage. "Won't he?"

"There was no sign of him," said Flaxfield. "Now, what about this litter?"

Cabbage spread his hands. "Look at this mess. There's nothing here."

Dorwin stared at Flaxfield. "Well?" she said.

"What?"

"You know what. Is it over? The wild magic?"

"It must be," said Cabbage. "You got here. There was no barrier." He drew a breath.

"Don't," said Flaxfield.

Cabbage turned his back to Flaxfield and snapped his fingers. A fine mist of gentle rain began to fall only on Cabbage and the space just around him. He turned his face up and closed his eyes, enjoying the soft relief. He pushed his hair back and let himself relax. Snapping his fingers again, he stopped the rain and looked at Flaxfield.

"That was a risk," Flaxfield warned him.

"Not really. I made stars earlier, and the cat. In fact, it was the cat who found her."

"What happened to the wizard?" asked Dorwin. "Slowin."

Flaxfield bit his lip. "That's what I've been looking for," he said. "And he had an assistant. They've both disappeared."

"Dead?" asked Cabbage.

"I don't think we'll be that lucky," said Flaxfield. "Perhaps. We'll find out eventually."

"Can you make a litter?" asked Dorwin. "We've Bee to look after and Leathort to pick up on the way back. And there's Perry."

"Your father's a practical man," said Flaxfield. "I suppose that's where you get it from."

He walked off and began prodding the ground with his staff again. "I don't like it. I don't like not knowing where they are."

"Well. Please can you hurry?"

Flaxfield stood over Bee. She looked so small.

"Come here, boy," he said. He held his staff out to Cabbage.

"I can't take that. It's yours."

Flaxfield smiled at him. "You know," he said, "I tell you off a lot, and I don't say often enough how well you're doing, do I?"

Cabbage looked away.

"But you're a good apprentice. You learn well. Today you're going to learn that there are some times when you have to do what you've been told you must never do. Understand?"

"Yes."

"What must you never do?"

Cabbage answered promptly and without needing to think. It was as simple as saying his five times table.

"You must never take or use anything proper to another wizard," he said. "You must never use his name as though it were your own. You must never take his staff and make magic with it. You must never . . ."

"That's enough for now," said Flaxfield. "You're going to take my staff and do as I say."

Cabbage allowed himself to be handed the staff. It was smooth and supple, made of willow, but darker, heavier.

"You're my apprentice," said Flaxfield. "So we're bound together in a way. You can use my staff with my permission. So. Make a litter from it, please. Like a hurdle. A willow one. From young wands: slender, yielding branches, that will bend but not break under Bee's weight."

"Why don't you?"

"Go on, boy. Or I'll tell everyone why you're called Cabbage."

It took a few tries before Cabbage made the litter exactly as Flaxfield wanted it. Then it wasn't easy lifting Bee onto it and fastening it to Dorwin's horse. The end dragged along the ground; the top was fastened to her saddle, so the angle was quite sharp and they needed to secure Bee firmly to keep her from falling off. Cabbage made special bonds that didn't cut into her.

The harvest took everyone's time,

now that the wild magic had blown itself out. And anyway, Flax-fold sent everyone packing.

"The inn's closed," she said. "So you'll have to find somewhere else to get together."

Finishing the harvest took two days. Cartford rolled a barrel of cider over the green and set it up on a table in the garden outside the inn. He encouraged others to bring food and more drink. When the sun was low and the crops were garnered, they gathered and sang and drank until Flaxfold opened the door.

"All right. You can use the front parlor and this garden. I'll serve you food and drink and you'll be gone an hour before midnight, and you'll leave us in peace. Agreed?"

"Agreed," said Cartford. "And we'll keep the noise down now. How is she?"

"As you'd expect," said Flaxfold.

"No worse?"

"No better."

As soon as she had sent the customers packing, Flaxfold looked down at the girl and she cried. No noise of sobbing, no heaving chest, just slow tears as though they would never end.

"We should have stopped this," said Flaxfold.

Flaxfield didn't cry. His face was blank. "We didn't know," he said. "There was no way we could have known."

The girl lay in a bed of moss and herbs. She was naked when they found her. All her clothes had flared up and turned to smoke and ash. Now the green tendrils and fronds curled around her and over her so that only her eyes and mouth and fingers could be seen. It was as though she had been carved from stone and left out in the weather, till lichen had possessed her and turned her into a green form.

"Will she live?" asked Cabbage.

"She may."

"I'm going back there. To take a look."

"You should stay here," said Flaxfold. "It's dangerous."

"I've got to find Perry," he said.

"I'll come with you," said Flaxfield.

"Better if you don't."

Flaxfield left the room.

"You should show him more respect," said Flaxfold. "He's your apprentice master."

Cabbage looked down at Bee. "How do you make the moss grow on her?"

"It wants to. It's that sort of moss."

"How much magic can you do?"

Flaxfold folded a towel and hung it over a rail. "Enough for this," she said.

"Will Flaxfield's magic come back?"

Flaxfold put her arm around Cabbage. "Think how bad it is for him," she said. "All his magic has gone. The wild storm took it. It's worse than being killed."

"What's a wizard without magic?" said Cabbage. "I'll see you later."

The stink of smoke made Cabbage want to throw up. It was greasy and hot. He made himself go on, into the low ring of bricks that marked where the perimeter wall had stood before the fire. He stepped over and into the ruins of Slowin's domain. His feet slipped on the cobbles, streaked with damp soot. All of the buildings were destroyed. The round bases of the towers stood like broken teeth, hollowed out by decay. At least the beetles had gone now.

He knew why he was there. To make sure that Slowin was dead, that he had been eaten up by the fire that had nearly killed Bee.

He couldn't rid his mind of the picture of Bee. He promised himself that whatever else he did, for the whole of the rest of his life, he would never give up until he settled a score with Slowin, who had done this to her.

But first he had to know if the wizard was even still alive. Cabbage felt him there. He felt something hidden in the yard. Something moving. Something growing and changing. All was dry and dead like a chrysalis. Cabbage knew what life lurked inside that dry husk.

There should be something, some remains of the wizard. Cabbage prodded heaps of ashes with his toe. They crumbled and drifted in the breeze, the backdraft carrying some onto his legs, leaving gray patches. Nothing had survived. If Slowin had died here, even his bones had been consumed by the savage heat. From tower to tower, Cabbage stepped and studied. Nothing. He stamped his feet in frustration, and something stirred. A shiny, black oval hauled itself up from between the cracks in the slate floor. It paused, took stock, and started to walk on crooked legs.

He kicked away the black beetle. It tumbled back, righted itself, raised its wing case, and clicked. The boy hesitated. The beetle was big, bigger than any he had seen before, the size of a walnut. He raised his foot to stamp on it, bracing himself for the wet crunch he knew would come when it crumpled under his boot. Another beetle hauled itself up through the crack. And another and another. They grouped around the one that he had kicked. He stopped. Waited. The beetles moved toward him. The walnut-sized one was the smallest. The biggest was the size of a man's fist. He left quickly.

"Is he dead?" Flaxfold's face was hard now. The softness of the tears had gone.

"I don't know," said Cabbage.

"Could anything live through that fire?"

He told her about the beetles.

"Really? Still there? Bigger than ever?"

"Do you doubt it?"

"Of course not. But I don't like it."

They sat on wooden chairs in the doorway to the inn, facing out.

"How is she?"

"I think she'll live."

Cabbage grimaced.

"It's better that she lives," she said.

"Is she in any pain?"

"Not now. But when she wakes."

"She's clutching something in her hand."

"Yes."

"Can you see what it is?"

"Not yet. Perhaps it's nothing."

"The beetles were talking to each other."

"That can't be right."

"The one I kicked called for help. The others came."

"Do you think it was his doing? Slowin?"

He stood up and walked away from her. He liked the scents of the garden. The stench of the fire wouldn't go away. He tried to fill his lungs with the green aroma of growth and life.

"Are you doing everything?" he asked. "For her."

Flaxfold did not bother to answer him.

"There must be some other magic that would help."

"Then you go and use magic on her," she said. Her voice was gentle. "See if apprentice magic is better than my way."

He reached down to a snapdragon, put his fingers to it as though he might break it from the stem. He squeezed the sides so that the jaw opened and closed, then took his hand away.

Flaxfold put her hand on his back. "We both want to help her," she said. "I know that. But she has been nearly destroyed by magic. More magic, even to try to heal her, would kill her. She is surrounded by magic, held by it. Magic is growing all over her, to protect her. But I can't let magic change her."

Cabbage moved away from her touch. "This isn't what I thought," he said, "when I set out to be a wizard."

"No," she said. "But it's what being a wizard is."

They watched Flaxfield walk up the lane toward them.

Cabbage broke the silence before the wizard arrived. "He looks tired."

Flaxfold nodded. "He's been helping with the harvest. He can't make the Harvest Spell, so he bends his back and stacks the sheaves. He can't stay away."

"That's not wizard work."

Flaxfold stopped smiling. "I think he knows what wizard work is better than you do," she said.

"What's that?" called Flaxfield. "Talking about wizard work?"

"I'll get you drink," said Flaxfold.

Cabbage jumped up. "I'll go."

She put her hand on his shoulder and made him sit again. "You and Flaxfield talk. I'll bring something cool for you both."

Flaxfield sat back and closed his eyes, enjoying the late-afternoon sun on his face. Cabbage tried not to wriggle and show impatience. Flaxfold was taking a long time with the drinks.

"Sorry," said Flaxfield.

"What for?"

"What are you angry with me about?"

Cabbage thought about it. "Perry," he said.

"We looked for Perry," said Flaxfield. "But I'm sorry we didn't find him."

"Is he dead?"

"What do you think?"

"I think we won't know unless we look for him some more."

Flaxfield wiggled his aching fingers, flexed his stiff shoulders, and sighed. "I'm not used to hard work," he said.

Cabbage glared at him.

"Cabbage," said Flaxfield. "Please can we talk?"

"We are talking, aren't we?"

"Good. Then we'll both listen."

Cabbage waited.

"How many things do we have to do soon?" asked Flaxfield. "Important things?"

"Perry," said Cabbage. He turned to face Flaxfield.

The old wizard nodded. "Go on," he said.

"We need to know what happened to him. Then there's Slowin. I know he's still somewhere. I just know it." He folded his arms and got ready to argue.

"What else?" asked Flaxfield.

Cabbage wasn't ready for this.

"Well, there's Bee, of course, but Flaxfold is looking after her."

"I thought you wanted more," said Flaxfield.

"Well, nothing's happening," said Cabbage.

"What else?"

Cabbage said nothing.

Flaxfield waited.

The sound of harvest had stopped.

"What did you do in the fields?" asked Cabbage.

Flaxfield explained, taking his time.

"Just like the others?" said Cabbage. "Cutting and lifting things?"

Flaxfield nodded.

"But you're a wizard."

"So I'm more tired than most." Flaxfield smiled. "I'm not used to such work anymore."

"What's a wizard without magic? And what will happen if there's no Harvest Spell?" asked Cabbage.

"We'll have to see," said Flaxfield.

The silence folded them into itself again. Cabbage felt choked by it.

"Flaxfield," he said.

"Yes?"

"Will you get your magic back?"

Flaxfield put his hand on the boy's arm. "I don't know."

"What will happen to you, if you don't ever get it back?"

"There are stories," said Flaxfield, "about wizards who lost magic."

"What happened to them?"

"The stories say different things. And the thing about stories is that they're stories."

Cabbage thought about this. "You mean they're not true?"

"I mean they're all true," said Flaxfield. "Especially when they're different."

Cabbage waited what seemed like a long time before he asked the next question. "If you never get your magic back, what will happen to me?"

"Ah," said Flaxfield. "Here are the drinks."

Perry was as anxious to see Cabbage

as Cabbage was to see him. He'd watched Cabbage run down the hill to Slowin's Yard; then he'd turned his face to the ground and lain still. He was deaf from the thunder, half-blind from the fizzing magic, unable to stand or move. Anyone else would have been killed by the onslaught from the wild magic. Anyone but a roffle.

A hand shook his shoulder. He lifted his head and saw a mouth shouting at him. Jagged lines crossed his vision, but he thought it looked a lot like Megawhim, his father. The mouth opened and shut again. Still no sound.

"I said, get up. Come on. No time."

Perry felt his arm dragged up, and he followed it, staggering to his feet. Now this person looked even more like his father. Perry stumbled. The fall jolted his head, and he whimpered with pain. Megawhim dragged his arm harder, and Perry slid across the grass, scraping his knees.

"Get in here."

He hauled Perry around the side of a large rock and down into the earth.

As soon as the light faded and the two roffles could smell the cool earth and touch the damp sides of the tunnel into the Deep World, Perry recovered as though he had never been hurt. All that was left of the wild magic was a small ringing in his ears and a slight fuzzy feeling in his head.

"You were following me," he shouted.

Megawhim walked on, deeper into the tunnel. Perry followed him, still shouting.

"What were you doing? You were supposed to leave me with Cabbage and Flaxfield, not go on sneaking after me."

They turned a corner, down a slope and through a door, heavy, wooden, and strapped with iron hinges and braces. Perry closed the door behind him and they were in the Deep World.

The light was constant in the Deep World, with no cloud or fierce sun. There was warmth that never burned, light that never dazzled. And the air was lighter, easier to breathe. A few deep breaths and all of Perry's discomfort had gone.

He half ran to keep up with Megawhim.

"Tell me," he demanded. "Why didn't you let me go on my own? You said you would."

Megawhim ignored him and carried on. Perry gave up the chase. He sat down, leaned back on his hands, turned his face up to the light, and closed his eyes.

He'd worked out that if his father hadn't been willing to leave him before then, he wasn't going to walk away now.

When Megawhim discovered that Perry wasn't following him, he turned and came back.

"Don't sit there all day," he said. "I want to be home by suppertime."

"I'll be back Up Top by then," said Perry, still with his eyes shut.

"You'd be dead if it weren't for me," said Megawhim.

"It couldn't hurt me. I'm a roffle."

"Do you think so? It looked to me like you were hurt."

"Only a little," said Perry.

Megawhim snorted. "You think you know everything, don't you? Well, do you know about Megarath?"

"Who?"

Megawhim nodded and smiled. "That's right. Who? You might ask who, all right."

Perry sat up and put his hands around his knees. "Tell me," he said.

"We'll eat first. Come on."

Hunger and curiosity are a powerful combination. Perry followed, taking care to make sure he paid attention to the way they were going so that he could get back again as soon as he was ready and go back Up Top to Cabbage.

Once you're in the Deep World, there are places to eat everywhere as well. When a roffle is hungry, all he has to do is knock on any door and ask for food. If you do this, the householder will invite you in, ask if you'd like to eat alone or with the family, and then provide what you need.

A very small person, even for a roffle, opened the door to them. She had flour on her hands from making pastry and some on her cheek where she'd brushed hair out of her eyes, and a smile like a soft breeze. Megawhim asked for a meal and a private talk with Perry, which the householder was glad to arrange.

"There's a new pie, just out of the oven," she said. "Or some cold salmon and thick lemon and dill dressing."

They had one of each.

"Megarath," said Megawhim, "went Up Top years and years ago. He said he liked it better up there, but really he'd had a quarrel with his neighbors and was too proud to make it up. He ate nothing but human food. He never breathed the air from the Deep World. The light from down here never brushed his face. He even met and married a woman from Up Top."

Perry stopped eating and looked at his father in amazement. "Can you do that?"

"What you can do and what you should do are two different things," said Megawhim.

"What happened to him?"

Megawhim stared at Perry.

"She died, of course. They don't live as long as we do. And then he was lonely. He tried to come back."

"I would," said Perry.

"Of course you would. Anyone would. But he couldn't find a roffle hole."

Perry started to laugh, then stopped suddenly.

"Really?"

"Yes. In the end, he got a roffle to show him one. He couldn't eat the food here. It made him sick. He couldn't stand the light. It hurt his skin. He couldn't breathe the air. It hurt his chest."

"That's silly," said Perry. "People like it down here. They love the food."

Megawhim shook his head. "They like it at first," he said. "But after a while, that's how it takes them. They can't live down here forever. And if they eat too much, too quickly, you know what happens to their tummies."

Perry giggled. "They go for a roffle holiday," he said.

"Exactly."

"Well, after all the human food and the air Up Top and the sun and everything, Megarath was more a person than a person is. He had to go back. And within a year, he was dead."

Perry gasped. "No."

"Yes. So think about it. You're young. Just a few weeks Up Top and the wild magic was already beginning to be able to hurt you. If I hadn't come to drag you back, well, who knows?"

"I'm still going back," he said.

"That boy left you to die."

Perry shook his head. "He left me to save someone who was in more danger than I was."

Megawhim scraped a corner of bread around his plate to get the last of the lemon and dill dressing. "Come home," he said.

"I will. But not yet."

The roffle put her head around the door. "There's syrup pudding," she said, and didn't wait for an answer.

There was thick cream as well, so the conversation stopped for a while.

"What are you going back for?" he asked at last.

"We started a job," said Perry. "You always told me that if I started a job, I should finish it."

"It has to be the right job," said his father.

"I know."

They thanked their host and walked back. Megawhim did not even try to persuade Perry not to go or to trick him into going to the wrong place. He opened the great door and held it for Perry to pass through.

"You won't follow me this time, will you?"

Megawhim put his hand on his shoulder. "Finish your job," he said. "Come home safe. Come home soon."

It was night when Perry stepped from behind the rock, but he didn't know which night. Time passes at a different speed in the Deep World. It might have been the same day, or a week or a month later. Sometimes, it was the day before. Perry looked up at the sky. The stars were back.

"What are you saying?" he asked.

They made no reply to him. None that he could hear. He was full and he was tired, so he curled up and went to sleep.

The line of black beetles trailed

down the road, a pen stroke on a creased page. Behind them, the ruin of Slowin's Yard. Ahead, miles of dust and the ruts from farm carts. By day their crooked legs felt the approach of every traveler long before he was in sight. They veered to the side, continued their way, hidden in the grass and vetch at the roadside, slowed down but never stopping. By night they never slept.

Flaxfold stroked Bee's green cheek. The moss was warm under her hand. She frowned, stooped to take a cloth from the bucket by the side of the bed, and dabbed it over Bee's face, her arms, her legs. She dipped the cloth repeatedly into the bucket, replenishing the water. When she was satisfied that the girl was cool, she pinched the tender tops of herbs that she had gathered. She rubbed the herbs into the moss. As they bruised against her hands, they released their scents, some sweet, some with a tang that made the mouth ache. Bee made no stir, no sound. Only the soft movement of her chest and the whisper of air from her nostrils showed that she was still alive. Flaxfold settled into an armchair that faced the window. Sometimes she watched the horizon. Sometimes she turned to look at Bee. Sometimes she slept.

The trail of beetles stretched back to Slowin's Yard. It had no end. Beetles popped up from the cracks in the slate flagstones and joined the end of the line. Thousands of them, shiny, smooth, clattering on the slate and cobbles. They had burrowed down when the fire blazed. Down where the heat did not scorch. Beyond the reach of the fingers of fire that had grabbed everything. Almost everything.

If Cabbage had not been driven away from the yard by the beetles, he would have found a pile of ash thicker than the others, raised in the middle in a stunted hump. If he had kicked at that pile as he had at the others, he would have found a boot, thick and black and buckled. This boot now moved, kicking away at the ash. The hump turned, revealing the shape of a creature attached to the boot. The beetles clattered around it, moving the ash, clearing a space, crawling all over the creature, touching it with a grim affection.

When the creature stood, it resembled a person. It was hunched, twisted, and squat. It wore the same clothes, heated to a high polish, gleaming and hard. Smoke drifted out of the areas where the nose and ears would be if there had been a face. Flakes of charred leather broke off as it moved; the boots cracked and splintered.

It straightened, and the clothes broke open. It grabbed the

jagged edges of the tear, ripped them apart, and shrugged. The clothes fell off like the shell of a chestnut.

A creature emerged from the husk. For a moment, it flared up, a blue flame, then, as quickly, died, leaving a gray sensation in the air, insubstantial.

The husk twitched, gathered, knit together, stood up.

Two things faced each other. A gray wisp of smoke and a blunt, squat, armored creature.

The armored creature moved. Black legs tapped on the slate, more than before, four, six. Beetles swarmed over it. Something like eyes in the smooth head turned to look at the other figure.

The smoke figure quivered. It leaned to the huge armored figure. "Brassbuck?"

The voice was softer than the sound of distant waves breaking.

The black figure clattered a reply, no words.

The smoke figure shuddered. "Not Slowin. Not anymore. New name. Soon. Come, follow."

The wraith moved away, drifting, deliberate, following the lines of beetles. Brassbuck stood a moment, her head tilted to one side, listening to the sounds of the beetles' legs.

She imitated the noise. "*Takkabakk, takkabakk.*" She seemed pleased with the sound.

The wraith passed over the ruined wall.

Brassbuck clattered after it. "Where are we going?" she clacked.

Flaxfold was asleep in the chair,

her face to the window, when she was woken by the noise.

She put her hand to her mouth, yawning. Outside, the night was just slipping away, leaving trails of mist over the fields. Less than an hour and the sun would break over the line of hedgerows. Till then, the world hesitated between night and day.

Flaxfold shook her head, blinked, and stretched. She smoothed her smock with small hands and looked at Bee.

The noise came again. Not a moan. Just the sound of air forced out with pain. Flaxfold felt the moss. It was dry. She started to move to the bucket to get the wet cloth; then she put her hand back. The moss was cool and dry.

"Bee?" Flaxfold put her face near to Bee's. "Can you hear me?"

She felt the movement of air from the girl's mouth. Strong now. Foul-smelling. Greasy and damp. Flaxfold pursed her lips in disgust and drew back.

She laid her hand on Bee's shoulder. The moss cracked and

fragmented. She took her hand away. Moss had clung to it, pulling away from the skin of the girl. She examined the place where the moss had been. The skin was shiny, puckered, not like a wound, but a scar.

"Bee?"

The girl shifted. The first time she had moved in days. More of the moss crumbled, fell away. Flaxfold lifted the shards from around Bee, brushed them away, cleared spaces. Everywhere the moss had been, the skin was dry and healed. In some places, the fire had not touched her, and the skin was pink and clear. In others, it was smooth as a laurel leaf. In others, shiny and creased. There were patches where the moss still clung, still damp. Flaxfold worked around those, leaving them to continue the healing.

She had uncovered just over half of Bee when the girl shuddered, her arms pressed close to her body, her fists clenched, and she coughed. Flaxfold leaned over, put her hand to Bee's cheek. Bee gasped, coughed again, a deep, grating cough that shook her whole body. She dragged in a painful breath, held it for a second. Then she vomited smoke out of her mouth and nose. It rose above her, a snot-green shape. Flaxfold backed away from it. It gathered to a clump, formed a sluglike shape, slid down onto the bed, slipped to the floor, and found its way to the fireplace.

Flaxfold put her hand to her mouth and nose. The stench was making her throat tight. The creature shuddered, then exploded, before it was sucked up the chimney and was gone.

Flaxfold hurried to Bee. She held her hand. "Are you all right?"

Bee's breathing was regular now. Flaxfold put her face to her lips. Her breath was strong, sweet, and steady. The woman hesitated, then peeled the moss from Bee's face.

When she saw it, her lips made a tight line. She held her breath. She found the wet cloth and dabbed it on Bee's cheeks, her forehead.

"It's all right," she said. "It's all right. You're better now. Ssshhh. It's fine."

Bee opened her eyes. Flaxfold smiled. Bee closed her eyes again and made a small noise.

"Does it hurt?"

Bee nodded.

"That will go away. In time. I can help that."

Bee turned her head away while Flaxfold removed as much of the moss as was left and would come free. She covered Bee with a fresh sheet she had washed and dried with no starch, so there would be nothing to rub against the skin. Bee's hand had relaxed. Flaxfold discovered a small iron seal, shaped like a bird. She put it carefully on the table.

"It's fine," she said. "You're doing well. I'll fetch you something to eat."

She turned away from Bee and, unable to prevent herself, her mouth moved, silently speaking, "Oh, you poor thing. You poor thing."

Bee heard the door close, then drifted, searching for a place where the pain was less.

. . .

A rabbit broke through the hedgerow and hopped clear onto the road. Halfway across, it stumbled on a black line that moved with relentless determination. The beetles swarmed over the rabbit. It kicked out, tried to run off, tumbled over, its legs flailing. The rabbit screamed. Less than a minute later, the clump of black beetles straightened out again and rejoined the column, leaving the stripped bones in the middle of the road. An army on the march.

Cabbage didn't like getting his hands dirty, so it was odd that he enjoyed the blacksmith's shop as much as he did.

On his first visit, Cartford had allowed him to stand and watch and to ask questions. The second time, the blacksmith had made Cabbage stoke up the fire and work the bellows.

"Once is a visitor," he said. "Twice is an assistant."

It wasn't hard work stoking the fire, but it was hot. The fuel was charcoal, which was light to shovel on. It was dusty though, and soon his hands and clothes were streaked with black. It burned with a sweet fragrance that reminded Cabbage of coppices and woods.

On the third visit, Cartford allowed Cabbage to hold a length of iron in the forge and hammer it on the anvil.

"You'd better put this on," he said, tying a leather apron around Cabbage. "That won't burn if the sparks fly."

The sparks did fly from the struck metal. Cabbage was so excited that he couldn't stop himself from making more sparks fly from his own finger ends to dance with them in the light of the forge.

"That's enough of that," Cartford warned him. "Magic doesn't mix well with this work."

Which reminded Cabbage that Perry had never heard the end of Flaxfield's story about the first-ever magic. And that reminded him that he still didn't know what had happened to his friend. And that made him sad.

"What do you mean?" he asked.

Cartford leaned against a bench. He flicked the handle of a vice.

"Magic is forbidden in blacksmiths' shops," he said. "Even play magic like your stars. Especially real magic."

"Why's that?"

Cabbage's iron had grown dull. It was still hot, so he held it in the bucket of water as Cartford had shown him. The man nodded approval. The bench was worn and chipped, as old perhaps as the shop itself.

"If I tell you, will you promise never to tell anyone else?"

Cabbage nodded.

Cartford leaned forward and lowered his voice. "It just is," he said.

"What?"

Cartford laughed. "Let's get that iron hot again," he said. "And you can tell me what you're going to do next."

"He's coming with me," said Flaxfield.

"How long have you been there?" asked Cabbage.

"Long enough," said Cartford. He scraped his hands down the front of his own apron. "Welcome." He shook hands with the wizard. "No danger of you working any magic here, is there?"

Flaxfield glanced at Cabbage before he answered. "You should keep a civil tongue, blacksmith," he said.

Cartford laughed. "Don't blame the boy. I've been watching you and it's obvious. You're not keeping your magic to yourself. You're not trying to protect us from the wild magic by controlling your own. Don't interrupt."

Flaxfield gripped his staff till his hand turned white.

"You've lost your magic. And now you're taking your boy off to find it again. Isn't that right?"

"We'll bid you good day," said Flaxfield. "Come on, Cabbage."

"Say good-bye to my daughter before you go," said Cartford. "She's grown fond of you. Do you hear me?"

Cabbage had been hanging up his leather apron. He looked at Cartford now.

"Yes, you. Don't be so surprised. I'm quite fond of you myself."

Cabbage blushed and wiped a smear of charcoal dust onto his cheek.

"Now, then, shake hands and say, 'Meet again soon.' And, Flaxfield." Cartford smiled at him. "We'll part friends as well. I'm fond of you, too, you old wizard."

They shook hands.

"We'll be gone before the harvesters get back from the fields," said Flaxfield. "Say my good-byes."

"I will."

Cabbage lingered longest outside Bee's room. No one but Flaxfold, Vella, and Pellion was allowed in.

He spoke through the door in a low voice that would hardly carry.

"Good-bye," he said. "We're going at last. I'll make sure Slowin pays for this. I promise."

Flaxfield took his arm. "We'll be on our way now," he told them.

Cabbage looked back one last time before the village disappeared behind them on the road.

"Where are we going?" he asked. "What are we going to do?"

"I'll tell you as we walk," said Flaxfield.

Flaxfold and Pellion and Vella stood side by side and watched them disappear.

"It's hard for him, saying good-bye," said Flaxfold.

"He's too young to go," said Vella.

"What do you think?" Flaxfold asked Pellion.

Bee's father thought hard about it.

"When there's something to be done, it doesn't matter how hard it is or how young you are, it has to be done," he said. "I think he has to do this."

"And what do you have to do?" Flaxfold asked after a silence.

Vella answered as quickly as she could. "We have to look after Bee."

Flaxfold looked at Pellion.

"Yes," he agreed.

"How will you do that?" asked Flaxfold.

Vella burst into speech with an angry flick of her arm. "I know what you mean," she said. "You mean we're useless. You mean that we can't do anything."

Flaxfold waited for her to finish.

"You've seen what she's like," said Bee's mother. "She just lies there, doing nothing. She doesn't even know who we are. She doesn't know we're there."

Pellion gave Flaxfold an apologetic look. "Don't think we're not grateful," he said.

"We're not," snapped Vella. "Why should we be grateful? Wizards! Look what they've done to our little girl. Look at her."

Flaxfold tried to put her arm out to Vella, but the woman smacked her away.

"Don't touch me."

"I'll be upstairs with Bee," said Flaxfold. "Come and see her if you want to."

She sat by the bed, dabbing a cool wet cloth on Bee's cheeks and forehead. "Is that good?" she asked.

Bee had made no response at all since the day she had vomited the slime of the wild magic out of her.

"I've made some fresh broth," said Flaxfold, "as soon as you want to eat."

She felt Bee's parents arrive in the doorway.

"When you start to eat, you'll start to get stronger," she said. "Look, here's your mother. Would you like her to do this?"

She stood and handed the damp cloth to Vella, who sat and took over from her.

"We're leaving now," said Vella. She dabbed Bee's face, then leaned down and kissed her cheek. "But if you ever want us to come back, just send word and we'll be here. As soon as you ask."

Flaxfold put her hand on Vella's shoulder and the woman allowed it to rest there.

"It was magic that did this to you," said Vella, "and it's only magic that can make it right again." She hesitated. "If anything can," she added.

"Can it?" asked Pellion.

"Perhaps it can change things," said Flaxfold.

Flaxfold left them alone and waited downstairs.

They all cried when they said good-bye.

"Why am I leaving her?" asked Vella.

"Because she was born for magic," said Flaxfold, "and that's how it has to be."

"Well, I pity any mother who has a child born for that," said Pellion.

"And I pity the child," added Vella.

Flaxfold didn't watch them walk away. She went back to Bee's room and put the cloth back to her cheek.

"Did you say there was broth?" asked Bee.

"Yes. I'll get some, shall I?"

"Yes, please."

"It's good to see you," said Flaxfold.

Bee's face, hard to read through the damage, showed fear and disgust.

"Something was in me," she said. "It made me sick."

"It's gone now," said Flaxfold. "Gone."

"Where to?"

The Palace of Boolat rose up above the plains and forest. Mattie stood far off and looked at it. He could have been inside days ago. Did he want to? Could he go anywhere else? The trade guilds who trained boys for commerce and gave them skills did not take ragged boys off the street. Villagers were suspicious of outsiders. Farms were family concerns. He could work. In his recovered body, he could work harder than ever before. There was just no work for him except kitchen work back at Boolat. And he didn't want that.

"I'll go back to her," he decided. "I don't care if she said I wouldn't be welcome. I'll make myself welcome."

A kitchen boy doesn't see many friendly faces. Most touches of a human hand are cuffs and blows. The little kindness Bee had shown him was the most he could remember. He wanted to see her again. She could be his friend.

Pleased to have made a decision, he decided he had earned a rest. He lay on his front, with his head propped on his arms, and looked for a last time at the palace.

"Just a new suit of clothes," he said. "That's all. I deserve that at least."

There's not much a servant doesn't know about the passageways and hidden corridors of the house where he works. Especially a young servant. More especially one who has grown up there. As soon as night fell, Mattie would creep in, find a good new set of clothes, sleep in a proper bed—there were many more rooms than people at Boolat. In the morning, just before light, he'd be ready to present himself at the wizard's yard for work.

It had no way of knowing what to do or where it was. The green slime hadn't really known *what* it was until Bee vomited it out. It was lucky for Bee that she didn't know that for over a day it tried to get back into the inn to crawl inside her again. As far as it could be said to have feelings, it had two. First, it wanted to be safe inside Bee again, keeping her from waking up. Second, it wanted to kill that old woman who had thrown it out. Between the longing and the fear, it had little time for anything else.

Something the old woman had done kept it out of the inn.

It could move, but it didn't want to.

Feelings aren't thoughts. It felt angry. It felt lonely. It felt confused. It felt hungry. So when a slug slithered over it, the green mess was glad enough to wrap itself around the gray body and absorb it. Then it felt pleasure. So it moved just enough to find another slug and another. This made it look quite like a slug.

Expelled from the inn and refused entrance again, it turned in a direction the way a compass needle turns to the north, and it started to travel. Slow progress for something that looks like a slug, yet all movement with a purpose cuts down distance. A mouse ran into it and was stuck fast to the sticky skin. It folded itself around the mouse and, because it had a slug's mouth now, it ate it, legs first. It moved on, ever in the same direction.

More mice. It grew fur and teeth. And it grew bigger. Now it could eat a rat. Now a weasel. Now a rabbit. The weasel bit back, but the slime thing didn't feel pain.

As it consumed animals with brains, it began to have a brain itself. It couldn't exactly think. It had more than feelings, though.

Swifter movement came with legs, and more purpose came with a brain. Now it was definitely seeking something, somewhere, someone.

It was soon big enough to eat a dog that was tied to a post while its owner went to work. Dogs are clever creatures, so that became part of its nature, too.

Now it could run. Now it could hunt. It tracked a shepherd boy, cornered him, and lunged.

Standing up on two legs, it looked across the hills. "Boolat," it said.

It shook its head, having no idea what it had said or why or what it meant. It recognized that the Palace of Boolat was the compulsion that had been drawing it, so it walked, unsteadily at first on the two legs, then with confidence, straight toward the towers. It still left damp green patches where it walked. It still made the slurping, slopping noise. Just not so much.

Though Cabbage was in a sulk,

the sulk didn't take the form of refusing to eat, and there were plenty of places to eat at Canterstock.

"We could eat for free at the college," said Flaxfield.

"Is the food good?" asked Cabbage.

"It's a long time since I visited," Flaxfield admitted.

"We'll eat before we go in then," said Cabbage. "Best to be safe."

It was the longest conversation they had spoken together since they left the village and the inn. Flaxfield had tried to talk, but Cabbage turned the attempts away. As soon as Flaxfield had told him where they were going, Cabbage refused to discuss it.

Canterstock was by far the biggest town that Cabbage had ever seen. He'd been with Flaxfield to markets and fairs. He'd seen villages and small towns, and he liked the activity of the streets, the noises and smells, the shops and stalls, the faces and the clothes.

Most of all, he liked the food stalls and the pie shops, the crumpet sellers and the hogs roasting in pits.

It wasn't market day in Canterstock; there were no food stalls, no hog roasts. It didn't take Cabbage long to find the shops and little alehouses that had the aroma of freshly cooked food drifting out into the street. Some of them had blackboards outside with the menus chalked on them. Cabbage read them as though they were the most precious and powerful books of spells.

"If you'd studied your work as hard as you study those, you'd be the greatest wizard the world has ever seen," said Flaxfield. "I'd rather eat food than read about it."

Cabbage thought the best-looking place with the finest food was one on the market square, right across from the college. He walked away from it, determined not to have his meal spoiled by the sight of the great building. They looked at more places and Cabbage sighed.

"We'll go back," he said.

"To the Goat and Cushion?" Flaxfield made a mock-surprised face.

"I'll sit with my back to the college," said Cabbage.

"Then you won't see what's going on. That's half the pleasure of a town."

The food was as good as Cabbage had hoped. The view was as bad as he had feared.

Canterstock College was the largest building in a large town. Honey-colored stone, high turrets, tall windows, some as wide as rooms, some just slits. The gate was as wide as most of the houses in the town. Cabbage watched several people come and go and the great gate was never opened. The visitors, or students, or whatever they were, used a wicket gate.

Flaxfield ate sparingly. A bowl of soup, bread, a glass of water. He watched Cabbage eat a huge meal and then drank some more water while the boy set about a big bowl of pudding.

When it was all gone, Cabbage leaned back and put his hands on the table.

"You're going to leave me there, aren't you?" he said.

"Is that what this sulk is about?"

"I know you are."

"Why would I do that?"

"Because you're not a wizard anymore. You've got no magic."

Flaxfield hitched up his cloak.

"If you've got no magic, you can't have an apprentice. And if I can't be your apprentice, you'll have to do something else for me."

"Shall I?" said Flaxfield. His voice reminded Cabbage of how Flaxfield had once treated him. He was a good master, and he didn't treat his apprentices harshly, but he did expect good manners and respect and obedience. And he got them. Cabbage's victory over the fire and his discovery of Bee had made him feel that he was important. His discovery that Flaxfield had lost his magic had made him feel that his old master was just an ordinary man, and that an apprentice wizard was somehow more important. Flaxfield had been patient on the journey, and Cabbage had grown even more confident. The sudden change in Flaxfield's tone of voice made him think again.

"Well," he said, "that's right, isn't it?"

"Which part of the story you've made up are you asking me about? Leaving you at the college? That all my magic has gone? That a wizard with no magic is no wizard? That I have to do something for you? Have I forgotten anything?"

"Well," said Cabbage again. "I mean you have to make arrangements, don't you? To let me finish learning to be a wizard?"

"I don't see why," said Flaxfield. "I could walk off and leave you here. I'd pay for my soup and you could pay for that banquet you've just eaten. How about that?"

"I've got no money."

"No. You haven't, have you? But you could work it off. And if they liked you enough . . ." He stared at Cabbage. "If they thought you were a very keen and hardworking sort of boy, though why they'd think that is beyond me, but if they did, they could keep you on in the kitchen as a pot boy."

"You wouldn't do that . . ."

"Or, as is more likely, if they thought you were a lazy sort of rogue, they could tip you out and let you fend for yourself."

"No. You wouldn't."

"Or, if I felt like it, I could take this staff from you and give you the sound beating that a sulky young dog who cheeks his master deserves, and then I could carry on looking after you. Which would you prefer, the kitchen work, or the beating?"

"Don't leave me here," said Cabbage. "Please."

"So you want the beating? To teach you a lesson?"

Cabbage sat in silence for a moment; then he nodded.

"Come on," said Flaxfield, in his usual voice. "I've never beaten an apprentice yet. I'm not going to start now."

Cabbage looked up.

The old wizard was smiling at him. "But you've given me a bit of a beating, young Cabbage. Not talking to me. Treating me like something you'd worn out."

Cabbage dragged his sleeve across his face. "I thought you were going to leave me at the college."

"Did I say I was?"

"Why else would we come here?"

"I tried to tell you, but you wouldn't listen."

"I'm sorry."

Flaxfield pointed across the square. "What do you think of it?"

"I don't know."

"You've been looking at it all through your meal. You couldn't take your eyes away from it."

Cabbage shrugged at being found out. "It's bigger than I thought," he said. "And I think it's lovely. Like a palace."

"Better than a palace," said Flaxfield. "It's a serious place, on serious earth. It has a purpose that palaces do not."

"Why have we come here?"

"To ask a question."

"Let's go and ask it then," said Cabbage. "If that's all right with you."

Flaxfield put his arm around Cabbage's shoulder. He left

enough money on the table for the meal and they set off across the square.

The sun washed the stone of the college, and for a moment Cabbage thought it might burst into flame from wild magic. There was no fizzle or crackle of the magic that swirled around them, and the yellow-cream walls of the college were alight with pleasure. Cabbage couldn't wait to get inside.

Flaxfield rapped on the gate with his staff. The small wicket gate swung open and he stepped through, indicating to Cabbage to follow.

"This is a bit of a step," complained Cabbage as he lifted his leg to climb in. "Why don't they open the . . . ?"

Something about the space inside the gate made him stop talking.

There was a silence he couldn't ignore, and it silenced him. It pleased him to stand there. He felt that something recognized him as he walked in and that he recognized something in return, though he didn't know what.

He didn't feel at home. And he didn't feel a stranger.

"Who've you brought today, then?"

Cabbage frowned at the breaking of the silence. To his right, just inside the gate, there was a small room set into the thick stones of the wall. A man leaned out of a hatch and stared at Cabbage.

"Introduce yourself," said Flaxfield.

"Good afternoon," said Cabbage.

The man laughed. He looked as though he laughed a lot, so Cabbage didn't mind as much as he thought he should.

"He's better mannered than your usual lot," said the man. He drew back from the hatch, stepped out through the door, and stood with arms folded.

"Very good," said Flaxfield. "Come on, Cabbage. We've got work to do."

Cabbage didn't say another word until they had crossed the courtyard, walked under the echoing arcade, and passed into the building and up the wide stairs. He was glad when the silence folded itself around him again.

At the top of the stairs, they followed a corridor, then another and another. It was as though Canterstock was inside the college as well as outside. The corridors seemed as numerous as the streets and sometimes as wide. Some of the corridors had doors leading off, with small windows in them. Cabbage stopped and looked through into classrooms.

"What are lessons with teachers like?" he asked.

"What do they look like?"

Cabbage checked the next window. The pupils were about his own age. They sat at desks in rows and faced a blackboard. Some were writing, others reading. A couple were in conversation with the teacher, who moved on after a couple of moments and leaned over another and pointed at his exercise book.

"It looks good," said Cabbage. "Quiet."

"Good, then," said Flaxfield. "Now, shall we go straight to the library, or ought we to go and say hello to the principal first?"

"You'd better say hello first," a voice called out, "or she'll want to know why you didn't."

Flaxfield raised a hand in greeting. "And there'd better be a good reason?" he asked.

"Exactly. Hello, Flaxfield. You've not been here for a long time. Hello, Cabbage. How do you like our college?"

Cabbage swung round and glared at Flaxfield. "You planned it," he said. "You planned all this to get me here and leave me."

Flaxfield spoke quietly. "I told you," he said. "There is no such plan."

Cabbage pointed at the woman who had spoken to them. "Then how does she know my name?"

Cabbage had not often seen Flaxfield angry. He had never seen him as angry as he was now. The wizard said, "I apologize for my apprentice, Melwood. It's my fault. I should have taught him better than this."

The woman smiled and touched Flaxfield's arm. "All apprentices should be a little bit cheeky," she said. "Otherwise they'd be wizards already."

She smiled at them both.

"You're welcome here, Cabbage," she said. "And please don't think that there are any secret plans about you. I certainly don't know of any."

Cabbage was embarrassed at his outburst in front of this stranger. Her voice seemed to belong in the college. It was the same color as the stone, and it had the same quiet strength, the same solidity.

"How did you know my name?" he asked, keeping his voice polite this time.

The woman drew close to him. When she spoke, he caught the scent of almonds, or sweet herbs.

"Those of us who know about magic always know the name of Flaxfield's apprentice. Didn't you know that?"

"Are you teasing me?" he said.

"Why would I do that? Did you think you lived secretly, obscure, unknown?"

He hesitated. "Yes."

She smiled. "It will be a strange day when no one knows who Flaxfield's apprentice is. Now, please come and have a drink with me before you go to the library. I think that there must be things I ought to know about."

She linked her arm with Cabbage's and led them away. Cabbage still had no idea who she was until she put her hand to the handle of the door with the sign PRINCIPAL on it and led them in.

"Make yourselves comfortable," she said, indicating chairs. She sat behind her desk and rang a small bell.

"What do you like to drink?" she asked Cabbage.

Perry had never been Up Top

on his own before. He missed Cabbage.

He looked back at the roffle hole. He remembered the floury woman and the smell of cooking.

"I'll go back," he said. "Every second day, I'll go back, just for a short time." Megawhim's story had frightened him a little. He didn't want to be trapped away from the Deep World.

He shook himself and started down the hill. That was where Cabbage had gone. Less than halfway down, he stopped. A black line snaked across the ground. It started at Slowin's Yard and continued up the road. From side to side a little. It rippled like a caterpillar. For a moment Perry thought it might be a giant snake. It had no end in the distance. As far as he could see along the road, the black line carried on.

He sat down and watched it, trying to work it out. A line of silk would shine like that, move in that sinuous way. A snake would not bulge and contract at the edges like this. He couldn't decide anything about it except for one thing. It frightened him. He couldn't get to the yard without crossing the line, and he was not going anywhere near it.

Perry had just about decided to give up the plan of going to the yard and to head instead back to the village and see if Cabbage had turned up there when a rabbit lollopped out from the edge of the field and, pausing, twitched its ears before trying to cross the road.

The black line broke near the rabbit. It swarmed over it. The rabbit struggled briefly and was gone, torn apart and consumed within seconds.

Beetles.

Now that he knew what it was made up of, Perry could see it clearly. The whole line, miles of it, was an army of beetles, on the march. And determined. They were a disciplined body.

Perry realized that the wild magic was no longer swirling all around him. In a strange insight, he recognized it in the beetles. The magic had clenched like a fist and had inhabited the beetles. It had found a way to concentrate its power.

Where the wild magic was, Perry expected to find Cabbage.

He sought high ground and kept to it. The beetles ignored anything that stood away, off. He moved faster than the army, overtaking all the time yet never finding the vanguard.

It was clear almost from the beginning where they were going. Like the slime creature, they had a goal.

The Palace of Boolat.

. . .

If the space where a person works reflects the sort of person they are, then Melwood was the sort of person Cabbage wanted to know.

The drinks had arrived: milk for Cabbage, something different for the others.

"Would you like some biscuits with that?" she asked.

"No, thank you," said Flaxfield. "We've just eaten."

Melwood looked at Cabbage. "I think your apprentice might manage one," she suggested.

Flaxfield grunted.

While the two of them talked and Flaxfield explained what had happened, Cabbage kept quiet and munched the very good biscuits. And he was looking around at the study.

I'll have a room like this one day, he decided. The light swam in through one of the high, broad windows. The walls were painted a delicate pink. It was a good pink, with a blush of rose. He liked pink. He wouldn't change the bookcases either. They went all the way up to the ceiling and there was a little wooden ladder to climb to get to the high ones. He thought about climbing it while they talked, just to see what it was like. He knew what Flaxfield would say if he tried, so he didn't bother.

The desk was good, too. The old wood shone. And the armchairs were very comfortable.

Best of all was the arrangement of shelves on the other wall, crammed with stuff that Cabbage wanted to pick up and have a closer look at. There was a bottle of something, no, three bottles that looked as though they were full of stones in green water. And a carved frog, darker green, with the vein of the stone looking like the real markings on a frog. And a hat, and a knife and a lot of boxes and a vase with irises in, blue with white throats, and a sunflower head cut out of paper, and jars and a picture of a dragon, a Green and Blue, the best sort. Cabbage tried to work out how hard it would be to climb up the shelves from the bottom left to the top right, and then work his way across the ledge over the pointed window and get back to the ground by climbing down the ladder.

"Cabbage," said Melwood in a voice that sounded like it was repeating itself.

"Wake up," said Flaxfield.

"I want to check on something," Melwood said. "Do you think you could get me that book, please? The blue one with the silver lettering on the spine."

She pointed to a shelf high up.

Cabbage stood up and brushed the biscuit crumbs from his chest. He shifted the ladder and climbed up. The treads creaked under him. The writing on the spine was in a language he didn't understand, and he decided to learn it as soon as he could.

"That's the one," she said. "Thank you."

He climbed down and handed it to her. She took it, put it on the desk, and ignored it. Cabbage sat down and waited for her to look at it. She didn't. When Flaxfield turned aside for a moment and looked out of the window, Melwood gave Cabbage a wink, patted the book, and looked at the ladder. He grinned and looked away.

"So," Flaxfield continued, "Cabbage here thinks I'm finished. And I'd like to change his mind about that. And then there's the problem of what's happened at Slowin's Yard. Is the wild magic blown out, like a storm, or has it just now found a way to do some real damage? And if it has, what can we do about it?"

"Flaxfield has always been a terrible tease," said Melwood. "You're still early in your apprenticeship, Cabbage, so you haven't worked out how to deal with it yet. Let me see, Flaxfield. What was it your master called you when you were an apprentice? What was your nickname?"

"We should get to work," said Flaxfield.

"I think it's coming to me," said Melwood. "Yes, I remember."

Flaxfield stood up and swirled round, his cloak catching the mug next to his chair, his foot banging into the stepladder. "The library," he announced. "Time to get to work."

"I'll walk you there," said Melwood.

"No need. I know the way."

"Of course you do, but I want to talk to young Cabbage here on the way."

"Why don't you show him around the college," said Flaxfield. "And I'll make a start."

"Would you like that?" she asked Cabbage.

"Yes, I would, please."

Flaxfield left the door open behind him and disappeared into the corridor.

"Where shall we start?" she asked Cabbage.

He thought about it. "Can you take me around everywhere and end up at the library?" he asked.

"A good plan," she agreed. "We'll start with the classrooms and work around through the magic labs."

"I know you can speak," said Flaxfold. "If you want to. You did earlier."

She picked up a rag rug from in front of the empty fireplace and took it over to the window.

"It's up to you," she said. "Talk or don't talk."

Sounds of workers relaxing after harvest soared in through the window. Flaxfold leaned out and shook the rug. Golden motes scattered in the evening sun.

"I don't know where dust comes from," she said.

She sat next to Bee, picked up the seal, and cradled it in her hands.

"I made that soup myself," she said. "And it's not soup you can buy downstairs. You know that, don't you? That's going to help to make you better."

She dipped the spoon in the soup, dragged the bowl of the spoon across the lip of the bowl, to prevent spilling, and held it to Bee's lips.

"But only if you eat it," she said. "The best soup in the world won't make you better if you just leave it to go cold at the side of the bed."

Bee stared up at the ceiling.

Flaxfold put the spoon back into the bowl. "I want to take a look at you. Is that all right?"

Bee ignored her.

"I know you can hear me, and I know you can speak, so if you don't say I can't, I'm going to look at you."

When she lifted the sheet, Flaxfold bit her lip. "There's nothing to you," she said. "Nothing at all. I've never seen a girl so thin."

She let the sheet fall softly back.

The moss and herbs and potions had done all the work they could. Bee's skin had healed up as much as it was going to. There was hardly a part of her body that had not been touched by the fire. Some was like smooth leather, some like wood with deep grain, some wrinkled and puckered, some deep red, and some cold white.

Flaxfold was glad that the final appearance of the girl's face had still been partly obscured by the healing cover when her parents had said good-bye. Now that it was free of Flaxfold's preparation, Bee's face was a child's painting, without definition or detail. Lips, nose, and eyelids were crude attempts at features. And the skin was a landscape after a cruel war.

Whatever Bee had looked like before the wild magic had destroyed her, whether she had been pretty or plain, now she was a new thing.

"Apart from anything else," Flaxfold said to her, in a business-like way, "we all have work to do."

In the days since Bee had first responded, the day that the green thing had left her, Flaxfold had sat and told the silent girl everything that had happened. Everything they knew. She told her story from the time she had been a tiny child at home. She told her how her parents had missed her when she went to Slowin's. She told her about the coming of the wild magic. She told her how the boy called Cabbage had found her and brought her here.

"And now he's gone off to find his friend and to see what damage the wild magic has done, and to see if there's anything left of Slowin," said Flaxfold.

She moved her chair to one side. The sun was low now and the light was falling directly onto her face.

"We need help," she said. She took Bee's hand. "We need your help," she continued. "You know things that no one else knows."

Something banged against the window. Small and not loud. Flaxfold ignored it. Evening in the country brings out many small noises.

"You can even stop them getting into danger," she said. "You can tell us so many things we need to know."

Something whirred behind her. She looked. A black beetle had flown against the glass, dropped onto the sill, and was opening its wing case and testing the gauze wings. Harvest activity disturbs many small creatures, and evening is their time.

Flaxfold stroked Bee's hand.

"And you need to get better anyway," she said. "Even if there's nothing you know, nothing you can tell us, we want to get to know you. You're safe here now. This is a good place for you."

The beetle buzzed its wings, took off, flew unsteadily for a moment, then fell onto the sheet, just below Bee's chin.

Bee screamed. Flaxfold jumped back, knocking her chair over. Bee sat bolt upright in the bed, screaming and screaming.

Mattie searched out and found

an empty bedroom. He chose one quite high up, because the best rooms were near to the great hall. It had been so easy to get in without being seen. He even had a look into the kitchens and watched his old master and the cooks and servants running around and shouting. Kitchens are very noisy, angry places.

It was enough. It helped. Back to Bee. Back to that yard. Never going to run around and be shouted at here again. It felt like a good decision.

Easy enough as well to get into the larder and take enough food for a feast in his room.

By the time he had eaten his fill, the sun was disappearing on the horizon. He wiped his mouth and clambered into bed. The long day and the hot walk led him into sleep before he had time to remember this was the very first time he had slept in a real bed.

· · ·

Age was always a thing with wizards. Cabbage decided there was no harm in actually asking Melwood how old she was.

She laughed.

"Is it rude to ask?" he said.

"Not really. I don't mind you asking."

And then she didn't tell him.

They walked the corridors slowly. Melwood stopped as often as Cabbage wanted to. She seemed to have nothing else to do.

"I'm sorry I can't take you into a lesson," she said. "It's a firm rule. No interruptions."

"Are they always as quiet as this?"

"Why wouldn't they be? How can you learn if you're not listening?"

"Well, I've never seen a school or anything before. But I've heard parents in the villages. They say that the children are naughty and make a row."

"How do you like our lights?" she asked.

Most of the light in the college came from the many windows. The corridors had some natural light, but there were passageways that didn't face outside. These corridors had a series of small globes set against the ceiling. Now that Cabbage came to look at them, he saw that they made patterns just the same as the ones in the night sky. They were star charts.

"Do they talk?" asked Cabbage before he could stop himself. He blushed at the stupidity of the question.

"Of course," she said. "If you know how to listen."

Cabbage decided she was younger than Flaxfield. He thought that if he could see his mother, she would probably be about Melwood's age. No. He didn't like that idea. If his mother had a younger sister, she would be Melwood's age. He knew that couldn't be true because that would make her too young to be the principal of a college.

"The stars stopped talking when the wild magic was abroad," he said.

"Have they started again?"

"I don't know."

"Why not?"

Her hair was shorter than he was used to. Women in the villages wore long hair. Hers was mostly bronze colored, with some small streaks of gray. So maybe she was older than he thought, in wizard years.

"I forgot to ask them," he said. "I was really angry with Flaxfield and couldn't think of anything else on the way here."

He found her easy to talk to.

"And I was thinking about Perry, too. I really have to go and look for him. I know he's all right. I know the wild magic didn't kill him."

He smelled the sweet scent of her breath again as she stepped closer to him.

"How do you know?" she asked. Before he could answer, she added, "And these stars have stopped talking as well. Listen."

He looked up at them. They were as silent as he expected such stars to be, not being the real ones.

"Don't tell Flaxfield," she said. "I don't want him to know. There are things I need to talk to you about alone, Cabbage. Is that all right?"

Cabbage felt the thrill of a secret about to be shared.

"Later, though," she said. "Tell me about your friend first. How do you know he isn't dead? Be honest."

Looking straight at her, Cabbage couldn't lie.

"I don't," he admitted. "I just can't believe he is."

Melwood led him to a wider corridor and a stone seat beneath a window. She patted it, and he sat next to her. She leaned in close.

"Learn this now," she said. "And never forget it. The worst things sometimes happen. Just because you can't bear the idea of something doesn't mean it won't happen. Just because you want Perry to be alive won't make him alive. And, most of all, just because you feel it was your fault he was left alone won't keep him safe. If you left him to die, he died. If he lived, it wasn't because you did anything to save him. Sometimes, the very worst thing that can happen happens."

Cabbage found it hard to breathe. As though he had been punched very hard in the stomach.

"Do you think he's dead?" he asked at last.

"I have absolutely no idea," said Melwood. "And neither do you. So don't pretend. Work with what's real."

Now she seemed as old as the stones from which the college was built. She touched his wrist.

"The wild magic came here," she said. "To the college."

"I don't feel it," said Cabbage.

"No. It fizzed and crackled. Not much. It was like the sea. Where you were, it was deep and strong. We felt the lapping only of the smallest waves. But it came here. And it found something. And I know it has stayed."

"Stayed here?"

She shook her head.

"No, not stayed. Not that. I was wrong to put it like that. But made a difference. As the sea draws back when the tide goes out but the sand is moved. Something moved here. The stars are a sign of it. I don't know what else."

"What harm will it do?" he asked. "Can you get rid of it?"

Melwood stood up. "Some things you just have to wait and see what happens. That's what it's like with the wild magic, I think. It may drain away, like sea water. Or it may burrow down into the college. Like woodworm or dry rot. It may live and grow and eat the college up from the inside."

"You must stop it," said Cabbage.

"Would you like to see the labs next?" she asked.

Two of the laboratories had lessons going on. Melwood passed by these and found an empty one.

There was a smell that caught Cabbage in the back of the nose, like vinegar, though it wasn't vinegar. Layered on top of that were other smells, cow's fart smells and toffee, the delicate scent of freesias and the dull, dead smell of meat.

The equipment and apparatuses were arranged around the room on shelves and benches. Glass jars and bottles, tripods, cabinets, tubes and stoppers, scalpels, gloves, flasks and distillation chambers. There was a cupboard, taller than Cabbage, with hundreds of tiny drawers, each one with a yellowing paper label with faded black ink.

"Magic is practical," said Melwood. "No number of books will teach you how to be a wizard. You have to practice."

Cabbage knew he shouldn't touch anything, and he couldn't stop himself. He loved it that Melwood didn't tell him to keep his fingers off the things.

"What sort of things do they do in here?" he asked.

She took a textbook from a bench, flicked through to the page she wanted. "Practical Magic, Book Three," she said. "To make a glass to see far off."

Cabbage leaned over.

"Get me"—she looked around—"that tripod, please, and a burner, a round flask, and a shallow dish."

Cabbage fetched these while she took the book to the cupboard and, keeping her finger on the page, chose drawers and took ingredients out of them.

She lit the burner, boiled the water in the flask, tossed in the ingredients in the right order, after weighing each one on a pair of brass scales.

"What are you saying?" asked Cabbage, seeing that she was whispering to herself.

"The words of the spells aren't in the book," she said. "You learn them in the classrooms. It stops people from stealing magic."

She threw in the last ingredient, covered the flame, and put a cork into the neck of the flask.

"Give it a few minutes to infuse," she said.

Cabbage scratched his head with both hands. "I've never seen magic done like this before," he said.

"Tell me."

"I just do it," he said.

"Then what's the point of being an apprentice?" she asked.

"Most of the time, I don't know," said Cabbage. "It's annoying. Mostly, Flaxfield just stops me from using magic."

"Does he say why?"

Cabbage looked at the flask. The water had turned brown when Melwood boiled up the ingredients. Now it had a layer of green on the top. As they talked, the green layer grew and the brown layer shrank. Then a blue layer capped them both so that there were three horizontal stripes of color.

"Flaxfield says it's like music," said Cabbage. "Say I can play the fiddle a bit. A teacher can show me how to put my fingers on the strings, to get better notes, new notes, and to stop me from using my fingers in ways that could hurt them. A teacher can show me all the old tunes that people have played before, ones I wouldn't know, and then I know them. A teacher can show me how to play scales, because they're the building blocks of music. A teacher can make new tunes with me. A teacher can let me try out new tunes of my own. Ones that no one has ever played before. Flaxfield says it's like that for wizards. The music is the magic."

Melwood shook the flask. There were stripes of red and yellow and all sorts of other colors now, and Cabbage expected them to mix together back into brown. Instead, the stripes broke up into thousands of particles of color.

"What do you want to see?" she asked.

Without knowing why, Cabbage said, "The Palace of Boolat."

She drew out the cork and poured the contents into the shallow dish. They leaned their heads close together over it and looked in.

The colors whirled around like water going down a drain.

Melwood murmured.

The colors formed back into stripes.

"Where is it?" asked Cabbage.

Melwood grimaced.

"Let's try somewhere else," she said.

"The inn," said Cabbage.

Melwood nodded and held her hands over the water. She moved her lips. The colors moved quickly, and Cabbage could see a small group of houses, and an inn, with trees.

"That's it," he said. "You can even see them in the fields, over there."

"So it works," said Melwood. "There's nothing wrong with the spell. Let's try Boolat again."

She repeated the movement with her hands and the words. The bowl shivered, then cracked and split and the water poured out, the colors covering the bench before they faded and turned to gray. Cabbage dragged his finger through and found that the bench was covered with a layer of ash.

"It's different at the college," said Melwood. "Here, we don't so much draw magic out of people as put it in."

Cabbage wiped his finger on a rag that was stuffed behind a pile of slates.

"I don't understand."

"You have to be able to do some magic to come here," said Melwood. "You have to have the gift. But it's not the same as your gift. It's a gift for learning magic, not making magic. It's the difference between someone who can hold a paintbrush and copy a picture and someone who can make a new picture in a new way. Not everyone can copy, but quite a lot can, and if you give them lessons, they can get very good at it. Only a very few people know how to make a picture that is different from anything that's ever been done before. Those are really great painters. They make you look at a thing in a new way, or feel something about it that you've never seen before. We take the copying people. You're not a copier. You can do something new. That's why you're with Flaxfield and not here."

Cabbage drew a shape in the ash. He didn't like getting his finger dirty in it. He couldn't stop himself from touching it. He wanted to show Melwood what he could do.

He wiped his finger clean again and put the rag away. Looking around, he found a textbook, battered and scuffed with the pages bent down at the corners. He had never seen a book like it before.

"Why is this like this?" he asked.

"What do you mean? It's just a textbook."

"It's injured."

Melwood smiled. "Pupils don't look after books very well," she said.

"Flaxfield does."

"I hope you'll approve of the way the books are cared for in the library," she said.

Cabbage opened the book and smoothed the pages down. He fumbled in his cloak and brought out another book, smaller, leather-bound, locked. Laying them side by side, he put one hand on each book, his left on his own, his right on the textbook.

He closed his eyes.

Slowly, with the sound of pages turning and with the gentle scent of new-polished leather, the textbook gathered its thoughts, remembered what it was, took pride in the dignity of being a book, and it renewed itself. The pages were crisp and clean. The edges were straight. The corners were sharp. The covers were upright and alert.

He opened his eyes and looked at Melwood, surprised to see, not just approval and praise, but something that felt like sadness as well.

"The Palace of Boolat," he said. "I've seen that, but only from a distance."

He closed his eyes again and turned a page in the textbook. It revealed a double-page drawing of a building with the heading THE CASTLE OF BOOLAT.

He looked.

"That's not right," he said.

"No," she agreed.

The Palace of Boolat was elegant and decorated. High turrets and graceful curves. Slender walls and bright windows. It reached into the sky. This building was squat and coarse, thick and solid. It clutched the ground and glared up.

"It's a palace, not a castle," said Cabbage. "This must be another place."

"No," said Melwood. "I recognize the woods and the fields, the ripple of the landscape. This is exactly where the palace is."

"What's gone wrong?" asked Cabbage.

Bee watched Flaxfold cup the beetle

in her hands and look at it carefully.

"Get it away," shouted Bee.

Flaxfold backed away from the bed. The beetle circled in her hands. It was a fine black beetle, with ridged wing case and delicate feelers.

"This can't hurt you," she said.

"Get rid of it. Kill it."

"I can't kill it," said Flaxfold. "It's done no harm."

She leaned out of the open window, spread her hands, and shook them. The beetle dropped and, finding itself falling, opened its wings, and flew off.

"It's gone," said Flaxfold. "Flown away."

"Flown?" said Bee.

"Of course."

"They don't fly," said Bee.

Flaxfold put her arm around the girl's shoulders and made

calming noises. "Let's get you to eat some soup," she said. "And then you can tell me all about beetles."

The soup wasn't very hot anymore. Bee didn't seem to mind. She let Flaxfold hold the spoon to her lips for three mouthfuls; then she took it and fed herself.

She noticed her arms, the mad skin, the scars. She ignored it, kept on eating until the soup was all gone. Flaxfold took the bowl from her and she lay back, suddenly tired again.

Flaxfold let her rest before she started to talk. "Have you heard what I've been saying to you?" she asked. "While you've been lying here."

"I want to see a mirror," said Bee.

"There isn't one in here," said Flaxfold.

"Fetch one."

Bee lay quite still.

"No. That isn't a good idea."

"Go away, then."

Flaxfold spoke softly. "Do you know what's happened to you?"

"I'm not talking to you until you fetch a mirror."

So Flaxfold left her alone.

Bee felt tears rise in her eyes. She wasn't upset. She was angry. Flaxfold had walked out on her, just as Bee was getting ready for a good fight.

She lay looking up at the ceiling. Against all expectation, she felt happy. A ceiling. When you have lived for years in a round stone tower with a ceiling out of sight in the darkness, there's a pleasure in lying beneath a clean, white surface almost within reach of your hand. Bee had imagined a ceiling would be as unbroken as a summer sky. Instead, she saw tiny cracks, lines and edges where the plaster was not smooth, a little dip in the left-hand corner farthest away from the window. The light played on the surface, emphasizing the roughness and individuality and character of the ceiling. It was a moment of revelation for Bee. Ceilings are as different as people.

It was easier than she had expected to stand up. Her legs wobbled a little at first. That soon passed. The floor was pleasant under her bare feet: polished oak, broad planks. She dragged the top sheet from the bed and wrapped it around herself.

It was good just to walk, so she made a circuit of the room, ending up at the window.

When she tried to see herself in the glass, the sun dazzled her. All the light was coming from outside, so there was no reflection. She leaned forward, then drew back quickly. The harvesters were outside, and if they looked up they would see her. She didn't want that.

She tried to listen to their talk. It was fractured and layered, no voice rising above the other, so she couldn't make it out. They seemed happy though, and she wasn't used to that, so she just let the sounds wrap themselves around her for pleasure.

After the vast towers she had lived in, the room seemed tiny. Comforting tiny. Not prison tiny. She felt enclosed and safe. Best of all, it was light and clean and empty.

Just as she was particularly enjoying being alone, Bee heard the door open. Flaxfold came in and closed it behind her.

"I'm not staying here," said Bee.

"That's your choice," said Flaxfold. She sat in the armchair and patted her hair. "Don't you like it here?"

"That's nothing to do with it," said Bee. "I didn't choose to come here. I don't have to stay."

"No, you didn't. And you can go whenever you wish. I can get some clothes for you, now that you're up and about. Where will you go?"

Bee pulled the sheet tighter around herself.

"Don't you want to stop me from going?" she said.

"We have no right to keep you here," said Flaxfold. "I wish you would stay. I'd like to get to know you. And there are things you could help us with. But if you won't stay, you won't."

Bee climbed back on the bed and sat on it wrapped up in the sheet. "What is this place?" she asked.

Flaxfold beamed at her. "It's different things all at the same time. It's an inn. And it's my home. And it's your home, if you'd like it to be."

"That's three things," said Bee. "Is that all?"

"You can stay as long as you like," said Flaxfold.

"I've got a home," said Bee. "A proper home. I'm going there."

"To your parents?" asked Flaxfold.

"What else do you think I meant?"

"Home changes," she answered. "I wasn't sure."

Bee tucked the sheet under her legs. "How long have you lived here?" she asked.

"So long that I can hardly remember anywhere else."

"That's not an answer."

"No, not really."

Flaxfold pulled herself up out of the chair and picked up a small blue vase with stocks in it. "I need to change the water in these," she said. "Can I get you anything else to eat?"

Bee shook her head.

"I'll be back in a minute with some clothes for you," she said.

She put her hand into her apron and took out a small round mirror. She put it on the mantelpiece, where the flowers had been.

"Before you go," she said, "we ought to see what magic you can do now, after the fire. Just in case."

She closed the door carefully.

The green slime creature's feet squelched only on hard surfaces. On the grass it was silent.

It liked to eat. It didn't like traveling, but it was drawn on toward the palace.

It liked changing shape. Sometimes, even when it had just eaten, it ate again, just for the pleasure of making a new shape. Foxes traveled faster. Rabbits were too weak. Weasels had sharp teeth and darted at rabbits. Best of all, and the one it kept coming back to, was the boy. Especially when it gave the boy the fox's sense of smell and the weasel's teeth.

Frogs and slugs were still good to eat, but it never used their shapes. Beetles tasted good, and it liked the crunch of their skeletons and the soft pulp inside that coated the tongue and the roof of the mouth.

It made itself into a beetle only once and quickly changed back. It had become accustomed to eyes and flesh. The beetle life scared it. So low to the ground, so blind, so scratchy, such small and concentrated pleasure. Beetles existed only to live. Even a frog felt the joy of water. Beetles felt no joy but moving forward, eating, and attacking.

It was mostly a fox when it came across the black line of beetles. It stopped and flicked its tail. It hadn't expected this. Not beetles.

It turned and slunk away, disappointed, into the new darkness. At least it could hunt and think of a new plan. One that didn't have beetles in it.

It trotted to its left, making more distance between itself and the beetles. Lifting its head, it saw the palace. It stopped. Listened. Sniffed. Two demands on its attention. The palace felt as though it was the right place. Something had been pulling it here ever since it had given up getting back into the inn. It really felt as though it was the palace drawing it. Or someone in the palace. It could see that. The scent pulled it in a different direction. It could smell boy.

It had killed only one boy so far. They were difficult to find alone. It wanted another. Keeping low to the ground, it circled the scent. It found a spot near to the trees where it was half-hidden. It could see the palace, with lights in the windows and blazing torches on the turrets. And, sitting, watching, waiting for some-thing, the boy.

Was a fox strong enough to kill the boy? It changed into a dog. Better. This boy was big, though. And he was in the open.

It had an idea. It was its first ever proper plan of its own. It shivered with pleasure and couldn't prevent itself from making a little yelp.

The boy's head turned.

It slunk back into the tree cover.

The boy stared and then looked away again. After a moment, he looked back. It would have to be careful. Definitely not the dog. It lay down, rolled on its back and breathed out. Twisting, it stood up, upright. A boy again. A boy could take another boy by surprise.

It stepped out into the open. The boy looked back.

It moved toward the boy.

"Hello," it said.

Perry's journey was over. He had reached the front of the line of beetles.

The head was encamped outside the Palace of Boolat. The tail was still catching up. The advance guard of the beetle army had stopped half a mile before the palace. A lookout in the palace might have noticed a stain or a shadow on the road, a trick of the light, an effect of the clouds. Perry, having followed the beetles, knew it for what it was.

He thought of trying to move ahead of the army of beetles, to enter the palace and warn them. But now that it had arrived at its destination, the army of beetles had become watchful. Perry had kept to high ground. In order to approach the palace, he would need to come down, to break cover. As soon as he tried, the front of the line rippled. A tendril grew out of it. A line of beetles, moving in his direction. Perry turned and ran. Looking back, he saw the tendril hesitate, then draw back, merging again with the mass of beetles.

"No, thanks," he said.

The day was ending now. Soon he would lose sight of the beetles in the darkness. He felt that they were concentrating their efforts on taking the palace. They would no more be bothered with him than they would with a rabbit or a fox.

Perhaps.

He didn't want to take the chance.

He moved farther away, keeping high, keeping the palace on his left. He found a patch of clear open ground, high enough to observe the palace, empty enough to be able to see any beetles that might be headed his way.

If he couldn't save the whole palace, at least he might be able to help any who escaped. And he could go back when it was over and see if he could find Flaxfield or Cabbage or someone who could come and . . . And there his plans ran out. He had no idea what anyone could do against this clattering army.

He sat and watched. A reluctant moon lifted itself into view.

Perry thought he heard a noise behind him. He turned and looked. Something seemed to draw back into the trees. That was all right. It would be a fox. As long as it wasn't beetles. Nothing could be worse than beetles.

Flaxfold didn't come back.

The daylight drained away. The voices outside called good-byes. Darkness and silence slid into the room. Bee let herself sink onto the bed, where she lay on her side, tightly wrapped in the sheet. She wiped her eyes on the linen.

She hated Flaxfold. The stupid old woman had given her questions she couldn't answer.

Did she want to look at herself?

Did she want to go back to her parents?

Did she want to stay in this lovely bedroom? So small, so white, so clean, so different from everything she had known at Slowin's.

Did she want to help the stupid woman to look for Slowin? Slowin was out of her life now. He could stay out. Helping the woman might bring him back, and what good would that do?

Biggest question of all: Could she still do magic?

If she could, did she want to?

If she couldn't, could she live without it?

If she couldn't, who was she?

So she lay and looked over at the mirror, on its side on the mantelpiece.

She could answer several questions at once. All she had to do was make the mirror rise by magic and come to her, bright side first. She could reach out and take it and, there you are, a magic girl looking at herself. What could be simpler?

She rolled over and put her back to the fireplace.

There was a knock at the door. Soft, repeated.

Bee ignored it.

It came again.

If the old woman wanted to come in, she could. This was her place, wasn't it?

After a pause, the knock was repeated. No louder, no more insistent.

This put Bee into a quandary. She was tired of being alone. She wanted company, but she wanted to be difficult. She didn't want to be polite to Flaxfold. She didn't want to invite her in, but she wanted her there.

"I'll come back another time," said a voice. "If you'd like."

Bee sat up. It wasn't Flaxfold.

"Wait," she said. "Who is it?"

"Dorwin."

"Who are you?"

"A friend. If you want one."

Bee snuggled back into bed. She pulled the sheet over her face so that only her eyes were showing. "Come in," she said.

Bee peeped over the sheet.

This woman was younger than Flaxfold, older than Bee. A real grown-up.

"May I come right in?" she asked.

Bee's *yes* was muffled by the sheet, but clear enough. Dorwin shrugged apologetically, as though she wasn't welcome.

"I've brought these."

She had clothes over her right arm, a plate in her left hand, and a lantern in her right hand.

"Where shall I put them?"

"I don't mind."

Dorwin kicked the door shut with her heel and approached the bed. She flapped her right arm.

"Can you help?"

"Put the plate on the table," said Bee. "Then you'll be able to work the clothes."

And that way Bee wouldn't have to move the sheet away from her face to take the clothes from Dorwin.

This done, the plate and the lantern on the table and the clothes on the bed, Dorwin hesitated, looking uncertain where to go.

"I can sit on the bed," she suggested.

"The chair," said Bee.

They played a little game of who would speak next and Bee won.

"Do you want me to pass you the plate?" asked Dorwin. "Are you hungry?"

Bee was, but she couldn't eat and hold the sheet over her face at the same time. "I'll have it later," she said.

Bee won the second round of the game as well. She wanted to talk, but Dorwin wanted to talk more.

"Flaxfold's a good person," she said.

"I don't care."

"No, of course."

"What did you say your name was?"

"Dorwin. I live in the village. My father's the blacksmith."

It was easy for Bee to listen to Dorwin. And it was easy for Dorwin to chatter on. The talk created a contact between the two of them. It wasn't important talk. It was all the better for that. Everything with Flaxfold seemed so important, so urgent.

"Do you like the room?" asked Dorwin when her flow of information slowed down. "I slept here for a week once. It's one of the best rooms in the inn. Good view from the window. It's not above the parlor, so the talking doesn't keep you awake. It's the other side from the kitchen, so you don't get cooking smells. And I never slept in a more comfortable bed before or since."

Bee sat up higher. "Why did you sleep here?" she asked.

"I was ill," said Dorwin. "Flaxfold made me better."

"Why?"

"She does that."

"How?"

"I don't know."

"Are you all right now?"

"Yes. Perfectly."

Bee looked at the clothes on the bed. She couldn't reach out and touch them without letting the sheet fall, so she left them there. They looked soft, comfortable.

"Were other people ill at the same time?" she asked. "Like with the plague?"

"No. Just me."

"That doesn't happen," said Bee. "You have to catch things from someone else."

"It was an accident, not a disease."

"Oh."

Despite what Dorwin had said, there was a little noise from downstairs. The parlor must be filling up with people wanting a drink.

"A boy found me," said Bee.

"Yes."

"He talked to me sometimes, when I was asleep."

"He came and tried."

"Where is he now?"

Dorwin tried to explain about Cabbage and Flaxfield and Perry.

"Is his name really Cabbage?" asked Bee.

"It's what he's called."

"That's not the same thing?"

"No. You know about names, though."

Bee looked sharply at her. "What do you mean?"

"You were an apprentice. You're going to be a wizard. I don't need to tell you about special names."

Bee lay back and stared at the ceiling. "I don't know anything about names," she said. "What was wrong with you, when you slept here?"

"I had an accident. In the smithy."

Bee felt herself grow tense. She coughed, and the back of her throat felt a burn of acid from her stomach.

"What happened?"

"I'll tell you another time. Why don't you eat? Here. Let me give you the plate."

"No. What happened?"

"I shouldn't have been in there. I was little. I wasn't allowed in on my own. I went in anyway. You know what children are like."

"No."

"No?"

"I've never been with children. I don't know."

"No. Well, children don't do as they're told. I didn't, and I went into the smithy. There was a special horseshoe hanging from the beam over the furnace. I wanted to play with it. I dragged a box over and stood on it. I could nearly reach it. Not quite. I stood on tiptoe, and still it was just out of reach. So I jumped."

Bee closed her eyes. She could see the horseshoe and the box. She could see the anvil. She could see the little girl jump up. She could see the furnace, hot and hungry.

"Don't say any more," she said.

"All right."

The silence was uncomfortable now. Dorwin stood and crossed to the bed. She sat and put her hand somewhere on the wrap of sheets that was Bee. The girl flinched. Dorwin did not try to move. After a while, the sheets moved. Bee burrowed through. A hand appeared and found Dorwin's hand. They sat in silence. The lantern glowed yellow. The wick needed trimming, and a thin veil of soot hung above it.

"Did it hurt much?" asked Bee.

"More than I thought possible."

"That's right."

Dorwin squeezed Bee's hand.

"Does it still hurt?"

"No, not at all. I can't even remember what it felt like."

"Where was it?"

"My arm. The right one. I was lucky. When I fell, I put out my hand to save myself. I fell toward the furnace and only my arm went in. The pain was enough to push me away."

"Not very lucky," said Bee.

"It could have been worse," said Dorwin and wished she could catch the words and take them back as soon as they were in the air.

"Yes," said Bee. "It could."

Dorwin lifted Bee's hand to her lips and kissed it.

"Don't." She pulled the hand away and hid it under the sheet. "I want you to go away now."

"I'm sorry."

"It doesn't matter."

"Can I give you the food?"

"Why do you keep on wanting to give me food? What's the matter?"

Dorwin tried to regain Bee's hand. Bee wasn't letting her, so she stopped. "I want to do something to help," Dorwin said. "And I can't think of anything that I can do except feed you."

Bee laughed and took them both by surprise.

"What are you going to do?" asked Dorwin.

"I'm going home."

"You've been very ill," she said. "Is it a long journey?"

"I don't know."

"I liked your parents. They were here."

"I know."

"I didn't know if you recognized them. Or if you were even awake."

Bee's hand appeared again and she took Dorwin's. "Let me see your arm," she said.

"You shouldn't."

"I want to."

Dorwin pushed her sleeve back, above her elbow.

"I can't see."

"I'll get the lantern."

Dorwin held the lantern while Bee leaned forward and looked at her arm. She trailed her fingers over the scarred flesh. She put her own arm out of the sheet and held it next to Dorwin's.

"They match," she said.

Dorwin was used to the appearance of her arm. The scars were older, calmer.

"Does it hurt?" she asked.

"All the time," said Bee.

"It will get less. It will go."

Bee said something that Dorwin couldn't hear.

"What's that?" she asked.

She could just make out the words.

"I'm like this all over," said Bee. "You're pretty."

Dorwin put her arms around the sheet and held Bee.

"I want to see my face," said the girl.

"Not now."

Bee pushed her away, let the sheet fall and sat in just the light undershift Flaxfold had put on when she was asleep. Her arms and neck and shoulders were bare. Her face was turned to look at Dorwin.

"Look," she said. "Everywhere. Now, give me the mirror."

"Leave it till tomorrow."

Bee just stared and waited. Dorwin moved the lantern to the table and fetched the small mirror, keeping the glass pressed against her side. Bee held out her hand. Dorwin handed her the mirror.

"Light," said Bee. "Bring more light."

Dorwin held the lantern and Bee lifted the mirror.

She looked directly at her reflection, holding her gaze steady. "My hair," she said at last. "Even my hair's burned away."

Dorwin took the lantern back to the table. Bee let her take the mirror and replace it. She lay down with her back to Dorwin.

"I'm going to sleep now," she said.

"Can I come and see you again?"

"Yes."

Dorwin leaned down and kissed Bee's cheek.

"Good night."

She drew the sheet up and tucked her in. She opened the door quietly.

"Dorwin?"

"Yes?"

"Tell Flaxfold I'm staying here. I'm not going home now. I've changed my mind."

"Don't you want to see your parents?"

"Slowin first," said Bee. "I need to deal with him first."

When Perry saw the boy

walking toward him from the trees, he thought it was Cabbage. He sprang up and ran toward him, only to realize that it was a completely different boy. He stopped and waited.

The boy stopped as well.

It was difficult, in the moonlight, to see what he was like. Perry stepped back.

The boy stepped forward. He was picking up his feet in an odd way.

Perry stood his ground.

The boy came nearer again, bending his knees too much, lifting his feet too high.

"Who are you?" asked Perry.

The boy growled.

Perry put out his hands. "Stop."

The boy kept coming.

"Stop now, or I'll stop you."

The boy stopped.

"What do you want?" said Perry. "Who are you?"

The boy smiled. Perry had never seen anything quite so frightening as the shape of the smiling lips.

He backed away.

"Answer me," he shouted.

The boy growled again.

"I'll fight you," said Perry. He picked up a stone the size of his fist, tossed it from hand to hand. "Come on."

The boy moved forward. Perry threw the stone and quickly stooped and picked up another.

The boy dodged. The stone glanced off his head instead of hitting him in the face. He growled again and bared teeth that belonged to a weasel. Sharp, yellow teeth, all pointed.

Perry threw the stone and quickly grabbed another. This one hit the boy on the neck. He roared in pain and lunged forward, head down. The third stone hit him on the top of the head. He fell and Perry ran, dodging around him, away from Boolat and skirting the woods. He kept in the open just enough to see, not to get lost in the trees, near enough to take cover if he needed to.

The boy half rose, stumbled, got up, and looked after Perry. He was about to follow when the sound of screaming from the palace caught his attention. He turned and listened. Still with his odd movements, he walked down the hill and toward the noise. It was as though Perry had disappeared, or never been thought of.

Perry watched him, all the way to the palace gate. He watched him go into the palace. He listened to the screams. He saw the beetles swarm through the gate. He saw soldiers rush for safety, only to be thrown back by some invisible barrier. He wanted to shut his eyes. He wanted to stop his ears. He wanted to run and leave the slaughter behind him. He stayed and watched and listened. He would need to tell someone about this, and he would need to tell them everything he could.

What he couldn't imagine was how he would find words to describe the two figures who appeared and walked through the army of beetles into the palace, officers joining the troops. It looked to Perry as though they had been directing them all along. As though the army of beetles was an advance guard. Perry peered at them. One was like a huge, hunched beetle. The other shimmered like a ghost.

Cabbage hadn't expected to be excited about going to the library. As far as he knew, it was just a room with a lot of books in it. He liked books, but you can only read one at a time, so a room with a lot of books was no better than a room with one book.

Melwood held the door open for him and he went in.

It was love at first sight.

As soon as he saw it, he knew he wanted to be able to come here always.

Flaxfield was there already, of course, sitting at a table with another man. They didn't look up.

"That's Jackbones," whispered Melwood. "He's the librarian."

Jackbones had his index finger on an open book. He was explaining something to Flaxfield. The wizard listened, then shook his head, turned the pages, put his own finger on the book, and explained something else. Jackbones shook his head and leaned back, then took another book and opened it.

"We're not interrupting, are we?" said Melwood.

"I didn't hear you come in," said Jackbones, jumping to his feet and holding out his hand. "Hello, Cabbage. Welcome to the library."

"Don't believe him, whatever you do," said Flaxfield. "No one has come into this library for two hundred years without Jackbones knowing it, even when he's asleep."

Jackbones pulled up a chair for Cabbage and gestured for him to sit down. Cabbage ignored the chair. He stood gaping around.

"Do you like it?" asked Jackbones.

"It goes on forever," said Cabbage.

"Clever boy," said Jackbones.

Cabbage glared at him.

"No, I mean it. I wasn't making fun. Most people, nearly all people in fact, ask how high it goes, how many floors it has, that sort of thing. You didn't."

Melwood took the chair that Cabbage had ignored. "Jackbones loves his library more than anything in the world," she said. "And he's pleased you like it."

"It really does, doesn't it?" said Cabbage. "It goes on forever."

Jackbones nodded.

"How does it do that? How can anything do that?"

"I'll tell you," he said. "Because you spotted it straightaway. But you must never tell anyone else. Promise?"

Cabbage looked at Flaxfield and Melwood.

"Oh, they know," said Jackbones. "Not many do, but these two are very special people."

"I promise," said Cabbage.

"It goes on forever," said the librarian, "because it contains every book that has ever been written about magic, every book that might be useful to magic, and every book that ever will be written about magic, but hasn't been yet."

Cabbage looked up. The library itself was circular and had galleries all around the sides going on and on out of sight.

"There are books in here that haven't been written yet?" he said.

"Yes. They're quite difficult to get to, but it can be done, if you know how."

Cabbage studied Jackbones. He looked more like a shopkeeper than someone who looked after a place like this. He was tall and slim, with short hair that stood straight up on the top and was cut close on the sides. He had the look on his face of someone who can sell you something. Again, the age was impossible to guess, but he'd been here more than two hundred years and wasn't old.

"Tell me," said Jackbones, waving a hand at the rows and rows of books. "I can get you anything you want. Tell me what it is."

Cabbage didn't even need to think of an answer; he knew immediately.

"I want my dinner," he said. "I'm hungry."

Flaxfield sighed. Melwood laughed. Jackbones clapped his hands together.

"Quite right," he said. "The perfect answer. Can't work while you're hungry."

He looked at the principal.

"I'll get them to send some up," she said. "I don't think Cabbage is ready for the dining hall."

"Then," said Flaxfield, "we need to work."

Mattie had managed to get a lot of crumbs on the bed and didn't mind because he wasn't going to stay around to clear it up. He lay for a while, brushing away crumbs and listening.

If there was a disturbance in the palace, he didn't want to be caught in a bed. He hopped out and made a not-very-bothered attempt to straighten the covers.

The shouting was clear now. Many voices. And screams.

Mattie moved to the window. His choice of a high bedroom gave him a wide view of the courtyard, the thick walls, and the outbuildings. The palace was a village really, with everything contained within its walls. It was a village in panic.

There were three barriers against attack. They were all in place. The gates were locked. The portcullis had been dropped, the drawbridge raised. No one could get through that. No person. No human being. Even a wizard would find it difficult because magic had been woven into the defenses when the palace was built.

The beetles swarmed under the gates, through the holes in the portcullis, around the raised drawbridge. Gaps the size of a fist, the size of a man's head didn't matter against an invading army. Against an army of beetles, they were as wide as highways.

The beetles crawled over everything. They stung and sucked. They nibbled and tore. They smothered and strangled. They ate their way through wood around the locks on the gate, and it swung open. They chewed the ropes, and the drawbridge came clattering down. Seeing an opportunity for escape, some of the men raised the portcullis and tried to run through. Mattie saw them stop as though they had run into a stone wall. They fell, dazed, and were at once covered with a cloak of beetles.

A taller figure drifted across the drawbridge, followed by another, squat and thick. They stopped in the gateway and watched the killing. The squat one ran forward and joined in. The taller one shimmered like smoke.

Mattie moved away from the window and opened his bedroom door. The screams in the corridor told him that the beetles were inside as well.

He couldn't fight them. He might be able to run later, when the gate was clear. Now, all he could do was hide. Well, he knew every passageway, every secret walk and hidden room, every arcane path. He would wait it out and hope.

The worst thing was not the screams.

The worst thing was how soon the screams stopped and all that was left to hear was the scratching of hard, black, spiky legs.

Morning,

and sunshine, and sleep. Bee had slept through the night without
disturbance. She woke to find last night's dinner still on the table.
The mirror was facedown on the mantelpiece. Bee jumped out of
bed and hurried herself into the clothes. Despite herself, she
couldn't help feeling pleasure at putting them on. Cleaner, softer,
and more graceful than anything she had worn at Slowin's.

There was a scarf, which she tied around her neck before she
remembered her reflection and moved it so that it was over her
head. She pushed the few straggles of hair that were left and
draped the end around her neck.

With long sleeves, a skirt that reached her ankles, and the scarf,
only her hands and face were visible. It would have to do. She had
stared at her own face last night and survived. Other people
would have to stare at it too. They might as well get used to it.

She looked out the window. The fields were all harvested,
save one. The red flames of the poppies in the wheat, the gold of

the grain, the green of the hedgerow, the blue of the sky. Bee realized for the first time that Slowin's Yard had been a world without color, a world of black shadows and blue-gray brick.

She had been expecting the knock on the door, so she was disappointed but not surprised when it came. She wondered if Flaxfold had some spy hole or other way of seeing into the room. She always seemed to know when Bee was awake or moving.

"Come in," she said.

"Can you open the door for me, please?" said Flaxfold. Bee did.

"You always have food when you come here," said Bee.

"And you never eat it."

She laid the tray on the table, took off the plate and cup and a small posy of flowers in a yellow pottery vase, replacing them with the plate from last night. She put the tray on the floor of the corridor outside, came back in, and closed the door.

"You're staying, then," she said.

"Yes." She hated Dorwin with a sudden rush of anger.

Flaxfold noticed the change in her and said, "That's all she said. Just that you're staying."

"I don't care what she said." Bee picked up the cup and drank it all down in one go.

"Well, whether you do or not, that's what happened. I don't know what the two of you talked about, but she said that you would be staying after all."

"How do I know you're telling me the truth?" she said. "You could make up anything and I wouldn't know."

Flaxfold smiled, disappointingly not offended.

"Because I will always tell you the truth," she said. "I will never lie to you."

"Never?" asked Bee.

"No."

Bee swallowed. She took a big bite of bread and pushed the scarf from her head. She stared at Flaxfold. "Look at me."

Flaxfold held the girl's stare.

"I'm ugly," said Bee.

Flaxfold said nothing.

Bee shouted at her. "See? You're lying to me. You won't say I'm ugly."

"I haven't said anything," Flaxfold answered. "How can that be a lie?"

"All right then, say I'm ugly."

Again, Flaxfold didn't answer.

"Liar," said Bee. "Your silence is a lie."

"I haven't answered because you haven't asked me a question yet."

Bee was used to these word games. She had been learning magic since she was six years old.

"All right," she admitted. "I haven't. I will now. Am I ugly?"

She found that although she knew the answer was yes, she was all at once afraid of what the woman would say. She waited.

"I don't know," said Flaxfold.

Bee put her finger under the rim of the plate and sent it spinning across the room. It landed in the fireplace and shattered. The eggs smeared the white wallpaper around the grate.

"Liar. I looked at myself. Anyone can see I'm the ugliest thing there ever was."

"Oh," said Flaxfold. "You mean your face?"

Bee looked at Flaxfold for a long time. The woman's eyes were such a pale gray. She had lines around them, creases from the years.

"I've just met you," said Flaxfold. "I'm just getting to know you. I don't know if you're ugly or not. You have lovely parents, so you should be lovely, too. But you have lived for as long with Slowin as you did with them, and he is as ugly as anger, so there is a good chance you will be ugly as well. I don't know yet. I hope you are not ugly. I'm going to act that way until I know differently. Now, shall I bring you some more breakfast? The last one is ruined."

Bee looked away. "You know what I meant," she said.

"Yes, I know what you meant. And I know what I said. If you want to talk about your face, we'll talk about that instead."

Through the window Bee could see the harvesters begin work on the last field. The stalks were toppling, sliced at the base. The poppies fell with the wheat. No distinction.

"Is my face ugly?"

"Your face is scarred," said Flaxfold. "It isn't like the face you were given. Now it's up to you. You have a choice. You can let the way your face looks make you look like that inside, or you can let the person you are inside show itself on your face. I'll get you some more breakfast."

It took Flaxfold a while to clear up the broken plate and wipe up the mess before she left the room. She didn't look at Bee.

She could hear her draw the scarf back around her head and shoulders. And she could hear her quietly crying.

Morning, and darkness, and silence.

Mattie's sleep had been full of noises and alarms, broken and fearful.

There was nowhere the beetles couldn't go. But they needed to know how to get there first. The palace had a maze of hidden tunnels and passageways and niches. Mostly they were the service alleyways that the builders had used when the palace was first put up. Walls that looked solid often had hollow centers to save materials. Roof voids and narrow stairs and ladders were set into the design so that out-of-the-way places could be reached for cleaning and repair.

The beetles swarmed everywhere on the surface. They cleared out nearly every living thing that belonged to the palace, even the cats and dogs. The mice and rats they left alone. There seemed to be some sort of vermin confederacy between them.

The beetles never slept. Never seemed to. He could hear them scrambling, their legs scratching. He thought they might sleep when light came. They didn't. So he would have to make his move now.

Everything in the palace was linked in one way or another to the high boundary wall. Mattie started high up and moved as far as he could in the hollows to the outer wall. He skirted this until he came to an iron ladder set into the stones.

"So far, so good," he said.

This took him down two levels. And so on until he came to ground level.

The beetle activity was worse here. They liked the damp earth. They liked the corners where the fleas bred in the pools the dogs made.

Mattie had worked his way around to the gate. There was a small opening he could just squeeze through, which carried one of the chains of the portcullis.

The road was clear. All the beetles were inside. A dead horse in the courtyard was keeping them busy. There was a straight run from Mattie's escape opening to the drawbridge. He took a deep breath, held it in, dropped down, and ran for it.

The gate was open in front of him. The road urged him on. He had only to clear the drawbridge and he would be free.

As soon as he drew level with the entrance, he felt as though he had run into a net stretched across it. He bounced back in, falling over, and grazing his elbow. With a frightened look around at the beetles in the courtyard, he ran at it again. Again he bounced back.

There was a net of magic, and he couldn't get through.

He knew when he was wasting his time. Before the beetles had a chance to notice him, he scurried back, clambered up to the opening, wriggled through, and out of sight.

"Now what?" he asked.

Morning, and books, and problems.

Cabbage's sleep was populated by hundreds of strangers lined up in rows on shelves. They stood in lines and looked down at him. He walked along the rows, deciding which to take.

The first was a woman in a green dress with gold embroidery.

"Herbs and plants which heal," she said.

He moved quickly on, not sure how to respond.

He selected a small man with a red nose, no shoes, and a gray beard.

"Caves," said the man. "And potholes and mines."

"What do you mean?" asked Cabbage.

"Dark places underground, but not the Deep World. That's a different book."

"That's me," said a voice to his left and up.

Cabbage replaced the small man and climbed up to see who was speaking now.

"Over here."

It was a man with his hand on a memmont and a roffle's barrel at his feet.

"Deep World," he said, "and things pertaining to roffles."

Cabbage stepped down and backed away, thinking of how he had betrayed Perry and deserted him.

He ran to the door of the library and tried to get out. The door was locked. He tugged at it as hard as he could and woke himself up.

"Perry," he said.

He was thirsty, so he drank water from the jug on the washstand. The room was small and high-ceilinged. He could see Canterstock far below him.

A rapping at the door brought him back. He didn't have time to open it before a small boy threw it wide and came in with a tray.

"Sausages, bacon, fried bread, tomatoes, mushrooms, three eggs, and bread and marmalade," he said. "And milk. They said you'd eat it all."

"I will," said Cabbage. "Who are you?"

"Doesn't matter," said the boy and ran away, leaving the door open.

Cabbage ate breakfast as fast as he could.

Jackbones was already at work when Cabbage arrived. Flaxfield and Melwood hadn't shown up yet.

"They sat up late, talking," said the librarian. "So they'll not be here early."

"How late?"

"Very late."

"How do you know?"

"I was with them."

"Then why are you here?"

Jackbones smiled. "That's the way," he said. "Ask everything. Especially in a library."

"Do we have to wait for them?" asked Cabbage.

"Yes."

Cabbage wandered off.

"What did you dream about last night?" asked Jackbones.

"I don't remember," said Cabbage.

"Really?"

"I never remember dreams," said Cabbage.

"Fair enough," said Jackbones.

Cabbage kept his face away so Jackbones couldn't see him.

"If you go up those steps," said the librarian, "and up to the first gallery, you can fetch me a book down."

The steps were iron, latticed, and delicate, and so was the floor of the gallery.

"Keep walking," said Jackbones. "That's it. Now stop. Look to your left. Up a bit. Along. Good. The book on herbs, please."

Cabbage drew down a book, green leather with gold lettering. He looked at the title: *Herbs and Plants which Heal*.

"Don't stand gawping. Bring it down," said Jackbones.

Cabbage put the book on Jackbones's desk and waited for him to look at it. Jackbones leaned back on his chair and put his feet on the desk. He leaned so far back that his chair must fall, and Cabbage understood for the first time that Jackbones was a wizard.

"Now, there's another book you could find for me," said Jackbones.

"You haven't looked at that one."

Jackbones raised his eyebrows. "Really?" he said.

"You haven't touched it."

"But I've read it before."

"Then why do you want to read it again?"

"I don't. Now, I'd like you to go to the third gallery and get me another book."

"*Caves*," said Cabbage, "*and Potholes and Mines*."

"I said you were a clever boy," said Jackbones.

"How did you know that's what I dreamed?"

"Why do you think I know?"

"Because those are the books I dreamed about."

"You said you'd forgotten."

"Who writes these books?"

"They come from everywhere. Some are by great wizards who have never seen the college. Some by blacksmiths and farmers. Some by teachers at the college. There is no end to the places where books come from. To be honest with you, and you must never tell anyone else this, some of the books aren't very good. We only have them because they're written by people who taught here and who like to have a book of their own on the shelves."

The back of the chair was nearly touching the ground now.

"You're showing off," said Cabbage.

Jackbones made the chair approach an upright position.

"I am." He sighed. "I can never stop myself."

"I remembered it when I took the book down," said Cabbage. He put a tentative finger on the green book. "It was a woman in a green dress."

"That's right."

"How did you know?"

"Now go and get me *Deep World* and *Things Pertaining to Roffles*."

"Where's that?"

"Have a look. See if you can find them."

Cabbage laughed. "The books go on forever," he said. "Where should I start?"

Jackbones waved a dismissive hand. "Get on with it. I'll give you five minutes."

Cabbage darted off.

After wasting time running around the first gallery and getting nowhere, he stopped and leaned over, looking down at Jackbones, who was leaning dangerously back with his hands behind his head and his feet on the desk, grinning.

"Two minutes left," he said.

Cabbage scowled at him.

"What's it called?" asked the librarian.

"*Deep World,*" said Cabbage, "and *Things Pertaining to Roffles.*"

Jackbones grinned.

Cabbage stood back from the gallery rail and whistled. Except he couldn't whistle and it was just a blowing noise.

He picked up a pen from a worktable in a niche, put it to his lips, and blew.

A soft whistle, melodious and inviting. He looked around. He blew again.

"Come on," he said. "Where are you? Come on."

A nose poked around the side of a bookcase, followed by eyes and ears set into and onto a furry head. It looked at Cabbage.

"Good boy," said Cabbage. "Good boy. Where are they?"

The memmont climbed three galleries. Cabbage followed. It went straight to the correct shelf, and Cabbage took down two volumes, identical in binding, the first one about the Deep World, the second about roffles.

Cabbage stooped and stroked the memmont. "Thank you," he said.

He nuzzled his face against the soft fur, enjoying the scent, quite unlike that of a dog or cat or any other animal at all. The odor took his mind back instantly to the inn yard and Perry. He hugged the memmont.

"Time's up," said Jackbones.

Cabbage leaned over the gallery rail and brandished the books.

"Got them," he said.

"Bring them down."

The memmont wouldn't come with him, preferring to climb higher.

When he reached the ground, Cabbage found Flaxfield and Melwood with Jackbones.

"There are memmonts here," he said.

"Of course there are," said Flaxfield. "Who else did you think kept the books tidy? Not Jackbones."

"I didn't know," said Cabbage.

"Why should you?" said Melwood. "Now, be nice, Flaxfield. We need to work together."

"How shall we do this?" asked Jackbones.

"I'll take trying to find out what's happened to Slowin," said Melwood.

"Then I'll concentrate on finding out how we can get this chap"—Jackbones nodded to Flaxfield—"to be a wizard again."

"I am a wizard," said Flaxfield. "Never forget it."

"Quite," said Jackbones. "Let's see how we can get your magic back, shall we? Now, which of you is going to work with which of us?"

"I'll work with Melwood," said Flaxfield. "It's best if someone else solves my problem."

"I want to work with her," said Cabbage before he could stop himself.

Jackbones grinned. "What's wrong with me?" he asked.

Cabbage felt very uncomfortable with the three of them looking at him, waiting for an answer.

How could he say that he liked being with Melwood better? He had hardly ever spent time with women and he enjoyed the gentler approach that she had. Jackbones was too much like Flaxfield, joking and sharp and expecting a lot in return.

"Nothing," said Cabbage. "I want to work with her because she's looking for Slowin and if we find Slowin we might find Perry. That's all."

"Good answer," said Jackbones. "Do we all agree that the lad should be able to look for his friend at the same time as we look for Slowin? Or better still, as we look for Slowin's remains?"

Flaxfield nodded. Melwood put a reassuring hand on Cabbage's shoulder.

"Good. We'll swap jobs then. I'll do the search for Slowin and Cabbage can work with me. Melwood can work with Flaxfield on Flaxfield's magic."

"Flaxfield has to look for Slowin," said Cabbage.

"No, no, no. It was never a good idea. If anyone can find something that's lost, it's the person who lost it. Flaxfield and Melwood, you and me, lad. Let's get started."

. . .

Morning, and blood and beetles and bodies.

The wraith that had been Slowin glided across the courtyard. It was more substantial now. The dawn light filtered through it with difficulty. It stooped, draped over the body of a woman in brocade and silk.

The wraith's clenched black companion clattered out a question.

"What are you cackling at?" whispered the Slowin thing. It stooped again and pulled away the gray silk dress.

"Slowin," the companion said, "are we staying?"

"Not Slowin," she replied. "Not anymore. Remember? Yes, we're staying. This will do very well." She examined herself, her arms, her flowing gray gown. "I didn't expect this," she said. "Not this."

Her companion clattered a warning.

A boy was approaching them on the drawbridge.

"How very interesting," she replied. She looked at the boy. "I don't think we'll need to worry about him."

The boy walked into the courtyard with an ungainly tread, bobbing up and down.

She beckoned him to her. "Come along," she said. Her voice was like the wind through dry reeds. "This way. Let me see you."

The boy came close, stopping two arms' length away. Out of reach. His feet made slurping noises on the cobbles, and he left a trail of slime.

The brittle companion laughed and mocked the sound.

"Smedge," the boy said, the word making trails of drool squish out of the corners of his mouth. "Smedge."

"Oh," said the wraith. "We like you."

"Like to eat," said the other.

"No," she snapped. "We don't eat this one. This one's different."

The boy raised a hand. "Who are you?" he asked.

This troubled the wraith. Who was she? She had so many names, Slowin, Ember, and something else. Which name was she?

"Introduce yourself," she said to her companion. It tried to say "Brassbuck" without success. It just didn't have the right mouth for it, and it came out, "Bakkmann."

"Bakkmann?" said the wraith. "Well, that's as good as anything."

Bakkmann jumped up and down and pointed at the boy. "Smedge," Bakkmann said. "Smedge."

She looked at the boy.

"I'm Smedge," he said simply.

"And who am I?" the wraith wondered aloud.

The boy stepped forward. He lifted the sleeve of her gown, gray and so light that a small cloud of dust blew from it. He took his hand away and looked at his fingers. "Ash," he said.

"What's that?"

"Ash."

"Yes," she said. "Bakkmann. Smedge. And Ash. Come. We'll go inside."

The three of them stepped over the bodies of the dead and went in. The beetles surged into the space.

"Are you sure that's all you remember about that day?"

Bee stared at Flaxfold.

"I'm sorry," said the woman, "but it's so important."

Bee picked up a stone and weighed it in her hands. She had spent four days going over and over the story of her life so far. All that she could remember. Flaxfold made her tell the story of Mattie in great detail.

"How did you know about the pebble and swallowing it?"

"If you have to ask that, you don't know anything about magic," said Bee.

"Even a very experienced wizard would be frightened to do that," said Flaxfold. "To eat the fire spell."

"Perhaps experienced wizards know so much that they don't know what to do anymore," said Bee.

Bee found a different stone, a flatter one. She stood and braced herself, then sent it spinning across the surface of the river. It bounced once and sank.

"Can we go now?" she asked.

"One more time, please," said Flaxfold. "After Mattie went away?"

"I went to sign the paper for Slowin."

"What did you put?"

"I told you. I can't remember."

"Tell me again."

Flaxfold was patient.

"All I remember is that the name he told me to sign wasn't right."

She took another stone. A heavier one.

"How do you know?"

"The same way I knew to eat the fire. The same way you really know anything. I just knew. It was the wrong name. And he wrote the wrong name for himself as well. I know he did."

"Yes," said Flaxfold. "I believe you. But what were the names?"

Bee looked at Flaxfold and looked at the heavy stone.

"Then everything ended and I was here. That's it. That's everything."

"I'm going to stop asking you now," said Flaxfold. "And I'll never ask you about it again."

Bee's scarf had slipped, and she adjusted it so that it covered her neck again.

"What?"

"Never."

"Why?"

"If you ever want to talk about it, then I'll listen. But you'll have to ask."

"Do you mean it?"

"I mean everything. I don't make foolish promises."

Bee found that she was hugging Flaxfold before she knew she was going to. She was hot in the autumn sun. The scarf was uncomfortable. She took her arms away, embarrassed.

"Flaxfield has to know this," said the woman.

"I know. And someone has to tell him. Will you?"

"I have to stay here. Dorwin will go, if you allow me to tell her enough."

Bee let go of the large stone and selected another, slimmer one. She skimmed it over the water. One bounce. "Just the last bit," she said. "Not the things about when I was little?"

"She really needs to know everything," said Flaxfold. "We don't know what's important and what isn't."

"Do I have to tell her?"

"If you like. Or I can tell her. Or no one tells her. She can take a message to Canterstock and bring Flaxfield back and I can tell him and he can go back again. That will take a lot of time."

Bee stood up. "You tell her," she said. "I don't want to tell it again."

"Help me up," said Flaxfold. She took Bee's hand and stood. Bending, she picked up a stone. She drew back her arm, flicked, and the stone skimmed across the surface of the water, two, three, four bounces.

Up Top or the Deep World?

Deep World or Up Top?

Not many people had the choice.

Perry watched the palace as night and day replaced each other three times.

He watched the last of the beetles march in. He saw lights

burn in turret windows far into the night. He heard no screams after the first attack.

Twice he stood up to leave. Twice he sat down again and watched and waited.

One person might escape.

One person might have hidden and survived.

One person might emerge and say what was happening in there.

He couldn't be sure, but it seemed to him that the building itself was changing. The tall, slender towers were thickening and shortening. The graceful walls were growing thuggish and brutal.

It wasn't possible, and he didn't believe it. He didn't see any change happen. He had helped his father in the garden, and he knew that you never saw a plant grow, but that if you looked at a row of beans after three days, they were very different, so, after three days, the building he saw was not the palace the beetle army had gone into.

And the beetles themselves. They made forays into the area outside.

Where they had all looked much the same when they went in, now there were a hundred different varieties. Some as small as a cockroach. Some as big as a fist. Some the size of a dog. And the biggest could have overpowered a donkey.

And the shapes. Some grew horns and mandibles. Their legs were angular and sharp. Some were squeezed into balls like bedbugs. Some jumped like fleas. Some stabbed. Some stung. Some whistled. Some clattered.

Rabbits and pigeons learned not to come near. The beetles were fast and deadly.

The worse of them all, the most cruel and quick, made a clattering noise. *Takkabakk, takkabakk, takkabakk.*

Even after it was clear that no one was going to come out alive, Perry stayed and learned all he could, to report back.

It was only after the takkabakk ones began to venture farther from the walls and to climb the hill in his direction that he decided it was time to leave.

Sometimes he could see three entrances to the Deep World all at the same time. Sometimes he went for over a couple of miles without seeing one, but he knew that if he stopped to look, they were there.

There had been one just behind the strange boy who wasn't a boy. Perry could see an escape all the time. The only trouble was he couldn't have taken it because the not-boy was in the way.

He could hear his father's voice telling him off for not going home. He could hear his father telling him that Cabbage had left him to die; he should forget about Cabbage. Perry knew better. Perry knew that Cabbage had gone to even greater danger.

Up Top or the Deep World?

Deep World or Up Top?

He stood at a door to the Deep World.

He was tired. He was hungry. He was lonely. He was still frightened by what he had seen of the beetles and the not-boy and the two figures who came with the beetles. He was homesick. All of these called him back to the Deep World.

On the other hand, he had never had a real friend before. He wanted to see if Cabbage had survived. He had started a job with Flaxfield and Cabbage and he wanted to see it through. He wanted to prove to his father that he was good enough.

Up Top or the Deep World?

Deep World or Up Top?

He could go to the Deep World, just for a little while. Eat, rest, come back and carry on.

It was a stone gatepost in a drystone wall. Perry rubbed his hand on the sun-warm lichen. He put his cheek against the stone, feeling the roughness of the sawed edge.

He heard the horse approach long before he saw it. He moved to the side of the gatepost, hidden from the road, ready to step down into the Deep World. Beetles, shadowy figures, not-boys . . . Up Top was a more dangerous place than he had expected. Who knew what a horse could bring riding on its back?

"We're getting nowhere," said Flaxfield. He stood up and stretched. "Cabbage," he said.

The boy looked up from his book.

"Do something," said Flaxfield. "Throw me some magic."

Cabbage grinned at the joke.

"No, I mean it. Throw me something. Anything."

Cabbage wondered what sort of test this was. He had experimented with magic since the storm, just to see if it worked. Sometimes it went wrong. The book and the vision of Boolat had been some sort of failure. Most of the time it worked perfectly. That still didn't make it right to do what Flaxfield was asking now.

"I don't work magic just for fun," said Cabbage. "I need to have a good reason. Otherwise it sets off a chain that can lead to trouble. Magic makes magic."

Flaxfield stood on his chair and shouted at Cabbage. "Throw me some magic, boy. Now. Anything you like."

Cabbage looked at Melwood and Jackbones for support.

Melwood lifted her shoulders in a tiny shrug. Jackbones grinned at him.

"All right," said Flaxfield, climbing down again. "It's not a game, is it? It's a practical test. Just throw me something."

Melwood spoke up, in a quiet, reasonable voice. "Why don't you tell us what you want?" she said. "Then we'll understand what to do. You can't spend six years teaching Cabbage not to use magic wastefully and then forget all his training and play games with it."

"All right," he grumbled. "I suppose so."

He paced up and down as he explained.

"We've spent what, three, four days, I can't remember, looking everywhere to find an explanation for what happened and to put it right." He stood still and pointed around him at the layers and layers of books rising up out of sight. "And I have to tell you that I don't think there's a single thing about magic in the whole of this library that I don't already know."

He looked splendid now, standing in command of all this, and Cabbage felt a sense of pride that Flaxfield was his master.

"Oh," said Jackbones, "so you know everything there is to know about it, do you? There's nothing these books can teach you?"

Flaxfield waited for the effect of this teasing to ebb away. He stood in silence until even Jackbones felt he might have gone too far.

"There will be incidents here I know nothing about," said Flaxfield. "There will be people I've never heard of, things that have happened, accidents and triumphs and failures and trage-dies. They may set up a trail we can follow that will lead us to an answer. But there is nothing"—he paused—"nothing," he said again, "about magic itself that I do not know."

He gave Melwood an apologetic look before saying, "I'm not one of your college wizards. I'm Flaxfield."

Jackbones snorted.

Cabbage went cold and his skin tingled.

Melwood nodded generous agreement.

"So why don't we give the books a rest for a while and try some-thing practical? Let Cabbage throw some magic at me. Remember what he said? Magic makes magic. It's worth a try."

"All right," said Melwood. "Nothing dangerous," she warned Cabbage.

"What shall I do?" he asked.

"Throw a wet sponge at him," said Jackbones. "That should teach him to have more respect for my books."

"Perhaps if you showered him with rose petals, it might cheer him up," said Melwood with wink.

"I can make him invisible," said Cabbage. "I've been working on that."

"Invisible and inaudible," said Jackbones.

Flaxfield snapped his fingers. "Invisible will do very well," he said.

"What will you do?" asked Cabbage.

"I'll make myself visible again," said Flaxfield. "Magic makes magic."

Cabbage stood up and faced Flaxfield. Melwood and Jackbones stopped talking and watched intently. Cabbage called to mind the spell and the way to do it. It was a strong spell and would take a great effort. He could have chosen something much easier, less of a strain, but he wanted to impress Jackbones and Melwood. As he began the working, there was a rush of air, channeled down from the higher galleries. It carried a sound as of thousands and thousands of pages rustling. Cabbage looked up. Although the galleries were empty, he felt as though thousands of eyes were watching him.

His lips moved. He raised his hands and turned the flat of his palms toward Flaxfield. He felt the floor move to one side, then settle. It shook him and made him stumble forward. Melwood put out a hand to steady him. He felt a shock at the subtle power of her touch. She had more magic than he had thought.

When his head cleared and he could see again, there was no one where Flaxfield had been standing. Either the wizard had walked away while Cabbage was unsettled by the spell, or the magic had gone wrong and Flaxfield wasn't there any longer. Or it had worked, and he was invisible.

If he was invisible, it was time for Flaxfield to undo the spell and appear again.

The three of them looked at each other for guidance. Jackbones had just opened his mouth to make a suggestion when there was a knock at the door.

"They mustn't come in," said Melwood. She moved quickly to the door to lock it. Before her hand could reach the key, the handle turned and the door began to open.

"Wait there," she commanded.

The door stopped moving.

"Who is it?" she said.

A head came around the door and smiled.

"It's Spendrill," said Jackbones.

"You can't come in," said Melwood. "We're busy. I'll come and see you later."

"There's a visitor," he called. "Says it's urgent. Got to see Flaxfield straightaway."

Despite the seriousness of the situation, and the danger, Cabbage couldn't stop himself giggling. Whoever it was, they certainly couldn't see Flaxfield now.

"Let them in," said Flaxfield.

Cabbage breathed a relaxing sigh. At least Flaxfield hadn't been vanished. He was still there. It was just that his idea hadn't worked.

Spendrill opened the door, stepped aside, and Dorwin came

past him into the library. She saw Cabbage, ran to him, and hugged him.

"It's so good to see you," she said.

Melwood coughed and Cabbage was surprised to see that she looked a little annoyed at Dorwin. He introduced them, and then Jackbones came and shook Dorwin's hand.

"This is very unusual," he said.

"Oh?" said Dorwin.

"Only members of the college and other wizards are allowed in the library. I think you are the first."

Cabbage began to apologize for her. "Dorwin's been very helpful," he said. "She was with me when we found Bee."

Dorwin stepped in. She was in no mood to make an apology. "I have important information," she said. "I rode all night. Did you want me to wait outside the gates like a tinker?"

"You are welcome," said Melwood, recovering her poise. "It is our honor that you come into the library."

Dorwin calmed down. "Thank you," she said. "I suppose you want my friend to wait outside, though?"

Spendrill put a hand behind him and ushered Perry through the door.

"Oh, a roffle," said Jackbones. "No, that's all right. Roffles have been here before. They're not people, after all, are they?"

Cabbage didn't know where to look; he was so ashamed that he had left Perry alone. He was so pleased to see him. He was so embarrassed at letting him down. He was so excited at seeing him again. He was afraid that Perry would be angry.

"You must be tired," said Melwood. "Let me arrange a room for you and some food."

"I'm fine," said Dorwin. "Later. Thank you. I have to deliver my message. It's urgent."

"Please arrange that," said Melwood to Spendrill. He nodded, waved a hand, and left.

While they were talking, the boys faced each other.

"Hello," said Perry.

"Hello," said Cabbage.

"You'll never believe what I've seen," said Perry. He came close to Cabbage. "Are you all right?"

Cabbage nodded.

"Sorry you got lost," said Perry.

"Sorry I left you there."

"What else could you do?"

"Will you all stop speaking at once and let me know what's happened?" said Flaxfield.

Dorwin looked startled. "Flaxfield?" she said. "Where is he?" she asked Melwood.

"It's a long story," said Jackbones.

"So is mine."

"Mine, too," said Perry.

Cabbage looked hopeful.

"Shall we listen to them while we have lunch?" he said.

Perry whispered to Cabbage, "And will he finish the story for me?"

"Story?"

"About the mirror and the magic?"

"Cabbage," shouted Flaxfield. "Get me back to normal."

Jackbones grinned.

Ash found the highest point in the building,

a tower with a view of the countryside that stretched beyond sight.

"This is for me," she said.

Smedge moved from one foot to another. His balance was getting better and he was walking almost like a real person.

"You'll have to stop leaving that trail everywhere," said Ash.

Smedge looked at the glistening slime. "It's nice," he said.

He was getting used to speaking as well. If only he'd had time to practice before he went over to the boy, he could have kept him off guard long enough to bite off his face.

"It stinks. It's slime. It's got to stop," said Ash.

Bakkmann clattered a harsh laugh.

"It hurts when I walk if I don't make the slippy," said Smedge.

"If you can't stop doing it, I'll burn your feet off," said Ash. "That will hurt more." She put her hand on his face and stroked him. "My own little Smedge," she said. "I made you. When I remade myself, I made you as well, didn't I?"

"I don't know. Perhaps the girl made me."

Ash slapped him. His face burst into flame. He fell to the floor, screaming.

"Oh, stop it," she said. She kicked his head. The fire went out. "Stand up."

Bakkmann laughed again. "Stand up," it clattered.

The left side of Smedge's face was burned away. His jawbone and eye sockets were revealed, and the eye had puckered and shriveled in the heat.

"Put it right," said Ash. "I can't look at that all day."

Smedge closed his good eye and remembered what things he had eaten. His face rebuilt itself, flesh covering the bone. His wasted side didn't match the other side. His face was half weasel, with ginger fur. He liked it. He liked weasel.

Ash slapped him again.

"No. Properly. I've got jobs for you. You'd better learn how to look normal."

Smedge made his face all boy. He was getting better at it.

Ash looked out of the window. The light didn't pass through her anymore. She was solid. Slim and tall, with a flowing gray dress.

"We'll stay here until we're stronger," she said. "I can already feel that I've got such power, and it isn't finished yet."

"Just us and the takkabakks?" said Smedge.

"We'll send them out for food," said Ash. "And they can fetch some servants for us. We'll need looking after."

Bakkmann crackled out a question. "Then what?"

"Ah," she said. "Then we can really enjoy ourselves. There are some old scores to settle. Flaxfield for a start."

She glowed white hot when she said his name.

"That old fool thinks he's so strong. He behaves as though magic were his own personal property. As though the rest of us weren't good enough. I'd like to put that to the test now."

She leaned out of the window and sent a torrent of fire streaming down the side of the tower. It splashed on the ground and poured out into a lake of flame.

"It's so easy," she said. "There's so much. I'm so new." She wheeled round and laughed at them. "I'm a new thing altogether," she said. "I'm the birth of new magic. I can do anything."

Bakkmann jumped up and down, beetle legs buckling and straightening.

"And I shall," she said. "I'll do everything I want. I'll do things I don't even know I want yet. And the first thing I want to do is get Flaxfield here and destroy him."

Smedge licked his lips. Green drool dripped from the sides of his mouth.

"Go on," said Ash. "Get out, both of you. Find yourselves somewhere to settle in. Bakkmann, you can take the kitchen. Smedge, I don't care where you go. Just go."

Perry and Cabbage sat together at lunch and whispered too much and prodded each other too often and giggled too noisily for the others. Melwood stopped Jackbones from giving them a telling-off.

"They're just boys," she murmured. "And they need to let off steam."

Jackbones grumbled. Flaxfield was too annoyed about being invisible to bother too much about a badly behaved apprentice and a roffle. He ate in silence.

It was the way he ate that made Cabbage and Perry laugh the most. The food floated up from the plate, hovered a moment, and just vanished.

"Why don't we see it when he swallows?" Perry whispered. "We can see through him."

"I don't know," said Cabbage. "That's just the way it is."

Flaxfield took a drink of wine and the boys collapsed in another heap of giggles as the red liquid hung perilously suspended in the air before disappearing.

"He's got some on his chin," gasped Perry.

The wine moved up and down in time with Flaxfield's chewing as it clung to his chin.

Melwood gave them both a warning look and dabbed her linen napkin on the patch of wine. She thought it was time they settled to some work.

"Let's make a start, shall we?" she said.

"I can't," said Cabbage. "Not for a couple of minutes. I need to concentrate on the food."

"You need to concentrate," she said, giving him one of those looks.

He blushed and elbowed Perry.

"Can we hear the end of the story?" asked the roffle.

"What story is that?" she asked.

Perry explained about the story of the way magic came into the world.

"You never finished it," he said to the empty chair where Flaxfield was sitting.

"No, I didn't. Well, I've finished eating, so I may as well tell you the rest now while you carry on."

Cabbage knew that Flaxfield was giving him one of his special teasing glares. He was glad the wizard was invisible and for a moment considered not ever remembering how to turn him back.

"Where did we get to?" asked Flaxfield.

"Smokesmith made the reflecting panel for the king," said Perry.

"That's right," said Flaxfield. "I remember now."

"Not the Smokesmith story?" said Jackbones.

"Why not?" asked Flaxfield.

"There are better stories than that about where magic came from."

"There are other stories," said Flaxfield. "This is the best one, and it's the one I'm telling."

When the mirror was ready, Smokesmith polished it in the dark so there was nothing for it to reflect. He wrapped it in leather and had it carried up to the king's chamber, high in a turret in the palace.

It was wide and round and spacious and the light fell in from all directions. It was perfect for reflections.

The mirror was put in place.

The queen was expecting a baby, her first. She was in her ninth month, and all the preparations had been made. The midwife was in place. The room was readied with clean linen, a crib, attendants, sheets, and towels, and a fire burning night and day with water always kept hot, ready. By strict reckoning, the queen had a week to go before the baby was due, but babies, and especially first babies, aren't very good at telling the time and can turn up early or late as the whim takes them.

The king decided to wait until after the baby was born. The queen wanted to see the mirror now. She kissed her husband and said it would be good to do it while the light was strong. It might be cloudy later; summer was going. She teased him and flattered him. He was so handsome, she said, that she wanted to see two of him. When that didn't change his mind, she just told him to get the smith and said they were going to look. The king did as he was told.

The king and the queen and Smokesmith assembled in the turret room. The door was locked and no one else was allowed in.

"Will you stand together?" asked Smokesmith.

"Yes," said the king.

"I want to be the first," she said. "On my own. I want to be the very first."

Smokesmith kept his mouth shut.

The king took her arm. "We should stand together," he said. "I'm the king."

"I'm having a baby. I'm doing it first."

So the king stood with Smokesmith and together they unwrapped the mirror and let the leather fall to the floor.

The queen stared at herself. The surface was flawless. No bends or curves distorted the image. No smears or smudges obscured it. It was a perfect, full reflection. The first ever.

The king waited and watched.

The queen smiled, turned first this way, then that. She crooked her finger to bring her husband to her side. As he moved to join her, she put hands to her belly, screamed, and fell.

The baby was on the way.

He unlocked the door, called for help.

Servants rushed in and knelt by the queen. Attendants seized Smokesmith and put swords to his throat.

"No," said the king. "Leave him. It's just the baby on the way."

Everyone who rushed in paused and gaped at the sight of themselves entering. The royal privilege of perfect reflection was now anyone's property. The unique gift was ruined.

They carried the queen to the prepared room and the delivery began. The king paid Smokesmith and sent him away. He stayed a long time in the room, looking into the mirror. He was not pleased with what he saw. He understood for the first time that many of his companions were better looking than he was. Even some of the servants cut a better figure. His wife was beautiful. She could have married someone more suited to her looks and she had chosen him. He began to suspect that it was because he was rich and powerful and a king.

The more he looked at the mirror, the more he hated it.

He covered it with the leather wrapping and locked the room behind him.

When he had opened the door with his wife, he had been a happy man. Now he was bitter and resentful and torn with doubts.

That night the baby was born. The midwife came to tell him the news.

"It's a boy," she said. "A handsome lad, like his father."

He looked at her as though she were mocking him.

"Let me see."

The queen was asleep. The baby was in a crib by the bed. The midwife led the king there and they leaned over to look.

Two babies, side by side, identical, backs to each other, lay in the crib.

"Is this a joke?" he demanded.

"I don't understand," she said.

The noise woke the queen.

"Which is my baby?" she shouted.

They uncovered the children. One was a boy, one a girl.

The queen grabbed for her son.

She held him close while the king showered questions on her and on her attendant women and on the midwife. They were frightened at his rage and tried to tell him what he wanted to know, rather than the truth.

One woman said the queen had given birth to a girl. Another said it was twins. Another said that the midwife had smuggled in the extra baby in case the real baby died.

"I had one baby," said the queen. "I had a son. See. This is my child."

She held the baby out for them to examine.

It was a girl.

The baby in the cot was a boy.

While the others flew about in a panic and the queen thrust the girl child from her, the king called in two guards. He took the child from the queen and handed it over.

"Get rid of them both," he said.

They took the other child from the crib and walked out.

Flaxfield stopped talking and raised his goblet to his lips. No one laughed when the wine disappeared.

"What happened then?" asked Perry.

"Then?" said Flaxfield. "The queen never had more children. The king hardly spoke to her again. They lived in separate parts of the palace. One strange thing was that anyone who had looked into the mirror found that things kept doubling. A servant would carry a joint of beef from the kitchen, and by the time he arrived at the hall there were two. A maid would pick up a candlestick to polish it, and when she put it down there would be two. People say that all the children who are born with some sort of magic gift are the descendants of the ones who looked into the mirror that day. The king kept the mirror wrapped in the leather. He sent it away to another of his houses, where it was locked in an attic, never to be unwrapped again."

"Is it true?" asked Perry.

"There are other stories," said Jackbones. "Most of them don't take as long to tell as this one."

"What happened to the babies?" asked Cabbage.

"The soldiers were told to take them into the forest and kill them," said Flaxfield.

"Did they?"

"The story says that's what they were told to do. Soldiers usually obey orders, especially when they come directly from the king."

"Is it true?" asked Perry. "Is that how magic first came?"

"I think all the stories about the start of magic are true," said Melwood.

"But they can't all be," said Perry. "Aren't they all different?"

"Of course."

"Then they can't all be true. Only one can be true."

"Where was the palace?" asked Cabbage.

No one answered.

Cabbage had an idea, a very bad idea. He looked at Melwood.

"Where was it?" he asked again.

"You say it," she encouraged him.

"Boolat," he whispered.

"Yes."

Perry tried to tell them about the beetles and Boolat, but before he could make a start, they had already pushed their chairs back, stood up, and started to leave.

"Just a roffle," Perry mumbled.

The river drew Bee to itself

day after day. She was getting better at skimming stones.

Swallows and swifts soared above it and dipped and dived, almost brushing the surface as they swooped for the insects that hovered over it.

Every morning and last thing at night, Flaxfold gave Bee an infusion of herbs that was supposed to stop the pain. It didn't. She carried the pain to the river as a milkmaid carries a yoke. It lay on her shoulders. It hung by her sides.

Once, she tossed the infusion into her washing bowl because she thought it was useless and didn't stop the pain. Before the sun was halfway up the sky, Bee had curled up in pain and couldn't stop kicking her legs and groaning. Flaxfold brought her another draft, stronger than usual. Bee slept through until the next morning, woke feeling dizzy, and drank her usual infusion without argument.

"Will I have to drink this every day?" she asked.

"I don't know. It depends on what Flaxfield finds out. And it depends on how well you heal."

"I've healed," said Bee. "Haven't I?"

"Yes."

"And the pain's still there, so it's always going to be there, isn't it?"

This was as much as they spoke. Flaxfold tried to spend time with Bee. The girl walked away. If Flaxfold came to the river to find her, Bee went inside.

"Perhaps it would be better if you tried some magic," suggested the woman.

Bee stared at her. "What do you think made me like this?" she said.

For some reason, the pain was less when she was at the river. She liked to take her shoes off and put her feet into the water.

Bee was frightened to work any magic at first in case it made the pain worse. But the day after she had thrown away her infusion, her head was still groggy and she wanted to put her feet into the water. It helped her. So she made a small spell to keep the patch of ground dry. She tested it with the palm of her hand, pressed down. The grass was dry, the earth unyielding as a field path at noon.

She sat and trailed her feet in the water. Her legs stayed dry. She watched fishermen on the far bank hauling their small craft out of the water and carrying them away upturned on their heads. Their legs dragged ribbons of river water as they waded ashore.

Bee considered the dry ground she sat on. It felt wrong now. The magic had upset the order of the river and its bank. River-banks are damp. They should be damp. If you sit on one, you get your legs damp.

Thinking this, Bee began to feel sick. She pulled her feet out of the water and walked away. The spell had spoiled the river for her. Where it should have made her forget some of the pain, now she had doubled it. Magic was more pain.

When Flaxfold came to her room that night to give her the infusion, she said, "Have you thought about trying to use some magic? There's still time to make you an apprentice."

"I've finished with magic," said Bee. "I'm never going to do it again. I'm never going to be an apprentice."

Perry leaned toward Cabbage and whispered, "Who are the other people in here?"

"Never mind who's here," said Jackbones. "Let's just get on." He laughed when the boys stared at him.

"Librarians hear every whisper," he said. "You should remember that."

This reminded Cabbage of something. Perry looked up at the high galleries and shook his head.

"How did you know what I had been dreaming?" Cabbage asked. "You did, didn't you?"

Jackbones cleared the table and arranged paper and pens for everyone to make notes. Flaxfield and Melwood, who had been dawdling and talking on the way back, came in. At least, Melwood came in talking to someone and Flaxfield's voice answered her. Dorwin came next and closed the door.

"Please," said Cabbage. "How did you know?"

Jackbones smiled. "Don't mind me," he said. "I like to tease. The books told me."

"What are you three gossiping about?" asked Flaxfield. "Undo this spell, please."

"I'm thinking about it," said Cabbage.

"Never tell lies in a library," said Jackbones. "This is a place for the truth."

"I will think about it," promised Cabbage.

They sat around the table. Cabbage quietly drew out his note-book. He was sure he had written a special page about invisibility.

Flaxfield's voice erupted from the empty chair opposite. "Don't tell me it's in that book?" he said. "I've never had such an apprentice for keeping a sloppy notebook."

Melwood came to his rescue. "It's not how neat a book is," she said. "It's how good the work is. I've known pupils with the neatest books and the dimmest minds. Sometimes mediocrity needs order; genius can't be regulated."

"All I'm saying is that if we have to wait for Cabbage to find something in his notebook you'll never see me again."

Cabbage ducked his head and turned the pages. Things weren't all in what other people would recognize as a proper order, but he knew where to find them. Most of the time. He flicked the pages.

"We're ready for your information," Flaxfield said to Dorwin.

Perry couldn't understand why she hadn't been asked to give it as soon as she arrived, so he asked.

Flaxfield said, "Whatever brought Dorwin here is important. We need some help. We need to hear. She had a long and hard journey, rattling along on a horse and rescuing roffles. That's no way to pass on knowledge. What she tells us now will be different from what she would have said the moment she walked in. Cheese and wine and wisdom need time to mature. She'll tell it better now."

"It isn't enough," said Dorwin. "Sorry."

"Let us decide that," said Melwood.

Perry moved his chair closer to Dorwin. She smelled good and he liked being close.

Dorwin told Bee's story as it had been related to her. Melwood listened with a look of deep sorrow. At times she held her breath. At the moment when Dorwin described how Slowin had stolen Bee's spells and sold them, she couldn't stop herself saying, "That's worse than theft, worse than beating someone. She was lonely and small and didn't know how wrong it was. Your magic is your life. It's the deepest, most secret part of you, and he stole it."

No one replied.

Dorwin continued. "She signed an indenture," said Dorwin, as the story reached its end. "And she knows that he cheated her there, too. He gave her his name and he took hers."

Flaxfield's voice interrupted. "He can't have done that. He can't."

The table shook under the impact of an invisible fist.

"What's the matter, Flaxfield?" asked Melwood.

"Slowin was the weakest, stupidest wizard there has ever been," said Flaxfield. "I'd watched him over the years. He was a fool and a bungler, but he couldn't do much harm. He wasn't a powerful wizard. He was greedy and vain and he wanted to be better than anyone else. I once had to correct him."

"What do you mean, correct him?"

"I mean, he was trying to take advantage of people with his magic. I corrected him."

"Like you correct me?" asked Cabbage.

Flaxfield's voice was soft and Cabbage could sense the smile.

"No, lad. I've never corrected you. Not in that way. I mean I had to show him what happens if you use magic for the wrong reasons. I'm afraid it may have hurt him. His pride, too."

"He won't have forgotten that," said Melwood.

"No. He doesn't forget. Anyway, I kept an eye on him for a while, to make sure he'd learned his lesson. He seemed to. And his power was even less then."

"But he found Bee," said Melwood.

"He found Bee," agreed Flaxfield. "And he tricked her parents and stole her from them."

Cabbage searched his notebook, listening with half an ear.

"He's kept a wall of silence around her," said Flaxfield. "He's hidden her very well. We had no idea what was happening. And the worse thing is that she's very powerful."

"What's he done?" asked Melwood.

"He's made a new order of magic," said Flaxfield. "By switching names, he's upset the reflected order. There will be changes. That's what the wild magic was. It felt the change coming. It boiled up all around him, and when the indenture was signed, it was ready. From now on, magic will be more dangerous than ever. We've always been careful with it, always tried to use it sparingly. From now, every act of magic will have a possible reflection. It's why we kept getting hurt when we used it. Magic is biting back."

Melwood asked the question that everyone was thinking.

"What about you, Flaxfield?" she said. "What happened to your magic? Was it sucked out of you?"

"That's what we have to find out," he said. "And Dorwin has brought us a chance to do something. We can make a start with the names. If we know what Slowin's real name is, we can get some power back. I'm convinced now that he survived the storm, and he's dangerous. We need to beat him. Now, Dorwin, continue. What names did they exchange?"

They all looked at Dorwin, ready for the one thing that could help.

"That's just it," she said. "Bee can't remember."

"What?"

"She remembers going into the tower and meeting Slowin. She remembers refusing to sign. She remembers being persuaded. She remembers picking up the pen and writing. Everything else is as though the tide had washed the sand clear. She remembers nothing."

"Then we're beaten," said Flaxfield.

Jackbones spoke for the first time

since Dorwin had begun her tale. "Don't be so weak," he said.

Flaxfield kept his voice under control. "We are weak," he said. "Slowin has grabbed magic to himself and he's on top. If we knew the names, we might have a chance. Without them, there's nothing we can do."

"Got it," said Cabbage.

He stood up with his notebook open in one hand. "I knew it was in there," he said. "It's so simple. How could I have forgotten?"

"Can you do it?" Flaxfield called.

"I think so."

"Come on, then."

Cabbage backed away from the table.

Perry spoke to Jackbones in a low voice. "I don't understand why Flaxfield couldn't just tell Cabbage how to reverse the spell. I thought he was the master."

Jackbones shook his head.

"There are different spells for the same thing. This one is Cabbage's own recipe. Only Cabbage knows how to undo it."

"Come and stand in front of me," Cabbage said to Flaxfield.

"I am."

"Oh. I didn't see you."

Perry giggled and Melwood fought not to join in.

"Look at me," said Cabbage. He was staring into nothing. "Right into my eyes. Are you doing that?"

"Yes."

"Don't say anything. Just look. Try to see yourself reflected in my eyes."

The library began to hum. It was coming down from the galleries. Like the sides of a windmill when the wind catches the sails and the grindstones are locked into position, rubbing against each other. It hummed and shook. Perry looked up again. Still the galleries were empty.

"Try to see yourself," said Cabbage. "I'm just a mirror. You're looking for a reflection."

The air thickened in front of Cabbage. It grew heavy. First his fingertips, then his shoulders, not attached, then his feet. Flaxfield was reappearing from the edges inward. Cabbage's lips trembled; his hands were clenched. He forced himself not to blink. At last they stood, face-to-face, wizard and apprentice, Flaxfield and Cabbage, man and boy. Flaxfield was entirely restored except for his eyes. Deep, empty sockets stared into Cabbage's eyes.

"Hold firm, lad," said Flaxfield. "Don't give up."

Cabbage bit his lips. His face was white as despair. His eyes fixed open.

"That's it," said Flaxfield, and stepped away. His own eyes gleamed at them. Cabbage gasped, staggered, and Jackbones pushed a chair beneath him as he fell. He sat with his arms on the table, head resting on the wood.

"Here," said Perry. "You dropped this."

He picked up Cabbage's notebook, which had fallen to the floor.

"Careful," said Flaxfield, reaching for the book and snatching at it.

Perry pulled his hand back and the pages fanned out.

"No one should touch an apprentice's notebook," said Flaxfield. "Put it down."

A pocket in the inside cover fell open and a sheet of paper tumbled out. Perry grabbed it. He put the book and the paper on the table next to Cabbage.

"What's this?" said Flaxfield.

"It fell out."

"I can see that. It's an indenture."

Cabbage lifted his head. His eyes were bloodshot. He rubbed his temples. "Headache," he said. "Bad one."

Flaxfield put a long finger on the table. "What's this? Did you sneak your indenture away?"

"Of course not. Why would I do that?"

"Well?"

Jackbones sat next to Cabbage. His face was eager and he grinned more than usual. "Give the boy a chance, Flaxfield," he said. "This might be what we were hoping for. I'll get you something for your headache, boy," he promised. "But tell us about this first."

Cabbage held the paper close to his face, then far away, trying to focus his eyes. "It was at Slowin's Yard," he said. "I picked it up. I thought it might be important."

Flaxfield smoothed it on the table. "It's Bee's indenture," he said. "It tells us everything."

They all leaned over. Flaxfield covered the paper with his hand.

"Off you go, Perry," he said. "Wait outside."

"What?"

"This is wizard work," said Flaxfield. "No one should ever see a wizard's real name except another wizard. Even then you shouldn't tell just any wizard. You'll have to go outside."

Perry moved to the door, looking over his shoulder. Cabbage took the indenture, folded it, and put it back into his notebook, which he closed with a snap.

"Hey, we need that," said Flaxfield.

"I'll look at it later," said Cabbage. "With Perry. I'll tell you what it says."

"We have to get on. Time's wasting. Give it here."

Cabbage knew that Flaxfield would never touch his notebook. As long as the paper was in there, it was safe.

"Perry's my friend. I'll look at it with him."

Dorwin and Melwood looked at each other and nodded. They knew how this would end. Flaxfield glowered. "You can't show names to a roffle," he said. "It's never been done."

"This is new magic," said Cabbage. "New times. New ways."

Flaxfield looked at Perry. The small roffle stood between them and the door, uncertain.

"Come on," he said. He put out his hand and Perry came over to him. Flaxfield put his arm around him. "I promised your father I'd look after you," he said. "I haven't made a very good job of it, have I?"

Perry put his own small hand on Flaxfield's. "You've been busy," he said.

Flaxfield helped Perry into his chair. "No. I've been angry," he said. "Angry with Slowin. And angry with myself. And angry about what was happening. I thought I was in command of magic, and all the time it was slinking about like a dog waiting for a chance to break in. I haven't behaved very well."

"Come on," said Jackbones. "Show us that paper, Cabbage."

Cabbage opened it up and laid it on the table.

"It's Bee's indenture, all right," said Flaxfield.

"And it's not been burned at all," said Melwood. "It doesn't even smell smoky. Not a scorch mark on it."

"Usual terms," said Flaxfield. "Nothing special; it's the names we want."

His finger ran down the page, stopping at the signatures.

"Here," he said. "She's signed her name Ember. That doesn't sound right."

"But look," said Cabbage. "Where he was supposed to sign. It's all a gray smudge."

Flaxfield beat his knuckles on the tabletop till they bled, smearing red on black on white.

"Careful," said Melwood, moving the indenture away.

"The magic hid itself," he said. "It's making fun of us. We need to know what the other name is, and we need to know what he was doing with the names. All we know is that Bee said it didn't seem right, and I can tell you, I believe her. Ember's no name for her."

"We need to know what Slowin's name is," said Melwood.

Cabbage jumped up. "We could ask his old master," he said. "He'll know. He'll have to tell us."

"There are two problems there," said Flaxfield. "First, he would never tell."

"He would if he knew how important it is," said Perry. "Wouldn't he?"

"Second," said Flaxfield, "he's dead. Third," he added, forgetting he'd said two, "I can't even remember who his master was."

"I can find out," said Jackbones.

"It's not a college matter," said Flaxfield. "He wasn't a college wizard."

Jackbones sighed. "All you old wizards with your apprentices, you think the college is nothing. This library collects knowledge from everywhere, not just the college. There's nothing worth knowing that isn't in here. If I tell you the answer's in here, then it's in here."

"Get it, then," said Flaxfield.

"I'll do that if you like," said Jackbones. "Just remember, everything has a price. And this is a high price."

"We haven't got any money," said Cabbage. "Have we?" He looked at Flaxfield.

Flaxfield's face was set hard. "Not that sort of price," he said. "Go on, Jackbones. Tell us."

Jackbones looked up at the galleries. Perry felt something up there move and remembered his question to Jackbones, about who else was in the library with them.

"If his old master is dead," said Jackbones, "then we'll have to go among the dead to find him."

Melwood shook her head. "No," she said. "Absolutely not. We're not opening the Finished World. Not for this or anything else."

"We have to," said Jackbones, "or we've lost."

"If we open the Finished World, the most likely end is that we'll all be drawn into it," she said.

"In the long run we're all dead anyway," he said. "So we may as well give it a try."

"We must," said Flaxfield. "But the boys can't be here when we do it. That's final."

Jackbones gave him an affectionate smile. "Flaxfield, old friend," he said. "You were so wise before all this happened. What's gone wrong? Don't you see, it will work only if the boys are here? They're what it's all about. They're the ones who will see this through to the finish, not us."

"They're not staying," said Melwood.

"He's right," said Flaxfield. "Of course he's right. Then they must choose."

He stood, and they all stood as though in obedience.

"What's it to be?" he asked. "There's a way we can look for the answer, a way we can try to beat Slowin, but it's the most danger-ous thing of all. We could all die trying. What do you say?"

"When do we start?" asked Perry.

Flaxfield smiled at the roffle. "Cabbage?" he asked.

"I'd like something to eat first," he said. "Just in case."

"I don't want to do this," said Melwood.

"Then leave," said Jackbones.

"If it happens, we all do it together," she said. "And stop get-ting above yourself. Remember who's the principal here."

The meeting broke up, and they went to get some fresh air, walk the aches out of their legs, think about the dangers just ahead.

Cabbage lingered till the others had gone.

"Can you really do this?" he asked Jackbones when they were alone.

"I think so."

"If we find out what we're looking for, what are we going to do then?" asked Cabbage. "About Slowin."

"That's easy," said Jackbones. "You'll have to kill him. Or if you don't, you have to make sure someone else does."

"Why me?" asked Cabbage.

"Don't ask. Sometimes you can't choose what you want to do. It chooses you. It's just up to you to decide whether to go along with it."

Perry looked around to say something

to Cabbage and discovered that his friend had stayed behind in the library. He was uncomfortable. Dorwin and Flaxfield had linked arms and were ahead of him. He didn't want to go back into the library and didn't know where else to go. It was all so formal, so ordered. Worst of all, there didn't seem to be any roffle holes he could slip into. Roffles like to think there's always a way out of trouble Up Top. He was just about to go back for Cabbage when Melwood came back down the corridor to him.

"All alone," she said. "Come on. I'll show you the garden."

"It's all right," he said. "I'll wait for Cabbage."

"Come on. This way." She scooped him up and led him down a spiral staircase and through a door into the sunshine. "What do you think of this?" she asked.

It was a wonderful garden. Like the library, it was far too big for the space allotted to it. The best thing though was that Perry could see three roffle holes straightaway, and he knew that there would be others if he looked around more.

Melwood tried to tease him. "How big do you think it is?" she asked.

They were in an area laid out to lawn, and on their right was another, bigger space, which had been cultivated with formal beds, trellises, low box hedges, herb borders, and banks of tall flowers. Perry could see an old wall that he supposed held a walled vegetable garden. To their left and ahead of them, long walkways and trees, a pond with geese and an island. Beyond that, landscape like muscle with deer and sheep.

Perry could tell that visitors always gasped with astonishment when they saw this for the first time, and Melwood was waiting for him to do the same. He had had enough of this. They had ignored him ever since he arrived, all except Cabbage. They had been so excited to hear what Dorwin had to say that no one had asked him what he might know. As soon as he told them that his father had snatched him out of danger, they turned away and didn't want to know anything else.

"Shall I tell you something?" he whispered.

Melwood smiled.

Perry lowered his voice even more. "You must never tell anyone."

"No," she said. "I won't."

"The Deep World goes on miles and miles and miles. No one has ever reached the end of it."

Melwood looked excited. Roffles never talked about the Deep World to people Up Top.

"But," he continued, "you could fit the whole of the Deep World into a cottage kitchen."

Melwood stared at him. Her face was blank with shock.

"It's a lovely garden," he said. "Why is everyone showing me things and telling me things but never asking me anything? Just because I'm small and just because I'm a roffle, it doesn't mean I don't know anything."

Melwood blushed. "I'm sorry," she said. "We've been too busy for you. We shouldn't have been."

"The thing is," said Perry. "I think I can tell you something about what you've been busy with. Why don't any of you think I might be able to help?"

So he told her what he had seen at Boolat. Melwood listened to the whole story without interrupting or asking him anything. When he was finished, she took his hand and said again, "I'm sorry. We have to tell the others."

"All right."

She led him to the door into the college. Before she opened it, she looked back at him. "Is it true?" she said. "What you just said about the Deep World?"

Perry smiled. "Can a ferret whistle like a wardrobe till the clothes fall out?" he answered.

Frastfil hadn't been teaching at the college for long. A lot of college wizards never forget how happy they were as pupils at Canterstock and they wish they could go back as teachers. Frastfil was one of those.

The trouble was, he discovered that it wasn't as much fun being a teacher as it had been as a pupil. He had never had many friends as a boy, and the lessons had absorbed him so that this didn't matter. He thought it would be the same now that he was a teacher. It hadn't turned out like that. The pupils didn't like his lessons much. And the other teachers weren't his friends any more than the other children had been back in the past.

He was lonely and wondered if he had done the right thing in coming here. Should he go back to being a working wizard?

The trouble with this was that he hadn't been very good at that either and was glad when the job here came along. It was all very difficult.

He went into the garden to think about it. He felt less lonely and useless in the garden because there were no other teachers there to ignore him, no pupils to tease him and cheek him.

He settled down on a bench behind a hedge and thought about what he should do. He was a shabby, crumpled sort of person, with a worried face that smiled too often when it wasn't happy. He came from a family of great wizards and he felt he should be a great wizard, too, and he couldn't understand why people thought he wasn't.

He was just wondering whether to toss a coin to see if he should stay at the college or leave when he heard the roffle and Melwood. He sank down lower on the bench and listened.

It was annoying. They were not quite close enough for him to hear properly. He gathered that there was a big problem and for some reason that he couldn't begin to understand, this roffle boy thought he could help to solve it. A roffle, imagine. And not even a grown-up roffle, but a boy. In his short time at the college, Frastfil had come to think of boys as the enemy. He knew they laughed at him, and he couldn't find a way to stop them.

He strained to hear. Whatever it was they were talking about, the principal thought it was important. And, to Frastfil's delight, he worked out that it was about Boolat. If there was anything he thought he knew about, it was Boolat. This was his chance to get noticed and to be important. He had a good idea that Melwood was not very pleased with him, that she thought they had made a mistake in giving him the job. This would be his chance to prove her wrong.

Frastfil's great-uncle had been the court wizard at the Palace of Boolat. Frastfil had often visited there as a boy. He knew it well. When Melwood and the roffle went back inside, he crumpled up his cheeks in pleasure. He was going to show the others what he could do. He'd offer his knowledge. He had heard that they were meeting later in the library. Good. He'd go and join in.

He stood up, pushed back his limp hair, put his hands into his pockets, jingled the coins, and squared up his shoulders, ready for work.

Mattie had eaten a rat,

a raw rat. He had hit the rat with a lump of stone and ripped the skin off.

It was all right.

It wasn't all right.

It had to be all right.

So it was all right.

He was going to do it again. He was going to keep on doing it until he found a way out of Boolat. Or he would die. Eat rats or die.

Water wasn't a problem. The sides of the passageways between the walls were all wet when you got to ground level, wetter still underground. Mattie could lick himself a drink anytime he wanted to.

Apart from the portcullis hole, he hadn't found any other escape possibilities. There wasn't anywhere he couldn't go as long as he stayed inside the tunnels. He watched the beetles colonize the palace. They liked the damper parts best. Once they had cleared the palace of people, they stayed away from the upper floors mostly.

Everything about them made him feel ill. Their hard shells. Their glossy bodies. Their crooked legs that could stab as well as support. Their clacking. Their rattling. Their swift actions. And they were changing all the time. Changing in all different directions. Some grew bigger. Some could rear up and look as though they walked upright. Some had more legs than others. There was no pattern to it, no reason. Except for one sort. They grew to be the size of big dogs. They developed a spiny armored shell and stabbing legs and many eyes and they walked on tiptoe. And they made a noise that Mattie thought was like talking. They chattered to one another—*Takkabakk, takkabakk, takkabakk*. It made him want to disappear.

Then there was the biggest one of all. The one who spent time with the gray ghost in the turret. Mattie was frightened of them, but because they were less like the beetles than anything else alive except for the rats, he spied on them. And because he thought that if ever he could discover the secret of how to escape, it would be from them. So he watched from inside the wall and he listened and he remembered.

"I think it was a woman," said Perry. "But I can't be sure."

They sat around the library table again. "I wasn't close enough, but you know how it is. Even from a distance, you can tell a man from a woman."

"Beetles?" said Jackbones. "What sort?"

"No sort I've ever seen before. Shapes and sizes I didn't recognize."

"And this boy?" said Flaxfield. "Tell us that again."

"It wasn't a boy," said Perry. "I'm sure of that. It was a thing pretending to be a boy. It couldn't talk, and it walked like a thing."

Jackbones laughed.

"I'm serious," said Perry.

"And I'm taking you seriously," said the librarian. "I'm admiring your choice of words. Someone like Flaxfield here would have wasted time trying to find a clever way of saying it. You did well. A thing walks like a thing, not like a boy. Good."

"It's not Slowin, then?" said Cabbage. "Slowin's dead?"

"What about the other thing?" asked Melwood.

Perry closed his eyes and opened them again quickly. "Like a beetle, like a man, like a monster," he said.

"Could that be Slowin?" asked Cabbage.

"It could," said Flaxfield. "We don't know what the magic has made or the changes it's brought. He deserves to be a beetle."

"And they killed everyone?" said Jackbones.

"I heard the screams. I saw things I don't want to tell you."

"All dead," said Melwood. "That's as much as we need to know."

"Where does this leave us?" said Jackbones. "The beetles survived the magic storm. More than survived, they thrived and multiplied. The magic has taken over Boolat. And something else survived and has gone with them."

"Survived or was created," said Flaxfield.

"Or was created," agreed Jackbones.

"What about the boy-thing?" said Cabbage. "That didn't come from Slowin's Yard."

"It might be dead already," said Dorwin. "It went into Boolat."

"So," said Jackbones, "as I said, where does this leave us? I vote we concentrate on finding out Slowin's name, forget about Boolat until we've done that."

"On the other hand," said Dorwin, "we need to find out what's happening there, just in case."

"If there are beetles there, then Slowin's there," said Cabbage.

"One thing at a time," said Jackbones.

Cabbage and Melwood looked at each other. Melwood nodded to him to speak.

"We tried to look at Boolat," he said. "Both of us. We couldn't see it. The magic was blocked."

"Why were you looking for it?" asked Dorwin.

"It chose us," said Melwood. "We have to keep Boolat in our minds. I think it's as important as Slowin's name."

"Of course," said Flaxfield. "Boolat has always been important. It would have to be Boolat. It's always Boolat. It will end there."

They stared at him.

"What do you mean?" said Jackbones.

"We may as well look for Slowin's name," said Flaxfield. "Boolat will intrude soon enough. What's your plan, Jackbones?"

The librarian shrugged. "You know what I'm suggesting," he said. "Are you prepared to do it?"

"We all have to agree."

"Agree to what?" said Cabbage.

"You tell him," said Flaxfield. "It's your idea."

Jackbones looked at Cabbage and Perry.

"You know about Finishings?" he said.

"Yes," said Cabbage.

"No," said Perry.

"Tell him," said Flaxfield.

"Where shall I start?" asked Cabbage.

"You decide."

Cabbage frowned. "You know," he said, "that there's the Deep World and there's Up Top?"

"Does a book of recipes taste as good as a pork pullover?" said Perry, reverting to roffle speech in his frustration.

"What?" said Cabbage.

"Of course I know," said Perry.

"Of course. Well, there are other places as well. And the Finished World is one of them."

"Where is it?"

"I can't tell you about it if you ask me questions and I lose my thread," said Cabbage.

"Do you know where it is?" asked Perry.

"Flaxfield," said Cabbage. "You tell him."

Flaxfield shook his head. "You're doing a good job," he said. "Go on. Let him tell it his way, Perry."

"When you die," said Cabbage, "you go to the Finished World. And you never come back. It's not a place. It's everywhere."

"Does everyone go there?"

"I think so."

"Do roffles go there?"

Cabbage put his hands on his head and gave Flaxfield a desperate look. "Help me, please," he said.

Flaxfield took up the explanation. "Roffles are different," he said. "You'll tell Cabbage about that one day. For now, just remember that the Finished World is everywhere. One of the things a wizard can do is help people as they go to the Finished World. If you die and have to make the journey yourself, it can be confusing when you get there. You may forget who you were, or you may be frightened because it's so strange. You may take a long time finding other people you knew. Wizards can help with this. They perform Finishings."

"Do you?" Perry asked Cabbage.

"I watch," he said. "And I help sometimes. A little bit. I'm learning."

"A Finishing makes the journey easier," said Flaxfield. "A Finishing gives a person things to take into the Finished World, things that help them to remember, things that they knew Up Top, things that tell others in the Finished World who it is that's coming to join them."

"Do the wizards take them into the Finished World, then?"

Cabbage recoiled. "No," he said. "No. We don't go through. We have to stay on this side."

"It's all right," said Flaxfield.

Cabbage tried to smile.

"We don't cross that border, Perry," said Flaxfield. "There's no way back. And it's wrong to go into the Finished World before you're called there. You would never be at rest. You wouldn't fit in. It's the worst thing that could ever happen. A wizard must be very careful to make sure he doesn't cross the border."

"What's the Finished World like?" asked Perry.

Jackbones leaned close and said quickly, "It's greedy. If it can snatch you, it will."

"Don't talk like that," said Melwood. "You'll frighten them."

"I'm frightened," said Jackbones. "They should be."

"I'm not frightened," said Cabbage.

Jackbones stood up. "We're never going to find what we want by looking through the books," he said. "There are too many. We don't know where to look. So I'm suggesting that we call up everyone from the Finished World who has written a book in here and we ask them. It's the only way I can think of. That way, the answer will come to us. We won't have to go looking for the answer."

"It's the quickest way," said Melwood, "but not the only way. We can carry on as we were."

Jackbones made an impatient and ill-mannered noise of exasperation.

"No," said Flaxfield. "Not after what Perry has told us. Something from Slowin's Yard has gone to Boolat, and there's going to be trouble if we don't stop it, and stop it soon. There's no time to look through here any more. Jackbones is right."

"So we open up the Finished World?" Melwood said. "Just like that? And see if we can stop it from grabbing us all? Is that it?"

She was nearly shouting at him, and she put her face close to his in defiance.

"Yes," he said. "Yes, that's what we do, Melwood. You know it is, don't you?"

He put his arm around her.

"One hour," she said. "We need to prepare ourselves. We'll meet here again in one hour."

"There's no need for Dorwin to stay," said Jackbones.

"Don't you dare try to keep me out of it," she said.

"It will be dangerous enough for wizards," he said.

"Wizards!" She said the word as though it meant something nasty you trod in. "I've seen enough of the mess wizards can make. You'll need someone ordinary to save the lot of you if it goes wrong."

"And a roffle," said Perry.

Dorwin hugged him. "And a roffle," she agreed.

"Who's going to do this?" asked Melwood.

"It's my library. I'll do it."

"Very well. One hour. We'll meet back here."

Frastfil had waited along the corridor

from the library door. Now he pounced.

"Flaxfield," he said, smiling. He was always smiling. "I want a word with you."

"Who are you?" asked the wizard.

Frastfil introduced himself, jingling coins in his pocket all the time and smiling till Flaxfield thought his cheeks would explode. Flaxfield did not smile much unless there was a reason, and he didn't like this constant smirk.

"My third cousin, twice-removed, was Cosmop," he said. "I come from a great family of wizards."

"I knew Cosmop," said Flaxfield. "He was a good man."

"I don't think you did," said Frastfil. "He lived a long time ago and has been dead for a long time."

Flaxfield let it go. "What do you want?" he asked.

"I want to help."

The coins jingled faster than ever and the smile grew more irritating.

"We're busy," said Flaxfield. "See the principal next week."

He started to walk off. Frastfil jogged along just behind him, smiling and jingling.

"No. I can help now. I know Boolat. My uncle was there. Court wizard."

Flaxfield stopped, turned slowly, and stared at him. "Have you been eavesdropping?"

"No."

"How do you know we're thinking about Boolat?"

"I was in the garden." He jingled. "I overheard."

"Did you tell them you were there? Did you walk away when they started talking? Or did you sneak around and listen in?"

Frastfil backed away. "I couldn't help hearing. My cousin was Cosmop. I know about Boolat. I teach here. I can help. I want to help. They were talking in loud voices. My uncle was a court wizard. Cosmop was my cousin."

Flaxfield waited for the drivel to run out. "I had a dog once," he said. "Best dog I've ever known. Gentle, playful, strong. He was a fast runner. A baby was safe alone with him. A thief would do well not to break in if he was there."

Frastfil looked confused. "I haven't got a dog," he said.

Flaxfield waved a hand to silence him. "When he died, I always had one of his pups in his place. Good dogs, but not as good as he was. When the next one died, I had a pup from his last litter and so on and so on. In his honor."

Frastfil tried to interrupt again. Flaxfield ignored him. "I knew they weren't as good as he had been, but I kept to the breed, out of loyalty. In the end, I could see that other people's dogs were better than mine. I stayed with the breed until one day, White-rime, the last of the line, showed me it was time to stop. He was clever enough, but sly and cowardly. He followed wolves. I think he thought he was a wolf himself. But instead of running with them, he ran after them. He scavenged what they had killed. He began to harry sheep and make them lose their lambs. He disgraced me and he disgraced his great ancestor."

"What did you do?"

"What do you think?" said Flaxfield. "He was no use, and he was dangerous."

Frastfil jingled and smiled.

"Now, go away," said Flaxfield. "And don't listen again or you'll wish you hadn't. This is too much for you. You'll get hurt if you try to help."

Frastfil turned his face away.

"Now, I've got things to do," said Flaxfield, "before the work begins. Run off and think about what I said."

The children in the village liked Flaxfold. She let them steal apples from her orchard and even left some on the trees for them without saying they were welcome to them. She gave them drinks at the kitchen door in the summer when it was hot, and she let them make snow-memmonts in the garden in the winter if they cleared her path of snow first. Then she let them sit by the huge fire in the kitchen and eat toast and jam while they held their hands in front of the hot coals to get the feeling back into their fingers.

So they were shocked when she took them to one side and told them off in a quiet, level voice that made them more ashamed than any amount of shouting would do.

Wilfmore tried to argue and soon gave it up. "She's like a monster," he said. "Her face is all . . ."

Flaxfold lifted one finger and he was silent.

"By the time you are forty," she said. "If I let you live that long, you will have the face you deserve. Do you understand?"

"No."

"No. You don't. If you keep making fun of people because of the way they look, or shouting at them, or being cruel behind their backs, you'll get the ugliest face there is."

"Sorry," he muttered.

The others mumbled their apologies.

"Bee isn't ugly," said Flaxfold. "She isn't a monster. She's had an accident. Do you understand?"

But the damage was done. The girl had heard the boys shout at her. She had seen their jeering faces. She had stared back long enough to frighten them, and their fear was worse than their mockery. The scarf had begun to loosen, but now it was folded tight and close. And so was Bee.

. . .

"What are the dead people like?" whispered Perry.

"I don't know," said Cabbage. "I mean, I know what dead people are like, but I don't know what Finished People are like."

"Why not? You've been to Finishings."

"You don't see them, after they've stepped into the Finished World," he said. "And the dead bit stays here anyway. Dead people and Finished People aren't the same thing."

"I don't understand," said Perry.

"No."

"Right," said Jackbones. "Let's get started."

"Are we all here?" asked Melwood.

Dorwin and Flaxfield stepped from behind a bookcase.

"I'm giving her one last chance to leave," he said.

"And I'm staying."

"You could take the boys," said Melwood. "They shouldn't be here for this."

Dorwin thought about it. Her face creased into a smile. "Yes," she said. "Yes. I'll leave. I'll take the boys and we'll wait outside, in the garden, perhaps."

The two boys shouted each other down in their eagerness to answer.

"No."

"I'm not going."

"We're staying here."

"You need a roffle."

"You'd be dead if it weren't for me."

Melwood frowned.

Jackbones gave a savage grin.

Flaxfield turned away to hide a smile.

Dorwin held up her hands for silence. "It looks as though we're staying," she said. "So what happens next?"

The excitement gave way to a tense silence. They all looked to Jackbones for a lead. Jackbones's grin had no humor in it. Cabbage was reminded of the wide mouth of a cornered dog.

"There are several ways to do this," he said. "We could perform a proper Finishing, and when the Finished World opens, we could send someone in to summon them."

"No," said Melwood.

"Calm yourself. That's just one way. We'd need a dead person for that anyway, and I wasn't intending to kill anyone today."

"Stop wasting time," she said.

Cabbage could see that Jackbones wasn't teasing. He was preparing himself. Getting his mind ready for what he had to do.

"I won't tell you the other ways, then," he said. "Just the one we're going to use. Help me with this, will you?"

They helped him to carry the round table to the very center of the floor. The circular galleries coiled above it, out of sight.

He cleared the papers from it, scooping them into a drawer. "Wait here."

He came back from his librarian's room with an assortment of objects, which he arranged on the table. A seal and a folded sheet of thick paper with a crinkled edge. A bottle of ink, which he uncorked and put by the side of the paper. A pen, simple, wooden handled with a steel nib. A board, divided into sections with lead discs for counters, each disc engraved with an emblem. Two dice, one of black wood, one of bone. A notebook, handmade, scuffed at the corners, the pages covered in diagrams and drawings and notes.

"What are you doing?" asked Melwood.

Jackbones put his finger to his lips.

"I won't allow this," she said.

Flaxfield drew her back and put his hand on her shoulder. She made a tight mouth and kept quiet.

Last of all, Jackbones put a book from the library onto the table. He opened it at the index at the back.

"What's he doing?" whispered Perry.

"These are the implements of his Finishing," said Cabbage. "If he had died, they would go with him to the Finished World."

"Are you ready, Flaxfield?" said Jackbones.

"Are you sure this is what you want?"

"I am. Do you know what to say?"

Flaxfield looked at the table and the objects. "No," he said. "Not yet."

"Start the Finishing Ceremony the usual way, then," said Jackbones. "By the time you get to the place, you'll know the right words for me."

Perry looked up into the galleries again. He had never been able to shake off his feeling that someone was watching them.

Cabbage concentrated on the Finishing. Jackbones's Finishing. A Finishing for a man still alive. It had never been done before.

It was forbidden. The Finished World was jealous, proud, severe. It would not like being mocked in this way.

Flaxfield's voice carried the familiar words common to all Finishings. They were old words. Sometimes they sounded harsh in their direct talk of death, sometimes fluid and gentle in their recollection of life, sometimes more than sad, more than lonely. They caught the listeners in a net of language. Before Flaxfield was halfway through the words, the galleries began to whisper. Echoes, thought Cabbage. For a second only. Not echoes at all. Whispers that found their origin in the galleries themselves.

Flaxfield faltered. Jackbones glared at him. The wizard continued.

The whispers grew more but no louder, more widespread but no more intrusive.

Jackbones was sweating. His eyes were bright and fixed on Flaxfield's. His hands were clenched. His jaw was set. If he was not in pain then he was in a different sort of agony.

The whispers were all around them now, like the wind in reeds, rustling and moving. Flaxfield neared the end of the common section, the words that were used at every Finishing. His voice was coarse, rough. It did not falter. It pressed on, against some opposition.

Melwood moved closer to Flaxfield. He let her touch his arm and his voice strengthened.

Cabbage remembered the crackling of the wild magic and the threat and the violence it brought. He felt something of that now, something wild and unknown. With an effort, he kept his mind on the Finishing. As Flaxfield reached the end, Cabbage realized that something was wrong. Flaxfield said the final words and stopped.

The whispering ceased in an instant, every voice silent at once. The silence filled the library more thoroughly than the sound.

"Go on," said Jackbones. "Finish it."

Flaxfield looked down at the implements on the table.

"I don't know how," he said.

"Finish it!"

Flaxfield hesitated. He took the notebook, held it out to Jackbones, tried to speak, shrugged and put it down again.

The whisperers sighed, began to speak again in a receding voice, withdrawing.

Jackbones grabbed Flaxfield. "We've nearly done it," he said. "Finish it. Just do it."

Flaxfield put the notebook down. "I don't know how to."

The whispers faded, waves far off.

Cabbage stepped forward, picked up the book, open at the index. He faced Jackbones.

The whispers surged back again.

"Your book is written," he said. "Your life is recorded. The index is complete. The shelf is your home. Go and be Finished."

Jackbones relaxed. He wiped the sweat from his face with his sleeve. His jaw loosened. He smiled. He took the book from Cabbage. All the color drained from him. His hair, face, clothes, eyes, everything. They could see through him.

The whispers grew harsh. Jackbones looked up to the galleries. The others let their eyes follow his.

Above them, at every level, around every rail, packed tight, pressed together, faces looked down at them. Thousands upon thousands. A host greater than any army fell silent and waited.

What's happening?"

asked Bee.

"Nothing's happening," said Flaxfold. "Why do you ask?"

Bee drew her shawl tighter around her face as she spoke to the woman. "Something's going on," she said. "I know it is."

Flaxfold drew a stool up to the table and sat next to her. The table was so big that it could never have been carried in through the door. It had been built in there. Scarred with the marks of knives and hot pans and many spills, it had served generations of villagers and travelers with many thousands of meals.

Bee ran her finger down the raised grain. "Someone's dying," she said. "Because of me. Because of . . ." She couldn't bring herself to say Slowin's name. "They've come for him. He's going to die, and they won't let him join them. He'll be dead forever. Because of me."

Flaxfold picked up a spoon and looked at her reflection, bulging in its bowl. "Are you sure?"

Bee nodded. "Well, I think so."

Flaxfold held the spoon out to her. "See?" she said.

Bee saw herself, swathed in the shawl, distorted by the contours.

"Does it look like you?"

"Almost."

"You see something," said Flaxfold. "You know something is happening. But it may be a reflection as in a spoon. Not quite a picture."

"You came here, then?" said Jackbones. His voice had not changed. It was as strong and mocking as ever.

The whispering crowd chose a voice. The others subsided while it spoke.

"Did we?" it asked. "Or did you come to us?"

"What does she mean?" whispered Perry.

"I mean, young roffle, that we may be in your library, or you may be in ours," she said.

Perry crouched as though hit. Dorwin put her arm around him.

"Stand up, little roffle," said the voice. "We won't harm you. Not this time."

Perry glowered. "I wasn't afraid."

The whispers laughed.

"Talk to me," said Jackbones.

"We shall," she said. "Oh, we shall, Jackbones. Have you come to join us? In the Finished World?"

"I want you to answer my questions," he said.

"Questions. All these questions. Well, we have questions for the boy, too. The Cabbage boy."

Cabbage was looking for someone to attach to the voice. No figure emerged from the throng. No one stood out. The voice was soft, musical, not a whisper like the others, a real voice.

"We want to know a name," said Jackbones.

The music faded from the voice. "You opened the Finished World to know a name?" she said. "A name?" Her voice was a knife.

Jackbones stared up as though he could see her.

"You think we wait here to answer your bidding?" she asked. "You can't be bothered to look for the book? You won't take the time to find the shelf and read the name? You opened the Finished World? For a name?"

Flaxfield stepped forward. "I opened the Finished World," he said.

The whispers gasped.

"Flaxfield," she said. The music almost returned, a melody half-remembered. "We're waiting for you to join us. Would you like to step through?"

"There is no time to look through the books," he said. "So I summoned you here."

"Not you. The boy. The Cabbage boy. He summoned us. You couldn't."

More whispered, mocking laughter.

"Leave the boy alone," he said.

"The boy opened the door, though," she said. "Let me see him."

Cabbage pulled clear and stood alone, looking up.

"Why do you want to know this name, boy?" she said.

"It's your turn. Let me see you now," said Cabbage.

The whispers grew harsh, then silent.

"Why not?" she said. There was a shuffle and a rearranging of the multitude. The spiral staircase to the first gallery creaked. First a foot, small and slender in a soft leather shoe, then a dress, green and blue and shimmering, then the whole figure, a woman, of no age and all age. She paused, looked at them, as though waiting for them to look at her, stepped softly down and stood a little distant from them, a single person, not of their group.

"Why do you want to know this name, Cabbage? Are you tired of yours?"

"I want to know your name first," he said.

The watchers in the gallery laughed.

"I could take you now," she said. "Don't you understand? I could take you by the hand and lead you up these stairs into the Finished World and you would never see your friends again. You'd be lost here forever."

"No," said Cabbage. "You won't do that."

She stepped toward him. The dress shimmered and clung, throwing light and shadow into her face.

"I won't?"

"No. You want to tell us. You know. You've come to help."

She came closer still and put out her hand.

"Leave him," said Flaxfield.

She laughed.

"You're not even here, Flaxfield," she said. "Your magic is folded up like a tent. Let me talk to the boy."

She took his hand. Cabbage felt as though he could see for the first time. He looked up. The hazy figures in the gallery were clear as noontime. He knew their names, the books they had written, the work they were doing now.

"You're called Springmile," he said.

"I am."

"Are you taking me with you?"

"Yes," she said. "I am."

Jackbones tried to lunge at them. He couldn't move his feet. "You're taking me," he said. "It's my Finishing."

"There is no Finishing here. No one has died. You're staying here, Jackbones, though you may wish you weren't."

She led Cabbage to the table.

"Take up the book," she said. "Not the notebook."

He picked it up. It was warm, dusty, light.

"Well?" she asked.

The book had transformed itself into a burned coal, dead almost, with just the smallest orange glow in the center.

"Tell me what you have?" she said.

"It's an ember."

"And there you have it."

"His name is Ember?"

"Be careful with what you hold," she said. "If you crush it in your hand, the living heart will burn you. If you blow on it and feed it, perhaps it will rekindle and grow into a blaze beyond your control. If you blow on it, you may rouse it to life or you may extinguish it forever. Ember is an end and it is a beginning."

"Can we use this to beat Slowin?" asked Cabbage.

"No. It will not help you."

Cabbage looked at her with defeated eyes. "This has all been for nothing?" he said.

"It will not help you," said Springmile.

"That's not true," said Flaxfield. "Knowing his name gives us power."

"You need both names," she said. "You need the girl's name, too."

"Do you know that?"

"Oh yes. We know that."

"What is it?" Flaxfield demanded.

"Where is she?" asked Springmile.

"You must know that, too."

"Of course."

Cabbage squeezed her hand.

"Have I got to go with you now?" he asked.

The porter held the door open

for Frastfil to go through.

"You're not leaving us, are you?" asked Spendrill.

"Oh, just, you know . . ." Frastfil smiled.

"We'll miss you," said Spendrill.

Frastfil jingled the coins in his pocket. "Perhaps I'll come back," he said.

"So you're still a teacher here?"

Frastfil smiled desperately. "Am I?"

"Where are you off to, then?"

"Oh, just a short trip. Or a long one. Or a new job."

Spendrill loosened his grip and allowed Frastfil to slip away. "Don't you know?"

"Ah." He smiled and jingled. "Maybe I do, maybe I don't, but I don't have to tell the porter, do I?"

Spendrill leaned forward and whispered into Frastfil's ear. "No," he said. "No, you don't have to tell the porter, but here's a funny thing. The porter always finds out."

"What?"

"Good-bye, then. I wish you a long journey."

Spendrill closed the gate.

Frastfil crossed the square, threaded his way through the narrow streets to the gate of the town. He stopped there, knelt and fastened his shoes, and set off on the road to Boolat, where he would be appreciated.

Springmile led Cabbage toward the spiral stair, its iron treads leading ever upward.

"Let him go," snapped Flaxfield. "He's staying here."

Springmile smiled down at the boy. "I want you to fetch me a book," she said. She whispered to him. He nodded. Without looking back, he climbed the stair, and the others disappeared from view as he turned the corner. Other faces were in front of him. The throng of the Finished People waited ahead. He kept his hand on the stair rail to stop himself from shaking. He kept his head down, not to look at them. As he reached the first gallery and made his path along the walkway, they fell aside to let him pass.

"Thank you," he said. He looked up without thinking, and his eyes met the eyes of a Finished Man. He was tall and gaunt, hair drawn back and tucked under a cap, a small beard just on the end of his chin, and shaved cheeks.

"You know where it is?" he asked Cabbage.

"Yes."

He reached the place on the shelf and took down the book. Why always this one?

At the bottom of the stair, he saw Flaxfield's face first and thought the old wizard was going to cry with relief. He lifted a hand in recognition. Flaxfield nodded and turned away. He handed the book to Springmile.

"That's the one," she said. "Never mind what Jackbones says, you're going to borrow this book. You're going to take it away from the library."

"I thought you were going to take me with you?" said Cabbage.

She put her face to his. "I shall," she said. "But not today."

"Oh."

"Are you disappointed?"

Cabbage looked at Perry and Flaxfield, at Dorwin and Jackbones and Melwood.

"Yes," he said. "A little."

"I know," she said. "Go and see your friend."

Cabbage trotted over to Perry, who punched him on the arm with pleasure.

Springmile stood tall and raised her arm. The whispering returned, more dense than before, more openly hostile.

"You've kept these people long enough," she said to Jackbones.

"Shall I go with them?" he asked.

"No. It was wrong to summon us, wrong to open the Finished World. We won't have you now. You must stay here."

The whispers approved and vanished, like spring rain. Alone of the Finished People, Springmile remained.

"You," she said to Dorwin. "Don't let them forget who you are. You"—looking at Melwood—"look after this place. Try to leave it stronger than it is. It is in great danger. You." She smiled at Perry. "Remember how to come and go. Do you understand, roffle?" Perry nodded. "You"—she smiled at Cabbage—"I shall see again one day." Cabbage gripped the book.

Saving her last message for Flaxfield, she turned now to him. "You," she said. "You told the story of the beginning of magic, of the boy and the girl. You of all people should understand what has happened, and you've let your grief over the loss of your magic cloud your thoughts."

Flaxfield argued with her. "There's a beauty and a power in clouds as well," he said.

"There is," she agreed. "There is. But you have forgotten the girl. You have your boy and his friend. You've let Jackbones do all this. And all the time, you've left Flaxfold and the girl as though they were nothing. They are everything. If you want to defeat Slowin, look to the girl. If you want your magic back, look to the girl. One will bring the other."

Cabbage watched her turn and mount the stair. The green and blue of her dress threw out a cascade of color that splashed the walls and floor. He wanted her to stay. He wanted to go with her. He felt as though a part of himself had died when she disappeared from sight.

The colors remained as the scent of flowers remains after they have been taken from a room.

Jackbones broke the silence, dragging a chair across the floor. His gray face was no longer insubstantial. Cabbage couldn't see through him. As the blues and greens faded from sight, Jackbones regained his substance, but no color. He was white and gray and black, neither of Up Top nor the Finished World.

"She's right," said Flaxfield. "We must get back. The answer to this is with Bee, whoever she is."

It was a solemn return to the village. And a silent one, for the most part. The boys kept together. Dorwin and Flaxfield rode alone. Cabbage tried to explain what it had felt like to walk among the Finished People. Perry couldn't understand what he was saying, and in the end neither could Cabbage, so they stopped talking about it.

"We'll meet again when I've spoken to Bee," said Flaxfield, and left it at that. He didn't even ask to see the book that Cabbage had taken from the library.

"Why don't you come with me?" said Dorwin when they reached the village. The boys were glad of the invitation and went with her to the forge house. Flaxfield rode alone the rest of the way to the inn. By the time he reached it, the evening was drawing on, the light beginning to fade.

"She's at the river," said Flaxfold. "She's always there now."

It was evening. Bee was sitting on the riverbank, watching the fishermen. They paddled to shore, picked up their little boats, and put them over their heads, walking back home like mushrooms. She didn't hear Flaxfield until he sat down next to her. She had been crying. She drew the scarf tight to her face. He picked up a stone and threw it into the river.

"I can throw farther than you," he said.

She found a stone, smooth and flat and skimmed it farther than his. His next throw outdistanced hers.

"See?" he said.

She took another stone. It was heavy, rough, no good at all for skimming. Underneath, the soil clung to it, and where it had been lying, tiny creatures scuttled for safety, exposed to the light. She threw it, without really trying, but used magic to keep it above the water. It went far beyond his, splashed clumsily into the river, almost halfway across.

"Very good," he said.

"I win," said Bee.

"Ah, no. I win. I challenged you to a throwing match. I won that."

"I won the magic match," said Bee.

"There was no match. I have no magic. You have so much. What are you going to do with it?"

"Nothing."

"You need to be an apprentice," he said.

"Being an apprentice made me look like this." She drew the shawl aside and stared at him. "Being an apprentice made me hurt all the time. Using the magic makes the pain worse."

"I know."

"I don't want to be an apprentice. Not unless it can make me better. Can it?"

Flaxfield took another stone. A smooth, gray stone, slender stripes of deeper gray running through it, not quite oval, but almost. "How badly does it hurt now?" he asked.

"Very much."

He gave Bee the stone. "Show me," he said, "if you can just do tricks, or if you can be a wizard."

"I don't understand."

"Hold it. Stop thinking about anything. Just let the stone be itself."

Bee thought he was mad, but he was interesting. So she did it. She looked down into the stone. She stopped thinking about herself, the way she looked, the pain, the terrible things that had made her like this. And as she held the stone, it seemed to melt into her hands, and her hands seemed to melt into the stone. Then she stopped being herself at all and, for a moment, she was the stone. And stones feel no pain.

"How did you know?" she asked.

"Let's go to the inn," said Flaxfield. "There's work we need to do."

He helped her to her feet. She walked alongside him, a new purpose in her bearing. A new resolve.

Flaxfold smiled to see them approach. She set food before them and watched them eat in silence.

"Do we need the boys for this?" she asked when they were done.

"It's up to Bee," said Flaxfield. "What do you think?"

Cartford didn't interfere

while Dorwin fussed over the boys, fed them and offered to make up beds for them if they'd rather stay there than go to the inn later on.

"We'd better go back," said Cabbage. "Thanks anyway."

"What's the book?" asked Cartford when they were done.

"I don't think I should talk about it," said Cabbage.

"That's all right. You don't have to talk. Just show it to me."

"That's what I meant," said Cabbage. He blushed. "Sorry. It's private."

Cartford took the book from him. He was big and quick and used to getting his own way.

Cabbage, caught off guard, flashed a spell across the table. A wasp the size of an apple flew past Cartford's head, buzzing in anger, hanging by his face. Cabbage expected the blacksmith to jerk his head back and drop the book. He ignored it. He opened the book, turned to the title page.

"*Caves and Potholes and Mines*," he read aloud.

The wasp darted at him. Cartford ignored it.

"Is this supposed to be important?" he asked.

Cabbage was frustrated at the failure of the wasp. He flicked his fingers. The wasp settled on Cartford's head, still buzzing, wings whirring, the sting poised to strike.

"If that thing stings me, I'll die," said Cartford. "You know that, don't you?"

Cabbage grimaced. The wasp lifted off and drifted out of the window.

"Don't make a threat unless you mean it," said Cartford.

"Give me back the book," said Cabbage.

"*Caves and Potholes and Mines*," Cartford read again. "What's this for?"

"We'd better go back," said Cabbage, standing up. "Thank you for dinner." He held out his hand for the book.

"Give it back to him, Father," said Dorwin.

Cartford sat back, the book still firmly in his hand. "Remember what I said about magic?" he asked Cabbage.

"What?"

"Don't be sulky. You used to like coming here."

"You've got my book."

"What did I say about magic and the forge? Think hard, now. It may be important."

Cabbage cast his mind back. "You said that magic didn't belong in a blacksmith's, but you wouldn't tell me why."

"Come on. I'll tell you now."

Cabbage and Perry had no choice. They either had to follow him or lose the book. They followed. Dorwin kept close to them.

He strapped on his leather apron, pushing the book into his pocket. The forge was glowing, and it took only a few pumps of the bellows and some extra charcoal to bring it back to heat.

This achieved, Cartford thrust a length of iron into it. "Magic was made in the blacksmith's shop," he said. "Remember?"

"That's just a story," said Perry. "There are other stories."

"There are indeed, roffle. Many other stories. But this is the real one."

He took another iron bar and hit it against the anvil. The sound rang out. "Bend that," he said, handing it to the boys.

They didn't bother trying.

"No," he agreed. "A waste of time."

He drew the iron from the forge. It glowed white. He placed it on the anvil, struck it with his hammer. The iron curled around. He straightened it again. With pincers and a vice, he twisted it around and around till it looked like barley sugar sticks.

He plunged it into a bucket of water. The steam hissed up; the water bubbled.

"See how the fire alters it," he said. "See how the iron moves and bends. See how the water turns to steam."

His face was bright in the forge light. His brow wet with sweat.

"Magic does that," he said. "It heats and bends the world. It disturbs the water. It affects all that is around it. It makes changes. That's why it was born in a blacksmith's shop. That's why you don't bring magic in here. For a start, there's no need. For another thing, the forge doesn't like magic, and magic doesn't like the forge."

"We should go," said Cabbage. "They'll be wondering where we are."

Cartford put the iron back into the forge. "You don't see the connection, do you?" he said.

Perry raised his hand to draw attention. "I do," he said.

"Go on, then."

"The first magic was made with fire. Slowin made the new magic with fire."

"Fire out of control," said Cartford. "Wild magic from wild fire. That's right."

Cabbage grabbed Perry's arm. "And we could make something here, in the forge, to control the new magic," he said.

"Let's go back and look at that book," said Cartford.

"I'll send a message to the inn," said Dorwin. "They can sleep here tonight."

Mattie kept close to Ash. The clacking and ticking of the beetles made him jumpy. He knew they were talking to one another and he hated it. For all that Ash frightened him, she had a human voice. He would have liked to speak to her. As it was, if he wanted to hear her voice, he had to endure the half-human clatter of the Bakkmann creature or the slopping speech of the Smedge thing.

In this way, Mattie learned all about how they had come to be there, who they had once been, and what their plans were.

Slowin. This woman was Slowin. Bee hadn't said Slowin was a woman. In fact, Mattie thought she had said Slowin was a man. But he had been ill, in pain. He might have misunderstood. Then the woman was Ash, not Slowin. Sometimes he thought they talked about Bee. He couldn't be sure at first.

"She's dead," said Bakkmann. "Has to be dead."

"You would think so," said Ash. "I find it hard to believe that she survived as long as she did. If it weren't for our little slippery friend"—Ash motioned to Smedge, whose lips slapped a wet smile back—"I wouldn't believe anything was left of her."

"She escaped," Smedge slopped. "They took her." He lowered a sad head. "I want to go back. Want to eat her up from inside."

"Perhaps you will," said Ash. "Perhaps you will."

They didn't call her Bee, though. Sometimes he thought they called her Ember. Sometimes he thought they called her Flame. It was very confusing, and the noise of the beetles rang around in his head even when they weren't there. It made it hard to concentrate.

Ash was substantial now, a proper woman, not a ghost. He couldn't see through her at all. And Smedge had more or less stopped shifting from one shape to another. He was a boy most of the time, without the bits of weasel and dog. He could walk and talk properly, except for the slimy trail around his mouth and the slurping sounds. Even these were getting less.

Bakkmann didn't change at all. Bakkmann was mainly beetle, partly human, entirely terrible.

Mattie's food was filth. His nights were fear. His days were spent searching for a way out, hiding from the beetles, eavesdropping on Ash, hugging his misery close.

Sometimes the beetles dragged people into the castle, travelers who came unknowing, or people who lived in the isolated houses in the neighborhood. They brought them to Bakkmann and Smedge, as a cat will bring a bird to the cottage door. Bakkmann and Smedge played with them, as the cat would play, until they grew tired and threw them to the beetles.

When he first saw Frastfil on the horizon, he wanted to shout to him to keep away, run, save himself. He couldn't, of course. That would have led to his own capture. So he watched the wizard blink and grin his way up to the door of the castle. The beetles heard him approach. They cleared the courtyard so he wouldn't see them. They crouched at the side of the portcullis and waited for him to cross inside.

Mattie heard the coins jingle in Frastfil's pocket. The man stopped just outside.

"Hello," he called. "Anyone there?"

His face took on a puzzled look. There should be people, horses, soldiers, servants, hens, and dogs. There should be noise and movement. It was silent. Still. Too quiet. Too empty. Perhaps he would turn and walk away. Well, it was too late now. The beetles would dart out and run after him.

Frastfil stepped forward, into the courtyard. The beetles pounced. Frastfil jerked back. He shouted a single word and stamped his foot. The beetles bounced back. Frastfil smiled at them. Mattie wondered if he was half-witted, smiling like that. They pounced again. This time Frastfil was knocked off his feet by the force of the attack, but they still bounced off. He pulled himself to his feet and turned to run. From nowhere, it seemed, Bakkmann stepped in front of him and blocked his escape.

"Look here," she clacked. "A wizard, is it?"

"Yes," said Frastfil. He still wore the same silly grin, even facing this monstrous black form. "Let me pass."

"Don't you like it here?"

The beetles crouched, ready to spring again.

"I can't keep this spell going," Frastfil said. "Let me pass."

Mattie watched Bakkmann lead Frastfil inside. He thought that the creature would play with him and then feed him to the beetles, and he didn't want to watch. He slid into his tunnels and crept away. He climbed the turret to watch Ash, needing the sight of something that wasn't a beetle and wasn't going to torture a person. So he was surprised when Bakkmann pushed open the door, threw Frastfil into the room, and clattered, "Look what I found. A wizard."

When Flaxfield arrived the next morning,

Cabbage saw his old master looking more like himself. Cabbage wanted to run over to him and give him a hug, and that was odd because he didn't think he'd ever hugged him. It would just be such a relief to have him back as before and for everything to be all right again.

It didn't last long. It soon became clear that the night had not brought back his magic. It was something else that had changed.

They were a strange crew, assembled in the parlor of Cartford's house.

The blacksmith dominated physically. It wasn't just that he was the biggest—Flaxfield stood almost as tall—but that he had a strength to him from hours at the forge. Flaxfield almost dominated in another way. He had the calm authority of old magic, even though it had fled from him. Dorwin had the advantage of being the one who controlled the house, and that gave her an air of being in charge. The strange one was Flaxfold. This dumpy woman with her gray hair tied back in a neat bun and her lined face looked as though she could take on any of them and win and not even be out of breath.

Cabbage thought back over the last few weeks. What a beaten, bedraggled bunch they had been, cowering from the wild magic, afraid to cast the smallest spell, distrustful of anyone strange.

What had happened overnight?

And what of the three of them? Perry and Bee and himself? Three children caught in a grown-up war?

He relaxed and waited for one of the adults to call them to order, take charge and sort things out, forget about Slowin, get Flaxfield's magic back, and go home. It was time it got back to normal and he could be an apprentice again, with time to himself. With any luck, Perry would be able to stay for a while.

Nothing happened.

No one spoke.

Cabbage began to grow uncomfortable.

"What are we going to do?" he asked Flaxfield.

"We're waiting for you to start," said Flaxfold.

"What?"

He looked around the room again. They were in two clear groups. Dorwin, Cartford, Flaxfold, and Flaxfield in one. He and Perry and Bee in the other.

"We weren't thinking about it in the right way," said Flaxfield. "Remember what Springmile said?"

"It's about Bee," said Perry.

"And Cabbage and you," said Flaxfold. "So tell us, please. What are we going to do?"

"That's your job," Cabbage argued.

Flaxfield shook his head.

"You have magic," he said. "You, Bee, you made the new magic. And you, Perry, well, to tell the truth, I don't know why you're involved in this at all, but you are, so you'd better stay with them."

Perry grinned. He was the only one showing any pleasure in this.

Into the gap left after Flaxfield's words, Bee inserted a statement. "Two things survived the fire," she said. "You have one." She looked at Cabbage. "The indenture. I have the other." She opened her hand and revealed the seal. "These were the two things strong enough to withstand the wild magic. They are the key to defeating it. Or controlling it, at least."

The shawl around her face muffled her voice. They strained to make out what she was saying.

"I think we should use these to . . ."

"I can't understand," said Cabbage. "Sorry, but I can't hear you properly."

Bee faltered. The authority fell from her. She drew the shawl tighter to her.

"Cabbage," Dorwin rebuked him.

"I'm sorry," he said.

Bee's eyes picked him out. She held him in her gaze for longer than he liked. Much longer.

"I'm really sorry," he said.

Bee unwound the shawl, dropped it to her shoulders, stared at him, bare-faced.

Her voice was strong and her look unflinching. There was a newer, greater strength. "I have a face," she said. "I'll not hide it anymore. And I have a name that I don't know yet. When I find that, I'll be well again. Well enough." She smiled at Cabbage. "Thank you," she said.

Cabbage didn't know what to say or do.

"Please," she said. "They say you have a book. What does it say?"

"Nothing," said Cabbage. "It doesn't help at all. It's just about mines and caves and potholes."

"Places underground," said Bee. "Where Up Top brushes against the Deep World."

"Yes."

"Where the iron comes from," she said. "That made the mirror that made the magic."

"That's right."

Bee looked at Cartford. For a second she hesitated to turn her face to him. The moment passed, and she looked him in the eye. "Do you have iron, blacksmith?" she asked.

"Does a roffle sing stars and sideboards?" He smiled.

"Shall we see what iron can make?" she asked him.

Cabbage gasped and pointed to Cartford. "You're not Smoke-smith, are you?" he said.

Cartford laughed. "I'd be hundreds of years old, if I were," he said. "What a question. Flaxfield, do you take half-wits for apprentices these days?"

Cabbage made his lips a straight line.

Flaxfield gave him a reassuring look. "There's nothing of the fool about Cabbage," he said. "As you well know."

"Ah, well," said the blacksmith. "I suppose that's good to hear. What do you want me to make for you, Bee?"

"I don't know," she said. "Can we just go and see?"

"Now?"

"As good a time as any," said Flaxfield.

"I have iron and fire," said Cartford. "Come and see."

"I'll go back to the inn," said Flaxfold. "Will you come with me? Boys?"

"Can we stay here?"

Flaxfield went with them to the forge.

"Show me how you make something from iron," said Bee.

"A horseshoe?" asked Cartford. "Just for a start?"

"Come on," Perry whispered to Cabbage. "I've got an idea."

The boys slipped away unnoticed.

Bakkmann clattered an angry jet of abuse at Ash.

Frastfil, who couldn't understand what Bakkmann was jabbering, didn't even seem to be able to interpret the feelings behind the outburst. He smiled at the creature and jingled the coins in his pocket.

"I want to eat the fool and spit out his stupid money," Bakkmann clattered.

Frastfil just managed to make out the word *money* and he held up a sixpence.

"What's the fool doing?" said Bakkmann.

Ash put herself between Frastfil and Bakkmann to block the wizard's view of the creature.

"Put your money away, Frastfil," she said. "Everything is free here."

"It's so different," said Frastfil, "from how it was."

"Is it?" said Ash. "No, I don't think so."

Bakkmann spat a gout of black slime on the wall.

"I want to play with him now," she said. "I want to stroke him."

"Go," said Ash. "Enough."

Bakkmann slouched out.

"What rough beast is that?" said Frastfil when he was sure Bakkmann was out of hearing.

"Nothing's different," said Ash gently. "See."

She took his hand and led him to the high window.

Beneath them in the courtyard, beetles scurried through dung and blood.

"Look at the horses," said Ash.

"I thought . . ." said Frastfil.

"Yes?"

He shook his head.

"No. It's stupid. I can't say it."

"Come," she said. "You must be hungry."

"Did I tell you?" said Frastfil. "I used to come here once."

"You did," she assured him. "You told me. Your uncle."

She led him from the turret, down to the great hall. The floors of the passageways and chambers were slippery with slaughter, the walls greasy with slime.

"Do you remember these tapestries?" Ash asked him.

"They're beautiful," said Frastfil. He ran his hand along the damp bricks. His fingers were sticky with blood.

"Sit here. At the place of honor."

Ash guided him to the oak board at the high end of the hall. She motioned for takkabakks to join them. They sat around, clacking and stabbing, hardly able to keep from killing him. Ash introduced them as family members, courtiers, servants, visitors. She found the ragged hunk of meat and put it before him.

"Delicious," he said. "The kitchens here were always wonderful. Such delicate flavors."

"We try our best." She smiled. "For special guests. Now, tell me all about the college and what you do there. Who is the principal now?"

"It's a bad place," said Frastfil. "They don't appreciate me."

"Perhaps we can do something about that," said Ash. "Tell me everything."

Bee felt Cartford watch her hammer

the hot iron, bend it on the anvil, and flatten it with the hard downstrokes. He nodded. She seemed to be at one with the glowing metal. She moved between anvil and furnace, reheating and beating until the iron took the exact shape she was striving for. She looked at it, turning it over and over to check, then plunged it into the water trough, where it sizzled and spat.

She watched Dorwin fish it out, cold now and hard.

"You've never worked metal before?" asked Dorwin. "At Slowin's? In his experiments?"

Bee shook her head.

"It's in her nature," said Cartford.

"Fire and iron," said Flaxfield.

Bee had been absorbed in her work, forgetful of the others. Now that they were examining her work and talking about her, she grew uncomfortable. Her hand went to her shawl to pull it over her face. She checked the movement and stared at them, uncovered.

"It was easy," she said. "Sorry. I don't mean that. I'm not show-ing off."

"You're not," agreed Cartford. "You can just do it. Like being able to swim if someone throws you in the river. Some people can, others can't."

"No one swims the way she did that," said Dorwin. "Was it magic that did it?"

Flaxfield took the horseshoe from her.

"It was magic and it wasn't," he said. "Magic's in her. She is magic, the way some people are tall." He held up the iron shoe. "She is fire and she is iron."

Bee had placed another iron rod in the furnace. She took the tongs, turned it, shook off the cinders, looked at it. It was red, going yellow. Cartford gently applied the bellows, stoking up the heat. Bee looked again at the iron. It was white now, almost pain-ful to look at. She drew it out of the furnace with the tongs and laid it on the anvil. After three strokes with the hammer, she put her hand to the hot iron. "No!" shouted Dorwin.

Bee twisted the iron in her fingers, pinched it, and made a slim knot. The iron was cooling now, turning back to red, not hot enough, not soft enough to work. Bee thrust it back into the furnace.

"Let me see your hand," said Cartford.

There was no mark where Bee had touched the hot iron. No blister.

"That would have taken my fingers off," said Dorwin. "Melted them like butter."

"Could you do that before?" asked Flaxfield.

Bee thought about the question. "Fire never hurt me," she said. "Only the wild magic fire."

"Do you want to make something here?"

"Yes."

"Do you know what it is?"

"I think so. Yes. I know what it is. But I don't know what it's for."

"That will come later," said Cartford. "Let's make it and see."

"How long will it take to get to Boolat?" asked Cabbage.

"Four days if we walk," said Perry. "A day and a night if we take horses."

"Can you ride?" Cabbage asked.

Perry had been on a horse only twice, both times as a passenger. "It looks easy enough," he said.

"So does swallowing a sword when you see it at a fair. I wouldn't like to try it."

"We'd better walk, then," said Perry.

"Four days?" said Cabbage.

"We'd better take some food," said Perry. "You know how hungry you get."

It was a joke, but Cabbage didn't smile.

"We can't take four days. That's too long."

"We could share a horse."

"You know that's not what I mean," said Cabbage.

The road from Cartford's house went across the river and into the trees. Half a mile along it, there was a watermill and a mill-pond with ducks. They walked in silence until they were at the mill. Cabbage leaned on the fence and pulled at a long stem of grass. He rested Flaxfield's staff against the fence.

"By the time we get there, it will be too late," said Cabbage.

"I'm not allowed to take anyone into the Deep World."

"If you went alone, how long would it take to get there?"

"We could be there, or near to it by evening. I don't know all the ways."

"So I wouldn't be in the Deep World long?"

"I'm not allowed."

"I'm not allowed to tell you about magic and show you secret things, but I have. I'm not allowed to talk to you about spells and where magic came from. Am I?"

"You won't tell anyone?" said Perry.

Cabbage punched him on the arm. He jumped off the fence and grinned.

Perry punched him back and laughed. "I shouldn't," he said.

Cabbage's face was alight with pleasure. "We have to. Can we really?"

"Promise you won't tell?"

"Come on. Where's the roffle hole?"

"I can't."

Cabbage gripped Perry's arm. "If we don't find out what Bee's name is we're never going to get things right again, are we?"

The mill wheel was still, disconnected from its gears. It was cool by the mill race, the sound of the water like laughter. Perry stepped up to the wheel and disappeared. Cabbage followed and found himself bumping into a stone wall. The wheel rose over him, twice as tall as Flaxfield. Perry was nowhere. He stepped back and looked at exactly the spot where Perry had disappeared.

"Come on," shouted Perry. "Over here."

"I can't find it," said Cabbage.

Perry reappeared, just to his left.

"Here. Come on."

And he was gone again.

Cabbage looked for the entrance to the Deep World. There was nothing.

"Here."

A hand appeared. Cabbage took hold of it. It tugged him forward. He stepped between the huge mill wheel and the wall, and all of a sudden there was a gap, obvious now that he could see it, hidden before by some odd geometry. He walked through and followed Perry down a short tunnel to a door.

"This way," said the roffle.

Bee worked the white-hot iron

in her fingers like clay. She couldn't leave it alone. She heated one end of a rod in the furnace until it was soft enough to cut off with a pair of shears. Before it cooled and grew hard, she rolled it in her palms and shaped it, tugging and twisting, feeling the stretch and bend. It set quickly, and she needed to heat each piece several times to soften it as she formed her shapes.

Cartford acted as her assistant, stoking the furnace, working the bellows, providing fresh supplies of iron. He showed her which tools would help her to shape the soft iron.

Bee made a bird, squat, flat, and smooth. It was just like the clay birds on sale in the markets, simple, with no feathers or eyes.

She made a fish, twisted in movement, arched sides, flat tail, sharp fins. Using the bowl of a spoon, she imprinted scales.

She tried for a pig, but the legs wouldn't work and it looked more like a badger in the end.

With each piece, she grew more skillful, more adept. She learned how much the metal would tolerate, what its limits were.

"Come and eat," said Dorwin. "Rest."

"Later."

Bee knew that Dorwin was frightened. She had grown up near the forge. Her earliest lessons had been to treat it with respect. Seeing Bee tossing glowing balls of molten iron in her hands filled her with terror. Bee knew this and was sorry for her, but she couldn't stop. The iron filled her with joy. When she put it back into the furnace to reheat, she felt alone, deserted. As soon as she had it back in her hands, she breathed more steadily, lost her anxiety. Best of all, the hot iron took away the pain of the wild magic. While she was working the metal, the hurt was kept at a distance, too far away to damage her.

At last it was Cartford who made her stop. He waited till she plunged a frog into the water trough and he damped down the furnace.

"Enough," he said. "We all need to rest."

"Just one more," said Bee.

"No. Not now."

The pain flowed back into her.

Flaxfield lined up her iron shapes on the bench. Some of them were still wet from the trough, glistening, gray-black. The bird was quite dry. Flaxfield weighed it in his hands. A casual passerby, seeing it in the ground, could be forgiven for mistaking it for a smooth stone. It was only when you picked it up and regarded it that the artistry was apparent, the bird was revealed. The frog and the fish were more finished, more detailed; they carried the mark of the hand more clearly.

"Is this one special?" he asked.

Bee didn't answer.

"They're all special," said Dorwin.

Flaxfield cradled the bird. "They are," he agreed. "But one has meaning. One will be right."

"None of these," said Bee. "Not yet."

"What's this one?" asked Dorwin.

It was an early piece, perhaps the first. Like the bird, it was unformed, suggestive rather than complete.

"It's a head," said Bee.

"I can't see it," said Dorwin.

Bee took it. "It's there, though," she told her. "I'll come back to it."

"What sort of head?"

"Can we eat?" said Bee.

The daylight was bleeding away when Cabbage and Perry emerged from the Deep World.

"You won't tell, will you?" said Perry.

Cabbage breathed in the air Up Top. It seemed thin and tasteless to him now.

"I wouldn't know where to start," he said. "I don't know the words to use."

"Still," said Perry. "You won't try?"

"No. No, of course not. I promised."

They stood between light and darkness. Night rode toward them.

"How far are we from Boolat?" asked Cabbage.

"Let's see. It's in that direction. I can tell from the sun."

"There's a house over there. We could ask."

It stood away from the road, nearly a mile off.

Perry shook his head.

Cabbage laughed. "Roffles don't ask for directions," he teased.

"It's serious," said Perry. "We're not allowed to. People are supposed to think we never get lost."

"I'll ask," said Cabbage. "You wait outside."

They were still out of shouting distance when Perry stopped.

"You can come a bit nearer," said Cabbage.

"Wait. Look."

"What?"

"Sh."

In the fading light, Cabbage could see a man and a boy walking toward the house. They were nearly at the door when they stopped. The man put his hand on the boy's shoulder. They backed away slowly. The boy stepped forward again. The man pulled him back. They struggled. The man grabbed the boy and jerked him back, turned, and started to run.

"What's going on?" said Cabbage.

Swift black shapes darted out of the house and fell on the man and the boy. They were not out of shouting distance after all, and Cabbage held his breath while the boy screamed his life out. It was over quickly. More beetles crowded around, mobbing the corpses. Soon nothing was left, not even bones.

"They're huge," said Cabbage.

"They're not the biggest."

Their meal over, the beetles moved away.

"Oh no," said Perry. "There's a woman. Coming out of the house."

"They're driving her," said Cabbage. "Like a sheep."

The boys followed, keeping a distance, hoping not to be observed.

"Well, at least we know which way is Boolat," said Perry.

"What are they going to do with her?"

"Food for the others?" said Perry. "A prisoner? I don't know."

The light had gone before the turret of Boolat appeared. The woman made a last attempt to run as the gates of the castle opened before her. The beetles closed formation around her and she was driven inside.

"I feel sick," said Cabbage.

"Perhaps we should go back," said Perry. "Tell them what we saw. Tell them the beetles are scavenging, raiding, that they're on the attack."

"No. We've come to discover Bee's name. I'm not going back until we do."

"We can't go in there."

"We have to."

Perry sat down on the grass and looked at the castle. Cabbage looked up at the stars.

"Tell me," he said. "How do we get in there?"

. . .

Mattie followed Frastfil through the castle.

He listened to Bakkmann's demands, holding his breath in expectation that the creature would lunge at Frastfil and jab a sharp leg into him.

He wanted to help Frastfil, but he couldn't find himself liking the wizard. There was something smug and self-satisfied about him that made Mattie want to slap him. He wished he would stop jingling those coins. He couldn't stay close when they were in the corridors, so he ran ahead and waited for them in the great hall. When he saw Frastfil tuck into the ragged haunch of meat, he felt sick. When he saw him greet the beetles like friends, he thought he must be mad. At last he understood that Ash was a powerful wizard and held Frastfil in a strong spell. He was enthralled, unable to see what was really happening around him. He thought himself in the Boolat of old.

"I'd wipe that stupid smile off your face if I could show you where you really are," said Mattie.

He drew closer and listened as Frastfil told Ash about himself and the college, and he listened even more attentively as Ash gave Frastfil his orders.

"There may be a roffle way," said Perry.

A cloud straggled across the moon.

"What?" said Cabbage.

"You asked me how to get in there," said Perry. "There may be a roffle way."

"I was asking the stars," said Cabbage.

The boys looked at each other, embarrassed.

"Sorry," said Perry.

He waited for Cabbage to speak. Cabbage lifted his eyes to the sky again. The cloud ran on, leaving the moon clear. Cabbage studied the patterns of the stars. He fished in the pocket of his cloak and drew out a notebook.

"I'm never allowed to show you this," he said.

"I'll sit over there while you look," said Perry.

"No. Come on. You took me to the Deep World. Come and look."

Cabbage opened the book, thumbed through it, and found a page with neat diagrams of stars. He had joined some of them up into shapes with lines of black ink.

"See?" He pointed to the book and up to the sky. "That's the cart. Like a farm cart."

Perry looked from one to the other. He saw the pattern.

"These nine stars make the gallows. Over there."

Four for the noose, the other five for the frame. Perry recognized it.

"There's the staircase, the mouse, the hand, the hourglass."

Where once the sky had been a random sprinkle of lights, Perry now saw an arrangement of objects.

"Did you make this up?" he asked.

"It's not made up," said Cabbage. "It's how they are."

Perry blushed. "Sorry. I mean, did you discover the shapes?"

Cabbage felt as though he had stepped out of the house undressed. He closed the book and stuffed it back into his cloak.

"Everyone knows the shape," he said. "All wizards anyway."

"All of the shapes?"

"Most of them."

"What did the stars tell you? When you asked them how we can get in?"

"They said there may be a roffle way," said Cabbage.

"I told you that."

"Why did you say it?"

"I remembered what Springmile said in the library. She said, 'Remember how to come and go. Do you understand, roffle?' I just thought of it. I think she meant that there's a roffle way into the castle."

"Come on. Let's look for it."

Perry trotted toward the castle, skirting away from the gate.

"So are the stars are talking to you again?" he said.

Cabbage looked up at the blackness, pierced by tiny dots of light.

Flaxfield ate his meal quickly

and left the others still at the table. He stepped out into the night, enjoying the feeling of the soft darkness against his face.

He had never known what it was to not have magic. He looked up at the stars and could hear nothing. The patterns were still there, unchanged. Their eloquence had gone. They were as silent for him as for any other man. He didn't hear Dorwin close the door behind her, didn't hear her approach. The first he knew of her was when she slipped her arm through his.

"What's it like?" she said.

He breathed in the scents of evening. "Partly, it's a relief," he said.

"Really?"

"Partly."

Dorwin tightened her arm in his.

"It's a relief," said Flaxfield, "not to have the responsibility of magic, not to be able to do anything even if I want to. To be out of that world of working. To be free of that rough magic."

"And the other part?" she said.

"Oh, the other part. That's like a death."

Dorwin tried to get him to look at her. He kept his face turned up, his eyes on the black sky.

"Whose death?"

Flaxfield began to walk, and she kept alongside him. They passed between the house and the forge and through into Cartford's orchard.

"You're a clever thing," said Flaxfield.

"I know." Dorwin smiled. "You were my teacher."

"Sort of," he said. "Whenever I passed through."

"Are you going to answer the question?"

"It's like the death of the person I've loved most of all in the world," said Flaxfield. "It's like saying good-bye forever to my heart's prize."

They stopped under an apple tree. The fruit needed another month before it would be ripe for harvest.

"Do you remember your mother?" asked Flaxfield.

"Of course."

"You remember what it was like when she died?"

Dorwin nodded.

"It's that," said Flaxfield. "And more. Because it's as though I've died, too. It's my own death. Without magic, I'm not who I am."

"There's more to you than magic."

"Is there? I don't know. Magic has been the breath in my body, the blood in my veins."

"If it was that," she said, "you'd die without it. And you're still alive."

Flaxfield took his arm from hers and put his hands on her face. She flinched, put her hands on top of his.

"You're so cold," she said. "So cold."

"The sun has gone."

"But the air's still warm."

She took his hands from her face and stepped back. "Is it really you?" she said. "Really alive?"

"For the moment. No one else."

"What will happen if your magic doesn't come back?"

"Well," he said. "There's the relief of being without it, as well as the sense that it's a sort of death."

"What sort of death? Can anything bring the magic back?"

"I don't know. Slowin and Bee made a new thing, a new magic. Perhaps the old magic had to die to make room for it."

"Cabbage has still got his magic."

"He has. But he was there at the birth of the new. I wasn't. I am the old magic."

Dorwin stepped forward again and took his hands, putting them back on her cheeks.

"I'm going to get your magic back for you," she said.

"We'll do our best. It's all we can do."

They looked up at the stars through the shifting canopy of leaves.

· · ·

The library was dark and empty, just the way Jackbones liked it. He moved along the stacks like a ghost. There was something insubstantial about him now. He couldn't walk through walls, daylight didn't drive him away, yet he had the presence of a man who had more than half left this world.

The college was asleep. The building never slept. Buildings never do. It creaked and cracked, settling down as the late-summer warmth seeped out of it.

Jackbones descended the spiral stairs to the lower level. He paused to see who was invading his kingdom.

Melwood closed the door and looked around. Anyone else who wanted to find him would have called out. She knew better than that. She knew even a muted call in his library would annoy Jackbones. She chose a book, apparently at random, and sat down to read it. She and Jackbones were old colleagues. He knew she knew he was there. She knew that she could wait all night if he didn't want to see her, but that he would appear soon if he was willing to talk.

Jackbones smiled. When Melwood had first been appointed as principal there had been complaints. Not everyone thought that a woman should have the job. Jackbones had been her first ally in the college. He never showed his approval to her face and treated her in the same harsh, faintly hostile manner that he treated everyone else. She recognized this as a compliment, and she soon learned that he was fierce in her support behind her back. As far as she could tell, he thought that she was a nuisance, but only in the way that everyone who wanted to disturb his library was a nuisance,

360 / TOBY FORWARD

not because she was a woman. She could live with that. She might have been surprised to learn that he liked her and thought she was a good principal. All of that didn't mean that he thought it was a good thing that she had disturbed the calm and emptiness of his library late at night. The sooner he spoke to her, the sooner she would leave him at peace.

Turning the corner of the stair, he tried to take the smile from his face and found himself surprised that it stayed there, a sign of welcome and friendship.

She put down the book and smiled back. "Jackbones. I'm sorry to disturb you."

"Then don't do it," he said. "Go."

"Sit by me. Talk for a while."

"I'm busy."

"It will wait."

He lifted the chair so that it would not scrape against the floor and sat down.

"You did a brave thing," said Melwood.

He waved a dismissive hand.

"If you hadn't gone through with it, if you hadn't summoned Springmile, we should all be lost. She brought us the clues, the means to defeat the wild magic."

Jackbones shrugged.

"What will happen to you now?" asked Melwood.

"Happen? Nothing. I'm still the librarian here. No need to change that."

"I mean, what will happen now that you can never enter the Finished World?"

"Have you heard from Cabbage?" he asked.

"Not yet. It's still early days."

Jackbones took the book from her and studied the title. He put it next to him on the table, ready to replace it where it belonged.

"You liked him, didn't you?" she said.

"Liked him? Liked a boy? Liked someone making a fuss in my library?"

"I thought he belonged here," she said.

"Apprentices belong with their masters, not in a college. You know that."

"If Flaxfield doesn't get his magic back then Cabbage will need looking after. He'll need teaching."

"It's never been done. We don't take apprentices."

"There's always a first time." She stood up, took the book, and put it back where she had found it. "Anyway, I just wanted to ask, if he did come back here, would you be willing to teach him?"

"What? Why?"

"He couldn't be a normal pupil; that wouldn't work. He'd need a master of his own."

"He won't be back," said Jackbones, "so you can forget about it."

"I'll leave you in peace," said Melwood. "I just thought you ought to be able to think about it."

She closed the door quietly behind her. Jackbones sat for a long time in silence at the table.

Flaxfold's normally cheerful face

was grim.

"You look tired," said Dorwin.

Flaxfold shook her head. She sat at the kitchen table and poured herself water from the earthenware jug. Dorwin put bread, butter, and cheese in front of her without asking, and apples and a jar of pickles.

"Bad news?" said Cartford.

"Travelers," said Flaxfold. "It's been a busy night at the inn. Not many locals. A lot of people on the move. Frightened."

"The wild magic's gone now," said Dorwin. "Didn't you tell them that?"

"Wait," said Flaxfield. He took an armchair near to Cartford. The two men sat side by side, listening.

"A village to the north has been attacked," said Flaxfold. "And isolated houses. It was hard to get them to talk about it. They didn't expect me to believe the stories at first. When

I did, they couldn't stop. The news poured out of them. Beetles. All sorts. Some like dogs. Some the size of men. And they talked to each other in a clattering sound. *Takkabakk. Takkabakk.*"

"Slowin," said Cartford.

"He's gathering strength," said Flaxfield.

Bee gripped the iron shape in her hands till her knuckles were white and stared straight at Flaxfold.

"They kill some straightaway," said Flaxfold. "And they're rounding up others and taking them away."

"Men? Women?" asked Cartford.

"Both."

"What for?" he asked.

Flaxfold drank deeply. "I don't want to think what it may be," she said.

"We've got to stop him," said Dorwin.

"We're trying," said Flaxfield. "That's what we're doing. Bee? What do you think?"

"I don't know who I am," said Bee. She still gripped the iron shape. It hurt her hand, and she liked that because it stopped her thinking about the other pain.

She saw that Flaxfold didn't know what to say to her. At last the woman spoke.

"You're who you've always been," she said.

Bee put the shape down.

"That's the problem," said Bee. "I'm not the same person I was. And anyway, I don't know who I was before."

"No," said Dorwin. "Don't say that. However you've changed, there's part of you that's still the same."

Bee smiled, a patient smile that excused Dorwin for her failure to understand. She looked at them all. None of them understood. When Flaxfield spoke, she turned her face away. Of all of them, he was the one she liked least, trusted least. He had been kind to her at the river, but he had challenged her there as well. And in some way that she didn't understand, she felt that the disaster was his fault as much as Slowin's.

"She's right, though," he said.

Bee felt a shock of surprise run through her. Flaxfield was the last person she had expected to agree with her. He had been so distant, so bad-tempered. He hadn't seemed to listen to anyone else.

"Having an apprentice is like having a garden," said Flaxfield. "You have to look after it. You need to make sure the ground's right for the plant. Then there's protection from the worst weather. You have to weed out the harmful plants that will choke the crop. You have to allow room for things to grow. And it's no good planting parsnips and expecting roses to grow. Things are what they are. I've never had two apprentices the same. A good master will learn from the apprentice as well as teaching him. Look what happened to Bee. Slowin never taught her anything, gave her no room to be herself, never let her be a real person. She was just a magic mine for him. He dug out the ore and took it for himself. He hollowed her out, stole her very being. Instead of becoming more of who she is, she grew to be less and less. It's a wonder she survived at all to be a good, real person."

Bee couldn't take her eyes from him, and he kept his on her. He wasn't talking to the others; he was speaking to her.

"She doesn't know who she was the day the magic went wrong, and she doesn't know who she is since she was remade by the wild magic. She hasn't even got a name. What's a wizard without a name? Nothing. What's any person without a name? Eh?"

"Stop it," said Dorwin. "You're too hard on her. Stop it, Flaxfield."

"It's all right," Bee whispered. "He's right."

Flaxfield stared Dorwin down.

"I have got a name, though," said Bee. "It's Beatrice. I want to use it again, please."

The silence was agreement.

"And I want to find my own wizard name," she said. "The one I should have signed on the indenture."

"I'm afraid you can't do that," said Flaxfield.

"Why not?"

"Because he stole it from you. He signed it himself. It changed him, and it changed you and it's changed everything. You can't have it back."

Bee felt as though she were falling through the air from a high turret.

"I need a name," she said.

"You do," agreed Flaxfield. He stood up and put his hands on her shoulders. All at once the pain went, absolutely. For the first time since the fire, no, for the first time in months, she felt free of all pain.

"You'll have a name," he said. "If we can defeat Slowin. And to do that, we need you to finish what you've begun."

He took the lump of iron. When he lifted his hands from her shoulders, the pain trickled back.

"What is this?" he said.

She shrugged.

"What were you making?"

"I don't remember."

Beatrice couldn't work out how she felt about him. One moment he was the only person who understood her; the next moment he was interrogating her. One moment he taught her how to live with the pain; the next moment he challenged her to work on magic, not to hide away and protect herself from more pain. His hands on her shoulders made her able to be herself again. His hands on the iron dragged her into a world of confusion and doubt. She didn't know whether she loved him or hated him.

"Think," he said.

She reached her hand out for the iron.

"I really don't remember," she said, "but that's an eye."

"Where?"

She put her finger on a small bulge.

"All right. Go on."

"That's the mouth."

She put the iron close to her face to see it better. She rubbed it on her puckered cheek.

"There's something coming from the mouth," she said.

"Is it a person, an animal?" asked Flaxfield.

Beatrice slammed it on the table. "Come with me!" she shouted. "I'll show you what it is. All right? Will that make you shut up?"

"I'll take the boys back to the inn and leave you to it," said Flaxfold.

They stared at her.

"I thought they were with you," said Dorwin.

"Then where are they?" said Flaxfold.

This time Cabbage could see the roffle entrance as soon as Perry pointed it out to him. Spending time in the Deep World had given him a better eye for roffle work.

"What if the beetles see us?" he asked. "What if they've found the door on the other side, in the castle?"

"Then we're dead," said Perry.

Cabbage nodded.

"Do you want to turn back?" asked Perry.

"I'll go first."

"No. It's a roffle hole. Roffle in first."

Perry pushed through, and they were in darkness for a moment before the way turned and opened up and Deep World light spread up from beneath their feet.

"This doesn't actually go into the Deep World," explained Perry. "It's an Up Top Passage, but there are chinks in places, to guide us."

The way narrowed again. They slipped around a doorframe and found themselves in a dark passage. The little light was not from beneath them now; it came from faults in the mortar and sly slashes in the stonework that the builders had put in for their own assistance.

"No sign of beetles," said Perry, and Cabbage relaxed a little, not having thought until then that he was tense.

They were in the secret tunnels and passageways in the walls.

"Let's go up," said Cabbage. "Away from ground level."

"Left or right?"

"It doesn't matter."

Cabbage hated enclosed spaces. The passageway was narrow, low, and alternately damp and sticky or dry and spidery.

"Ugh," said Perry. "I hate being closed in."

"What if they know we're in here?" asked Cabbage. "What if they're waiting for us?" He stopped. "I'm going back," he said. "Come on."

Perry grabbed his arm. "What if they're following us?" he said.

"Don't say that," said Cabbage.

He was trembling. His hands were wet with sweat. The walls of the passageway were closing in on him, the ceiling lowering.

"All right," said Perry. "Stop it. All right."

Cabbage put his back to the wall and breathed deeply.

"Relax," said Perry. "We'd hear them, wouldn't we? They scratch and clatter."

Cabbage nodded. He let his hands fall to his sides. Small stars trickled from his fingertips and the tiny cat appeared and started licking them up. Cabbage smiled. The cat rubbed against his leg.

"I'm all right," said Cabbage. "Sorry. Panic. It's gone now."

The last of the stars dealt with, the cat walked into the wall and disappeared.

"Let's press on," said Cabbage.

Perry shook his head and put his finger to his lips. "There is something scratching," he whispered. "Listen."

"They'll have gone to find Slowin," said Cartford.

"What are you talking about?" said Dorwin.

"I saw them slink off," he said. "I knew they were up to something, and I thought about it and decided that's where they were going."

"Why didn't you stop them?" said Flaxfold.

"Not my business to stop them," he said. "Anyway, I thought they were right. Someone has to keep an eye on him. You're all too busy here."

"That's irresponsible," said Dorwin. "You should have told us earlier. We'll have to go after them."

"Never mind that," said Cartford. "I'm going to the forge with this girl here. We've got work to do, haven't we?"

Beatrice smiled at him.

He put a huge arm around her shoulders. "Bring that lump with you and let's see what you make of it now that you know where you're going."

"He's right," said Flaxfold. "One thing at a time. They've made a choice. I'm going to the inn. I'm packing food and supplies, getting the horses ready, and then I'm going to sleep. First thing tomorrow, I'm setting off to Boolat. There'll be horses for everyone who wants to come with me."

She went to Beatrice. "Whatever you're making," she said, "do it quickly. Then get some sleep. You've practiced enough. It's time to act."

Beatrice let Flaxfold hug her. She felt abandoned when the woman left. In such a short time, she had come to rely on her.

"I'm ready," she said.

Cartford added more charcoal and pumped the bellows. Bee placed the lump of iron in the heart of the fire. She didn't bother with tongs now, plunging her hand deep into the hottest part to retrieve it.

With small calipers and prongs, flat-edged shaping tools and curved curettes, she formed the soft iron into a finished shape. Again and again she heated it and worked it until it was perfect. She cooled it in the water trough to harden it and appraised her work. The others leaned over to see what she had made.

A dragon's head, mouth gaping, flames streaming out.

"It's a dragon," said Dorwin.

"Not just any dragon," said Flaxfield. "It's a Blue and Green, the best sort of dragon."

"Is it?" said Beatrice. "I've never seen a dragon. I'd love to."

"You shall," said Flaxfield.

"Is it a charm?" said Dorwin. "Or a neck pendant? What's it for?"

The neck of the dragon was rough and unfinished. Beatrice ran her finger over it. She put it back into the furnace.

"You're not going to melt it down?" said Dorwin. "It's finished."

Beatrice took the white-hot iron, turned it around in her hand, and squashed the unfinished end on the anvil. It made a perfect circle. When she picked it up to examine it, Beatrice was astonished to see that it had the shape of a bird engraved into it.

"I didn't do that," she said.

"You did," said Flaxfield. "You just didn't know you were doing it."

Beatrice put it to her lips. "I didn't choose to make a dragon," she said. "It just happened."

"Nothing just happens," said Flaxfield. "You didn't choose the dragon; the dragon chose you."

"It's a seal," said Dorwin.

"It is," said Flaxfield. "Of course it is. What else would it be? Cartford, have you got a length of leather? Like a bootlace?"

Cartford had most things in the forge, and it didn't take long to find some. Flaxfield threaded it through the curled iron flames and tied it around Beatrice's neck. She felt the same momentary cease in the pain as he knotted the leather and his hands brushed her neck; then it returned.

"Just for now," he said.

He stretched and yawned.

"I'm going to bed. I've got a long ride tomorrow."

Smedge sniffed in the corner,

which was damp with rat and green with mold. He licked it and rubbed his cheek against it. His sense of smell was very keen, a legacy of the dogs and weasels he had been in his journey to becoming more or less a boy. Behind and beyond the lovely aroma of urine and decay, he could smell something else, something unpleasant, yet interesting.

"Boy," he whispered.

He put his face close to the crevice in the stone and drew a deep breath.

"Boy."

His mouth twisted into a smile.

He scratched at the wall, seeking a way to dislodge a stone, to break through and look for the boy, if there was a boy.

He lay flat on the wet ground, pushed his face along the dirt, poked his nose as far as he could into the loose stonework, and drew in a deep breath.

"Boy."

In a frenzy of greed, he clawed at the stones.

"Listen," mouthed Perry. "Something's looking for us."

He put his head to the wall and pointed along the tunnel. "That way," he whispered.

The boys moved as quietly as they could away from the scratching. Perry put his hand in front of him to grope the way, fearful of bumping into the wall at a sudden turn.

Cabbage held one end of Flaxfield's staff and Perry held the other, making sure they didn't get separated.

"I could make a spell," he whispered. "Just a little light. Enough to see by."

"Anything that's here will see it," said Perry. "It will bring them to us."

Cabbage nodded, followed. "Are you sure the noise came from behind us?" he asked.

"I think so."

The tunnel grew tighter, lower. They had to stoop to move through it. Pace by pace, they were walking into a space too small for them. There was no room to turn, no chance to run back.

Perry slowed down. He stopped, listened. He moved forward a step, hand outstretched. Something nearby stank. He hesitated, braced himself, moved another step, and his hand touched not the wall, but something soft, irregular, damp. A face.

Beatrice loved the smell of the horses. The journey on horseback took less time than Perry had predicted. Dorwin, Flaxfield, and

Cartford were experienced riders, and they urged their horses on, stopping only briefly for food, water, and enough rest for the animals to get a second wind.

Beatrice rode with Cartford.

Flaxfold had not argued when Beatrice told her to stay at the inn.

"I want to come back here," said Beatrice. "And I want you to be safe to come back to."

So Flaxfold waved them off and waited.

Flaxfield spotted the first ruined house. The door was wrenched from its hinges. The walls were charred and scratched, the garden churned and wrecked. He pointed to it and made no comment. Though the takkabakks had left, Beatrice felt the shadow of their presence and it redoubled her pain. She almost cried out, disguising the noise as the effect of a jolt on Coaldstamp. Cartford tightened his grip on her and rode on.

The single house was followed by a cluster, shortly after by a hamlet, all destroyed. Isolated houses along the way looked the worst, the saddest, the most painful.

"We're getting closer," said Cartford. The last house they passed still had smoke curling from its windows.

They reined in and gathered into a circle.

"We'll be there in less than an hour," said Flaxfield. "Just before dark."

"And then what?" asked Dorwin. "Do we ride straight up to it and demand the boys?"

Beatrice made sure she got her answer in before anyone else. "I'll decide when we get there," she said. "And I want to ride ahead with Cartford now. I want to be the first to see it."

"You've got an idea?" asked Cartford.

"No, not at all," said Beatrice. "It's just that I was there when Slowin started this, so I think I'm the only one who can do anything now."

"You're right," he agreed. "But I'm not letting you out of my sight. As long as you understand that?"

Beatrice was seated in front of Cartford. She put her hand on Coaldstamp's neck. The horse's mane was lifted by wind and movement, and as she touched it, flames spread along its length. Coaldstamp faltered for a second. Beatrice left her hand on his neck and he settled, unhurt by the flames, untroubled.

"Do you think you could stop me?" she asked Cartford. "I'll do what I need to do."

Cartford made no reply. Coaldstamp clenched his teeth down onto his bit and twisted his head to one side. Beginning at the forelock, the flames trembled, diminished, and died.

Beatrice looked over her shoulder. "Did you do that? How?"

Cartford rode on. At last he answered. "I made that bit in my forge. I chose the iron. I fanned the flames. I shaped it and cooled it."

It was a while before Beatrice dared to ask her question. "Are you a wizard, too?"

"I'm a blacksmith," said Cartford. "Here we are."

He reined Coaldstamp in, and they looked down the slope to the ugly, squat shape of Boolat. Flaxfield and Dorwin drew alongside.

"I wouldn't have known it," said Flaxfield. "It's so changed."

"It's Boolat, right enough," said Cartford.

"You would know," said Flaxfield. "Well, Beatrice, we're here. Now what?"

"Wait," she said. "Let me look at it. Let me think."

Mattie jumped back and fell over. The tunnel had narrowed to a cramped passageway. Utter darkness ahead. He had heard something in his tunnels. He needed to know if the takkabakks had discovered his secret, breached his defense. Or if the Smedge creature had found a way in and was trespassing in his spaces. He thought he might be able to kill the Smedge, if he could bear to bring himself to touch him. Either way, he had to know. So he inched forward, heart racing, breath tight. And, without warning, the hand touched his face.

He shouted and scrambled back, clumsily, wedged in the tight space. Perry shouted out. Cabbage said, "Light," and the staff in their joined hands glowed. In its blue light, the three of them looked at one another.

Mattie recovered, stopped shuffling back, and stared at the other two. Perry steadied himself against the wall. Cabbage was the first to regain speech, now that he knew they were not facing a takkabakk. "What are you doing?" he demanded.

Mattie's voice shook. "I thought you were the slime boy," he said.

"What's that?" asked Cabbage.

"Follow me. Quietly."

Mattie couldn't turn around, so he backed up until the passageway grew wider.

Perry turned his head and mouthed, "He stinks."

Cabbage nodded and extinguished the light from the staff. They continued in silence until the way was wide enough to walk easily, two abreast. As the passage grew higher, the light returned, through crevices and gaps, and drafts of air, which relieved some of the stench coming from Mattie.

"We'll go to the bedroom floor," he said. "They don't go there much. It's too dry, too clean. They like filth." He held a hand out for them to stop, and he took his time looking through a gap, waiting and listening.

"It's clear," he said.

He pushed against a large stone, and the boys were astonished to see it swing silently away, making a door into a room.

"Come on. Don't close it behind you."

He sat on a bed, which had its own ceiling. If you lay down on it, you looked up at fields of golden wheat, a unicorn, and a girl. He patted the bed for them to sit next to him. Cabbage hesitated. Perry took a deep breath and joined Mattie, glaring at Cabbage to make him follow. Cabbage made a small spell to clear the air. Perry gave him a grateful smile, and the three of them sat in a row.

"I'm so glad to see you," said Mattie, "but you're in danger. How did you get here? And how do you know about the tunnels?"

"How does a hangman get a box of tadpoles?" said Perry.

Mattie blinked.

"He's a roffle," said Cabbage. "They know lots of secret places, and they all talk like that. Tell us what you're doing and then we'll tell our story."

Mattie began with the meeting with Bee on the hill outside Slowin's Yard.

"No? Really? You're Mattie?" Cabbage interrupted him.

"How do you know about me?"

So that led into Cabbage having to tell Mattie about Bee and the inn.

"You mean she's really burned? Was that because she swallowed the fire?" said Mattie.

"No." Cabbage banged his hand against his head in frustration. "She was in a sort of explosion of magic."

Perry raised his hands for silence. "Let Mattie tell his story," he said, "without anyone interrupting him; then you tell yours, and then I'll tell mine. Otherwise we'll never get anywhere."

Cabbage sat back with his elbows on the bed. "All right," he agreed. "But I'm hungry. Is there anything to eat?"

"Only rats," said Mattie.

"Tell your story," said Cabbage. "I'll be quiet."

And so they each told their stories.

"Where are your friends now?" asked Mattie.

"Miles away," said Cabbage. "They don't even know we're here."

"And Bee. Is she all right?"

Cabbage shook his head.

"We really need to know about that turret room," said Perry.

"Who's in charge here?" asked Cabbage. "And why are they attacking with the beetles?"

Mattie began to squirm, and he climbed down from the bed, paced the room, which was large enough for him to put a lot of distance between himself and the others. He went to the door and put his head to it, listening. He looked through the window. He came back, stood in front of them, leaned forward, and whispered, "They're going to kill people. They're going to kill your friend Flaxfield. They hate him."

"Why?" said Cabbage. "How?"

Spendrill watched Frastfil

cross the square in front of the college. He made a little spell to keep the wicket gate locked, just for his amusement. Frastfil rattled the handle, trying to get in. He leaned his shoulder against it. He grinned as though everything was just fine. He muttered a spell to force the gate open. Spendrill smiled and watched him through the porter's spy hole. Frastfil kicked the door, smiling all the time. He put his hands in his pockets and jingled his loose change. He lifted the knocker and rapped out a summons.

Spendrill hummed a little tune to himself. He was enjoying the game. He particularly enjoyed defeating Frastfil's magical attempts to force the gate.

"Is that all you've got?" he muttered. He shook his head.

"What's going on?"

Melwood stood at the hatch in the gatehouse.

"Good evening, Principal," he said, giving her a deferential smile.

"Don't try that innocent act with me," she said. "Who's outside?"

"Outside?" Spendrill cupped a hand behind his ear and listened. "Is there someone outside?"

Frastfil heard voices and he slammed the knocker against the door and shouted, "Let me in!"

"I think there is," said Spendrill. "Now that you mention it, I think there is."

"Then let him in," she said.

Spendrill looked downcast. "Are you sure?" he asked. "Really sure?"

Melwood turned and walked away quickly before she could burst into laughter and disgrace herself. "Let him in, Spendrill."

Spendrill released the spell and the gate opened, causing Frastfil to fall through.

"Oh dear, oh dear," said Spendrill. "Let me help you up, old chap. Dear, oh dear. Are you hurt?"

Frastfil staggered to his feet and wriggled out of Spendrill's grasp. "I'm fine. I'm absolutely fine."

He rubbed his shoulder and glared at the porter. "Why did you lock me out?"

"Were you trying to get in? I'm sorry. Were you, really? Oh dear. Well, the gate does seem to have been locked, but only a simple spell. Any wizard should have been able to spring it open."

Frastfil glared again. "Are you telling me you didn't hear me? Are you?"

"You know," said Spendrill. "It's a funny thing. Sometimes noise doesn't travel properly in the college. Have you noticed that? Still, you're here now."

Frastfil thought about asking him again if he had heard him and ignored him. Spendrill put his finger to his lips. Frastfil snorted and walked off.

Cabbage jumped off the bed and grabbed Mattie's arms. In his excitement, he forgot to keep the clean air spell going, and a swift waft of Mattie's stink overpowered him. He stepped back, coughing. Mattie blushed.

"I know," he said. "I know. I've lived in the tunnels and I've eaten rats, and there's no reason to wash and keep clean. I'm sorry."

Cabbage made the spell again. "It's all right. We'll get you out soon. But let me be sure. You say the gray woman is called Slowin?"

"Sometimes, but she doesn't like that. She says that she's called Ash now."

"Right, and the beetle thing is called Bakkmann?"

"That's right."

"This is the most important," said Cabbage. "You say that she's got another name. A secret name. A name no one is allowed to know?"

"Flame," said Mattie. "And it used to belong to someone else, and she stole it."

Cabbage jumped up and down with pleasure. "We've got it," he said. "We've got it."

Mattie grabbed him. "Stop. You're making noise. You'll bring them here."

"What about the slime boy?" said Perry.

"Yes," said Mattie. "There's him, and there was a wizard, a man, who came here, and Ash gave him a job and sent him away."

"Slime boy first," said Perry.

"He's not a boy at all," said Mattie. "He changes shape. His name is—"

The door crashed. Something outside was trying to break in. Mattie crouched down and curled himself into a ball on the floor. Cabbage watched the door strain against the lock and the hinges. The nails creaked. The timber bent. Between blows to the wood, the boys could hear clattering and clicking.

"Takkabakks," whispered Mattie. "They'll break through." He crawled away.

Perry ran across and lifted him to his feet.

"Come on," he said. "Show us the way out."

Cabbage grabbed Mattie's other arm and dragged him to the secret door.

"You know the passageways," he said. "You have to show us."

Mattie collapsed again. "It's too much," he said. "I can't do it anymore. I've had enough."

Cabbage saw that all of Mattie's courage and resourcefulness were used up. Spending time with him and Perry had reminded the boy of human contact and friendship, talk and touch.

"We'll get you out," he promised. "The roffle way. We'll take you with us. But hurry. Show us the right direction."

Mattie gathered his wits and tried to smile. He led them through the secret door and closed it behind him.

"What about the slime boy?" asked Perry. "What if he's in here?"

"Got to take the chance," said Cabbage. "Come on."

Mattie led them back a different way.

"Tell me as soon as you see a roffle way," said Cabbage. "One that will get us out of here."

The light outside had almost gone now, so Cabbage had to make the staff glow when they reached the lower levels.

"Here," said Perry. "There's a way here."

Mattie's face was set hard now. His panic had disappeared. "I'm sorry," he said. "About that, up in the room. I don't know what happened."

"It's all right," said Cabbage. "I was more frightened than you were."

Mattie gave him a grateful smile. "They haven't followed," he said. "There's no sound of them in the tunnel. They're not very bright. They forget quickly. It's how I've survived this long."

"Well, it's over now. We're going out," said Cabbage. "Show us the way, Perry."

Perry ducked to his left and disappeared. Cabbage stood aside for Mattie to follow. When Mattie couldn't find the gap to the roffle hole, Cabbage took his hand and led him. Cabbage was half in and half out. Mattie stumbled and came to a halt.

"Can't you see it? I've got your hand."

Mattie tried again. Again his way was blocked.

"I can see it now," he said. "I just can't pass through."

Perry hissed back at them, "What's going on? Hurry up."

"We can't," said Cabbage. "Mattie's stuck."

He stepped back and examined the entrance. He ran his hand around the edge.

"I couldn't get through the gate, either," said Mattie. "I tried, and the same thing happened."

Cabbage rapped the staff against the wall. The sides of the roffle hole glowed.

"It's sealed," he said. "The whole castle is."

"Why can you get out, then?"

Cabbage shrugged. "We got through to Slowin's Yard," he said. "Maybe there's something about us. Or perhaps Slowin or Ash or whatever she calls herself only made a spell to keep the people in who were here already. I don't know."

Mattie leaned against the wall. "Can you make a spell to break it?"

"I've tried. Just then. It's fixed fast."

"What shall we do?" asked Perry.

"Go," said Mattie. "You have to. I'll wait and see if you can come back for me."

Cabbage banged his fist against the wall.

"No," said Mattie. "Don't do anything to attract attention. I need these tunnels to be safe."

He stood upright.

"Go now. I'm going to find a bath, get clean and tidy, and be ready for when you come back for me. Go on."

"There has to be something," said Cabbage.

Mattie turned and walked away.

The stars looked down on them

and they looked down on the castle.

"Have you decided?" asked Cartford. "What we're going to do?"

Beatrice drew her scarf around her face so only her eyes were visible.

"I have," she said. "I have to see Slowin. I know he's in there. I can talk to him. He can't harm me."

"Of course he can," said Flaxfield. "I shan't allow it. You can't go there, even with us to protect you."

Beatrice put her finger to her lips, pressing the scarf to her face.

"Alone," she said. "I'm going alone."

"Out of the question."

The girl and the wizard confronted each other, glaring, voices raised, stubborn.

"Look," said Cartford.

Takkabakks streamed out of the gate of the castle. A river of black, swelling and spreading, searching. They ran first one way and then another, testing patches of wall, crawling up and dropping back down.

"Something's roused them," he said.

"They're hunting," said Dorwin.

"What for?"

"For them," said Cartford.

He pointed to the right-hand corner of the castle. Two small figures appeared from an aperture at a level with the top of the gate, Perry and Cabbage. They dropped to the ground, turning over to break their fall, stood, looked around, saw the army of beetles, and began to run up the hill.

As one, the beetles turned and raced toward them.

The boys were fast. The beetles were faster. The boys had a start on the shiny army of takkabakks; the beetles gained ground all the time.

Cabbage raised a staff high above his head and aimed a sheet of fire at them. They clacked and clattered and made swifter ground. When the flames died down, the beetles were nearer than ever.

"He's feeding them," said Beatrice. "They love fire. They're made from fire."

"So are you," said Flaxfield. "Can you stop them?"

The four of them ran down the hill toward the boys, arms waving, shouting threats and encouragement, urging them on. Cabbage summoned a wave of fire that burst up from the ground between him and the beetles. The rocks melted, the earth became a river of flame. The beetles ran through it, gaining strength and speed.

"No," said Beatrice. She killed the fire with a sweep of her arm. For a moment, as the ground and stones solidified, the beetles were trapped, their legs caught fast. A river of fire gushed down from the turret, softening the ground, strengthening the takkabakks. The boys had drawn away a little, but not enough.

"They won't make it," shouted Dorwin. "And neither will we. There's nowhere to run to."

They ran toward the boys as fast as they could without falling. The gap between them and the boys was bigger than the gap between the boys and the takkabakks. The beetles would overwhelm them first. Beatrice was shaking. She had lived with the small beetles for so long, with dread and disgust. Now she saw what the wild magic had achieved. It struck her like a hammer.

"Come on," shouted Cartford. He grabbed her arm and dragged her onward, toward the boys, toward the battle, toward the beetles. The force of his urging shocked her and drove her on with him.

"They're gaining ground," said Dorwin. "The boys are fast, good runners. They may make it to us in time."

As she spoke, Perry stumbled and fell. Cabbage stopped to drag him to his feet.

"Can't," said Perry. "I've twisted my ankle. You go."

Cabbage turned and faced the takkabakks, bearing down on them at speed, with vicious clacking and hissing. "I'm not leaving you again," he said. He brandished the staff, not knowing what to do with it, knowing that fire made them stronger.

"Go on!" shouted Perry. "Run."

Cabbage shook his head. He swept his arm in a circle all around them. Small stars tumbled from his fingertips and lay gleaming on the grass. He swept again, again. Stars tumbled out and heaped up.

The first of the takkabakks ran up to them, its legs flicking the line of stars. As soon as it made contact with them, it exploded, showering yellow slime in the air. The takkabakks reared back, regrouped, and poured forward. With each leg that touched a star, a takkabakk exploded. Nothing stopped them. They had no fear. No sense of self.

"More stars," said Perry. "More stars."

The explosions were breaching the wall of stars.

Try as he might, Cabbage couldn't keep making them. The takkabakks kept coming. "They can see we're losing," said Cabbage. "They won't stop."

He looked down, and a black cat rubbed against his legs, eyes bright and filled with fear.

He flung his arm out again, but he was almost spent. A few stars trickled out, not enough to fill up the breach in their defenses.

"We're finished," he said. He stood over Perry, his staff held out, ready to strike at the takkabakks with the last of his strength to defend his friend.

A hand banged him on the back. Flaxfield looked down at him.

It had been enough. The wall of stars had not held, but it had won them time.

Cartford's strong hand seized Perry, hauled him to his feet, and helped him stand. Dorwin put her arm around him and stood facing the onslaught. Beatrice looked at Cabbage, only her eyes visible.

"Hello," she said.

Cabbage tried to smile at her. She drew the scarf aside and let it fall to her shoulders. She turned her face to the advancing beetles, so close now that they could see their thousands of clustered eyes.

"Run or fight?" said Cartford.

"Fight," said Beatrice.

Cabbage looked over the tops of the takkabakks at the castle turret. Something in there was directing the army, informing them, controlling them. He took Beatrice's arm and directed her gaze.

"It's Slowin," she said.

"Can you stop him?" asked Cabbage.

Before Beatrice could gather her thoughts, a line of fire broke through the tree cover to their left. With a swiftness that shocked them all, a counterarmy of burning lanterns advanced toward the takkabakks, bouncing and swaying unevenly.

"What is it?" asked Dorwin.

The takkabakks paused, swerved, and deflected their attention from the group of Flaxfield and the others and moved toward the fire.

"It's memmonts," said Perry. "Hundreds of them."

Lanterns were lashed to the backs of the memmonts on a sort of harness. They leaped across the grass, agile, swift. The lanterns bobbed. The memmonts sprang forward. They spread out and ran toward the takkabakks.

Close behind them, pouring from the forest, roffles, with blazing torches. Cabbage could see their barrel-packs on their backs, their short legs driving them on helter-skelter toward the enemy.

"They'll be slaughtered," said Dorwin.

"Will they?" said Flaxfield.

The advance guard of the memmonts reached the front line of the takkabakks. The black beetles reared up, sharp-pronged proboscises poised to strike.

"Please, no," said Perry. "No."

The takkabakks lunged at the memmonts, stabbing out. And as their spikes struck, the takkabakks burst open. The roffles cheered and careered down at them. The memmonts ran through the ranks of takkabakks, jumping over them, lanterns banging against the black armored sides. As soon as the flame from a lantern touched a takkabakk, it exploded and died in a sticky mess of its own insides.

"But takkabakks love fire," said Beatrice. "What's happening?"

The roffles followed the memmonts. Thrust their torches at

the takkabakks and shielded their eyes from the filthy spume that burst out from them.

"Look at Slowin," said Beatrice.

The figure in the turret was too high for them to see clearly. At the window, where the woman had stood, there was a consuming blackness, as intense as moonlight, as cold as ash, as dead as dust.

The takkabakks retreated, scuttling back into the gates, pursued by the roffles. The memmonts showed them no mercy, leaping on them, bursting them, and leaping again. The roffles, more cautious, still advanced, stabbing their torches, ruthlessly driving them back into the castle.

"They've given up," said Cabbage. "I thought they'd keep coming till the last one was dead."

"I think they would," said Flaxfield. "If it was left to them. It's Slowin. He's called them back. He needs them for another fight, another day."

"It's over," said Cartford. "For now."

The memmonts, their task of disruption finished, wandered off aimlessly, grazing and sniffing the ground. The light from their lanterns was dying fast.

"Flaxfield, come on. We need help, before the roffle fire dies."

Flaxfield looked down at Megawhim. He put out his hand and the roffle shook it. "You saved us all," said Flaxfield.

Megawhim looked anxiously at Perry. "Are you hurt?"

Perry broke away from Dorwin and came to his father. "No. I'm fine."

Megawhim looked down. "We thought you needed help," he said.

Perry nodded. "Does a pig need a poultice on a pie tin?" he said. "Thank you."

Megawhim smiled, relieved. "We haven't got much time," he said. "Roffle light doesn't last Up Top."

"How did you know it would work?" asked Cabbage.

"We've fought with them in the villages. We learned it by chance. There's no magic in the Deep World, and their light comes from no sun. These creatures are not natural. They're freaks of magic, made from magic. Magic can't hurt them, but the roffle fire is deadly to them. You needed help, and it was all we could think of. But they'll come back when the light dies. We've been watching how they attack the villages. They won't stay in there for long."

"We should get away," said Perry.

Flaxfield took Beatrice by the hand. He reached out and took Cabbage's as well.

"Remember Springmile," he said to him. "Remember what she said. If we want to defeat Slowin, look to Beatrice. If I want my magic back, look to Beatrice. I want both of those, so let's see how we do it."

"Her name," said Cabbage. "The one Slowin stole. It's Flame."

"Flame," said Beatrice. "I love that."

"The one he gave her is Ember," said Flaxfield. "New fire can spring from ember."

"Then let it," said Beatrice. "Come on."

She led them to the very gate of the castle. The roffles stood aside to let them pass. The takkabakks squatted in a ragged army within the gates, glaring out at them.

She took the seal from around her neck. The dragon's head glinted in the starlight. The flames from its mouth shone with light from within.

"I need wax," she said, "or something, to seal the castle. What shall I do, Flaxfield?"

Flaxfield shook his head. "Springmile told me that you were the answer. You must decide."

Dorwin stepped forward. "She told me to remember who I am," she said. "I'm Cartford's daughter. I'm the blacksmith's daughter. I think this place needs to be sealed with fire and with iron."

"If you seal it," said Perry, "will Mattie ever get out?"

Beatrice stared at him. "Mattie? What do you mean?"

"He's in there. He's trapped."

"Mattie," called Beatrice. "Are you there?"

A small face appeared at the side of the portcullis, above the level of the takkabakks. He almost smiled at her.

"Come down," she called. "The takkabakks won't hurt you now. Please. Come to us."

Mattie moved forward and stopped. "I can't. It's already sealed this side."

They stared at each other.

"Look at you," he said.

"I know."

"You made me better and now look at you. I'm sorry."

Beatrice put her hand to him. "It's not your fault. It's something else that did this."

"I'm so sorry."

Megawhim tugged her sleeve.

"The light is dying. Do it quickly."

The takkabakks were pushing back at them, testing the effect of the fire. Perry held the last of the roffle torches, swinging it to and fro to keep them back. Its flame was already spluttering.

"Shall I see you again?" asked Beatrice.

"I want that," said Mattie.

"Then I shall," she said.

She lifted a hand, but he was gone, back into his passageways, back into hiding.

"Come back," she said.

Dorwin touched her.

"He's gone," she said. "Come away."

"No," said Beatrice. "We can't leave him."

"Mattie chose to go in there," said Flaxfield. "And now he's chosen for you to leave him there. Sometimes things choose us; we don't choose them. We have work to do. Perhaps he has work there."

"Here," said Cabbage. "You want something to seal?" He struck Flaxfield's staff against the portcullis and sheared off a pointed end. It fell to the ground with a clang that rang through the stones of the castle. He touched it with the end of the staff. It melted and pooled into a near circle. Before it could cool again, Beatrice took the seal and pressed it to the soft metal. When she took it away, it left the imprint of a bird.

"Flame," she called. "Fire changed you and fire binds you. This place is your limit. Yours and the creatures you brought here. Stay here forever."

She stepped back.

The roffles waited. The light from their torches was spent. Darkness defined them.

The takkabakks lunged at them, hurling themselves into the gateway. At the edge of the sealed mark, they fell back, injured and hissing in pain.

"They can't get through," said Flaxfield, "but it won't hold forever."

Beatrice stared at the place where Mattie's face had last been seen.

"Come on," said Dorwin, taking her arm. "Let's go home."

Beatrice nodded. She weighed the seal in her hand. Cold now, the light gone from the iron flames. She was shaking again. Her face was white beneath the scars. Her breathing was labored.

"I don't want this," she said. The words cost her more breath than she could spare. She turned aside, stepped away and, bending, her face down, vomited and coughed. She put her hand to her chest to control the pain. The seal dangled from its cord.

The others turned their faces away, to spare her. All except Cabbage, who put one hand on her shoulder and waited for her to recover. His own hand was unsteady. She felt the cost the spell had taken from him, too, and was comforted.

When she stood upright again, she almost managed a smile at him.

She held the seal out to Flaxfield. He put it around his neck.

"Whenever you want it back," he said. "It's yours."

"No. Keep it. Or pass it on. You decide. You'll know."

He slipped the seal inside his shirt.

"I want to see Flaxfold," she said.

"Soon," he said. "And we should get away from this place, but there are things to settle first."

The roffles were rounding up the memmonts and driving them back to the edge of the forest, to the roffle holes and home to the Deep World. All except Megawhim, who stayed close to Perry.

"Lead us up the hill," said Flaxfield. "We'll see your memmonts safely home."

The company assembled high on the hill, in the undergrowth that announced the forest. The last of the memmonts squeezed back into the roffle hole, and the only ones left from the Deep World were Perry and Megawhim.

"Well," said Megawhim, "I'll be saying good-bye."

"You'll stay one more day, won't you?" said Perry. "Please. I promised you a harvest pie. Stay and eat it with us at the inn."

"I don't know," he said. "I could, I suppose."

"And then we'll go home," said Perry.

"Both of us?"

"Of course." He clasped Cabbage's shoulder. "You've got work to get on with. And I can come and visit you, can't I?"

"Yes. Yes, please."

"And Cabbage can visit us, can't he?"

Megawhim started to argue. Perry looked at him steadily.

"Yes," said his father. "I'd like that. There's lots to show him."

"The inn, then," said Cartford. "And harvest pies."

In the turret room, Ash flung herself on the floor and clawed her fingers into the stone slabs. The pain was a relief from the fury that was devouring her.

"Flaxfield!" she howled. "Always Flaxfield."

She recovered herself enough to run down to the keep, pushing through the hunched takkabakks. She propelled herself at the gate, only to be flung back by the sealing spell.

She grabbed the leg of the nearest takkabakk, ripped it off, and launched herself at the creature, snapping legs, wrenching slabs of shell, breaking it open like an egg. She hurled it aside, half-dead, and ran again at the gate.

Bakkmann watched her mad rage and clacked away, to wait.

One creature alone escaped the castle. A slow slide of slime slipped from a gap in the stonework. It pooled at the foot of the wall, shuddered, rose up, and formed itself almost into a boy. Smedge watched the victorious gathering at the rim, the wizard and the boy, the roffle and his son, the woman, the big man. And the girl. Smedge lost form and flickered through weasel and slug, fox and toad. He regained almost the shape of a boy, the mouth the last to conform.

"I'll find you," he slopped.

He returned to slime and slid back into the castle, to look for Ash.

The harvest feast made Cabbage

tingle with joy. He felt the hairs on his arms rise up and the hair on the nape of his neck prickle with pleasure.

Everyone he loved was in this room.

And the food.

He had never seen such food.

Never tasted such food.

When he looked back at that night, his delight at what had been prepared and presented was always blighted by a small, silly regret that he had not been able to eat everything that was available. Not that he wanted all of everything. He couldn't even eat a little of everything. He reached his limit long before he had tasted the roast ham hock or the pressed ox tongue. Sometimes, when he conjured up the feast in his memory, the chicken and bacon pie that he had been saving till last came to haunt him. He left it too late. By the time he went to get a portion, he couldn't eat another thing.

Cartford managed to eat more than he thought a human being could find room for. He was astonished at how much food a roffle managed to put away. Perry served Megawhim a huge portion of the pie, "Just as I promised," he said. Perry sat on his recovered barrel-pack. Even Dorwin had a good appetite. Flaxfold didn't seem to eat anything, but she had overseen all of the preparation, and Cabbage decided that not a little magic had gone into the work.

Beatrice made only a small repast, though she enjoyed what she had.

Flaxfield ignored everything set out on the tables, and Flaxfold brought him a trout, pan-fried in butter, with toasted almonds on top. His own meal at a harvest feast.

Beatrice, Perry, and Cabbage sat apart from the others. Beatrice was silent for the most part, while Perry and Cabbage jabbered on excitedly, recalling the battle with the takkabakks. She listened, weighing their memories.

"You kept them away with the torch," said Cabbage.

"You broke off that iron spike," said Perry.

"It was Flaxfield, though," said Bee. "It was the power of Flaxfield through his staff that did it."

"No," said Cabbage. "It was you. It's you that all this is about. Springmile told us that, and she's right."

Perry chewed and swallowed politely before he added, "Cabbage is right. You knew what to do. And it was your magic through Flaxfield's staff that did it in the end."

"How was that?" asked Cabbage.

"Because she was bound to Slowin," said Flaxfield, who had appeared at their table with Flaxfold by his side.

"Some more?" she said, her arms full of dishes of food.

The boys looked on with appreciation as she spooned meat and gravy onto their plates. Beatrice raised a hand to indicate that she had had enough.

"Some greens?" asked Flaxfold.

Perry watched her serve him some cabbage.

"Not for me, thanks. It gives me wind," said his friend.

Perry looked up from his plate. Flaxfield winked at him. Cabbage blushed and changed the subject.

"What do you mean, bound to him?" he asked.

Flaxfold moved away. Flaxfield drew up a chair and joined them.

"They were made together, Ash and Beatrice," he said. "Made by the wild magic. Made by Slowin's great theft of her name."

He moved aside to make room for Dorwin. Beatrice let the newcomer slip her hand on hers. She counted the people at the table. Five of them. A woman. A wizard. An apprentice. A roffle. And her. A nothing. Taken from home, no longer an ordinary girl. Indentured to a thief and immediately sundered from him. Not an apprentice. Not a wizard. A nothing.

"What will happen now?" she asked.

"It's a hard truth," said Flaxfield. "But it must be told."

"Tell it quickly, then," she said.

Flaxfield smiled at her. "You're the strongest of all of us," he said. "You want to face the worst without delay."

"I face my face every day," she said. "If I can live with that, I can face anything. What happens next?"

"We part. Perhaps forever. Perhaps to meet again someday. I don't know."

"I'm going to see Perry again," said Cabbage.

Beatrice held up her hand for silence. "Go on," she said.

"Slowin, or Ash, or whatever, he or she, or whatever, is locked away safely for now. It won't always be so. She'll look for ways to escape. She'll try to get revenge. The magic will decay. It will weaken. There will be a time when we have to defeat her. Until then, the way to keep the magic strong is never to talk about it. Not even to one another. Keeping Boolat in mind will feed it. If we meet, we shall remember. So we must not meet. As far as possible, we should even try to forget it, not even let it live in our minds.

"Dorwin will stay here," said Flaxfield, "looking after the forge. Perry, tomorrow you go home, with your father. Yes?"

"Yes," said Perry.

"That leaves us three," said Flaxfield.

Cabbage put down his knife and crust of bread. "What can you do now?" he asked.

"See," said Flaxfield.

He held his hand outstretched over the table, dipped his finger in a beaker of water, traced a shape on the tabletop. A star. Holding his hand a little higher, he closed his eyes. Small stars dribbled from his fingertips, drifting like snow, settling on the table.

Beatrice caught a glimpse of a garden and a cottage, snow-flakes becoming flames, her father returning from the fields. These stars were already alight. Flaxfield opened his eyes. When he saw the stars, he laughed.

"It works," he said. "See?"

"You can't leave them there," said Cabbage.

"I can't get rid of them," said Flaxfield.

Cabbage clicked his fingers. A tiny cat, the size of a mouse, scrambled over the rim of the table, ran across to the stars, and licked them up. Beatrice wished she could scoop her up in her hands and put her to her face. The stars gone, the cat licked her paws, looked at the faces around the table, ran to her left, jumped off, and vanished.

Beatrice looked from Flaxfield to Cabbage and back again. "Is that it?" she asked.

"More or less," Flaxfield admitted. "It's a start."

She looked at Cabbage. "It's not enough," she said.

A fiddle struck up at the other side of the room. With a scrape and a clatter, the villagers pushed the tables and chairs aside. Cartford came and took Dorwin by the hand and led her away to start the dancing.

"I told you once that magic would kill the village if it was used to collect the harvest, and you asked me why," said Flaxfield.

"That's right," said Perry.

"Do you know the answer?"

"Because if they didn't work for the harvest, they wouldn't have tonight," said Perry.

"And if they didn't have tonight, there wouldn't be a village," said Flaxfield. "Just people in their own houses."

They sat and watched the villagers, red-faced from sun and work and food, broad-smiled from success and safety and music, their feet moving to the fiddle and drum.

"It's time we left," said Flaxfield. "We don't belong here."

Megawhim detached himself from a large mug of cider and came over to them.

"We'll be going, then," he said.

"Thank you," said Flaxfield. "Without you and your roffles, we'd all be dead."

Megawhim shook his hand.

Perry and Cabbage shook hands. The roffles hauled their barrels onto their backs. Beatrice stepped back before anyone could try to say good-bye to her.

"I'm going upstairs," she said.

She paused at the door to the corridor and watched the two roffles leave. She saw that Dorwin noticed them go, saw her sadness. She used just a little magic to eavesdrop. A forbidden skill, but one she felt she had a right to use just this once.

"What do you want to do?" asked Flaxfield.

"I'm your apprentice. I want to stay with you."

"The little magic I have is not enough for that. We would be like Slowin and Beatrice. I would steal magic from you, not teach you. I can never allow that."

"What else can we do?"

"What do you want?"

Cabbage looked at the dancers, the inn parlor, the bright glass and soft oak. "I want to ask the stars," he said.

Flaxfield opened the door. The last Beatrice saw of them was as silhouettes in the doorway framed against the starry night.

She climbed the stairs to her room, with its cracked, uneven ceiling, and sat at the window looking out at the night. The seal from the yard was on the table. She picked it up and felt its weight. A knock at the door disturbed her.

"Yes? Come in."

Flaxfold brought her a small cup with her potion against the pain. "Would you like this?"

Beatrice smiled and nodded. She drank the draft gratefully.

"It never goes away," she said.

"No."

Beatrice gestured to Flaxfold to sit.

"They've all gone," said the woman.

"I watched them leave."

"What will you do?"

"I'm sorry I spoke to you as I did," she said. "May I stay?"

"Yes, please."

"I don't have a name. Not a real one. Mine was stolen."

"What would you like to be called?"

Beatrice thought this through.

"What sort of name would you like?"

"Not Beatrice. I think she died when she left home. And not Bee. She died when the fire came. I won't be Ember; that's Slowin's name. I can't be Flame. He stole that."

"So you need an everyday name?"

"Yes."

"Choose anything you like."

The girl thought again. "I want a name that will help stop the pain," she said. "Flaxfield showed me how to use the stones to help it. I do that sometimes. And when I do, I think of the stones in the winter. I think they store up the cold the way they store heat in a fire. I think of a stone, lying under the snow, taking winter into itself. And it helps to cool the pain inside."

"A stone name, then?"

"Not that."

Beatrice took Flaxfold's hand. "Names are given, not chosen," she said. "Please, can you give me a name?"

Flaxfold squeezed her hand gently. "December," she said. "It's a winter name, with all the joy of winter as well as the cold. It's not dead like a stone. It's the end of the year and its beginning."

"December," said the girl. "I love it. Thank you."

After her quick smile, her face grew sad.

"What is it?"

"I had the other name," said December. "The name that would have made me a wizard. Slowin stole that forever. I'll never be a wizard now."

"You told me that you didn't want magic in your life anymore."

"I'm sorry. I was unhappy. Of course I wanted it. I still do."

Flaxfold smiled and let go of her hand. She opened the little cupboard near to the bed and took out a pen and ink and a sheet of paper. It was just like the one Slowin had shown her.

"Read this," she said. "Carefully."

"I don't want to be Flaxfield's apprentice," said December. "And even if I did, his magic has gone."

"Ah, it's gone for now. But it's coming back. But, no, not his apprentice. Do you agree to the contract, though, if the person was the right person?"

"Yes."

Flaxfold took the paper, uncorked the ink, dipped the pen, and signed it, with two names, as Slowin had done. She pushed it across the table to December.

"If you like," she said. "You can sign this here and here. You put December on this line, and underneath you write, Fireborn."

December looked at the indenture and looked at Flaxfold. The dumpy, gray-haired woman with crinkled lips and eyes looked steadily back at her.

"It's real, isn't it?" said December.

"Oh, it's real," said Flaxfold.

December took the pen and signed.

Cabbage and Flaxfield walked alone

through the corridors of the college.

The library door was closed, as usual. Cabbage wondered whether they should knock or go straight in. Flaxfield put his hand to it and thought again.

"You try it," he said. "It's a game Jackbones plays. If he doesn't want you to come in, there'll be a spell, and he'll keep you waiting. See what happens."

Cabbage took the door handle, twisted it, and the door moved open. Flaxfield nodded. They went through.

Once again, there was something about the quality of the silence that Cabbage felt was welcoming him. It made him want to be silent in return. It was everywhere in the college but no more so than here, among these rows of books. He looked for Jackbones.

Ever since the day they had conjured up the hidden readers in the library with the Finishing, Jackbones found himself looking ever more and more up to the galleries. It was as though he were expecting to see someone there. Whenever he lifted his eyes from his work, he let them keep moving up, scrutinizing the rows of iron. They were always empty.

So it took Cabbage by surprise when the librarian looked up at him and smiled. Not the predatory grin he usually gave, but a proper smile, as of pleasure.

"How did you get on?" he asked, pushing a chair to him.

"We can't talk about it," said Flaxfield.

"You old crow," said Jackbones. "Leave him here with me for the afternoon. I'll soon get it out of him."

"In your library?" said Flaxfield. "Wouldn't that be a nuisance?"

Cabbage looked at these two men. He saw something similar in them. Something gentle covered in a harsh shell. Jackbones had more of a shell than Flaxfield, seemed less disposed to pleasure. Flaxfield, though, was not the person Cabbage had always known. The wild magic had made him angry somehow, more concerned with his own troubles than he had been.

And Jackbones. Since the Finishing, Jackbones had lost some of his sharpness, his bite. They were, Cabbage thought, two edges of the same sword.

"I could put up with him for a while," said Jackbones.

This was the moment the stars had told him about. This was the conversation Cabbage wanted and dreaded. This was when his life would be plotted.

"How long?" asked Flaxfield.

The door opened and closed quietly, and Melwood was with them. "We've been expecting you," she said.

Before he could stop himself or reflect on what he was doing, Cabbage moved away from Flaxfield to take her hand, offered in welcome. The old wizard lowered his head.

"He needs a master," said Flaxfield. "I'm like a house that's burned out. The walls are still sound, and the roof hasn't fallen in, but there's nothing inside."

"Can you rebuild it?" she asked.

"Who knows?"

"In the meantime," she said, "there's Cabbage."

"Will you take him?"

Jackbones leaned his chair back beyond the tipping point, letting it hover. He looked up at the gallery, keeping his eyes away from Flaxfield.

"Do you want to be with us?" Melwood asked Cabbage.

"I want to be a wizard," he said. "I want to stay as Flaxfield's apprentice. I don't want to get in his way. He has to find his magic again, and I'd stop him. The first time I walked into the college, I felt as though I were coming to a place that I knew, that I wanted to be in. I want to be with Flaxfield. I want to be here. I can't do both."

Melwood walked along the bookcase, brushing her fingers on the spines. "You can't be a pupil here," she said. "You would never fit in. We can enroll you, but you won't go to classes. You would have to be taught on your own."

"It's the only way he knows," said Flaxfield.

"Hush. This is not your concern," she said. "Will you come here?" she asked Cabbage. "There is work for you here, as well as learning."

Cabbage looked at the three faces. His gaze lingered longest on Flaxfield. "I will," he said. "If Jackbones asks me to."

The chair swung back to upright. "It's not for me to ask," he said. "I don't ask pupils to come here."

"Jackbones," said Melwood. "Remember our talk."

He grimaced. "I need someone to take over the library," he said. "One day. I could teach you, if you want."

"Jackbones," she repeated.

He sighed.

"I'd like you here," he said. "Melwood can look after your training, and I'll show you the library."

Cabbage shook his head. "No. If I stay here, you'll take over from Flaxfield. It's the only way."

Flaxfield's voice was uncertain as he asked, "What do you say, Jackbones? Will you be his master?" He took Cabbage's indenture from his cloak and spread it on the table. "We can tear this up. I'll release him from his contract. You sign a new one." He cleared his throat and could not meet Cabbage's eyes. Cabbage felt his own eyes grow damp.

Jackbones pushed Flaxfield's hand away. He examined the paper. "This is clumsily done," he said. "Look at all this space here, beneath the names. Do you always draw up an indenture like this?"

"It's elegant," said Flaxfield. "Not your cramped, librarian card."

"Are you sure you want this?" Jackbones asked Cabbage.

"Yes."

"Speak up."

"Yes."

"Then we'll do it like this," he said. Taking a pen, he signed his name beneath Flaxfield's. "We won't tear it up. And we won't cross anything out. I'm doing it, but I'm not doing it alone." He brandished the paper and shook it under Flaxfield's nose. "See, you old crow. Your name's still on here. You're still responsible. Understand?"

Flaxfield nodded.

"And you'd better come back here often to take your share. Is that clear?"

Flaxfield put out his hand to Jackbones. The librarian refused it, and Flaxfield had to take his arm.

"Thank you," he said. "Thank you. Cabbage, come here."

Cabbage came and put his own hand on Jackbones's arm so that his hand and Flaxfield's were joined in grasping the librarian.

"Thank you," said Cabbage.

"Oh, just get on, will you? Flaxfield, you'd better clear off and find out how to get some magic back. Cabbage, you'd better start sorting out some books. I've got a lot to do if I'm going to have to take you on."

Melwood prodded his shoulder. "Stop showing off," she said. "You're pleased as poppy seed. Now, haven't you got something in your private room you can offer us to drink?"

"Pleased?" said Jackbones. "I'd be more pleased if I could just sort out this library and stop having all these interruptions. As you mention it, though, there is something in my room I could give you if you'd all like that."

"Another time," said Flaxfield. "You were right. It's time I was off."

Cabbage felt his hands start to shake. His throat was hurting. "Flaxfield," he said.

The wizard held up his hand for silence. "Jackbones is right. The sooner I leave, the sooner I'll come back to see how you are."

Cabbage bit his lip. "Perhaps I should go with you," he said. "The magic might come back quickly now."

"There's one other thing," said Melwood. "Cabbage is not a dignified name. We'll have to call you something else. What's your real name?"

"As we are all his masters now," said Flaxfield, "there's no hurt in knowing. Jackbones knows already, from the indenture. His name in magic is Waterburn. His public name is Vengeabil."

"Vengeabil it is, then," she said.

"Come on, Vengeabil," said Jackbones. "Help me to find something to drink."

Vengeabil started to go into the librarian's room to help him, stopped, and turned to say a proper good-bye to Flaxfield. The library door closed, and he was gone.

Melwood slipped her hand into his. "I'm glad you're back," she said. "The trouble I told you about, the ripples of the wild magic, we'll need you to deal with them."

"How will I do that?" he asked.

"It will be a long job."

"Here you are," said Jackbones. "Drink up. Good health."

Vengeabil raised his glass, looked at the closed door, and drank.

THE END

Envoi

"Where did magic come from?" she asked.

"Oh," said the man. "There are lots of stories about that."

"Tell me the best one."

"There's Smokesmith."

"What's that about?"

"A blacksmith."

"Is there another one?"

"There's one about a little girl."

"Tell me that one."

A man was growing old. He lost his teeth, his hair, his mind. He thought he could escape death. He thought he could grow young and strong again.

He lived all alone in a dirty yard, with only a half-mad helper to look after him.

One day, his last tooth fell out and he couldn't eat anything but bread soaked in milk. He was at the point of turning his face to the wall and surrendering to death when a beetle crawled over his hand. He seized it, squeezed it, ate it. He liked the taste, and he liked the wet stickiness, so he looked for another. He got his servant to catch them in the yard and bring them to him.

All day he ate them, throwing away the husks.

He felt stronger. He got up and decided not to die today.

When evening came, he sat by the fire. He always sat very close to the fire because he was always cold. He threw an empty beetle case into the fire and it flared up, melted, reshaped itself, and scuttled out again.

He picked it up, popped it into his mouth like a hot chestnut, and ate it.

He threw the shell back into the fire and out it ran again, a new beetle. He ate this one as well and threw it back. And so he spent the evening before he went to bed.

The next day, he had two teeth, one at the top and one at the bottom so he could bite.

Now he set about eating the beetles as fast as he could. He crunched them up, threw them into the fire, caught them as they ran out, and ate them again.

The next day he had seven teeth and his hair had begun to grow back.

"I thought you said it was about a little girl."

"I'm coming to that."

"Can you do it soon?"

"All right, well, to cut the story short, after a while the beetles stopped nourishing him and he started to eat slugs and frogs and weasels and things."

"Ugh."

"Yes, ugh."

"When does the little girl come into it, and the magic?"

"Shall I continue?"

"Yes."

By eating the living beetles, the man had broken into the sealed life of an animal. He had released something new. It was the first trickle of magic ever seen. And so he ate all the other animals alive as well. The bigger the animal, the greater the magic that he released. And when he swallowed the animal, he swallowed its magic.

Every time he ate a bigger, more complicated animal, he grew younger and stronger.

But the magic wore off as soon as he stopped eating them. After just a few days, he would grow old again very quickly and the magic would dribble away.

The servant had watched all this and she tried eating the beetles, too. She liked them so much that she never bothered to eat anything else, and, little by little, she turned into a beetle herself.

Every day was a contest with death. If he stopped eating

living things, he aged so quickly that he knew he would be dead by morning. It was a race to survive.

And so he made a plan.

He killed a dog, and as soon as it died, he threw it into the fire. The dog blazed up, barked, and ran out again and out of the yard before the servant could catch it.

"I don't like this story. And there's still no little girl."

"She's just about to come into the story."

"I don't want her to now."

"It's too late. Here she comes."

So he captured a little girl, killed her, took her to the yard, and threw her into the fire.

The sky split open. Magic rained down from the stars and drenched everybody in the yard, the old man, the girl, the servant, the beetles.

As the old man had expected, the girl came straight back to life in the fire. Only she couldn't run out. He lunged forward to pull her clear, so that he could carry on making magic from her. He fell in and they both burned terribly.

The servant was more a beetle than a woman by now. She dragged them from the fire. The old man had crumbled to ash, and the girl was scarred and burned all over. But they were both full of magic. The cloud of ash formed into a shape like a woman and ran off from the crime, followed by the servant. They locked themselves away for shame, and no one ever saw them again.

They built themselves a castle of magic and lived there, with the beetles, and never grew older and never died. People say that one day they will come out and eat again.

The girl recovered, in a way. She lived and she was so full of magic that she could do anything, only you would never know by looking at her ruined face. People say she's waiting some-where, ready to act if ever the ash person comes out of the castle.

The magic that spilled from the sky that day rained down on other people as well. Every time a star shoots across the sky, another baby is born with the gift of magic.

He finished his story.

"And that's how you were born," he said. "When a December star shot across the sky. Well, that's the story, anyway."

"Shall I be burned and ugly?"

"No. Wizards don't look like that anymore. Only the little girl."

"Is it true?" she asked.

"It's a story. The blacksmith story is nicer, but there isn't a little girl in it. There are babies, though."

"But it is true?"

Acknowledgments

Crossing the Atlantic has never been without danger or discomfort. My thanks to Michelle Nagler for her patience, good humor, and kindness in looking after *Fireborn* and me on our journey over.